Advance Praise for *The Oppenheimer Alternative*

"I loved it!"

—**Lee Smolin**, bestselling author of ***The Trouble with Physics***

"An imaginative restructuring of a phantasmagoric life into an alternative phantasmagorical story. Oppenheimer fans will be intrigued."

—**Martin J. Sherwin**, co-author of the Pulitzer Prize-wining biography ***American Prometheus: The Trumph and Tragedy of J. Robert Oppenheimer***

"A truly science fictional work of alternate history which turns on the decisions—and discoveries—of the great physicists who wrote the history of the 20th century: Einstein, Fermi, Gödel, and Oppenheimer. They are the vividly realized, all-too-human characters who people this novel, and give its brilliant speculations human life and blood Bravo!"

—**S.M. Stirling**, author of ***Dies The Fire***

"Incredibly realistic: the characters, locations, the era, and even the science. I felt like I was back in Los Alamos—and I should know: I worked there! Breathlessly riveting; Sawyer pulls it off masterfully."

—**Doug Beason**, former Associate Laboratory Director, **Los Alamos National Laboratory**

"The feel and detail of the Manhattan Project figures is deep and well done. I knew many of these physicists, and Sawyer nails them accurately."

—**Gregory Benford**, author of ***The Berlin Project***

"I enjoyed it tremendously! Really great, a page turner. I was hooked from the beginning to the end. Another fine addition to the Sawyer canon!"

—**Andre Bormanis**, producer, ***The Orville*** and ***Cosmos***

"Sawyer's impressive use of scientific and historical detail and Sawyer's characterization of the man himself pull back the layers of Oppenheimer's morals, genius, and grief. Science fiction fans will devour this smart speculative tale."

—***Publishers Weekly***

"An expert and engrossing knitting of the threads of history, with genuine characters of the mid 20th Century, to weave out a compulsive fictional narrative."

—**Jem Rolls**, author of the play ***The Inventor of All Things***

"Sawyer portrays brilliantly and poignantly the struggles of the scientists who started it all and were consequently obliged to bear an unbearable burden."

—**James Christie**, Chair, Project Ploughshares,
member organization of the Nobel Peace Prize-winning
International Campaign to Abolish Nuclear Weapons

"You can call this alternate history or alternate astrophysics (or both). Whatever term you choose, it's a terrific story."

—**Eric Flint**, author of ***1632***

"Sawyer has outdone himself! No one could have taken on this project with such gusto and with such a search for the truth as this outstanding author. I've never read such a complete and thrilling account of Oppenheimer's world.

—**Jonas Saul,** author of the ***Sarah Roberts*** series

Praise for Robert J. Sawyer

"A new Robert J. Sawyer book is always cause for celebration."

—***Analog Science Fiction and Fact***

"Sawyer not only has an irresistibly engaging narrative voice but also a gift for confronting thorny philosophical conundrums. At every opportunity, he forces his readers to think while holding their attention with ingenious premises and superlative craftsmanship."

—***Booklist***

"Can Sawyer write? Yes—with near-Asimovian clarity, with energy and drive, with such grace that his writing becomes invisible as the story comes to life in your mind."

—**Orson Scott Card**, author of ***Ender's Game***

"Robert J. Sawyer is by any measure one of the world's leading (and most interesting) science-fiction writers. His fiction is a fascinating blend of intellectually compelling big ideas and humane, enduring characters."

—***The Globe and Mail***

"Sawyer, an articulate fountain of ideas, is the genre's northern star—in fact, one of the hottest SF writers anywhere. By any reckoning Sawyer is among the most successful Canadian authors ever."

—***Maclean's: Canada's National Magazine***

"Robert J. Sawyer is a writer of boundless confidence and bold scientific extrapolation."

—***The New York Times***

"Sawyer's books—always rich in science, action, and profound thinking—never fail to surprise, delight, and cause us to transcend our ordinary thinking. I've read Crichton, Asimov, Heinlein, Clarke, King, and Koontz—and Sawyer outdoes them all."

—**Clifford A. Pickover**, author of ***Time: A Traveler's Guide***

"A polished, exciting writer. Sawyer writes with the scientific panache and grandeur of Arthur C. Clarke and the human touch of Isaac Asimov."

—*Quill & Quire*

"Cracking open a new Robert J. Sawyer book is like getting a gift from a friend who visits all the strange and undiscovered places in the world. You can't wait to see what he's going to amaze you with this time."

—**John Scalzi**, author of ***Old Man's War***

"Sawyer is Canada's answer to Michael Crichton."

—*The Toronto Star*

"No reader seeking well-written stories that respect, emphasize and depend on modern science should be disappointed by the works of Rob Sawyer."

—*The Washington Post*

"Sawyer is a terrific writer. He can write about the most sophisticated science while giving readers the room to understand what's happening and follow the plot."

—*Winnipeg Free Press*

Novels by Robert J. Sawyer

Golden Fleece
End of an Era
The Terminal Experiment
Starplex
Frameshift
Illegal Alien
Factoring Humanity
FlashForward
Calculating God
Mindscan
Rollback
Triggers
Red Planet Blues
Quantum Night
The Oppenheimer Alternative

The Quintaglio Ascension Trilogy
Far-Seer
Fossil Hunter
Foreigner

The Neanderthal Parallax Trilogy
Hominids
Humans
Hybrids

The WWW Trilogy
Wake
Watch
Wonder

For book-club discussion guides, visit sfwriter.com

THE OPPENHEIMER ALTERNATIVE

A Novel

ROBERT J. SAWYER

SFWRITER.COM Inc.

THE OPPENHEIMER ALTERNATIVE

Cover and interior: Bibliofic Designs

SFWRITER.COM Inc.
Mississauga, Ontario, Canada

ISBN (Print): 978-1-988415-24-6
ISBN (Kinde): 978-1-988415-22-2
ISBN (ePub): 978-1-988415-23-9

The Oppenheimer Alternative is available as an audio book from Audible and Recorded Books.

sfwriter.com

Dedication

For

Alisha Souillet

Who made this a better book
And me a better person

Acknowledgments

Special thanks to the late Manhattan Project physicist and Nobel laureate Luis W. Alvarez, who graciously spent an afternoon with me in 1983, a meeting I'll never forget; to Dr. Doug Beason, former Associate Laboratory Director, Los Alamos National Laboratory; to Alex von Thorn, whose great-uncle, Brigadier General Thomas F. Farrell, was an assistant to Manhattan Project leader General Leslie R. Groves; to Liz Cano, who first introduced me to the work of Leo Szilard via Jem Rolls's one-man play "The Inventor of All Things," and to Jem Rolls himself.

Many thanks to Sharon Fitzhenry and Richard Dionne at Fitzhenry & Whiteside in Canada and Shahid Mahmud at CAEZIK in the United States who rose to the almost-impossible challenge of getting this book out in time for the seventy-fifth anniversary of the birth of the atomic age. Special thanks to my editor, Adrienne Kerr—it was wonderful to be working with her again. Adrienne used to be my editor at Penguin Random House Canada, but Fitzhenry & Whiteside engaged her on a freelance basis to edit this book; you can hire her, too: see adriennekerr.net.

Thanks for help along the way to Alisha Souillet, Roy Ashton, Gabor Bagi, Gregory Benford, Jerry Bokser, Dave Brohman, David De Graff, Paddy Forde, Marcel Gagné, James Alan Gardner, Gerald I. Goldlist, Dominick Grace, Judith Hayman, Steve Hoban, Matt Kennedy, Michael Lennick, W. Thomas Leroux, Chris Lotts, Donald Maass, Brian Morey, W. Maynard Pittendreigh, Lezli Robyn, Jensenne Roculan, Robin Rowland, Daryl Rybotycki, Stephen W. Saffel, James Snyder, Laura Frankos Turtledove, Vince Gerardis, Alex Wellerstein, Elizabeth Westbrook-Trenholm, Andreas Wolz, and George Zebrowski.

Beta readers for this novel were Robb Ainley, Keith Ballinger, Denise Bérubé (who read the manuscript while in Hiroshima!), Ted Bleaney,

Andre Bormanis, Aleksandar Bradaric, Stephanie Bradfield, Wayne Brown, Nixie Byrd, Jon Caruana, James Christie, Fiona Reid Cosgrove, Melissa L. Cox, Irene Dutchak, Andrew Edmunds, Talisa Edmunds, Shayna Feldstein, Hugh Gamble, Michael Jäger, Andrew Zimmerman Jones, Herb Kauderer, Wouter Lagerweij, Clare Levijoki, Joel Lee Liberski, John Lynch, Michael Mariani, Erik Maronde, Ryan McCarty, Margareta Mina, Andrea Mitchell, Chris Nolan, Colin Porter, Karin Porter, Lou Prosperi, Natalka Roshak, Judy Sanders, Larry Schoeneman, Georgina Scott, Lee Smolin, Lynne Stonier-Newman, Lou Sytsma, Gord Tulloch, Keith Ward, Bret Wiebe, Stephanie Wilson, and Len Zaifman.

For the first time in over twenty years, I've written a novel without first securing a publishing contract. My Patreon supporters made that possible, including, most generously, Arioch, Christopher Bair, Keith Ballinger, Kelly Barratt, Jennifer Blanchard, Ronda Bradley, James Christie, Genevieve Doucette, Hugh Gamble, Gregory Koch, Joel Lee Liberski, Gillian Martin, Christina Dawn Monroe, Carol Richards, Robin Schumacher, Timothy W. Spencer, Andrew Tennant, Scott Wilson, Joshua Paul Wolff, and Brian Wright. If you'd like to join them in supporting my work directly, please visit **patreon.com/robertjsawyer**.

Most of all, thanks to Carolyn Clink, the strong nuclear force that keeps everything from flying apart.

Dramatis Personae

Luis Alvarez (1911-1988): American physicist; 1968 Nobel laureate.

Stepan Zakharovich Apresyan (1914-1990): Russian diplomat and spy; vice-counsel at the Soviet Consulate in San Francisco.

Kenneth Bainbridge (1904-1996): American physicist; director of the Manhattan Project's Trinity test.

Hans Bethe (1906-2005): German-born American physicist; 1967 Nobel laureate.

Patrick Blackett (1897-1974): British physicist; Robert Oppenheimer's tutor at Cambridge's Cavendish Laboratory; 1948 Nobel laureate.

Niels Bohr (1885-1962): Danish physicist; 1922 Nobel laureate.

Vannevar Bush (1890-1974): Head of the U.S. Office of Scientific Research and Development.

James F. Byrnes (1882-1972): Secretary of State under Harry S. Truman.

Barbara Chevalier (1907-2003): First wife of Haakon Chevalier.

Haakon Chevalier ["HOKE-on SHEV-al-EE-eh"] (1901-1985): American-born professor of French literature at the University of California at Berkeley and translator at the Nuremberg Trials.

Robert Christy (1916-2012): Canadian-born physicist.

Arthur Holly Compton (1892-1962): American physicist; 1927 Nobel laureate.

Edward Condon (1902-1974): American physicist.

Watson Davis (1896-1967): editor, Science Service.

Peer de Silva (1917-1978): Manhattan Project security officer.

Major General Walter Dornberger (1895-1980): Military leader of Germany's V-2 rocket program.

Helen Dukas (1896-1982): Einstein's live-in secretary.

Freeman Dyson (1923-2020): British-born American physicist.

Albert Einstein (1879-1955): German-born Swiss/American physicist; 1921 Nobel laureate.

George C. Eltenton (1905-1991): British chemical engineer (or so it was thought at the time; actually a physicist) for Shell Development in California who approached Haakon Chevalier on behalf of Russia.

Ward V. Evans (1880-1957): member of the 1954 Atomic Energy Commission security-review board.

Enrico Fermi ["FAIR-mee"] (1901-1954): Italian-born American physicist; 1938 Nobel laureate. In 1942, he produced the first-ever controlled nuclear chain reaction at the University of Chicago.

Richard Feynman ["FINE-man"] (1918-1988): American physicist; 1965 Nobel laureate.

Lloyd K. Garrison (1897-1991): American lawyer; represented Oppenheimer before the 1954 Atomic Energy Commission security-review board.

Kurt Gödel (1906-1978): Austrian-born American logician.

Gordon Gray (1909-1982): chairman of the 1954 Atomic Energy Commission security-review board.

General Leslie R. Groves (1896-1970): Head of the Manhattan Project.

Bourke Hickenlooper (1896-1971): United States senator and past chairman of the Joint Committee on Atomic Energy.

Verna Hobson (1923-2004): Robert Oppenheimer's secretary at the Institute for Advanced Study.

J. Edgar Hoover (1895-1972): Director of the Federal Bureau of Investigation.

Dieter Huzel (1912-1994): German rocketeer working under Wernher von Braun.

Lt. Lyall Johnson (1914-2006): American counter-intelligence officer stationed on the campus of the University of California, Berkeley.

Lyndon B. Johnson (1908-1973): 36th President of the United States, in office 22 November 1963 to 20 January 1969.

George Kistiakowsky (1900-1982): Ukrainian-American chemist, leader of explosives group at Los Alamos.

Anne Wilson Marks (1924-2006): Robert Oppenheimer's secretary at Los Alamos.

Herbert Marks (1907-1960): Robert Oppenheimer's lawyer (and Anne's husband).

Lt. Col. (and later Major General) Kenneth Nichols, Ph.D. (1907-2000): General Groves's assistant, and, later, general manager of the Atomic Energy Commission.

J. Robert Oppenheimer (1904-1967): American physicist, scientific director of the Los Alamos site of the Manhattan Project; director of the Institute for Advanced Study.

Katherine "Kitty" Oppenheimer (1910-1972): German-American botanist; wife of Robert Oppenheimer.

Katherine "Tyke" Oppenheimer (1944-1977): Robert and Kitty's younger child, known as "Toni" when she was older.

Peter Oppenheimer (1941-   ): Robert and Kitty's older child.

William S. "Deak" Parsons (1900-1953): associate director of the Los Alamos laboratory under Oppenheimer; weaponeer on the *Enola Gay;* promoted to Rear Admiral following the war.

Lt. Col. Boris Pash (1900-1995): American military intelligence officer; commander of the Alsos Mission into Germany.

Isidor Isaac Rabi ["ROB-ee"] (1898-1988): Austrian-born American physicist; 1944 Nobel laureate.

Roger Robb (1907-1985): attorney for the Atomic Energy Commission.

C. Arthur Rolander, Jr. (1920-2017): First, the Atomic Energy Commission's deputy director of security, then vice-president of General Atomic.

Robert "Bob" Serber (1909-1997): American physicist; Robert Oppenheimer's close colleague.

Rita "Pat" Sherr (1916-1997): wife of physicist Rubby ["ROO-be"] Sherr; looked after Robert Oppenheimer's daughter.

Robert Sproul (1891-1975): President of the University of California, Berkeley.

Henry L. Stimson (1867-1950): Secretary of War during both World Wars.

Lewis L. Strauss ["Straws"] (1896-1974): Chairman of the Atomic Energy Commission.

Leo Szilard ["LAY-o SIL-ard"] (1898-1964): Hungarian-born physicist.

Jean Tatlock, M.D. (1914-1944): American Communist Party member; Robert Oppenheimer's mistress.

Ted Taylor (1925-2004): Mexican-born American physicist who worked at Los Alamos and then headed the *Orion* project.

Edward Teller (1908-2003): Hungarian-born physicist, often called "the father of the hydrogen bomb."

Charles Tobey (1880-1953): United States senator.

Harry S. Truman (1884-1972): 33rd President of the United States, in office 12 April 1945 to 20 January 1953.

Harold Urey (1893-1981): American physical chemist; 1934 Nobel laureate.

Joseph Volpe (1914-2002): legal counsel for the Atomic Energy Commission.

Magnus von Braun (1919-2003): younger brother of Wernher von Braun.

Wernher von Braun ["VAIRN-er fon Brrrown"] (1912-1977): German rocketeer.

John von Neumann ["von NOY-man"] (1903-1957): Hungarian-born American mathematical physicist.

Henry A. Wallace (1888-1965): vice-president of the United States under Harry S. Truman.

Author's Note

Every character in this novel was a real person and, with the exception of Peter Oppenheimer, is now deceased. The Manhattan Project and Project *Orion* both really existed as described here, and the Institute for Advanced Study still exists.

The chapter-head quotes are all real, and, thanks to the published recollections of the participants, official transcripts, illicit recordings, and so on, some of this novel's dialog is real, too.

That is what novels are about. There is a dramatic moment and the history of the man, what made him act, what he did, and what sort of person he was. That is what you are really doing here. You are writing a man's life.

—I.I. Rabi,
testifying at Robert Oppenheimer's security hearing

Prologue

What pithy words should one use to sum up the life of J. Robert Oppenheimer before dropping the urn with his ashes overboard?

Do you wax poetic about the precocious child who, at age twelve, gave a lecture to the venerable New York Mineralogical Club? Perhaps you'd discuss his rise to fame in 1945 as "the father of the atomic bomb"—and then lament the McCarthy Era witch-hunt that later sought to strip his security clearance? You might even include a word or two about his supposedly quiet twilight overseeing the monastic Institute for Advanced Study in Princeton.

In the end, Kitty Oppenheimer, the compact alcoholic for whom Robert had been the fourth—albeit longest-serving—husband, said nothing while raindrops fell like bombs from the heavens. She let go of his urn seconds after dangling it over the gunwale of the motorboat that she, their twenty-two-year-old daughter, and two friends had taken out from the Oppenheimer beach house on Hawksnest Bay that monochromatic afternoon in February 1967.

Surprisingly, the urn didn't sink at once. Rather, it bobbed up and down as if empty, the waves themselves giving the storied physicist a final sinusoidal eulogy before the container, taking on water, at last sank beneath the choppy surface.

Chapter 1

1936

I have to explain about Oppie: about every five years, he would have a personality crisis; he would change his personality. I mean, when I knew him at Berkeley, he was the romantic, radical bohemian sort of person, a thorough scholar ...

—Robert R. Wilson,
American physicist

"You're bad luck for me," said Haakon Chevalier. "I hope you know that."

Robert Oppenheimer looked at his friend, seated next to him on the pink-and-green living-room couch as the party bustled about them. Oppie's sense was the exact opposite: Hoke had brought him nothing but good fortune, including getting him into this offbeat rooming house here on Shasta Road. "Oh?"

"Absolutely. When I go places without you, *I'm* considered the attractive one."

Oppenheimer made a small chuckle. Chevalier, who had just turned thirty-five, was three years his senior, and was indeed movie-star handsome: gallant, as befitted his last name, and long of face, with wide-spaced eyes and sandy hair swept back in a slight pompadour.

By comparison, Oppie knew he himself was scrawny, his tall body angular, his coarse black hair a wild nimbus, and his duck-footed gait awkward—one friend had described it as a constant falling forward as if he were forever tumbling into the future.

"See that one over there?" continued Hoke, with a subtle nod. "She hasn't glanced at me once since we got here, but *you*—" Chevalier shook his head in good-natured exasperation. "It's those goddamn eyes of yours, I tell you. Fucking opals."

Oppie was used to compliments about his pale blue eyes: he often heard them called "transparent" or "luminous," but this metaphor was new to him. He smiled as he turned to look at the woman Hoke had indicated, and—

And, my God, he'd seen that lovely face before—he was sure of it. But where? "Wow," said Oppie softly.

"Wow, indeed," agreed Hoke. "And she keeps looking your way. You should go over and say hello."

"I ... um ..."

"Oh, for Pete's sake, Robert, go! You study the mysteries of the universe; girls are simple by comparison."

Hoke taught French literature at the University of California's Berkeley campus; Oppie was a professor of physics there. Normally, members of such diverse faculties would have little to do with each other, but Oppie loved French poetry, and the two men had become great friends. One advantage Hoke had was a lot of female students—he'd married one, in fact—whereas in Robert's circles, women were rare. "Come on," said Hoke. "Give me a story to tell Barb when I get home. Go try your luck."

Luck. Einstein said that God didn't play dice with the universe—but, then again, God probably wasn't itching to get laid. "All right already," Oppie said, unfolding himself from the couch. Of course, he couldn't just go up and say hello, but Mary Ellen, his landlady, was swirling by in one of her floor-length batik dresses. She threw many parties, often as fund-raisers. This one was for the Republicans in Spain—or maybe it was for the Spanish Nationalists? Whoever the good guys were, anyway; Oppie had come downstairs from his room for donuts and drinks, not the cause.

"Say, Mary Ellen, I wonder if you might—"

"Robert! So good of you to pull your nose out of your books and join us! But your glass is empty. Let me—"

"No, no; I'm fine. But if you could ..." He gestured feebly at the busty young woman seated by the fireplace.

"Ah!" said Mary Ellen, her wide face splitting in a grin. "Yes, of course!" She took Oppie's hand and pulled him across the crowded room. "Jean," she said, and the woman looked up, "this is my best tenant—oh, hush, Fred; you know I love you, too! This is Robert. He teaches physics. Robert, Jean here is studying to be a doctor." Mary Ellen managed to make an art-deco chair appear out of nowhere and maneuvered Robert onto it so that he was facing Jean. "Now, let me get you a drink!"

"A doctor," said Oppie, impressed, smiling at Jean.

"Yes. A psychiatrist, in particular." Jean's voice was warm. She was, as he'd noted from across the room, beautiful—even more so close-up. "I'm fascinated by Freud," she continued. "Do you know his work?"

Well, well: look at those dice. Six the hard way! "I do indeed. In fact, I know Ernest Jones."

"Oh my!" said Jean. "Really?"

"Yes. We, ah, met when I was at Cambridge in 1926." Jones, a great friend of Freud, was the first English-speaking practitioner of psychoanalysis and had become its chief proponent in the English world.

"Tell me—my God, tell me everything about him!"

Mary Ellen fluttered by again, giving Oppie a bourbon and a wink, then went upon her way. "Well," said Oppie, "he was practicing in Harley Street ..." As he spoke, he continued to study her smooth, classically beautiful face and striking green eyes, emeralds to his opals. Jean wore her black hair short and had a slight dimple in her chin. She was probably a decade younger than he was.

They talked for most of an hour, and the conversation slipped easily from topic to topic. He was enthralled by that hauntingly familiar beauty of hers *and* by her nimble mind and ready wit, and yet she was mercurial. One moment she'd seem animated and boisterous, the next fragile and sad. Still, against a noisy background of someone banging away on the piano, dozens of overlapping conversations, and the clink of glasses, he listened attentively, although at one point he had to hold up his hand to stop her. "My family," she said, "moved out here from Massachusetts just before the crash, and—"

"You were in an accident?"

She looked at him for a moment, puzzled. "No. The stock-market crash."

Oppie shook his head slightly.

"The stock-market crash of 1929. The beginning of the Great Depression."

"Oh—ah, yes. Yes, of course."

"You don't know, do you?" Jean looked amazed. "Where have you been?" He wished she'd gone on to add the words *all my life,* but instead she finished by observing: "Born with a silver spoon in your mouth, were you?"

"Well, I—I mean, my father did all right." Then he added, as if somehow it explained his ignorance: "He invested, but mostly in art, not stocks."

She tilted her head again, and the light from the porcelain table lamp hit her just *so,* and he suddenly realized where he'd seen that face before. Oppie's favorite book was Baudelaire's poetry collection *Les Fleurs du mal.* The shape of Jean's face and the curve and length of her nose were identical to that of the woman in the etching accompanying Baudelaire's heartbreaking *"Une Martyre"* in the glorious 1917 edition. He frowned, ousting the thought. That etching was gruesome: the woman's head had been severed, a beauty cut down in the flower of youth as her older lover traveled the world.

The evening at last wound down, and Oppie, four drinks in, was ready to ask the young lady out. "And so, Miss ..." he began.

"Tatlock," she said, and the crisp syllables hit him like bullets.

"Are ... are you related to John Tatlock?"

"He's my father."

"John Tatlock? The medievalist at Berkeley?"

"Yes, why? Do you know him?"

Oh, yes, thought Oppie. John Strong Perry Tatlock was an expert on Geoffrey Chaucer, a towering presence at Berkeley faculty-association meetings, a loud voice often heard booming across the Faculty Club dining hall—and a raging anti-Semite. That wasn't unusual at Berkeley; when Robert had tried to get his student Bob Serber a job there, the physics chairman had said that having one Jew in his department was quite sufficient. But ... *damn.*

"Ah," said Oppie, his stomach knotting; he hadn't mentioned his own last name. He got up from the funky chair. "Well," he said sadly, "it was nice meeting you." He made his way toward the staircase that led up to his lonely room.

Jean was present at the next party Mary Ellen hosted, and the one after that, each time just as lovely, just as magnetic. Finally, her father's prejudice be damned, Oppie mustered the courage to ask her to dinner.

"Where would you like to go?" she replied, and he was flustered again. Did that mean her acceptance was a given, or that it was now contingent on him naming a suitably posh place? "I, um, well—"

"Oh, it doesn't matter!" she said, smiling. "Do you like spicy?"

"Very much so."

"There's a place over in San Francisco, the Xochimilco Café. Do you know it?"

He shook his head.

"Well, good! Then it can become *our* place! Saturday night? Or—or do you ...?" The question, he realized, was a belated reference to his Jewishness.

"No, Saturday is fine."

And it *was.* The café, which had a name more appropriate to the Southwest he'd loved in his youth than the Northern California he was in now, was a dive. Not that it mattered; she'd been right that money wasn't a concern for him—he'd happily have taken her to the most-expensive seafood place on the wharf. But the booth they found was suitable for conversation, the *carne adovada* agreeably piquant, and the tequila strong and plentiful.

She was, he discovered, a member of the Communist Party and wrote for its newspaper, *The Western Worker.* When she spoke of downtrodden people, of the fight for liberty—common coin on the Berkeley campus, stuff he'd previously tuned out as background noise—he found himself listening, nodding, and repeatedly interjecting, "Yes, yes, yes!"

That night, he walked her home. After a block, she reached over and took his hand. When they arrived at the entrance to the small building she lived in, they could hear a jazz recording through a neighbor's open window; she told him it was Benny Goodman's latest, "The Glory of Love." Oppie pulled her near and, bending his head down, he kissed her for the first time, starting slowly, gently, but, as she responded, growing more and more passionate.

They began dating regularly. A few years before, he'd given a talk entitled "Stars and Nuclei" to the Caltech astronomy club; he'd studied the largest and smallest of objects, but, until Jean, he'd missed seeing the human world all around him.

Still, it wasn't long before he learned of the darkness that chased her inner light—her mood swings, her nightmares; she was a chimera, angel and demon in one body, the would-be psychiatrist who had long seen a psychiatrist of her own. Despite it all, he came to love her unwaveringly, and she, with the deeper feelings both high and low that heaved and tossed her spirit, perhaps loved him even more.

After only a few months, they were engaged ... and then, bewilderingly, Jean broke it off. "Not ready," she said, and "Too soon." They continued to date, though, and he finally worked up the courage to ask her a second time to marry him. She agreed, but then, weeks later, once again changed her mind: she did love him, she insisted, but said he deserved more, better, and his protestations failed to sway her. Robert, heartbroken, started seeing other women, including Kitty, the petite temptress, the flirtatious vixen, the skilled horsewoman who could, or so it seemed, break any stallion. To his surprise at the time, she was soon pregnant. He did the honorable thing—did his duty—and married her.

But it was winsome, bittersweet Jean Tatlock, not Kitty, who was forever in his heart, his mind, the soulmate he could never have.

Chapter 2

Six Years Later: 1942

Question: What is an optimist? Answer: One who thinks the future is uncertain.

—Leo Szilard

Leo Szilard, still cherubic at forty-four, had been warned about this visit. General Leslie Groves was coming to the Metallurgical Laboratory, the drab code name given to the facility at the University of Chicago that studied the fissionable elements uranium and plutonium. The man who'd been merely a colonel days ago had apparently leveraged a promotion to go along with being appointed head of—what the hell were they calling the overall bomb effort now? Ah, yes: "The Manhattan Engineer District."

Leo suspected he'd soon have some obscure code name himself. His preference would be "Martian Number One." Enrico Fermi, who believed the universe should be teeming with intelligent life, had exhorted Leo to explain the absence of these advanced visitors, which, for lack of a generic term, Enrico had taken to calling "Martians." Leo had quipped, "Oh, we are here—but we call ourselves Hungarians."

Szilard had already bestowed nicknames on others, which he mostly kept to himself. His largely platonic girlfriend Trude, a dozen years younger, was *"Kind,"* the German for "child." Eugene Wigner, a fellow Martian, was

"Pineapple Head," in honor of his oddly prolate noggin. And he'd decided the best name for this general who had burst into their seminar room in Eckart Hall was "Bumpy," commemorating both his lumpy exterior and his bumptious nature. Leo couldn't fault a person for being overweight; his own fondness for pastries and rich sauces had made him, as Trude affectionately chided from time to time, more than a little rotund. But a man's clothes should fit, for God's sake, and this blustering martinet's jacket seemed at least one size too small.

The general and his military aide had been brought to see this group—the Met Lab's fifteen most-senior scientists—by Arthur Holly Compton, the jutting-jawed director of the laboratory. The seminar room was large and luxurious with built-in glass-fronted bookcases, plush maroon leather furniture, and two blackboards, one wall-mounted and another that had been wheeled in. A central mahogany table was strewn with papers, dog-eared journals, and coffee mugs.

Thirty-two-year-old Luis Alvarez, lanky and intense, was trying to answer the general's slew of questions by writing equations on the built-in blackboard, but that oaf had the gall to interrupt him. "Just a second, young man. In the third equation, you've got the exponent as ten-to-the-minus-five, but then it magically becomes ten-to-the-minus-six on the next line."

"Oh, yes, yes," replied Alvarez sheepishly, rubbing out the mistake with his thumb and writing in the correct value. "Slip of the chalk."

"That raises a question," Groves said to the whole group. "Your estimates for how much fissionable material you'll need—how accurate are they?"

Leo, with his shoeless feet propped up on a vacant chair, shrugged slightly. "Within a factor of ten."

"A factor of ten!" exploded Groves. "That's idiotic! That's like telling a wedding caterer to prepare for a hundred guests when the real number could be anywhere from ten to a thousand. No engineer can work with sloppy figures like that."

"General ..." said Leo, giving him his newfound title in hopes of placating the brute, "you have to understand—"

"No," snapped Groves. "All of *you* have to understand. This isn't a theoretical project; it's a practical one. I have to build actual working bombs."

He took a deep breath then let it out loudly. "Now, you lot may think engineers are just technicians"—Leo had the good sense not to interject—"and you may know that I don't have a Ph.D. Colonel Nichols here has one, but I don't. But let me tell you that I had ten years of formal education after I entered college—*ten full years*. I didn't have to make a living or give up time for teaching. I just studied. That'd be the equivalent of about *two* doctorates, wouldn't it?"

Leo swung his feet off the chair and leaned forward. "Sir," he said, the word almost a hiss, "I would never claim your rank—even if you have only just attained it—as my own. But forget doctorates; everyone in this room, save you, has one."

"Leo ..." cautioned Compton, thin eyebrows drawn together in a don't-do-this glare.

"No, no, no," said Szilard. "We're trotting out credentials here, are we not? And you, Arthur, you are none other than the winner of the 1927 Nobel Prize in physics." Leo locked his gaze on Groves. "Maybe you saw him on the cover of *Time* a few years ago?" Szilard then indicated a slender, balding man seated on the opposite side of the table. "And him? That's Enrico Fermi. He won the 1938 Nobel. And next to me?" He pointed to an egg-headed man with a mustache. "Say hello to James Franck, the 1925 Nobel laureate. As for me, I have collaborated with—and share patents with!—Albert Einstein."

Groves rose, fuming. "I'm going to Berkeley," he snapped, "but I'll be back in a few days." He jabbed an accusatory finger at the blackboard. "And I expect *precise* answers when I return." His footfalls on the hardwood floor shook the bookcase glass as he stormed out.

Leo got up, turned to face his colleagues, and spread his arms. "I warned you how it would be if the military were allowed to take over! How can we work with people like that?"

Compton had calmed down a bit. "Well, once Groves gets to Berkeley, Oppie will set him straight on the theoretical issues."

Szilard frowned. Oppenheimer? Too eager to please, too much of a climber. Oh, sure, charismatic in person—who hadn't felt that? But as the champion of science and reason against Bumpy Groves? "May God have mercy on our souls," Leo said, shaking his head.

Robert Oppenheimer gazed out the mammoth window in the university president's living room, lost, as often, in thought. Of course he was thinking about the vexing problem of isotope separation, but—

Isotopes were the same element but different—both *this* and yet each separately *that.* Just as it was with the women in his life, both beautiful and brilliant, but different, too: Kitty, who demanded to be satisfied, and Jean, whom he could never fully satisfy. The same and yet not: Kitty, who had been married to someone else when she first began dating Robert and who he'd now learned from friends had bragged that she'd gotten him to marry her "the old-fashioned way, by getting pregnant," and Jean, still there, still in his social circle, occasionally still in his arms, who ran away from commitment.

Robert hadn't been blind as time went on. His former landlady, that whirlwind of energy named Mary Ellen, and the delicate, moody Jean, now indeed an M.D., were more than casual friends. In just one of many ways in which Jean was pulled in multiple directions simultaneously, Mary Ellen—always confident where Jean was often diffident; always a confidant, as close as Oppie himself was—had also taken Jean to bed.

"Robert?"

The voice had been that of the reception's host, President Sproul. He turned. "Yes?"

Sproul—panther-lean, bespectacled, and wearing a gray three-piece suit—indicated the uniformed man next to him, and Oppie beheld the visitor. "General Leslie Groves, meet Dr. J. Robert Oppenheimer."

The term "fission" describing how a uranium nucleus could split into two had been borrowed from biology, and Oppie had a sudden flash of micrographs he'd seen of a dividing cell: an entity pinched in the middle to form bulbous halves. Groves's belt was the constriction and an ample gut billowed out above and below it.

The general was almost as tall as Oppie, with an elongated head weighed down by jowls and crowned by swept-back hair. Groves sported a short, bristly mustache that had grayed at either side, lending the more-prominent dark part—inadvertently, Oppie was sure—a Hitlerian aspect. Binary stars adorned each side of his khaki collar. Oppie offered his hand, and Groves shook it firmly.

"You're the head theoretician here," the general said as if it were an accusation.

Oppie nodded. "My actual job title is—if you can believe it—'Co-ordinator of Rapid Rupture,' but, yes, that's right."

"I'm a nuts-and-bolts man myself," said Groves. His voice reminded Oppie of the sound stones made in his lapidary tumbler. "An engineer."

Oppie nodded amiably. "You're in charge of building the Pentagon." The massive new structure in Virginia was nearly finished.

The general's eyebrows creased his forehead, clearly impressed that Oppie knew this. "Indeed I am." Oppie left unspoken the fact that Groves had also been in charge of building the internment camps for Japanese Americans. The army man looked around the vast room, apparently uncomfortable with the opulent surroundings. "I was hoping that I'd have earned my pick of assignments after the Pentagon—I wanted to see action overseas—but they gave me this thing."

"This thing," Oppie knew, was being in charge of the atomic-bomb project, including the work here at Ernest Lawrence's Radiation Laboratory and that at Arthur Compton's Metallurgical Laboratory in Chicago.

President Sproul apparently knew the way to this particular man's heart, at least: "Lunch will be served momentarily." Groves smiled at that, and Oppie smiled at Groves's smile.

"I'm glad they put an engineer in charge," Oppie said, turning on the charm as Sproul was beckoned away by another guest. "We scientists can spend far too much time woolgathering."

The general's eyes, a darker blue than his own, fixed on Oppie. "Are you free this afternoon? I'd like to talk to you some more."

It was all falling into place; Kitty would be so pleased. "Your wish is my command, General."

Chapter 3

The gravitational deflection of light will prevent the escape of radiation as the star contracts. The star thus tends to close itself off from any communication with a distant observer; only its gravitational field persists.

—**J. Robert Oppenheimer** and **Hartland Snyder**

Groves arrived at Oppie's office in Le Conte Hall accompanied by a colonel with thinning hair and round glasses—"Nichols," the general called him, and that let Oppie put a face to the name. This was Ken Nichols of the Manhattan Engineer District, whose office in New York had now lent its name to the entire American atomic-bomb effort. The British counterpart was code-named Tube Alloys, and heaven only knew what bland moniker the Soviet undertaking, if there was one, lurked behind.

Groves removed his army jacket, revealing a pressed shirt with crescent moons of sweat on either side. He handed the outer garment to Nichols and said, "Get this dry-cleaned."

Oppie took a drag on his cigarette. He knew that Nichols had a Ph.D. in hydraulic engineering from Iowa State. Once one received a doctorate, the grad-student lot of being an errand boy traditionally ended—but perhaps, to give him the benefit of the doubt, the general merely wanted privacy. Oppenheimer's assistant, the shy and lisping Bob Serber, finally granted a job here despite his religion, was working away on the office blackboard. Oppie took the opportunity not only to ensure they were alone but also to reset the karmic balance. "Say, Bob, why don't you take Dr. Nichols here over to the Faculty Club for a drink? You can leave the dry-cleaning with Becky."

Oppie caught Nichols's eye, hoping for a grateful nod. Instead, what he saw on the man's bespectacled face was anger that Robert had witnessed his petty humiliation. Serber assented as he rubbed his hands together to disperse chalk dust.

Once the other two were gone, Oppie sat on the edge of his desk. The ceiling of the white-walled office consisted of two angled sections joining in a central peak. Groves moved to stand against the far wall, the low roof there making him seem even more imposing. "I saw Ernest Lawrence this morning," the general rumbled, "and his vaunted Calutron. You know how much uranium-235 he's managed to separate from 238 so far?"

"None?" ventured Oppie.

"That's right, none. And I was in Chicago a few days ago. That buffoon Leo Szilard and the rest are still just blue-skying instead of getting down to specifics. I'm knee-deep in physicists, and not one of you seems to understand *time.*"

Robert admired Szilard's bounding intellect, but he could certainly see how these two would clash. "Well," he said, "Einstein wrote FDR in August 1939, urging the development of an atomic bomb. It's now October of '42, over three years later, and we've barely started on that bomb. I'd say it's awfully late in the day, General."

"At last a practical man!" exclaimed Groves. "All right, Mr. Rapid Rupture, tell me: *can* it be done? Atomic fission?"

Oppie frowned. "It's a sweet problem. The answer is ..." He paused deliberately for dramatic effect, then, firmly: "Yes."

Groves nodded, impressed. "How fast?"

"If we maintain a concentrated effort? Two years."

"Straight answers," Groves said. "I like that." He eyed Robert for a moment. "Okay, let's get this out of the way right now. Are you a member of the Communist Party?"

Oppie had been prepared for that question and kept his tone completely flat as he brushed ash from his cigarette with his pinkie. "No."

"Have you ever been?"

"No."

"Your wife was. And your brother Frank."

"True and true. And you'll find I've supported just about every left-wing cause there is, from the Teachers' Union to the Republicans in Spain over the last few years. But I've never belonged to the Communist Party and I've left all of those other things behind. There's work to be done."

"There is indeed," said Groves, "and there's no room for Communists in it."

"General, I give you my word: I'm not a Communist." A pause. "I'm an American."

"That you are," said Groves. "Born and raised—but so many of these others aren't. Germans, Hungarians, Italians, you name it. But Americans like you and me? We're thin on the ground."

Oppie tipped his head to one side but made no reply.

"All right, Professor, given how much catching up we have to do, how would you get us on track?"

"A central laboratory," Oppie said, playing his first card. "Get all us scientists together at one location." And then, laying the trump: "That'd make security a hell of a lot easier."

But Groves surprised him by *not* being surprised. "Yes, I've been thinking of that. Last month I ordered the acquisition of 59,000 acres in Oak Ridge, Tennessee, for uranium processing. Might be a good spot."

"No, no. It can't be seen as merely an add-on to an isotope-separation plant. We're talking about the heart and soul of the bomb effort. It should be a stand-alone facility."

The general stroked his jaw. "Maybe you're right. Who would you put in charge?"

"My boss here at Berkeley, Ernest Lawrence, is the logical first choice," said Oppie, pleased that the general and Lawrence had already clashed over the failure to produce any uranium-235. "Then there's I.I. Rabi at Columbia, or Edwin McMillan." But Oppie knew they couldn't be spared from their secret radar work. He threw out a couple more names, just for appearance's sake: "Or, from Caltech, Wolfgang Panofsky, say, or Carl Anderson."

Groves nodded at the mention of Anderson. "He won the Nobel for discovering the positron."

"True," said Oppie.

"And that raises a point. As I told those clowns in Chicago, I don't have a Ph.D., but in this project I have to be the leader of countless people who do. That's not a problem for me as I made it quite clear to them that I've got more than the equivalent in post-secondary education. But suppose I decide I want to put *you* in charge of this hypothetical out-of-the-way lab? You'd be a thornier case. Many of the men you'd be leading have already won the Nobel Prize, but you haven't."

Oppie raised his chin. "Not yet."

Groves leaned back and barked a laugh. "I admire a man who has faith in himself."

"It's not a question of faith, General. The work has already been done. In 1938 and 1939, I published three papers in the *Physical Review*, each with a different one of my grad students. Now, it sometimes takes the Swedish Academy a while to recognize an achievement as Nobel-worthy, and, unfortunately, we were hit with quite a stroke of bad luck: the very day the final and most important of the three papers was published, Hitler invaded Poland, and this damned war began."

"September first, 1939," supplied Groves.

"Exactly. And the world has been preoccupied ever since. However, once the war is over, those papers will be rediscovered, and their import noted. Then it's only a matter of *when* I'll get the Nobel, not *if*."

Groves made an impressed face, but then shook his massive head. "Well, for my purposes, if you don't get it until after the war, it doesn't help. But, okay, I'm curious. What's this great breakthrough that nobody noticed at the time?"

"There's a terrific Russian physicist named Lev Landau. He believed he'd figured out what causes the heat of the sun. He thought the center of the sun is a condensed neutron core. That is, at the sun's heart, all the orbiting electrons have been crushed down to combine with protons to become neutrons, and those neutrons, plus the ones that had already been part of the atomic nuclei at the core, are *all* that's left: solid neutron-degenerate matter. It was a great notion and explained wonderfully how the sun stays warm—the kinetic energy of in-falling matter being pulled down by the ultra-dense core. But Bob Serber—that's the fellow who I sent off just now with Colonel Nichols—Bob and I realized that Landau had failed to take into account the strong nuclear force. If you factor *that* in, the sun would give telltale signs of having that sort of core, and it doesn't."

Groves looked at Oppie, clearly unimpressed, but before the general could voice an objection, Oppie raised a hand. "Now, as I said, that was the *first* paper, and, yes, it wasn't all that much in itself. But it led directly to the *second* paper, which I wrote with George Volkoff. In that one, we determined that sufficiently heavy stars will, at the end of their lives, contract *indefinitely.*"

Groves frowned. "Indefinitely? What does that mean?"

"Good question," said Oppie with a grin, "and the answer was what the *third* paper was about, a collaboration with my grad student Hartland Snyder. Indefinite contraction, we showed, will lead to a point of zero volume and infinite density, with gravity so strong that nothing, *not even light itself,* will be able to escape the pull. That's a whole new class of astronomical objects, and one with properties nobody had guessed at before. A few kilometers from the center, at what's called the Schwarzschild radius, time itself will freeze, thanks to relativity but, for an in-falling observer, it will continue to pass. There's nothing intuitively obvious about these ... these ... 'dark abysses,' if you will, but they absolutely must exist."

Groves leaned back, an expression of awe on his face. "And *that's* worth a Nobel," he said softly.

Oppie nodded and crossed his arms smugly. "That's worth a Nobel."

"Jim, you'll be interested to know that the Italian navigator has just landed in the New World."

It was code, of course: the Italian navigator was Leo Szilard's colleague Enrico Fermi, who had led today's successful experiment. After months of labor, Fermi's team had created that which Szilard himself had been the first to envision nine years previously: a controlled nuclear chain reaction. This afternoon, the world's first atomic reactor had run for twenty-eight minutes—the first, that is, unless Nazi physicists had beaten them to the punch.

Szilard stood near his boss, Arthur Holly Compton, in the latter's office at the University of Chicago. Arthur was on the phone with James Conant, chairman of the National Defense Research Committee, the organization in charge of secret war technology for the United States. Conant must have asked how the natives were because Arthur's reply was, "Very friendly."

Silence while Arthur listened for a moment. "No," he said into the mouthpiece, "I suspect he's gone ... back to port." A pause. "Yes, he's here; let me put him on." He handed Szilard the black handset. Never one for formalities, Leo said, "Hello, Jim." His Hungarian accent made the name sound a bit like "Yim."

"Congratulations, Doctor!" The voice was warm although there was much static crackling behind it. "None of this would ever have happened without you."

Szilard rubbed his forehead with his free hand and said, because he knew it was what he was supposed to say, "Thank you," and then he handed the phone back to Arthur.

Leo liked to think either in his bathtub—he often soaked for hours—or quite literally on his feet. He excused himself and headed out into the cold evening air while Arthur went back to his oblique conversation. As Leo ambled across the campus, he passed many students, some clutching textbooks, a few holding hands, and he felt twinges of guilt. If something had gone wrong today, all these young people at the beginnings of their lives, along with, quite possibly, almost everyone else in Chicago, could easily have been killed.

Leo's breath blossomed into clouds in front of him. He hadn't had a destination in mind, but his feet brought him across the width of Stagg football field. There'd been snow earlier in the week that had melted, leaving the brown grass dry. He made his way toward the concrete rows of angled seating that ran along the west side. The brick structure beneath these bleachers housed various athletic facilities; Leo greeted the guards at the north end and headed into the doubles squash court that had been their experimental working space.

A short figure with a receding hairline and an oblong face was looking down from the court's spectator gallery at the giant cube of graphite blocks. The other scientists, doubtless in a mixture of elation and exhaustion, had all left, but Enrico Fermi leaned on the railing, just staring, apparently lost in thought.

The beast below was hibernating, all fourteen cadmium control rods having been shoved back in, *picas* into the hulking body of *el toro.*

Leo approached and solemnly offered his hand; Enrico took it. Their names had already been linked forever in history—or would be, once the security was lifted—thanks to the letter to President Roosevelt that Leo had drafted three years ago. That letter, signed by Einstein himself, had begun:

> *Some recent work by E. Fermi and L. Szilard, which has been communicated to me in manuscript, leads me to expect that the element uranium may be turned into a new and important source of energy in the immediate future.*

"Well, we did it," said Enrico, with his Italian accent. But this was only the beginning, and they both knew that. The Einstein letter had gone on to say:

> *This phenomenon would also lead to the construction of bombs, and it is conceivable—though much less certain—that extremely powerful bombs of a new type may thus be constructed.*

"Yes," Leo replied, "we did." He let go of Enrico's hand and shook his head slowly, looking at their creation below. "This will go down as a black day for mankind."

Chapter 4

1943

History, though coy, needs truth to be her handmaiden.

—Haakon Chevalier

"*. . . Some sunny day!*"

Kitty Oppenheimer and Barbara Chevalier reached the song's rousing conclusion. Their husbands applauded, Oppie clamping his cigarette between his teeth so he could do so with gusto. Kitty rose from the piano bench, and the two women bowed theatrically.

Oppie got up from the living-room couch, clutching his empty martini glass, and said, "Another round?" He knew the answer: their two dinner guests considered his martinis legendary; Oppie himself took them as evidence that although he'd settled on physics, he'd have made a damn good chemist, too.

Kitty, a brunette, merely raised her thin eyebrows in a "need you even ask?" expression, and Barb, blonde with green eyes, declared an enthusiastic, "Yes, please!"

Oppie collected the other glasses on a sterling-silver tray. He was about to turn toward the kitchen door when, to his surprise, Haakon Chevalier, an inch taller than Oppie's six feet, lifted himself from the couch. "I'll give you a hand."

"Forsaking the company of two beauties for me?" said Oppie. The tension between Haakon and Barb had been palpable all evening; the singing had helped, and Oppie hoped his remark would lighten the mood even more. He motioned with his head for Haakon to get the door, and the two of them entered the spacious kitchen, the smell of an almost-ready suckling pig greeting them. The heavy wooden door swung shut.

"We're going to miss you," Haakon said as Oppie put down the tray of used glasses, Kitty's and Barb's obvious by their bright-red lipstick marks. "Berkeley won't be the same without you."

Oppie had a second set of long-stemmed conical glasses in the freezer. He pulled them out and—his signature flourish—pressed each one facedown as though it were a cookie cutter into a shallow pan filled with lime juice and honey. He was conscious of Haakon's eyes on him, watching the master at work.

"Any hint of where you're going?" Haakon asked.

Having now set the glasses down, Oppie poured Black Bear gin into his cocktail shaker then, with a practiced flick of his wrist, added a splash of vermouth. He thought about replying, "Somewhere even drier than my martinis," but, no, that witticism had to die unspoken in the name of security. It was such a strange thing to get used to—and, really, if he couldn't trust Hoke, his closest friend, whom could he? "Sorry," he said affably. "My lips are sealed."

Haakon smiled but tipped his head toward a vodka bottle sitting next to the sink. "Genuine Russian, I see. Thank God we're not at war with *them.*"

"Ha," said Oppie as he expertly manipulated the shaker.

"Speaking of the Russians, Robert, do you know George Eltenton?"

Eltenton was a chemical engineer at Shell Development. Was Haakon taking a dig at Eltenton's Communist leanings? That wouldn't be in character; Hoke was as Red as anyone. "Not well," Oppie replied, apportioning his potent mixture among the four glasses. "But he's been to this very house. He's a member of FAECT"—the Federation of Architects, Engineers, Chemists, and Technicians—"and came to a meeting here a couple of years ago; I was trying to get the boys at the Rad Lab to join the American Association of Scientific Workers."

"A good union man," Haakon said, nodding his approval, but Oppie wasn't sure if he meant him or Eltenton.

"It didn't go anywhere," continued Oppie. "Just as well. Lawrence blew a gasket when he found out—wanted me to give him the names of those who'd been at the meeting. Naturally, I refused."

"Commendable," said Haakon. "Anyway, it's good you know George. He and I move in some of the same circles"—meaning, Oppie knew, the Communist Party—"and a fellow at the Soviet consulate in San Francisco had a word with him."

"Yes?" said Oppie, deploying olives now.

"Well, we're all on the same side, and the Soviets—no, one is plenty—well, the Soviets have gotten wind, I guess, of what's been going on at our university. You've never said, but everyone assumes it's of great importance."

Oppie made no reply.

"And so George was wondering if, you know, in the spirit of openness, if you were so inclined—that is, if you wanted to—well, any technical information that went to him would very discreetly find its way to your scientific colleagues in Russia."

The wall clock ticked off seconds. Oppie kept his tone as even as he could. "That's treason."

"Of course, of course," said Chevalier. "I just thought you'd want to know."

"I want nothing to do with anything like that."

Haakon nodded and helped himself to one of the glasses. He took a sip. "Perfect, as always."

In May 1943, Oppie, Kitty, and their son Peter, who had just entered the terrible twos, arrived at the place that would variously be called Site Y, the Hill, the mesa, or, in commemoration of the poplar trees that abounded here, Los Alamos. Oppie knew this part of northern New Mexico well. He'd spent the summer of 1922 here, an eighteen-year-old kid in need of toughening up following a string of illnesses before entering Harvard that fall. He had learned to ride horses then and ever since had been in love with the austere, feral countryside.

He'd returned to this area with his younger brother Frank in the summer of 1928, leasing a rustic cabin made of halved tree trunks held together by adobe mortar, a cabin Robert continued to rent to this day. Upon first learning of its availability, he'd exclaimed "Hot Dog!" and the Spanish equivalent, *Perro Caliente,* had become the place's name.

So, when he, Leslie Groves, and a few others had begun scouting a location for their secret atomic-bomb lab, Oppie had led them to what he and the general quickly agreed was the perfect spot: a boy's ranch school situated atop the two-mile-long Pajarito Plateau, 7,300 feet above sea level. Groves acquired it by eminent domain, and Oppie snared for his family one of the six existing houses, originally occupied by the school's masters, on what came to be known as Bathtub Row. Other accommodations—rude and shoddy since they were only expected to last the duration of the war—were soon under construction; they would have only showers.

General Groves could have claimed one of the Bathtub Row houses for himself, but he wouldn't normally be on the mesa; his principal office was in the War Building in Washington. But he was there the day Robert chose the Oppenheimer abode. "Very good," he said. "I'd have picked that one, too." The general paused—something he rarely did—then said, "I've got you a little house-warming present." He handed a small tin case, less than an inch wide, to Oppenheimer.

"Snuff?" said Oppie. "General, I—"

"No, not snuff." And then Groves made an odd sound, which Oppie supposed was his chuckle. "Well, it's *for* snuffing, but ..." He pointed at it. "Open it up."

Oppie dug a fingernail under the case's cover. It hinged back, revealing a small brown oval capsule surrounded by soft padding.

"Potassium cyanide," said Groves. "You're to carry it with you until the war is over, and, yes, before you ask, I've got one, too." He patted a pocket. "Everyone at the top levels is getting them."

"Good grief, General, isn't that a little melodramatic?"

"What do you think all this talk of security has been for? The Germans are doubtless trying to build an atomic bomb; so, I'd bet my life, are the Russians. But *we've* got the best minds, and the easiest thing for them to do is kidnap you or other key members of your team. If you're captured, they *will* torture you, and they *will* succeed in getting you to talk—unless you take that first. It's glass, covered in rubber to help keep it from breaking accidentally. Don't swallow it; it'll go right through your system intact. Instead, chomp down on it. You'll be dead in a matter of minutes."

Oppie looked at the capsule. It was only the size of a pea, but it reminded him of an apple from long ago.

Chapter 5

To those who loved me and helped me, all love and courage.

—Jean Tatlock

Groves and Oppenheimer soon realized that their original plan of having only a few hundred people on the mesa had woefully underestimated the complexity of the task they were undertaking. Los Alamos quickly became a town of thousands, albeit one surrounded by barbed-wire fencing.

Although Oppie had been open to commissioning the scientists into the military, most of them had objected to that notion. Still, they were living on a *de facto* army base. A shrill siren sounded at 7:00 a.m.—"oh seven hundred," as he was learning to call it—to rouse the scientists; they were expected to, well, to be sciencing by oh eight hundred. Oppie had quickly fallen into the habit of being the first to arrive at the technical area each morning and very often was the last to leave, coming home by moonlight or the blaze of the Milky Way. There were no street lamps allowed, lest the facility they were taking such pains to keep secret be noticed by an airplane.

By the time he got back to Bathtub Row one particular summer evening, he found Kitty on the white couch, her legs, in blue jeans and bobby socks, swung up on the upholstery, a tumbler in hand, and a bottle of bourbon on the oval table in front of her, next to an overflowing ashtray.

She didn't get up. "Dinner takes forever to cook at this altitude," she declared. Water boiled at just 198 Fahrenheit; bread never rose. "If I don't know when you're coming, I can't have anything ready."

Robert put his porkpie hat down and poured himself a Scotch. "Sorry. Work was difficult today."

"*What* work?" she demanded.

"You know I can't tell you that. We're not supposed to discuss—"

"It's *me,* for God's sake."

"Yes," Robert said, taking a sip. It was indeed her: the volatile and capricious hellion he'd married on the rebound after Jean had dumped him for the final time—but also the fiercely intelligent nonconformist who had devoted herself to his career. "You know my field," he said. "You can ... guess what we're working on."

Kitty lit a cigarette. "'Guess,'" she repeated derisively, sending the word aloft in a plume of smoke.

"There's a war on."

"I *know* that," snapped Kitty. She'd been born in Germany, although her family had come to the States when she was two. Her mother's first cousin—estranged from her even before the U.S. had entered the war because Kitty had married a Jew—was a Nazi field marshal named Wilhelm Keitel; he was chief of staff of the *Wehrmacht.*

"Many other women have husbands who have gone overseas," Oppie said. "At least yours is home each night."

"Don't take that line with me, Robert. I lost Joe in a war, remember." Kitty's second husband, a staunch Communist, had left her behind to go fight alongside the loyalists during the Spanish Civil War.

"I'm sorry," he said. "I didn't mean—"

"— to be dismissive? No, of course not," she said in the tone she sometimes used that left him unsure of whether she was being sincere or sarcastic.

"The war can't last forever," Oppie said. "And, when it's over, things will be so much better for us. I do wish I could tell you just how important my work is."

"I can do important work, too. I was embarking on a Ph.D. in botany when I was with Richard." Husband number three, the one she'd divorced after getting pregnant by Oppie. "I could make a real contribution here."

"You *will* make a contribution. You're my wife. You'll host parties, be the center of the community we're building."

Kitty poured herself more bourbon and took a swig. "For Christ's sake, Robert."

Soon, the sprawling mesa was feeling crowded. Thousands had moved here: scientists and soldiers; doctors and domestics; those in makeshift offices who counted beans, those in well-equipped labs who tallied Geiger clicks; children who found it all a grand adventure, adults who grumbled about the lack of even rudimentary comforts. Jeeps careened along winding dirt roads, while people hustled on foot between semi-circular Quonset huts and slapped-together cubic structures.

The chill and hoarfrost of winter gave way to spring and its pointillist wildflowers. Then May—had Oppie and Kitty really been here a year already?—followed by the long days and short nights of June.

As time went by what would have been outrageous indignities became the accepted norm: Oppie now thought nothing of receiving each day's mail already opened. He was surprised, though, to get a note with his own former residence on Shasta Road in Berkeley as the return address. Ah: it was from Mary Ellen, his erstwhile landlady and inveterate party hostess. And bless her heart for trying to be discreet: she'd written, "JT needs to see you." Of course, Peer de Silva—who, Oppie thought, had a rather appropriate first name for a security officer—had surely checked the contents before releasing it, and would have cross-indexed the initials with a list of Oppie's known associates. Although there were a few who sported that pair, only one of any closeness was in Berkeley: Jean Tatlock.

Jean, who had broken his heart.

Jean, who had twice refused to marry him.

Jean, who he saw each night in his dreams, needed to see him—in person. In the middle of war-time, while he was sequestered here, among the literal eagles and figurative hawks, when every day counted and every hour was crucial.

Of course, he'd demur.

Of course, he'd stay at his post.

Of course ...

She had wanted to see him one last time before he'd departed for here, but Kitty had thrown a fit, leading to Oppie leaving Berkeley without so much as a goodbye.

But he knew Jean and she knew him. They *had* made a distinction, clearly understood by both of them, between those times when one of them *wanted* to see the other and those when they *needed* to. And Mary Ellen, writing on behalf of Jean—why? Because Jean was so low, so far down, that she couldn't compose a letter herself? Mary Ellen *would* have conveyed Jean's precise intent: Jean *needed* to see him.

Of course ...

Of course he would go.

What else could he possibly do?

For safety's sake, General Groves forbade key personnel to fly, and Robert couldn't book a train ticket to San Francisco, where Jean lived, without arousing suspicion. But to nearby Berkeley? That wouldn't raise eyebrows; it was easy to concoct a list of tasks for him to do at the Rad Lab, including conferring with Ernest Lawrence.

After his long Pullman trip from New Mexico (and, for appearance's sake having first done a couple of things on campus), he slipped away from Le Conte Hall in the evening and took the streetcar across the Oakland Bay Bridge.

Jean had driven to the terminal to meet him. It was a quarter to ten when his long legs, running now, closed the distance between them, and he swept her into his embrace. They drove in her green Plymouth coupe along the Embarcadero then turned onto Broadway. Oppie noticed in his side mirror that behind them a brown Ford, so studiously unremarkable as to be the Platonic ideal of nondescript, made the same turn.

She posed no questions about where he was living now, and he didn't volunteer. Someone—Hoke, perhaps, or maybe even her father—had probably whispered that he was involved in a secret war effort that he couldn't talk about; she might ask him to compromise his marriage but never his work.

In the seven years they'd known each other, Jean had changed little physically, although she was now a resident pediatric psychiatrist at Mount Zion Hospital. But Oppie had given up his former wild mass of wiry hair in favor of a close-cropped look better suited to his new role as the scientific director at Los Alamos.

They arrived by 10:00 at the Xochimilco Café—their place—and, after drinks, inevitably, no other alternative ever being discussed, they left for her home on Telegraph Hill. Walking arm in arm from her car to the front steps, laughter lubricated by liquor, Jean dropped her key, and Oppie gallantly picked it up for her.

They climbed to the house's top floor, which contained Jean's rented room, little more than books, a bed, and a couch. Clothes slid off. His long-fingered hands lifted her heavy breasts, thumbs brushing her hardening nipples. Soon she was flat on her back, and he climbed atop, slid inside, and joined with her.

When they were done, with her nestled into his shoulder, she said wistfully, "I feel so ... so paralyzed sometimes."

"I know," he replied softly, stroking her thick hair, his heart fracturing as it always did when he knew he'd have to leave her. He remembered a poem she'd shared with him years ago, written when she'd been just sixteen but somehow apropos:

> *Is even this*
> *Not enough to appease your awful pain*
> *You gaunt terrible bleeding Jesus*

"I love you," he added, and he felt her cheek move against his shoulder as she smiled her shy, tenuous smile.

Late the next day, having missed his train back to New Mexico, she drove him to the airport, and he booked a flight to—no, not to home, nothing could be more home than this, but to Santa Fe.

On the way to the airport, he noticed the same, or a similar, brown Ford a few cars behind them. Ah, well; he'd doubtless catch hell for violating General Groves's no-flying edict.

Chapter 6

God knows I'm not the simplest person, but compared to Oppenheimer, I'm very, very simple.

—I.I. Rabi

It had been six weeks filled with frenzied work since Robert had spent that night with Jean. The tasks he performed on the mesa were urgent regardless but the harder he went at them the less time his mind had to wander back to her, to that night, to the life he could have had, his life that might have been.

And now he had returned to Berkeley again, in part to deal with security matters, including a certain laxness at Ernest Lawrence's Rad Lab and the indiscretions, which had caught the attention of Army Intelligence, of his former grad student Rossi Lomanitz, still at U.C.B. Every atom of his being wanted to take the Bay Bridge west once more, to hold Jean in his arms again, but ...

But. He had indeed been observed the last time, and a scandalous report had been filed. Even after Groves had given him the pill to carry around, he hadn't been conscious before that trip of just how truly pervasive security would be on this project—or, perhaps, as Jean the Freudian would say, he had been suppressing the thought that should have come to any rational man.

And yet if only he could *see* Jean again. For her good. For his. And, yes, for the good of the project: get it out of his system, clear his mind, energize his body, reassure himself. The army had always understood the value of a furlough; even General Groves had capitulated when Oppie had insisted back on the mesa that the scientists get Sundays off from their labors.

Robert drank in the warm August air, pulling it into his lungs. Gaseous diffusion: a molecule or two of oxygen that had once been inside her, living scant miles away, had surely now come within him.

He could scarcely ask his military driver to take him there now, and he had no car of his own—and the streetcar would be far too easy to tail. But a cabbie should be happy for the fare, happier still with his tip, and in what—an hour?—Jean could be tight in his embrace once more.

Goddamned security! There *were* matters that needed to be classified, and he never slipped in those. Although each had its beauty and rhythm, he'd recite only poetry to her, not formulae. Both his work, physics, and hers, psychology, would be left unmentioned, the former because it was now forbidden, the latter because it, too, was explosive where she was concerned. Her intricate, delicate psyche was as fragile as a blown-glass flower.

Still, it *was* good to be back in Berkeley, back among deans and dons, classicists and economists, surrounded by young, questing minds. He hadn't realized that he'd been missing people in their late teens, but their mere presence, their laughter, their raucous talk, was invigorating. The university wasn't as crowded as it would be next month when the fall term began, but it still buzzed with the fervor of a thousand lines of inquiry and a hundred specialties, instead of a monomaniacal focus, all for one and one for all.

Robert strode through the granite-clad main entrance to Durant Hall. Oppenheimer's students were famous for imitating him, down to his gait and gestures, not out of mockery, he knew, but genuine admiration. But in one crucial area they could no longer afford to be copying him: whereas he'd gotten away with his aborted effort at unionization before the war, Lomanitz was pushing for one again now. Oppie had beseeched all his past students to set aside politics for the duration of the hostilities, but hot-headed Rossi was hell-bent on forging ahead.

As Oppie headed down the corridor toward the room Lomanitz used, he passed by the office of Lieutenant Lyall Johnson, the ex-F.B.I. man who was the army counter-intelligence officer now permanently stationed on campus.

Or, that is, he *should* have passed by, but ...

But the door was open, as were its windows, the occupant trying to get a cross-current going in the sizzle of August. And, well, it probably wouldn't hurt to check in first ...

And so he entered, finding Johnson doing a newspaper crossword puzzle. Reading upside down, Oppie offered that six across was "Rubicon," and added, "I'm going to have a talk with Rossi Lomanitz, if that's all right with you. He's a good kid and a good physicist; I'm sure he'll listen to reason."

Johnson offered his blessing for Robert to try to straighten the boy out. Oppie turned to go, but then he thought a sundae needs its cherry, a martini its olive. Yes, disciplining Rossi certainly would show that Oppie had moved beyond his own Red past, but being back here in Berkeley had reminded him of Haakon Chevalier's visit to his house shortly before he and Kitty had left for Los Alamos. And so, just to drive home the fact that he really was wholeheartedly part of the team, he turned back to Johnson and added: "By the by, there's a chemist at Shell Development—you know, in Emeryville? Fellow named George Eltenton. Might be worth keeping an eye on him."

Johnson had already looked down at his puzzle again, but his head snapped back up. "Oh?"

"I mean, I don't *know,*" said Oppie, "but before I moved to Site Y, I heard a rumor he might have been looking for info about what's been going on here at the Rad Lab. Eltenton used to live in Russia, so ..." He let the lieutenant connect the dots.

"Thank you, Professor," Johnson said, using his fountain pen to jot the name on a piece of buff-colored paper. Again reading upside down, Oppie noted that Johnson got the spelling right on the first try.

"Anyway, I'm sure it's nothing, but ..." He tipped his trademark porkpie hat in farewell and headed on down the corridor to see Lomanitz. Behind him, through the open door, he thought he could hear Johnson dialing a phone.

Later that day, Oppenheimer received a message from Lieutenant Johnson, asking him if he wouldn't mind popping by his office the next morning. Oppie slept alone that night in his Spanish-style one-story villa on Eagle Hill overlooking Berkeley, a 2.5-acre property kept for the day when he, Kitty, and Peter could return to it for good.

It had been a restless night, the sheets knotting as his angular limbs flailed. Poor Jean was so close, so very close. Through his window he could see bright Altair. It was sixteen light-years from Eagle Hill to Alpha Aquilae as the photon flies; he could see *it,* but he couldn't see *her.*

When morning came, he showered, the plumbing taking a while to come to life after weeks of disuse, dressed, and returned to Durant Hall. This time, Johnson's door was closed. To avoid drawing attention to the secret work being done at the university, regular campus police instead of MPs guarded things, and one was stationed today outside Johnson's office. The man was apparently expecting Oppie since he acknowledged his approach with a curt "Professor," opened the door, and gestured for him to enter.

Johnson wasn't alone.

"Dr. Oppenheimer," said a fit-looking man in his early forties. He had round wire-frame glasses and a receding tawny hairline. "I'm Lieutenant Colonel Pash."

Robert had heard the name before. Working out of the Presidio, Pash was in charge of counter-intelligence for the Ninth Army Corps here on the West Coast. Oppie also knew that his first name was Boris, of all things. Although San Francisco-born, the teenager then known as Boris Fedorovich Pashkovsky had spent the First World War in Moscow with his father, a priest in the Russian Orthodox Church. When the civil war broke out after the Bolsheviks seized power and denounced the church, eighteen-year-old Boris had joined the White Army to fight them. His hatred of Communists, Oppie had heard, bordered on the pathological.

Pash rose from behind the desk Johnson had used yesterday; the young lieutenant had taken a creaky wooden chair by a filing cabinet. "This is a pleasure," Pash said, extending his hand. "I don't mean to take much of your time."

"That's perfectly all right," said Oppie, enduring the crushing grip. "Whatever time you choose."

Pash sat back down and motioned for Oppie to take the vacant chair, a twin of the one Johnson was on, in front of the desk. Oppie did so, balancing his hat on a knobby knee.

"Mr. Johnson told me about the little conversation you had yesterday," Pash said. "It's had me worried ever since he called."

Oppie's meeting with his ex-grad student had not gone well. "I wanted to tell him that he'd been foolish. Some people might have been embarrassed to be confronted thus but, to put it bluntly, he doesn't seem capable of being embarrassed, so—"

Pash was frowning. "What are you talking about?"

"Rossi Lomanitz. He was—"

"I'm not interested in him," said Pash with a dismissive gesture. "There's something more serious. Mr. Johnson said there was a possibility that some other ... *entities* were interested in our work here?"

Oppie felt his heart move in his chest, and his mouth was suddenly dry. "Oh, I have no firsthand knowledge that would be useful."

"But you had heard something concerning a chemist named George C. Eltenton?"

Oppie hadn't supplied the middle initial; clearly, some work had already been done. "Well, yes, apparently Eltenton had, um, had indicated that he was in a position to transmit, without danger of a leak or scandal, any, ah, technical information that one might supply."

"Indicated to whom?"

Oppie fished out a cigarette. His hands were shaking as he lit it. "To members of this project."

"Did Eltenton approach these project members directly?"

"No, through an intermediary." Oppie spoke quickly, trying to move the focus of the conversation. "Now look, to put it quite frankly, I would actually feel friendly to the idea of the Commander in Chief informing the Russians about what we are working on—they're our allies, after all, fighting the Nazis, too. But I do *not* feel friendly to the idea of moving information out the back door."

Oppie saw Pash jot the word "friendly" followed by an exclamation mark on the pad in front of him, and then he added "back door" below it, circling the term. "Could you give me more specific information about this ... this 'back door,' as you call it? You can surely see that the existence of such a thing would be as interesting to me as the whole project is to you."

Damn. He stubbed out the cigarette, only half gone, in a green-glass ashtray and lit another, using the bit of theater as a chance to collect his thoughts. "Well," he said, looking not at Pash but out the window behind him at sun-baked grass, Sather Road, and Wheeler Hall, "the approaches were always to people who were troubled by them. I feel that to give more than the name I've already given you—Eltenton—would be to implicate people whose attitude when approached was bewilderment rather than co-operation."

"Yes, but—"

"No, no. To go beyond that would be to put names down of people who are not only innocent but whose attitude was one-hundred-percent appropriate."

"But they *were* approached. When? Where? Any information would be helpful."

"These incidents occurred on the order of five, six, seven, months ago. There were, um, three cases, and, ah, two of the men were with me at Los Alamos, men very closely associated with me."

Irresistible force; immovable object: "All right, Professor. I understand you wanting to protect the innocent who were merely approached. But surely you see the person *doing* the approaching on Eltenton's behalf was complicit. Can you give me his name?"

Oppie's voice had risen in pitch. "I think that would be a mistake. I have told you who the initiative came from. Anything else would involve people who ought not to be involved."

"I really must insist, Professor. This intermediary poses an obvious security risk. I need you to tell me about him."

"Well, he's ... he's a man whose sympathies are very far left."

"Obviously. And ...?"

Oppie pulled in more smoke, hoping it would calm him. It didn't. "I'm sorry," he said, "but I would regard it as a low trick to involve someone when I would bet dollars to donuts that he wasn't really a problem."

"With due respect, that's not your judgment call to make." Oppie said nothing. "Professor?" His job title had never before sounded quite so menacing.

Oppie sighed. "He's a member of the Berkeley faculty but not part of our project. That's really all I can say."

"And he approached these three scientists simultaneously?"

Three scientists. Fuck. He *had* said that. "No, no." Grasping at straws, gasping for air: "They were contacted within a week of each other but not in each other's presence."

Pash steepled his fingers. "Look, Robert—may I call you that? Look, Robert, without your help, we are going to have to spend a lot of time and effort trying to track down this intermediary. As you can imagine, we'll all be hot under the collar until we find him; this is a very serious thing. So, again, do you suppose you could help me with the name?"

"The intermediary thought it was the wrong idea to transmit information; I don't think he supported it." Rallying some strength now: "In fact, I know he didn't."

"Now, look, Professor—"

Oppie cut Pash off, and words spilled out of him. "No, *you* look. You know how difficult the relations are between these two allies, Russia and the United States. Even though our government's official policy is one of co-operation with Russia, a lot of our secret information—our radar and so on—just doesn't get to them. But they're battling for their lives over there—thousands of their boys are dying every day along the Eastern Front—and they'd surely like to have an idea of what is going on here in America. This overture was just to make up for the ... the defects of our official channels, the fact that there are a couple of guys in the State Department who might block such communications. You see? *That's* the form in which it was presented to people."

Pash had an incredulous expression but said nothing.

Oppie really wished he could get the pitch of his voice down to normal. "Now, yes, an overture to share information with the Nazis would have a different color—"

"Not in my book," said Pash.

"— but, even so, I'm sure everyone approached decided that back-door communication with the Russians should not be taking place. No one would have provided Eltenton with what he wanted. It is treasonable."

"It most certainly is," said Pash. "Now, I am not persistent, but—"

"You *are* persistent ... and it is your duty. But I take *my* duty seriously, too. I feel responsible for every detail of this sort of thing down at Site Y, and I will say that everything is one-hundred-percent in order there; that's the truth." Oppie pointed in the direction of Le Conte Hall, where Lawrence had his office. "That doesn't go for this place up here, which is why I came to see Lomanitz, but I would be perfectly willing to be shot if I had done anything wrong."

Pash made another note on his pad. "Oh, I doubt it will come to that."

Chapter 7

The [Oppenheimer] I had known was gentle and wise, a devoted friend, the soul of honor, a student, a humanist, a free spirit, a man dedicated to truth, to justice, passionately concerned with human welfare, and emotionally and intellectually committed to the ideal of a socialist society.

—Haakon Chevalier

"Thank you for coming, Robert. Have a seat."

"My pleasure, General." Leslie Groves had his own office here at Los Alamos, reserved for his frequent trips from Washington. It had a picture of President Roosevelt on one wall, a giant Mercator map of the world covering most of another, and, on his desk, angled enough that Oppie could see it, a photo of the general's wife, twenty-year-old namesake son, and fifteen-year-old daughter.

"Robert, I think you know that I trust you; I've put enormous faith in you."

"I'm very grateful, General."

"And I suspect you're attentive enough to realize that not everyone approved of my choice of you as director of this facility. Some of your ... previous associations, you understand."

Oppie had heard much more than that. His employment history included no administrative positions at all; he'd never even been a university department head. When he'd gotten this assignment at Los Alamos, many had been stunned. One of his colleagues at Berkeley had muttered he didn't think Oppie could even run a hamburger stand. "So I've gathered."

"But I was sure I was right then," said Groves, "and I'm sure I'm right now. You're the best person for the job." He chuckled. "Don't let Colonel Nichols know I said that; he thinks I'm chary when it comes to praising—" there was a slight pause, giving a hint of emphasis to the next word, which otherwise was spoken in Groves's normal gruff tone "— subordinates."

"Thank you," said Oppie, stiffly; the lines were being drawn.

"And, you know, it's been fifteen months since we first met, you and I, and look at what we've accomplished." He lifted and spread his arms, a gesture Robert took to encompass the entire mesa.

"It *is* remarkable."

"And in all that time, I've never once given you an order, Robert. You know that."

The general, son of a Presbyterian army chaplain, didn't smoke, and Oppie tried to respect that by not indulging often in his presence, but he felt the need growing. "True."

"So, please, Robert, don't make me do so now. I'm asking you, man to man. We need to know the name of the intermediary you mentioned to Lieutenant Johnson and Colonel Pash. The colonel's people have done a lot of digging, and they've come up with a list of likely candidates. I'm going to hand you this list, and I'm hoping you will circle the name of the one who was Eltenton's go-between." He rotated a sheet of paper in front of him a half turn and slid it across the steel desktop.

The first name was Joseph Weinberg, one of Oppie's favorite ex-students; eight other names were listed below Joe's, one per line—colleagues all. Oppie looked up from the page. "General, in good conscience, I simply can't."

"I'm asking you as a friend, Robert."

"And I'm replying as one."

"All right, then." Groves took a deep breath and let it out noisily. "All right." He locked his gaze on Oppie. "Dr. Oppenheimer, I order you to reveal the name."

Oppie closed his eyes, took a deep breath. Hoke, he knew, had repeatedly read Victor Hugo in the original French; he'd understand that you couldn't let an innocent man take your place.

"Chevalier," he said, very softly.

"Who?" snapped Groves.

"Haakon Chevalier."

Groves pulled back the paper and grabbed a pen. "Spell it."

He spelled both names, and the general printed them in capital letters. "Never heard of him."

"He's not a scientist. He teaches French literature."

"Good grief," said Groves. "No wonder they couldn't find him."

"Also," said Robert, "he's taken a leave from the university. I honestly don't know where he is now, but I'm sure he was against all this."

"'Chevalier,'" said Groves, reading his own note. "So, not an American?"

"Actually, he was born in New Jersey."

"Good."

"Oh?"

"American subject," said Groves. "American justice."

Oppie felt his gut clenching. He rose. The general looked up at him, surprised, then barked, "Dismissed"—one last twist of the knife.

The following week a letter arrived for Oppie, addressed, as all mail for those on the mesa was, to P.O. Box 1663, Santa Fe, New Mexico. The postmark, canceling the three-cent stamp, was New York. The envelope, as usual, had been opened.

Oppie slipped the two typed pages out and unfolded them. His heart kicked his sternum. It was from Haakon Chevalier and began, *"Dear Opje."* Robert had acquired his nickname in 1928, when he was twenty-four, during the term he'd spent at the University of Leiden, and his friends of long standing continued to use the Dutch spelling. Oppie read on:

> *Are you still in this world? Yes, I know you are, but I am less sure about myself. I am in deep trouble. All my foundations seem to have been knocked out from under me, and I am alone dangling in space, with no ties, no hope, no future, only a past—such as it is. I am close to despair, and in such a moment, I think of you and I wish you were about to talk to.*

Haakon's first source of woe, he said, was ongoing strife with Barb. His second source was—

Hoke must have no idea of what had transpired; none. If he had gotten wind of it, if he'd had a clue, his tone would have been harsh, the French professor shouting *J'accuse ...!* But instead he seemed genuinely perplexed and forlorn. Chevalier wrote that he'd taken a sabbatical and gone to New York in hopes of landing a translating job with the Office of War Information. He'd cooled his heels in the Big Apple for three months waiting for his security clearance to be processed—something that should have been a routine matter—only to have it denied for reasons no one would discuss, mystifying him. In the interim, with no work, he'd exhausted his funds. The letter concluded:

> *I don't know if this will reach you, which is the reason why I do not write you more. I should like to hear from you if you can spare time for the personally human, in these days when the human seems to become depersonalized.*

And then his signature—first name only—the letters leaning, in a way that Robert used to find amusing but could summon no smile for today, to the left.

Oppie supposed the acid at the back of his throat was what guilt tasted like. With a shaking hand he set the page down, wondering what *Schadenfreude* Peer de Silva—who must have been briefed by Boris Pash by now—had felt in sending the letter on to Oppie with nary a word struck out.

Chapter 8

1944

I wanted to live and to give and I got paralyzed somehow. I think I would have been a liability all my life—at least I could take away the burden of a paralyzed soul from a fighting world.

—Jean Tatlock

"Can I have a moment, Doctor?"

Oppie prided himself on being able to recognize anyone he knew by their voice, and the one belonging to this speaker, deep, a tad oleaginous, made his stomach tighten. He swiveled his desk chair around. "Certainly, Captain de Silva."

Peer de Silva had the distinction of being the only West Point graduate stationed at Los Alamos; he'd earned the enmity of the scientists not just by censoring their mail but by confiscating their personal cameras, too. In his mid-twenties but with the brittle demeanor of a cynic a half-century older, de Silva was one of those prickly souls who took offense at everything. He'd once burst into a group-leaders' meeting to complain that a young engineer had had the effrontery to perch on the edge of his desk. Oppie probably shouldn't have used the tone he had—the one he normally saved for the thickest of undergraduates, the benighted fools who proved there were indeed such things as stupid questions—when he'd snapped back, "In this lab, anybody may sit on anyone's desk—yours, mine, *anyone's.*"

As he beheld de Silva now, Oppie noted something odd in the man's bearing. His face—handsome enough but always lifeless, like a Roman statue—was cocked at a strange angle, and his hands were apparently clasped behind his back as if he were willing himself to appear at ease. "I have ... news," he said, and Oppie noted the small gap where an adjective—good, bad?—had disappeared under a mental stroke of the captain's thick black marker.

"And if you share it," Oppenheimer offered, trying for lightness, "then we'll both have news."

"It's about your—" The younger man aborted that run and started again. "It concerns Miss Tatlock."

Oppie felt his heart begin to race. He knew that the security people were aware of his relationship with Jean; knew that they knew she was, or had been, a member of the Communist Party; and—yes—knew that seven months ago, when he'd taken that unauthorized trip to San Francisco, he'd spent the night with her. A lot of poker was played here on the mesa, but Robert rarely joined in; still, he was conscious that he was being scrutinized for tells. "Yes?" he said as nonchalantly as he could.

"I figured you'd want to know," de Silva said. "I'm sorry, sir, but she's dead."

Oppie's first thought was that this was some ruse, a test, to see if ... if what? He would flout security again? Surely Jean couldn't be gone. He'd have expected to hear through mutual friends—the Serbers, perhaps—or directly from her father John, now an emeritus professor.

"Word just came in," de Silva said as if he'd read the suspicion in Robert's eyes. "Honestly, sir, it's true."

That it was de Silva breaking the news meant it was the fruit of surveillance. Had her phone been bugged? And, if so, had that jackass Pash ordered it because of Robert's last visit—his last visit *ever,* he realized now—to her back in June? Oppie sagged in his chair. Jean was just twenty-nine and had been in good physical health. That meant something like an automobile collision or—

Good *physical* health ...

"Did she k—was it an accident?"

"I'm sorry, sir, but she took her own life."

Both legs and arms went numb, and the world blurred in front of him.

"Tell me ... tell me the details," Oppie said, fishing a Chesterfield from a crumpled pack and lighting it.

"Apparently, she'd agreed to phone her father last night but failed to do so. He went by this morning to check on her and had to break in through a window. He found her body in the bathtub."

Robert exhaled smoke and watched it rise toward the ceiling. Thoughts—some inchoate, some in words—percolated through his mind. Last year, he had paid his fifteen cents to see a recent flick called *Casablanca* in the base theater; he knew full well that the problems of two little people didn't amount to a hill of beans in this crazy world. But, still, he'd all but abandoned her, except for that one furtive night, since his move to Los Alamos. Had his desertion—his dereliction of duty—led to that complicated, conflicted woman, the only woman he had ever truly loved, taking her life?

His heart felt like a crumpled-up kraft-paper bag, each expansion of it scratching his innards. He couldn't talk to Kitty about this, but he had to talk to *someone.* "Are you as good at keeping secrets as you are at discovering them, Captain?" De Silva opened his mouth to reply, but Oppie raised the hand holding his cigarette. "No, I don't expect you to answer that. But let me tell you, Miss Tatlock—Jean—is a remarkable girl. In years gone by, we were close to marriage two times, but ..." Oppie trailed off, surprised by the way his throat caught—more than his usual smoker's cough; a constriction as if his very core were loath to let out the words. "But both times she ... she took a step back."

That much he'd say, but no more—not about her ... or about him. She'd retreat each time she realized she was also attracted to women. And yet they shared so much: tastes, interests. And he could hardly fault someone else for being indeterminate, for being uncertain, for being both simultaneously *this* and *that.*

"I'm sorry," de Silva said, and Oppie chose to accept the words as sincere.

"She'd wanted to see me before I came here," Oppie continued, "but I couldn't, not then. It was three months before I ..."

"Yes," said de Silva softly. "I know."

"Of course you do." Oppie nodded curtly. "I am deeply devoted to her. And, yes, as you also surely know, even after my marriage to Kitty, she and I have maintained ..." He stopped, drew a breath. "... *did* maintain an ... intimate association."

Such measured words, Oppie thought. Why couldn't he just *say* it, loudly and clearly? He loved Jean, loved her supple mind, loved her passionate convictions, loved her gentle, artistic spirit, loved—

The wetness on his cheek surprised him, and Oppie lifted his empty hand to wipe the tear away. But another replaced it, joined soon by many more. "Forgive me."

De Silva's voice was gentle. "There's nothing to forgive."

But there was. He had failed her. He'd known all about her bouts of depression. They had discussed them often, and he had talked her back from the brink more than once, even at last sharing the one time he'd contemplated taking his own life, in the summer of 1926, whisked to Brittany by his parents after what had seemed to his twenty-two-year-old self a disastrous year socially and scientifically at Cambridge's Cavendish Laboratory. And still, despite his candor, despite his support, despite his love, Jean was *gone.*

She had introduced him to the poetry of John Donne, reciting it often from memory. *Batter my heart, three-person'd God,* she'd say, and now he knew what that truly meant, the trinity he didn't believe in inflicting a sorrow he was sure would never pass.

"Well," said de Silva—a man's man, a soldier unused to emotional displays—"I should leave you to your work. Again, doctor, my condolences."

"Thank you," Oppie said. De Silva left, gently closing the naked wooden door behind him.

The tears were coming freely now. He rarely paid much heed to his chronic cough, but the combination of sniffling and hacking was ghastly, and his hand wasn't steady enough to operate his silver lighter; it kept spitting flame near but not near enough to the tip of his next cigarette. He swiveled his chair to look out the window, but the view of the mesa was as blurry as it was during a thunderstorm, even though it was a cloudless day.

There was a rap on his inner office door. He didn't want to see anyone and so he remained quiet. But the door swung open anyway, revealing Bob Serber. "Have you heard ...?" Serber trailed off as Robert swung around and he took in his face, doubtless red and puffy. Bob was silent for a moment, swimming in Oppie's vision, then: "Can I get you anything? A drink, maybe?"

Robert snorted, pulling mucous back up his nose. He shook his head. "It's just awful, isn't it?" Serber said. "She was so ..." But no single word could encapsulate Jean, and he settled on "sweet," Oppie's own favorite description for an irresistible problem in science. Robert nodded, and, after a moment more and with a wan smile, Serber withdrew.

Oppie sat for a while—it felt like an hour, although his wall clock said it was only fifteen minutes—then got up. His secretary Vera had returned from wherever she'd been when de Silva and Serber had visited, and she, too, could see that he was distraught, but when she asked what was wrong, he simply said he was going for a walk.

He headed outside and immediately ran into William "Deak" Parsons, the forty-two-year-old head of the ordnance division and second in command here at Los Alamos. "Hey, Oppie," Deak began, but he, too, clearly saw the pain on Robert's face. A good Navy man, conservative and tradition-bound, Parsons was often at loggerheads with the freewheeling civilian George Kistiakowsky, who was spearheading a revolutionary implosion-bomb approach. Oppie, hardly in the mood to hear another plea for arbitration, held up a hand before Deak could speak further. "If it's about explosive lenses, Kisty wins; if it's anything else, you win."

He continued walking and, even with his splayed-foot gate, he felt unsteady on his feet. There was a *crème brûlée* crust of snow over the frozen mud, and now that he'd finally managed to light up again, the clouds emerging from his mouth were equal parts smoke and condensation. Ashley Pond was frozen, a giant cataract-covered eye staring heavenward.

He made his way toward the stables, left over from the Los Alamos Ranch School. There were horses for rent here, but Oppie and Kitty, both accomplished riders, each owned their own. He saddled up Chico, his sleek fourteen-year-old chestnut. On a Sunday, when he had hours to kill, Oppie would take the gelding from the east end of Santa Fe west toward the mountain trails. But he didn't want to bother with off-site security today. Instead, he rode Chico around the perimeter of the mesa, just inside the barbed-wire fence. Getting out to the edge took care, but Oppie was deft, playing Chico like a musical instrument, bringing each hoof down individually in the perfect sequence to negotiate even the roughest terrain.

They trotted at first as the horse warmed up, then cantered, then, at last, galloped, faster and faster, and faster still, circumnavigating the facility, an electron in an outermost orbit—no, no, a proton hurtling in a cyclotron: building up speed with each lap, wind whipping Chico's mane, slapping Oppie's cheeks, flinging tears from his face and wails from his lungs. He urged his mount to even greater velocities, the horse responding with grim conviction, skeletal poplars racing by them as if one could outrun pain, outrun guilt, outrun love.

Chapter 9

1945

I am about the leading theoretician in America. That does not mean the best. Wigner is certainly better and Oppenheimer and Teller probably just as good. But I do more and talk more and that counts too.

—**Hans Bethe**,
in a letter to his mother

As the months wore on, Oppie struggled to keep his emotions private. He was in charge here; everyone looked to him. When he saw Jean's face in one of the clouds above the mesa, in the swirl of grain on a desktop, in the dreams that came as he tossed and turned each night, he kept the sadness to himself.

Days bonded into weeks, weeks fused into months, his sorrow, and maybe even his guilt, lessening slowly, but he knew both were asymptotes: they would continue to abate infinitely but could never fully disappear. Still, here, fifteen months after Jean's passing, he was functioning, and functioning, surely, was the best one could hope for. And so today he did what he usually did, walking down the corridors of the laboratory section, enclosed by its own additional fence; even the MPs were forbidden entrance. There were always sounds here: equipment chugging, pumps whirring, typewriters clattering, and a welter of voices with accents drawn from across two continents.

And one of those voices—deep, rumbling—came to Oppie louder than the rest. "No, I have *not* made a mistake!"

The accent was Hungarian, and the voice was that of Edward Teller; it was coming out of the open door to Teller's office, just ahead.

As Oppie closed the distance, he heard Hans Bethe striving for a soothing, reasonable tone. "Well, you were wrong about the sky possibly catching fire." In 1942, Teller had suggested that a single blast of a fusion bomb, or even a fission one, might ignite all the hydrogen in the oceans or all the nitrogen in the atmosphere, destroying the world. The then-nascent atomic-bomb effort was almost halted after that, but Bethe had shown that Teller had underestimated the radiative-cooling effects that would prevent such catastrophes.

"One error in three years!" exclaimed Teller. "*These* figures are correct." Teller and Bethe had collaborated on a theory of projectile shock-wave propagation before the war, but Teller was miffed with Oppie for having appointed the sturdy Strasbourgian as head of the Theoretical Division instead of him. Bethe laughed easily at himself and others, while Teller brooded and held grudges.

Oppie had settled on what he'd now been told was the "management by walking around" style: being seen to be seen, poking his head into this lab or that workshop all over the mesa to check on things—so neither Bethe nor Teller were surprised when he appeared in the doorway. Teller was hunched in a wooden chair. Bethe was taller anyway but as he stood near Teller's desk he loomed over the Hungarian. "But they can't possibly be right. Don't you see, Edward—"

"What's up?" asked Oppie, leaning against the doorjamb. As always, he scanned the blackboards in any room he entered. Teller had created a chart labeled "Weapon Ideas," with columns including "Yield" and "Delivery Method." The final and most-powerful entry, Oppie noted, had its mode of delivery listed as "Backyard." Ah: if that device had the yield specified, it would destroy all life on earth—so there'd be no need to transport it anywhere before use.

Teller turned his steel-gray eyes toward Oppie. "Hans thinks my solar-fusion math is wrong," he said in the same derisive tone he might have used to declaim a ridiculous notion such as "Hans thinks the world is flat."

Oppie turned to Bethe. Hans, not Edward, was the authority on solar fusion. In a pair of 1939 *Physical Review* papers, Bethe had analyzed the reactions by which hydrogen can be fused into helium, and he'd worked out the math for fusion via the carbon-nitrogen-oxygen cycle, which he'd concluded was the sun's main way of producing energy. "This *is* Bethe's field," Oppie ventured.

"Irrelevant," snapped Teller; his accent was as thick as his massive eyebrows. "I've gone over and over the figures. There's nothing wrong with my equations."

Oppie was getting irritated. From the very beginning of this project, Teller had insisted that the focus on a fission bomb was a mistake. At the initial gathering of the group Oppie had dubbed "the Luminaries" at Berkeley almost three years ago, in July 1942, Robert had begun by taking the scientists through the devastation wrought by what was, hitherto, the largest human-caused explosion ever: the 1917 Halifax disaster, which had occurred when a French munitions ship collided with a Norwegian vessel in waters near that Nova Scotia port city. The resulting explosion—equivalent to 2,900 tons of T.N.T.—killed 2,000 and injured 9,000 more. What they were hoping to build, Oppie had said, would be two or three times more powerful: a weapon so dreadful Hitler would surely immediately stand down as soon as its destructive potential was demonstrated—assuming that the Nazis didn't build one of the damn things first.

But that wasn't enough for Teller. He had stood up before the others, who were in folding chairs arranged in a ragged circle on the top floor of Le Conte Hall, and declared, "A fission device is surely possible. Easy, in fact. But there are more interesting problems."

Oppie remembered leaning his seat back and taking a deep, calming breath of the summer air coming in through the open French doors that led to the balcony. He'd brought all those people to California to exchange ideas, but it had turned out to be akin to herding non-Schrödingerian cats; keeping such peripatetic minds focused took constant cajoling. "Such as?" he'd asked.

"Enrico Fermi has this notion," Teller said. "A fission weapon, trivial though it is, could be used to ignite deuterium, creating a *fusion* bomb. I've been doing the math." He indicated sheets of paper in front of him. "If we used a fission bomb to ignite just twenty-six pounds of liquid heavy hydrogen, the resulting fusion explosion would be equivalent to *millions* of tons of T.N.T."

"Millions ..." repeated Bob Serber in his soft, lisping voice.

"Exactly," said Teller. "Forget reproducing this Halifax explosion—a trifle. Think of the Tunguska event!" In 1908, something exploded in an unpopulated part of central Siberia, flattening over half-a-million acres of forest. It was twenty years before the first Russian scientific expedition made it to the center of the devastation. They found no blast or impact crater, leading them to conclude that perhaps an in-falling meteor or comet had exploded just before hitting the ground. They estimated the force of the airburst had been between ten and thirty megatons—ten and thirty million tons of T.N.T.

"Good God," said Oppenheimer. "What good would such a thing possibly be? You could only use it for genocide."

"Our foe," Teller had replied simply, "is a genocidist." He'd looked around that seminar room. Teller was Jewish; so were Oppenheimer, Serber, Bethe, and several of the others who'd been present.

"An atomic-fission bomb," Teller had continued, "is straightforward; your grad students could make one. But a bomb based on nuclear fusion, capable of Tunguska-scale devastation? *That* is a challenge worthy of *us.*"

Ever since then, Oppie had been indulging Teller, letting him work on the fusion-based bomb the Hungarian had dubbed "the super" while everybody else had been solely devoted to the more-tractable problem of creating a fission bomb. After they'd all moved here to Los Alamos, Oppie had also ignored the numerous complaints about Teller playing his grand piano—he'd refused to come to the mesa without it—late at night. As Oppie had said to one maddened housewife, "It'd be objectionable only if he didn't play so well."

"Okay, you two," said Robert, looking first at Teller then at Bethe. "Let's keep the noise down, shall we? And, Hans, you've got important work to do."

Teller clearly got the slight. He detected slights even when they *weren't* there; he never missed an actual one. Edward glared at Oppenheimer, but Robert was used to that by now. He headed on down the corridor, looking for the next fire to put out.

Chapter 10

A Faust of the twentieth century, [Oppenheimer] had sold his soul to the atom bomb.

—Haakon Chevalier

Another fatiguing day finally came to its close. Oppie, his duck-footed gait helping him keep his balance on the dirt roads, returned to his home on Bathtub Row. It was tiny compared with his place at One Eagle Hill, but, for all that, it now seemed vast, empty. His infant daughter was in a friend's care, and neither Kitty nor his son Peter had been home for many days now.

He supposed he should have foreseen Kitty's need to flee. This time, at least, she'd lasted four months before bolting rather than just six weeks: that's all she'd managed after their son had been born. He wondered if other women suffered such ... melancholy, he supposed it was, after giving birth. In any event, that first time, upon seeing that Kitty was overwhelmed, Robert had asked Haakon and Barb Chevalier to look after Peter for them while he spirited Kitty away to their Perro Caliente ranch. It had been two months before Kitty had been ready to return to Berkeley. With luck, that would be all she'd need this time, as well. Perhaps she'd be home tomorrow or by the weekend.

He always hoped that when he opened the front door—never locked here on the mesa—that he'd see his family back within, but, no, tonight was no different than last night, or the one before, or the one before that.

He missed the smell of cooking in the small kitchen Kitty had insisted be added to the place. He missed the *zoom-zoom* engine sounds Peter used to make as he pushed his toy trucks across the linoleum. And he missed the scent of Kitty's endless string of Lucky Strikes, the sound of her chipping ice for her drinks, the sight of her—bantam, brisk, vital—swooping about the house, a dervish soused in gin.

But all was quiet now, all empty. When Oppie moved, his footfalls echoed; when he sat, as now, there was nothing but silence so total that he could hear his heart beat.

Heart; they called the nucleus the heart of the atom, but in an atomic nucleus there were only two kinds of particles: protons and neutrons. Oppie's heart, though, consisted of at least three. First, there were the particles that drove him to lead, to control. Perhaps, he thought, that drive stemmed from a mortifying experience when he was fourteen. His parents had shipped him off to summer camp where the other boys, appalled by his prissiness, had stripped him bare, painted his dick and ass green, and locked him overnight in the icehouse. If there was to be a hierarchy, he'd vowed, never again would he be at its bottom.

Then there were the nucleons of ambition. His mind was unfettered, his interests myriad; as General Groves had observed, he could talk expertly about anything except sports, and do so in multiple languages. Yes, he didn't have a Nobel, not yet, but if his team succeeded here—if the damn thing worked—glory and fame greater than any medal could confer would come to him.

And, finally, there were the particles of ...

What to call it?

Regret? Longing?

It was both and neither. Jean was irretrievably gone; the *Bhagavad Gita*, which Oppie had discovered in his twenties, may have told of endless cycles of reincarnation, but he no more believed in them than he did in Ptolemy's planetary epicycles. Beautiful intellectual constructs, to be sure, but merely that. She existed no more, and nothing could change the past.

And Kitty? Kitty, whom he'd married instead of Jean? Whom he'd built some sort of life with? Kitty, the woman he was expected to say out loud that he loved? What of her?

She would return. Surely she would. She *had* to.

Oppie sighed in the moonlit room. He smoked so many cigarettes even he got tired of them, so from time to time he switched to a pipe; he selected a straight-stemmed billiard one from his rack and lit it, the wooden match hissing in the quiet, walnut tobacco glowing red, the smoke lost in the darkness.

Oppie had often thought about suicide and had come particularly close once—the event related to his time at Cambridge's Cavendish Laboratory he'd told Jean about. There was a fundamental instability in his heart, his core, his nucleus; no slow neutrons were needed to perturb it. He was a genius, damn it all, a thundering intellect. But under pressure, he did, he had to admit, unfathomably stupid things.

In the fall of 1925, Oppie's tutor at the Cavendish had been Patrick Blackett, just seven years his senior, and, like Oppie, tall, thin, and refined, with an extraordinarily elongated head as if his chin had grown as a counterbalance to his heightening brain. Robert had had—he could admit this to himself if never to Jean or Kitty—a sexual attraction to the man. Oppie had been a poor experimentalist at the best of times, and when Blackett hovered over him, he found himself constantly flustered and forever dropping things; to this day, the sound of shattering glass terrified him.

Eventually, his desire for Blackett and the man's clucking disapproval at his ineptitude proved too much. He bought an apple from a greengrocer and—Oppie's head shook as he recalled it—he slowly and carefully painted potassium cyanide on the skin, then left it on Blackett's desk.

Whether the fruit symbolized the stereotypical gift from pupil to teacher or a stymied offer of forbidden knowledge—the congress they'd never share—Oppie couldn't say; once again, it was both and neither. Oppie had been late, he realized, to sexual awakening—and this, *this,* was not what he'd expected. It was bad enough to discover that he was as much animal as intellectual, driven by urges, but *this* urge could not be allowed to endure.

And so, logically, necessarily, rationally, the best thing was to eliminate the temptation, to remove the object of his perverse affection.

Fortunately, another student suspected the apple was poisoned, and Blackett was warned. Oppie's father Julius begged Cambridge not to press criminal charges. The university finally relented on condition that Oppie come under the care of a psychiatrist. The doctor, Ernest Jones—yes, *that* Ernest Jones, the one he'd regaled Jean about on the night they'd met, the first English-speaking practitioner of Freudian psychoanalysis—had diagnosed him with *dementia praecox;* in the twenty years since, that term had been deprecated in favor of schizophrenia. Jones soon discharged Oppie as "a hopeless case," adding that "further analysis would do more harm than good," leaving Robert looking for his own answers in the *Gita* and other mystical Eastern texts.

Despite his high price and posh office, Oppie doubted the accuracy of Jones's diagnosis, but he knew that *something* had been and continued to be wrong with him. Still, with a force of will, he kept it all together, just as the strong nuclear force kept positively charged protons from exploding away from each other. That force was the most powerful known to physics; oh, yes, with a carefully orchestrated chain reaction, nuclei could be made to split, but even the mighty stars thought that too much work; they preferred to fuse smaller nuclei into larger ones—the strong force was not easily defeated.

But Oppie's force of will? *That* was growing ever more rickety. So much was pulling at him—pressure and pain; duty and sorrow. Everything depended on this lab, their work, him.

He drew on his pipe and thought of gooseflesh and green paint, of broken beakers and poisoned apples, of Patrick Blackett and Jean Tatlock.

At last, he made his way to his bedroom, undressed, lay down on the hard bed, and wrapped a cool sheet around his bony frame, a winding cloth for the dead.

Chapter 11

This is absolutely intolerable. We defeated Nazi armies, we occupied Berlin and Peenemünde, but the Americans got the rocket engineers. What could be more revolting and more inexcusable?

—Joseph Stalin

Wernher von Braun fiddled madly with the tuning controls on the wood-encased tabletop radio in his hotel room, high up in the Alps, trying to get the station back. His heart was pounding because of what he thought he'd heard a moment ago, but before he told the others he had to be sure. If he were wrong, a station playing a waltz would be proof enough; if he were right, then *every* broadcaster should be carrying the same story. The Bakelite knob spun under his thick fingers.

Static.

More static.

And then: "*— our glorious Führer fell this afternoon in Berlin, fighting to the last breath against the accursed Bolshevik hordes. Born in Austria on April twentieth, 1889, Adolf Hitler, the greatest leader the world has ever known, was just fifty-six ...*"

Wernher collapsed back onto the room's sole chair, its pine seat creaking under his two hundred and fifty pounds. A broad-shouldered and beefy thirty-three-year-old, six feet with sandy hair and blue eyes, he looked more like an American footballer than the lead engineer of the Nazi rocket program—except for his recent injury. Wernher's left arm, broken in two places during a car accident, was encased in a heavy cast, half raised, a stillborn *Sieg Heil.*

Von Braun had met the Führer four times, the first in 1939 and the last just shy of two years ago, in July of '43. He'd felt the man's preternatural charisma; everyone who'd ever encountered him had. Wernher liked to think of himself as apolitical but he had worn the S.S. uniform as part of an equestrian unit with, if not fascist pride, at least a certain appreciation of its sexy black leather and metal fittings.

That Hitler would die this year had been inevitable, whether as now, gloriously in battle, or later in front of an Allied firing squad. Many would grieve his passing but von Braun, ever the engineer, quickly turned his analytical mind to the problem at hand. He'd been sure the war was lost as far back as the beginning of January 1945, five months ago, and had called his rocketry team together then, baldly declaring that Germany would be defeated. Anywhere else in the Reich, before any other group, such a statement would have seen him sent to a concentration camp, if not executed, but his rocketeers were practical men, even if their heads were in the stars.

Indeed, in March of last year, Wernher and two of his subordinates had drunk far too much wine at a party in the spa town of Zinnowitz, and Wernher had let his tongue flap about his growing belief, even then, that Germany was heading for overwhelming defeat. That had been damning enough, but he'd also revealed something else he normally kept to himself, loudly exclaiming *"Ist mir scheißegal"*—*I don't give a shit*—about the military uses of rockets; *his* goal was manned space flight. Himmler's agents arrested all three of them for putting far-off dreams ahead of war production, locking them up for more than a week.

But now that the Führer was dead, Wernher was sure the authoritarian regime would unravel quickly. Most Nazis had sworn allegiance to Hitler personally; many who yesterday would have called surrender treason today were doubtless preparing to do just that. Von Braun had no intention of letting him or his colleagues be imprisoned—what they knew was far too valuable. But to which of the triumphant countries should they entrust their precious heritage? Who among the victors deserved the gift of space travel?

He'd already discussed this with his staff. They'd agreed that when the time came they would surrender as a unit, rather than let the Allies pick whom to employ—and whom to execute. They'd also agreed that they couldn't stand the French (who could?); that the Soviets were animals; and that the British wouldn't be able to afford anything as grandiose as a peacetime British Experimental Rocket Group. That left the Americans. Most of the rocketeers had never met a Yankee and what knowledge they had of their country came from movies—but the Germans knew a real devil here; one they didn't know surely could be no worse.

There was no American Prometheus—no brilliant scientist or engineer who had taken fire from the gods; it was conventional warfare, pure and simple, that had ground the Reich down, like bone crushed under an apothecary's pestle. But there *was* a German Prometheus, and he—Herr Professor Doktor Wernher Magnus Maximilian Freiherr von Braun—was it: his V-2 rockets traveled so fast they struck London *before* the roar of their engines could be heard there; a godlike fire indeed! And that power—the ability to make the most sophisticated rockets the world had ever seen—would be their deliverance.

Wernher rose, the bedroom chair squeaking its relief, and headed down to the beer hall of Haus Ingeburg, the ski lodge on the German-Austrian border in which he and his coterie of a hundred and seventy men were hiding out. Weeks ago, they'd secreted their fourteen tons of papers and blueprints in a deserted mine shaft in the Harz mountains, lest the S.S. destroy them rather than allow the material to fall into enemy hands. Then they'd abandoned the Peenemünde Rocket Base, where they would have been sitting ducks for Allied bombers. Here, in the rarefied air of the Alps, along the winding road that was currently known as the Adolf Hitler Pass but surely would soon revert to its pre-war name of Oberjoch, they had been biding their time.

The moment he entered the beer hall, pungent with smoke and schnitzel, Dieter Huzel, an electrical engineer a year younger than von Braun, caught him by his good arm. *"Mein Gott,"* he said, eyes wide. His face was drained of color as he pointed to the hall's radio, which had been turned off but must have recently been on. *"Mein Gott."*

"We have to move fast," Wernher said. "Where's Dornberger?"

Huzel pointed to a booth, and Wernher made his way over. Although von Braun was the (more-or-less) civilian head of the rocketry program, the top man was Major General Walter Dornberger, who had personally recruited Wernher despite others' misgivings. Von Braun had successfully maneuvered Dornberger to choose Peenemünde, a place dear to his family, as the site of the rocket works. Still, they did clash from time to time, with Wernher interested in *die schöne Wissenschaft*—the beautiful science—of rocketry whereas the general was obsessively focused on building weapons.

Dornberger, his thin comb-over no more defense against baldness than the German ground forces had proven to be against the implacable Russian troops, had his head bent; he was apparently staring at the green painted wood of the tabletop. "General," Wernher said softly.

The older man, a veteran of both world wars who had seen the Fatherland fall twice now, slowly looked up. It seemed to take a while for his gray eyes to focus. "Yes?"

"It's time. There's no choice."

Wernher had expected a protest, but the fight had gone out of Dornberger; he looked deflated, a study in concavities. "No," the general said. "No, there isn't, is there?" He moved to get up but, apparently discovering he lacked the strength just then to do so, instead gestured for von Braun to sit opposite him. Wernher did that, laying his heavy cast on the table, bright white covering green, the same color scheme they'd all seen on the springtime Alps these past weeks.

"I know you get intelligence reports ..." Wernher said softly.

Dornberger nodded but said nothing.

"And ..." prodded von Braun. "There must be something useful, no?"

Dornberger made a visible effort to focus, to rally. "Yes," he said at last. "A unit of American soldiers has set up a base at the bottom of this mountain."

"Which side of the mountain?"

"The Austrian."

Wernher nodded. "Tomorrow, then?"

"Ja," said the General softly, looking down at the painted wood once more. *"Morgen."*

Wernher rose. Across the room, Dieter Huzel had moved to the piano bench. He started to play the *Deutschlandlied.* Others gathered around, including, Wernher saw, his own younger brother, Magnus. He went over to join the group, and Magnus asked Huzel to go back to the beginning. He did so, and Magnus, who had a choirboy's warbling alto, sang: *"Deutschland, Deutschland über alles, Über alles in der Welt ..."*

Germany, thought Wernher, would never be above all again, but he, or someone else, riding one of his rockets, would soon indeed be above all in the world.

He didn't join in even though he knew that for him, as for the rest of them, it would be the last opportunity ever to sing that song.

Sometimes it's the simplest things that make the biggest impression. Wernher von Braun had enjoyed every bite of the sumptuous meal the Allied soldiers had prepared for him and his men now that they were all down at the base of the mountain, but once that meal was over, he found himself reaching for the bread again—a loaf of a whiteness to rival the mountain snows. It had been—*Gott!*—four years since he'd tasted white bread. He slathered butter on a slice and took a bite. After the hardtack of war-time privation, this was heavenly; even he would have admitted just now that there really hadn't been a greater invention than sliced bread, at least not when it was of such perfect hue and texture and softness, the crust yielding easily, the center practically melting on the tongue.

Two dozen of his senior men sat around the table, enjoying beer, wine, coffee, and cigars. But all eyes were on his brother Magnus.

"And then what?" prodded Wernher.

Magnus raised a pint of beer to his lips, wiped off the foam mustache, and continued. "I'd tied a white handkerchief—thank you, Dieter!—to the bike's handlebars. It's a *long* way down to the foot of the mountain, but I was able to coast almost all the way; you, dear brother, never could have made the trip with your arm like that. Anyway, there's never an enemy soldier around when you want one! I looked and looked. Plenty of pretty girls; what they say about the Alpine air is true. And some dairy farmers, and a local boy who wanted to know where I'd gotten the bicycle. And then, at last, there he was, just wandering down the street." Magnus pointed at one of the three Americans who were also at the table.

He must have understood some German because he said, “Yes, that was me!”

“*Ja*, that was him. A private from the 44th American infantry division. I rode closer, lifting my hands up off the handlebars, and called out in English, ‘My name is Magnus von Braun!’”

The private, apparently recognizing where Magnus was in the story, joined in, shouting the rest: “‘My brother invented the V-2! We wish to surrender!’”

The private and Magnus both laughed, and Wernher, his cast resting on the linen tablecloth, shook his head; even he hadn’t expected it to be that simple. “And that was it?”

“Well,” said Magnus, “the private had never heard of me, or even you, brother, but the V-2? *That* he had heard of.”

A Bavarian barmaid came by with fresh steins. Wernher downed the last of his previous drink in order to snare one of the new ones. “My friend here,” said Magnus, indicating the private, “didn’t speak much German, and I had only so much English. It took a bit but—”

“Tell me you said, ‘We come in peace,’” quipped Dieter Huzel, who had enjoyed borrowing Wernher’s copies of the American magazine *Astounding Stories* before the war.

Magnus laughed. “Not quite, but I got the gist across, and the private led me—I walked my bike beside him—to the camp, where a colonel was available. His accent was so thick—or mine was, I guess, from his point of view—that we had trouble communicating ...”

“All the while the rest of us were shitting bricks waiting for word!” Dieter said.

“I was as quick as I could be,” said Magnus, “without, you know, being inhospitable.” He raised his beer. “Naturally, we had to drink on it before the colonel drove me back up the mountain.”

The colonel was at the head of the long table: a red-haired middle-aged man perhaps of Irish stock, with freckles. “We had a list,” he said in English, and Magnus did his best to translate for the rocketeers. “We called it the Black List—all the top Germans our science and engineering specialists wanted to talk to.” He nodded affably at Wernher. “Of course, your name was at the top of it.”

Magnus went on. “The colonel had told me they weren’t set up for so many prisoners of war, and it was clear we *wanted* to be with them; we weren’t going to run off. So why not let us enjoy this place's hospitality until it's time to leave?" *This place* was a sprawling Bavarian mansion in the market town of Reutte that had been commandeered by the American infantry.

Wernher raised his stein in a salute to the colonel. *"Danke schön."*

The colonel briefly frowned as if searching his memory for some appropriate German to reply with, then he made a little shrug, conceding that what he'd come up with wasn't exactly the right thing, but would do in a pinch: *"Guten Tag."*

Wernher smiled. It was indeed.

The colonel switched back to English again, and Magnus translated: "He says, 'I had my doubts, of course. The name von Braun I knew, but I'd expected some weak-looking gray-haired egghead, not—" he gestured, encompassing both Wernher's youth and physique "— Li'l Abner here.'"

Laughter erupted when Magnus finished conveying this to his colleagues; their Wernher was indeed both a *Wunderkind* and an *Übermensch.*

"Of course," said the colonel, "others are on their way here to take charge of all of you. I can't say what reception you'll get, but for now ..."

When Magnus finished the translation, Wernher nodded and reached for another white slice of heaven. For now, at least, he wouldn't worry about what the future held.

Chapter 12

For me, Hitler was the personification of evil and the primary justification for the atomic-bomb work. Now that the bomb could not be used against the Nazis, doubts arose. Those doubts, even if they do not appear in official reports, were discussed in many private conversations.

—**Emilio Segrè**,
winner of the Nobel Prize in physics

Blood of Christ.

Perhaps an odd thought for a Jew, Oppie reflected, but, then again, he wasn't much of a Jew. But he *was* a polyglot, and although the name of the mountains to the east was just a mellifluous phrase to many of those he'd brought here, Oppie couldn't think of *Sangre de Cristo* without its attached meaning.

He knew the debate surrounding the naming of this sub-range of the Rockies. Yes, it might have been to acknowledge the reddish hue the peaks often took at sunrise, or later at sunset, but Oppie preferred the story that *"Sangre de Cristo"* were the final words uttered near here by a Catholic priest mortally wounded by Apaches.

Germany was a largely Christian country—damn near exclusively so, after the Nazi slaughter—and so Oppie had long imagined that when the atomic bomb was finally dropped on one of its cities, many who didn't die instantly would pass on while mumbling some similar invocation. The German version was instantly in his consciousness: *Blut von Christus.*

But that wasn't going to happen now; there would be no atomic-fission fireball over the Fatherland. Hitler and his mistress had committed suicide two days ago, on April 30, 1945.

Oppie's strength, he knew, was in making connections, but the image of Jean dead in her bathtub that came back yet again was one he could have done without at this moment. He tipped his head, the brim of his hat momentarily eclipsing the jagged mountains, as he tamped down that memory. Other notions, though, weren't so easily banished.

They had failed.

He had failed.

As young Richard Feynman had said last night, "Damn it, Oppie, Hitler was evil personified. He was the whole fucking *point.* You told us—everybody told us—that what we were doing here was the key to defeating the Nazis."

But, in the end, conventional troops pressing in on Berlin—and maybe, Oppie mused, Hitler having learned of Mussolini's corpse being strung up by its ankles and stoned and spat upon by those who had suffered under his regime—had moved *Der Führer* to accomplish with a single bullet what Oppie's multi-million-dollar gadget was supposed to do: end the war in Europe.

Feynman wasn't wrong, and he was hardly the only Manhattan Project scientist questioning whether they should continue. Leo Szilard in Chicago was telling everyone that there was no need now to go on with bomb development, and although General Groves hated the pear-shaped Hungarian, Oppie was fond of—and, more importantly, respected—Leo.

But if they *did* continue their work, the target now would be Japan, not Germany. Oppie knew Germany well from his years at Göttingen studying under Max Born, but he didn't know Japan or its language at all except to say that there were few Christians there. If the bomb were dropped on Tokyo or Kyoto, no one would invoke the blood of Christ as their lives ended. But suddenly, overnight, the notion of killing Germans—in some ways an altruistic venture for Americans, who, after all, had little direct stake in the European theater—had shifted to killing Japanese, an act that had more than a whiff about it of being revenge for Pearl Harbor. Hardly what a graduate of New York's Ethical Culture School should be striving for. "Deed before creed" indeed!

Yes, the Pacific war was brutal and, yes, it needed to be finished as quickly as possible; American boys were dying over there every single day. But there was no hint that the Japs might have an atomic-bomb program of their own and so no reason to counter it with one of ours.

Oppie took another long look at the Sangre de Cristo mountains then turned and started walking back toward Site Y, the random alphabetic assignment suddenly seeming appropriate: a road with a fork in it—and they were now heading along a new path. His early-morning shadow stretched across the mesa in front of him, long and dark.

Later that May, Oppie traveled to Virginia for the first gathering of what Secretary of War Henry Stimson had dubbed "the Interim Committee," a nice, non-threatening name for the group that would advise Harry S. Truman—who, as vice president, had been blissfully unaware of the Manhattan Project until he was sworn in a month ago as FDR's successor—about the first use of atomic weapons.

Leo Szilard of the Chicago Met Lab had gotten wind of the fact that Oppie was out East, although he probably didn't know why; still, he insisted on a meeting. Robert obliged; he had the use of a small office with sickly yellow walls at the War Department when he was in town. He told Szilard to take the train there; Leo did so, and an MP escorted him to the appropriate room when he arrived.

Szilard had a way of wearing his trench coat unbuttoned that suggested a cape; there was a theatricality to him that some found gauche, but Robert rather enjoyed. As he took off the coat, Leo said, "Did you not get my letter? I wrote you!"

Oppie had indeed received the typed missive back at Los Alamos. Szilard had droned on about his concern that "if a race in the production of atomic bombs should become unavoidable, the prospects of this country cannot be expected to be good," adding, "I doubt whether it is wise to show our hand by using atomic bombs against Japan."

Oppie nodded. "I did, yes."

"You did not reply."

There had been no point in signing anything that defined a position except when he had to in official reports for those above him—Groves, Vannevar Bush, Stimson, or the president himself. "I have little time for correspondence."

Szilard harrumphed, sat himself down on the unpadded wooden chair opposite Robert, and waved away some of the smoke in the air. "Urey, Bartky, and I saw some character called Jimmy Byrnes two days ago. Einstein wrote a letter for us, and—"

Oppie cocked his head. "Did he, just?"

"Well, all right, *I* wrote it, but Albert *signed* it. And it was enough to get us an appointment to see the new president, this Truman. But when we arrived, they fobbed us off with a—a backwoodsman!" Oppie had heard that Byrnes was about to be appointed Secretary of State, but it wasn't his place to leak that to Szilard. "Still," continued Leo, "I tried to make him understand that it would be morally reprehensible to use the bomb against Japanese cities." He shook his head. "But he knew nothing of morals, this man. He said using the bomb now would make the Russians more manageable after the war. I told him it wasn't savvy to prod the Soviet bear thus. But he had been listening to Groves—*Groves!*—who had told him that it would take the Russians twenty years to build their own bomb."

"Oh, it won't be that long," Oppie replied, making a diligent effort to exhale smoke away from Szilard.

"No, no, no, of course not! But that fool Groves had told him there was no uranium in Russia. First, how would he know—how would *anyone* know, a country that big? And, second, there *is* uranium in Czechoslovakia! No, I said, if we provoke them, the Soviets will be sure to have the bomb before this decade is out."

"What did Mr. Byrnes say to that?"

"He dared tell me I should think of Hungary, saying I should not want the Russians to occupy my homeland forever. Hungary? Robert, I am thinking of the whole world! The post-war environment in which we all live ... or die."

Oppie looked at him for a long moment. "The atomic bomb is shit," he said flatly.

Szilard's dark hair was combed back from his wide forehead; his eyebrows climbed toward his hairline. "What do you mean by that?"

"Well, put it this way: it's a weapon with no military significance. It will make a big bang—a very big bang—but it's not a weapon that'll be useful in war."

"How can you say such a thing?"

Oppie waved his empty hand as he sought a comparison. "It's like the gas warfare of the Great War: once people saw how ... how unconscionable its use was, they outlawed it. But no one bans the theoretical, only the practical. Surely you can see once we use the bomb against Japan, the Russians will get the point."

"Absolutely they will get the point—they will get the point only too well."

Oppenheimer didn't like the sarcastic tone. "What do you mean by that?"

"They will feel threatened, don't you see? Us *having* such a bomb is one thing, and, yes, since we cannot keep that fact a secret, we should tell the Russians. That will gall them but it won't galvanize them. But the fact that we are willing to *use* such a bomb against people? This *will* trigger an atomic arms race, mark my words."

"Well, you know I'm on a committee here."

"Yes, yes. You, Fermi, Compton, and Lawrence as the scientific contingent. Pointedly, *not* me or anyone else who will strongly speak against—"

"We're not puppets, Leo."

"No, no, no. I didn't mean—"

"But we *are* scientists. Not policy makers or politicians. We've no claim to special competence in solving military or political problems."

"Of course we have special competence! We are learned men, we are *thinkers!* And, practically alone of all the peoples of the world, we have devoted our thoughts, day in and day out, for years now to the question of atomic bombs."

"To the *technical* questions of—"

"Not all of us have had our heads buried in equations. You know that. Bohr, myself, many others have been deeply contemplating the ethical and political ramifications of this ... this monster we've unleashed."

Oppie lifted his hands slightly. "All I want is to see the war in the Pacific over in the shortest possible time."

"The war could end today, tomorrow—as soon as the bomb is ready—with a demonstration, as I said in my letter. *Show* the Japanese; invite a contingent to a remote area. Let them see what the bomb can do."

"And if it's a dud?"

"The uranium-gun design can't fail; you know that. The physics is—"

"Solid, yes. But still, there's a chance ..."

"A chance!" Leo threw up arms in disgust. "Bah! When the time comes, you will play ball, Robert. You have become like *them*"—the special sneer reserved for Groves and his ilk. "You want your 'big bang.' You want to use the bomb on a city; you want the whole world to know what you've accomplished."

The words stung. Two years ago, Enrico Fermi, visiting Los Alamos from the Met Lab, had said to Oppie, "My God, I think your people here actually *want* to make a bomb!"

"It's not like that, Leo."

"No? What *is* it like, then?"

"The bomb can end the war decisively and quickly. If we don't use it, there will have to be an Allied invasion of Japan, with huge casualties on both sides." Oppie had been hearing that daily from Groves and others ever since the fall of Berlin—and the Japanese were fighting on in every jungle hellhole with an insane tenacity, down to the last man.

"Your horizon is too short, Robert—much too short. Japan is finished regardless. You know that; *everyone* knows that. But if the bomb is used, it'll start a stone rolling that'll gather enough poison moss to kill us all."

"No one spends two billion dollars making something *not* to be used."

"Two billion? And here I thought the going rate was thirty pieces of silver."

Oppie placed his hands flat against his desktop and took a deep breath. When he felt he could speak again in an even tone, he rose, ending the meeting. "Give my regards to the others back in Chicago."

Chapter 13

Kitty was a schemer. If Kitty wanted anything she would always get it. I remember one time when she got it into her head to do a Ph.D. and the way she cozied up to this poor little dean of the biological sciences was shameful. She never did the Ph.D. It was just another of her whims. She was a phony. All her political convictions were phony, all her ideas were borrowed. Honestly, she's one of the few really evil people I've known in my life.

—Jackie Oppenheimer
(Robert's sister-in-law)

Oppie strode along, the brim of his hat shielding his eyes from the June New Mexico sun. General Groves had ordered a new billboard put up here on the Hill. *"Whose son will die in the last minutes of the war?"* it asked, with a picture of dead American soldiers strewn upon a battlefield, and, beneath, in larger type, the exhortation *"Minutes count!"*

Oppie made eye contact with each person he passed—scientist, soldier, servant, spouse—and nodded or smiled. It was a key part of keeping this vast machine well lubricated. When they'd begun here, the responses had always been in kind, but frayed nerves, exhaustion, and foul moods were pervasive now. The excitement of the early days had turned out not to be self-sustaining; rather, it had fizzled as weeks stretched into years. Oppie had been here for twenty-seven months; many others had passed their second anniversaries as well.

Kitty was still gone. She had left—no, not him, never him, but the mesa—ten weeks ago, declaring she simply *had* to get away. She'd fled to her parents' house near Bethlehem, Pennsylvania, taking their son Peter, now nearly four, with her. But she hadn't taken her namesake Katherine, their daughter, just four months old then. Oppie didn't approve of the child being named for her mother. He always told people his own first initial stood for nothing because being called Julius after his father was likewise a violation of Jewish tradition; you don't give the name of one still living to another. But Kitty had asked this of him, and, as with so much else, including their marriage, he found himself incapable of denying her. But he had taken to referring to the infant as "Tyke," and his wife had soon followed suit. Still, Robert, the director, the boss, the man at the center whose letters and phone calls were monitored, would not give the security people the satisfaction of hearing him asking, begging, Kitty to return.

"Groves will never let you go for any appreciable length of time," Oppie had said when Kitty had blind-sided him by announcing her plan to depart. The general was now allowing civilians to take leave for the odd weekend, or occasionally even a week, but more was unheard of. "By the time you get to Pittsburgh, you'll have to just turn around and come back here."

Kitty was on the couch, legs crossed, dark hair unkempt. "Dick says I can go for as long as I like."

Dick. For God's sake, even he didn't call the general by that name. Oppie came to wonder if such familiarity had something to do with her earning an unlimited furlough—but Groves was as strait-laced as they came. Perhaps he'd simply decided life would be easier for a lot of people if the frenetic—and fermented—Kitty weren't here for a while, or maybe he felt security would be better with one less ex-Commie around.

"He's letting you go?" Oppie had repeated then, struggling to make sense of it all.

"That's right."

"To stay with your mother?"

"With both my parents."

"Your mother, whose cousin is Field Marshal Wilhelm Keitel?"

"*I* don't interact with people I'm not supposed to."

And there she was: Jean, tossed into the conversation without even having to be named. Dead fifteen months now but omnipresent here, in the house she'd never visited on Bathtub Row, spicing his dreams each night while tainting his every conversation with Kitty.

"When will you be back?" Oppie had asked.

She'd looked out the window into the darkness. "When I'm at peace or the world is," she had replied. "Whichever comes first."

So far, neither had occurred. He locked the door to his office and headed out into the June twilight with Venus, the goddess of love, low on the horizon.

Oppie couldn't take care of an infant on his own *and* run this vast lab, and so the camp's pediatrician had suggested a solution. As Oppie continued his walk home, leaving the T-Section laboratories and heading to the Sundt apartments, the incongruity of there being a person with that specialty here hit him. Ten or so new babies appeared each month, much to the chagrin of General Groves, who had asked Oppie if he could do something to restrain matters. Robert had replied that his duties as scientific director may have included rapid rupture but there was nothing he could do about naked rapture—or its consequences; birth control wasn't part of his job.

And neither was being, in effect, a single parent. The pediatrician proposed that Pat, the twenty-four-year-old wife of physicist Rubby Sherr, should look after Tyke until Kitty returned, and so the baby had moved into the Sherrs's home. Pat and Rubby had a four-year-old daughter of their own and Pat was expecting again. She'd also lost a little boy this past winter, and the pediatrician thought that having another infant to care for would cheer her up. That made no sense to Oppie—atoms were fungible but surely babies were not—but the conceit served his ends and so he'd decided not to question it.

Robert made a point of stopping by the Sherr apartment twice a week. Homes weren't fungible either, even if all the ones in this part of the base had been hastily thrown together from the same blueprint. Pat had done what she could to make hers distinctive, with red-and-yellow throw rugs bought from the Pueblo Indians in Santa Fe, a bouquet of mariposa lilies in a glass vase on a small wooden table, and a few framed Audubon prints; Rubby was an avid bird watcher.

"Well, look who's here," Pat said as she opened the apartment door after he'd knocked, in a tone that implied she felt it had been too long since his last visit. She was wearing a loose yellow blouse and beige slacks.

Oppie gestured toward the tiny kitchen. "Dinner smells good."

"You should stay," Pat replied. "You're skin and bones."

Oppie was down to an admittedly skeletal hundred and fifteen pounds; Pat certainly wasn't the first to comment on his weight loss. Groves had declared that he'd become scrawny, a term Robert hadn't thought was in the general's vocabulary, and Bob Serber had lisped the word "emaciated" in reference to him last week. Meanwhile, his secretary had scolded him for living on tobacco and gin. Months now without Kitty, a year and a half since Jean had taken her own life, and, yes, the war in the Pacific still to be won and the weight of that on his shoulders. Just today, he'd received by military courier minutes of the most-recent meeting he'd attended of the Interim Committee, concluding: "The bomb should be used against Japan as soon as possible."

And Los Alamos—his purview!—was the bottleneck: "as soon as possible" meant as soon as Oppie's boys finished their job. There was no time for *anything* but the work that needed doing. "I'm sure it'll be delicious," he said to Pat, "but no, thank you. I'll be heading back to my office shortly."

Oppie had chaired the Target Committee meetings, assembling the list of Japanese cities suitable for bombing. Groves had only attended the first session—although his deputy, Brigadier General Thomas Farrell, came as his eyes and ears to the others—but Oppie had heard that Groves was livid that Secretary of War Henry Stimson had just vetoed the Committee's top choice, Kyoto. Stimson and his wife had visited Japan's ancient and beautiful former capital in 1926 and considered it too spiritually important to the Japanese to be obliterated. For his part, Oppie didn't care what cities were bombed; they were all just names on a map to him. But he *did* care about not being the holdup.

Pat invited him to sit on the couch, and he did so, air escaping from him in an audible sigh.

"Coffee, at least?"

"No, I'm fine."

"You don't look it. Oppie, what happens to all of this if you get sick?"

Robert lifted his shoulders. His superior, Groves, and Oppie's designated successor, Deak Parsons, would do their best to push through to the end, but they didn't know a tenth of what they needed to. It didn't all come together in the T-Section labs; it came together in Oppie's mind. "I'm fine," he said again.

She looked dubious but took the chair opposite him and had a sip from a mug that had been sitting next to the vase.

"I want to thank you," Oppie said, as he did on every visit, "for doing this for us."

Pat opened her mouth to say something, closed it, then, apparently deciding she *did* want to ask the question, opened it again: "Any idea when Mrs. Oppenheimer will be back?"

"Soon," he replied and then, shrugging, added, "I imagine."

She shifted in her chair. Oppie had seen that expression on many a face here: a job needed doing and one's personal feelings had to be set aside; even the civilians had to soldier on. He looked out the east-facing window. This building was casting a lengthy shadow, and a blazing ball of light, like a second sun, reflected back at him from a neighbor's windowpane. He could no more discuss the work he was doing with Pat than he could with his own wife, but chitchat was fine. "Did you hear Truman on the radio today?" he asked. "Honestly, I don't know how he's going to fill FDR's shoes. He simply—"

"Oppie?" A hint of reproof in the two syllables. He turned back to face her, his eyebrows lifted. "Don't you want to see your daughter? She's growing so fast."

He worked on opening his fourth Chesterfield pack of the day. "Yeah," he said, surprised by the question. "Sure."

Pat stood again and returned moments later carrying the little girl, clearly ready for a nap, wrapped in one of those blankets that had caused so much fuss early on: stamped upon it in bold, black letters was "USED." Oppie had lost a day and a half calming outraged wives, explaining to each in turn that it was an acronym for United States Engineer Detachment.

Pat proffered the child, who had brown eyes like her mother, and Oppie took her, adjusting his posture to better accommodate his burden. Although the little girl didn't put up a fuss, she turned her head to look back at Pat.

There was a small clock on the same table that held Pat's coffee cup and the wildflowers. Oppie dutifully watched the second hand click through sixty increments, bouncing his knee on every fifth one, then moved to give the child back to Pat. She shook her head slightly but did indeed take Tyke, stroking the girl's thin hair soothingly.

"You seem to love her a lot," Oppie ventured.

"I love all children," Pat said, "but this one's a perfect angel. And when you take care of a baby, whether it's your own or someone else's, it becomes a big part of your life, you know?"

"Would you like to adopt her?"

Pat's mouth dropped open and her hand stopped moving mid-stroke, only resuming its comforting action when Tyke mewled a protest.

"Well?" prodded Oppie.

"Of course not. Dear God."

"But you're so good with her."

"Jesus, Robert. She has two perfectly good parents already. Why would you even ask such a thing?"

Perfectly good? One physically absent; the other ... Oppie looked out the window again and took a long drag on his cigarette. "Because I can't love her."

Pat got up and carried the baby to the next room, putting her in her crib to sleep—and maybe to keep the child from hearing any more of her father's words. When she returned, she sat again.

"Robert." He turned, and she went on. "It's ... I mean, I can understand. You're *so* busy, so wrapped up in—in everything. And you have all of us to take care of, not just your daughter. But—look, I know Dr. Barnett thought this arrangement would be good all around, but if you'd just spend a little more time with Katherine, I'm sure you'd become attached to her."

She didn't understand; she *couldn't* understand. Sickly and unathletic, Oppie hadn't had any real friends as a child; he never learned how to relate *to* a child. And, besides, when you *do* become attached to someone, they just—

He shook his head, dispelling that thought. "I'm not the 'attached' kind."

"Oh, Robert. Robert, Robert." Her frown was deep. "Have you discussed this with Mrs. Oppenheimer?"

"No. I felt it prudent to feel you out first. Every child deserves what you and Rubby have managed to make here, amidst all this madness: a loving home. We can't provide that."

"I'm sorry." She touched her own protruding belly. "Soon it's going to be too crowded and ..." She trailed off, and Oppie sensed that she'd decided no excuses were necessary, a supposition confirmed when she shook her head and said a final word: "No."

"Well, then." Oppie, weary to the core of his being, rose from the couch. "I need to get back to work."

Chapter 14

Daran habe ich gar nicht gedacht!

—Albert Einstein

Edward Teller was convinced his solar-fusion equations were correct—and that the same process he'd detected in the sun could be used to make his proposed super bomb. He still refused to believe Hans Bethe, who was adamant that Teller was wrong about how the sun fused atoms heavier than lithium. And even though Oppie's own pre-war research on neutron cores made him an expert on stellar physics, the smug Hungarian wouldn't believe him, either.

Exasperated, Oppie had finally gotten Teller to leave a copy of his solar-fusion equations with him and he'd sent them by military courier to the one person even the irascible Edward couldn't gainsay: the genius that, with the passing of Freud six years ago, was the only living scientist who was a household name, the Grand Old Man of Physics himself, Albert Einstein.

Teller told Oppie he was confident that Einstein would see his brilliance. "If *Leo* could confound Einstein, surely *I* can," Teller had said, folding arms across his wide chest; Teller had long known Szilard, a fellow Martian.

Oppie had made a little shrug; over the years they'd all heard Leo repeatedly recount, with great relish, the two times he'd astounded Einstein. Early in 1922, Szilard had approached Einstein after a seminar to say he'd figured out how to account for the random motion of thermal equilibrium within the framework of the original pre-atomic form of phenomenological theory. Einstein had replied, "That's impossible. This is something that cannot be done." But the famed professor had heard Szilard out and soon became convinced Leo was right. When Szilard had handed in his impromptu paper on this topic—startling his supervisor, as it wasn't at all what Leo had agreed to research—it was deemed so original that it was accepted the next morning as his Ph.D. thesis.

Even more remarkable had been when Szilard and Eugene Wigner—old Pineapple Head himself—had gone to see Einstein at his two-story cottage on Long Island in July 1939. They'd outlined their belief that uranium, properly bombarded by neutrons, would split, releasing spectacular energy that could be used in a devastating bomb. *"Daran habe ich gar nicht gedacht,"* Einstein had said, according to Leo. *I never thought of that!*

Oppie was irritated enough by Teller's insistence on pursuing fusion; he'd be damned if Edward would pursue it *incorrectly.* He spent plenty of time babying him as it was, letting Edward come to his office for a private meeting every week. One-on-one time with the scientific director was *almost* as big a status symbol as was the division-head title that Teller so resented having gone to Bethe.

And, as it happened, Oppie and Teller were engaged in one of these conferences—Teller sitting, Oppie standing by the opened window—when a soldier brought them an envelope from Einstein. Although it was addressed in Einstein's hand to Oppenheimer, Oppie knew better than to be the one conveying bad news. He handed the mailer to Teller and let the man remove the page from the end that had already been slit open by Peer de Silva.

Oppie watched as Teller's eyes zipped not just left and right but up and down, taking it all in. And then, to Oppie's surprise, Teller's normally downturned mouth inverted into a wide grin. "You see!" he crowed, rising and handing the letter to Oppie. "You see!"

Oppie took the paper. Einstein always stretched words horizontally as if they were being pulled by some invisible mass off to the right. The letter, in German, not only affirmed that Teller's math was impeccable—something, Oppie had to admit, rarely said of his own—but that, having been moved to go to his bookshelf and consult his back numbers of the *Physical Review,* Einstein had spotted the fundamental flaw in Hans Bethe's pioneering work. Bethe had believed the temperature at the sun's core was some twenty million degrees Celsius, which would indeed have allowed for the much-more-efficient carbon-nitrogen-oxygen-cycle fusion he'd assumed for his equations. But old Sol (and here Einstein added a puckish parenthetical saying he was referring to our star, not his great-uncle) wasn't quite as massive as Bethe had thought and so likely has a core temperature of "merely" fifteen million degrees, which could support only inefficient proton-proton fusion. Teller's model used the correct solar mass, Einstein said, and was therefore more accurate.

Oppie looked up from the page. Teller was staring at him, shaggy eyebrows raised expectantly. "Just as I said, is it not?"

"Yes," replied Oppie and he tried to muster his most charming smile. "Well, I guess congratulations are in order."

A short time later, Oppie stepped into Bethe's lab. "I thought I'd give you advance warning, Hans, before you run into Teller. Einstein has written back about his fusion equations."

Bethe spread his arms. "Don't worry about bloodshed here on the mesa. I shall be magnanimous in victory."

Oppie held a match to the bowl of his pipe and, between puffs to get it going, said, "I'm afraid ... that good doctor Einstein ... has concurred with ... our friend Edward."

"What? That can't be."

Oppie had brought the letter with him—after convincing Teller there was no chance Hans would rip it up. "Here," he said, proffering the sheet.

Bethe's blue eyes scanned the page, and his normally unwrinkled brow creased below his short, stiff hair. *"Nein,"* he said. *"Herr Einstein ist ein—"*

"If you're about to call him a *Dummkopf,* Hans, you might want to think twice."

"But what he says cannot be!"

"Don't take it so hard. We all make mistakes with our figures."

"You make mathematical mistakes," Bethe said. "Teller makes such gaffes. But *I* do not."

"Well, Einstein says you had the sun five million degrees too hot." Oppie shrugged slightly. "You must have guessed wrong about its temperature."

"Guessed?" repeated Bethe. "I do not guess. I based my studies on specific, actual solar spectra. I derived the temperature I cited *from* the spectra."

Oppie frowned. "Did you analyze the spectra yourself, or did one of your grad stu—"

"Of course myself. Absolutely. At Cornell."

"Well, when the war is over, you can double-check ..."

"I will double-check now!" declared Bethe. "I'll get one of my colleagues there to send the plates here."

"It's not that important—"

"Have you seen Teller gloat? It *absolutely* is that important. If, as Einstein says, the sun is too cool for CNO-cycle fusion, then what accounts for the carbon lines I detected?"

"Well, assuming they are actually there—"

"They *are,* Oppie!" Bethe's frown deepened to a protractor-like semi-circle. "But if the sun has always been that cool—just fifteen million degrees—then ..."

"Then there should, at best, be only trace amounts of carbon in its spectra, inherited from the protostellar nebula," supplied Oppie. He took a contemplative draw on his pipe. "It never should have been able to produce any of its own."

"Exactly!" said Bethe.

"So the carbon spikes you think you saw?" Robert shook his head. "Impossible."

"Eppur si muove," said Bethe, throwing in an Italian accent for good measure.

Oppie snorted. *And yet it moves.* What Galileo reputedly whispered after being forced to recant his claim that the earth revolves around the sun. *Facts are facts,* Bethe was saying.

"All right, Hans. But when your spectra arrive from Cornell, show them to me first, not Edward. I'd rather this whole fight went away, and if you shove them in his face we'll get to see up close what one of his super explosions would be like."

And suddenly, Kitty's voice, airy and bright: *"Honey, I'm home!"* She bustled through the doorway on Bathtub Row hauling a suitcase.

So fucking prosaic. So goddamned ordinary. Like she'd just nipped out to the corner store for a loaf of bread. But there was no corner store—just the two base PXs—and Kitty had been gone almost three months now. There'd been news of her family—her first cousin once removed, Field Marshal Wilhelm Keitel, had signed the final terms of surrender on V-E Day in Berlin—but nary a word from her.

Oppie stubbed out his cigarette, rose from the living-room couch, and started toward the front door, but was intercepted by Peter barreling in toward him. His son, whose fourth birthday had passed while he was away with his mother, had grown in height at least as much as Oppie had lost in girth; he'd had to drill new holes into his belts again last week. Robert wanted to lift the boy up—really, he did—but he just didn't have the strength. But as Peter's arms encircled his legs, he tousled his son's hair.

Kitty, in a beige blouse and green slacks, looked rested and well fed, and Oppie was grateful for that. He thought, perhaps, her first question would be about Tyke, but, no, of course it wasn't. Closing the distance and giving him a kiss on the cheek, she said, "So, how about a drink?"

Had she known, he wondered, that she was ill-suited to being a mother when she got pregnant the first time? The first time with *him,* he meant, although she had also told him of her actual first pregnancy, which occurred when she was married to husband number one, the musician Frank Ramseyer. The security man here, Peer de Silva, would have laughed at the simplicity with which Ramseyer had tried to keep his dark secrets: he had composed his diary in mirror writing, Leonardo da Vinci fashion, with backward characters written from right to left. Kitty stumbled across it (literally: when drunk, one doesn't remember which nightstand is one's own), got a mirror, and—talk about falling through the looking glass!—discovered who her husband really was: a drug addict and a homosexual. Both the pregnancy and the marriage were dispensed with in short order.

Marriages two and three produced no children. But Kitty had deliberately gotten pregnant early in her relationship with Oppie. She'd wanted him then, and, apparently, she'd wanted the child—the boy who turned out to be little Peter—too. But theory does not always conform to reality; hypotheses are as often disproven as they are validated.

Not the attached kind. Like neutrons in a nucleus; oh, they'd hang around together unless perturbed, but they had no charge, no positivity on one and negativity on the other to draw them together, no bonding, no binding. Just a mysterious strong force, a literal and figurative chemistry that acted solely when they were in very close proximity.

Oppie got up to get his wife the drink she'd asked for, and to make one for himself, ice cubes, most of their substance below the surface, clinking in the glasses. "Welcome ..." he said but made a tiny mental edit before he added "home," since it really wasn't much of that. "... back."

Chapter 15

I am sure that at the end of the world—in the last millisecond of the earth's existence—the last human will see what we saw.

—George Kistiakowsky

At 5:29 on Monday morning, July 16, 1945, the one-minute-warning rocket twisted up into a predawn sky, adobe-pink to the east, stygian to the west.

"Lord, these affairs are hard on the heart," Oppie said as much to himself as to the other men present—and then, tilting his head, conceded that there really had never before been such an affair. He gripped a rough-hewn oak beam with one hand, his fingers wraith-like. With his other hand he held the four-leaf clover Kitty had given him before he'd left for this test site, a place he himself had code-named "Trinity." Although a trained botanist, his wife still felt there was luck in a mutant plant.

Thirty seconds later, four blood-red lights flashed on the console in front of Oppie in the concrete bunker ten thousand yards south of—a neologism, words shoved together like protons in a nucleus—"ground zero." On his right a young physicist from Harvard stood by the knife switch that if opened would abort the test. The thing had its own momentum now, an electric timer ticking away; no one would go down in history as the individual who had set off the first atom bomb, but one man could still stop it.

The team at Los Alamos had come up with two different bomb designs. The first was a simple uranium-gun scheme deemed so foolproof that, as Leo Szilard had observed to Oppie, it didn't require any testing. But Uranium-235, despite all efforts to efficiently separate it from U-238, was still available in such minuscule amounts that a second system was developed that instead used plutonium, which could be produced in comparatively large quantities. The alternative design required much more complex bomb hardware, and that was what they were about to test. Bob Serber had dubbed this spherical bomb type "Fat Man," after the Sydney Greenstreet character in *The Maltese Falcon.* It used a revolutionary implosion system perfected—or so it had seemed until two days ago—by George Kistiakowsky. But a trial run early Saturday in the Pajarito Canyon, using a dummy Fat Man with a core of conventional explosives, had failed.

In the real Fat Man to be fired today, the plutonium core had been molded into a sphere the size of a softball. Surrounding it was a shell of thirty-two explosive castings called "lenses" because they'd been engineered so that the force of their explosions would be focused on the central sphere. With each lens detonating simultaneously, the spherical shockwave blowing inward should implode the core to tennis-ball size, forcing the plutonium into criticality. But the lenses in Saturday's test bomb had apparently developed astigmatism.

Leslie Groves, military head of the Manhattan Project, and Vannevar Bush, in charge of the Office of Scientific Research and Development, and therefore its civilian head, had arrived as scheduled Saturday noon, and both were furious at the news.

Oppie tried to keep his cool in front of them—in front of everyone—but it finally all proved more than he could take. So much work, so much time, so near to success, but instead of a bloom of light, nettles in his fist. He'd broken down in front of Kistiakowsky, his tears the only moisture this desiccated area inauspiciously known as *La Jornada del Muerto,* The Workday of the Dead, had seen in weeks.

Kisty contended the failure was perhaps due to the use of substandard lenses, the best castings—free of significant bubbles and cracks—having been saved for the real thing, and he bet Oppie a month's salary against ten dollars that everything would go fine today.

Late last night, Oppie, having recovered his composure enough to wax philosophic, had shared his own translation of a passage from the seven-hundred-stanza *Bhagavad Gita* with long-faced, bespectacled Vannevar Bush and visiting advisor I.I. Rabi, compact and trim, who had won last year's Nobel Prize in physics:

> *"In sleep, in confusion, in the depths of shame,*
> *"The good deeds a man has done before defend him."*

But rain, sheets of it, torrents, had begun at oh-two-hundred hours, the very heavens weeping.

Right now, Truman, Churchill, and Stalin were arriving at Potsdam, near Berlin, for the first Allied-leaders' summit since the Nazi surrender. Truman desperately wanted a successful test so that he—the Commander in Chief, as Oppie had said, not some back-door sneak—could tell the Soviet premier that the Americans now had a working atomic bomb whose imminent use on Japan would surely end the Pacific war. The test had to go ahead *now*—but rain would drive radioactive particles down to the ground instead of letting them dissipate.

Groves loudly excoriated the meteorologist—who had, in fact, clearly warned the general days ago of the impending storm. Still, the man now felt the torrent would abate by dawn. Groves growled, "You'd better be right or I'll have you hanged," and he made the hapless soul sign his written forecast.

Then, just before 3:00 a.m., Groves got on the phone to the Governor of New Mexico, a servant rousting the sixty-six-year-old from bed. Oppie heard only the general's side of the conversation: he told the governor, who was learning of the imminent test for the first time, that he should be prepared to "invoke martial law come dawn if the thing does more damage than we anticipate."

Oppenheimer and the rest stepped outside, leaving only the person manning the abort switch. Groves, Teller, Feynman, and Fermi—the Italian navigator himself, who had moved to Los Alamos from Chicago last year—were scattered along with many more men at three of the cardinal points; the general had insisted on dispersal of the team so that if something *did* go wrong at least some essential personnel might survive.

At 5:29:50—with a mere ten seconds to go—a final warning gong sounded, an Oriental instrument signaling looming American triumph. Oppie took his piece of #10 welder's glass from his pocket. *"Five!"* said a male voice over the external loudspeaker. *"Four!"* Oppie found his lungs paralyzed. *"Three!"* His heart, though, was pounding hard enough to shake his whole body. *"Two!"* He held the deep-amber glass up, his blue eyes reflecting back at him as green—*"One!"*—the same green, he realized with a start, as Jean Tatlock's.

Light! Fierce. Pure. Blinding.

The cruel brightness, immediately unbearable, kept increasing. Silent light, holy light—not a sound to it yet but an intensity no one on earth had ever before experienced. For the first time, humans were doing what only the stars themselves had previously wrought, converting matter directly into energy, Einstein's $E=mc^2$ graduating from mere textbook formula into a devastating weapon.

The dome of blinding light grew and grew; Oppie estimated it was now a mile, now two, now three in diameter. And the color, which had started as pure white, then yellow, then a cacophony of hues, had now settled on an actinic purple, a radiant bruise on the firmament.

And then the light *rose up*—by God, yes, on a giant stalk, the hemisphere being pushed higher and higher, hell meeting heaven. Oppie hadn't expected that; no one had. It looked for all the world like an incandescent parasol, a mushroom of flame, miles tall.

And, at last, a thunderous *crack!* as the sound of the explosion hit them. Hands flew up to ears; eyes that had endured the brightness behind opaque glass winced at the volume. Oppie had done the math in advance: he knew it was therefore now twenty-five seconds after the timer had reached zero, but it felt like many minutes.

Next came the blast's scalding wind. Robert, incredibly, managed to keep erect; the more substantial Kisty, off to one side, was blown over but soon picked himself up and pushed against the gale to make it over to his boss. "You owe me ten bucks!" he shouted, his balding head split by a wide grin as he slapped Oppie on the back.

Oppie pulled out his wallet only to find it empty. "You'll have to wait!" he shouted.

Someone else was making his way over to him: Ken Bainbridge, the test-site director, with a serpent-like mouth. "Now we're all sons of bitches!" he yelled over the roar.

Yes, thought Oppie. *We surely are.* We've changed the world, won the war, and thrown down a marker in time: the whole, vast past was prologue; everything henceforth is part of a new epoch, a new period, a new era. The previous eras had been named for the ever-more-sophisticated animal life that had emerged in them: Paleozoic, Mesozoic, Cenozoic. But this new one had as its hallmark not unbridled biology but harnessed devastation.

The crowd around him was jubilant. Everyone was going to want to speak to him, he knew: to shake his hand, to offer congratulations, to share their views. But he needed a moment of peace as the weapon to end all war continued to assault the very sky in front of him. Oppie stepped away, walking sideways, keeping his eyes, no longer requiring the protective glass, on the great bulbous apparition.

Now ...

Such a devilish thing! There were still afterimages, true, but there was also, superimposed in Oppie's mind, a conjured city centered at ground zero, ceasing to be, incinerating into nothingness.

Now I am ...

Robert's primary education, at Felix Adler's Ethical Culture School—the abstract made concrete, that school of philosophy given brownstone-and-mortar reality—had elevated his thinking, and Hindu mysticism had given him insights few of his Western contemporaries shared.

Now I am become Death ...

Oppie had studied Sanskrit under the great Arthur Ryder so he could read the *Bhagavad Gita* in the original, and he thought as easily in that Hindu tongue as he did in English ... or French, or German, or Dutch. He suspected that whatever language he used shaped his thoughts: German, with its compound nouns, was appropriate to the unification of physical forces; English, with its heavy freight of adjectives, was about one thing modifying another.

But Hindi—the *Gita*—was about deep connections, and its words, those terrible, portentous words, erupted in his consciousness as the towering maelstrom continued to roil the sky.

Now I am become Death, the destroyer of worlds.

Chapter 16

Three Weeks Later: August 1945

I have no hope of clearing my conscience. The things we are working on are so terrible that no amount of protesting or fiddling with politics will save our souls.

—Edward Teller

Oppenheimer had been waiting impatiently in his office for the call; for God's sake, the bomb should have been dropped on Hiroshima yesterday. Why hadn't Manley phoned? Oppie had dispatched his assistant to Washington precisely so he could let him know the moment word arrived there from the B-29 that apparently had undergone a last-minute name change to *Enola Gay.*

When his phone finally did ring, Oppie managed to knock his overflowing ashtray off his desk as he scrambled to snatch up the handset. It was the base operator. "A long-distance call for you, sir. Mr. Manley."

"Yes, yes!" Oppie exclaimed. "Put him through."

Some clicking and then: "Oppie—"

"Damn it, John, why the hell do you think I sent you to Washington?"

"I'm sorry, boss. Groves wouldn't let me call until Truman announced the news. He'll be going on the air in just a minute, and—"

Oppie didn't bother to cover the mouthpiece as he shouted to Bob Serber: "Radio! The president's coming on!"

There was a small Bakelite-encased radio on top of a half-height bookcase. Serber clicked it on and the unit began to warm up. They only got the Santa Fe station and the mesa's own one, KRS; Oppie could tell that Serber had tuned in Santa Fe.

"And?" demanded Oppie. "And?"

"It worked!" said Manley.

Oppie sagged back in his chair. *The goddamn thing had worked!* Serber was staring at him, waiting for some sign. Oppie gave a thumbs up, and Serber's face broke into a wide grin, an expression Oppie thought gauche under the circumstances until he realized his own cheek muscles were similarly pulled tight.

Manley went on: "Deak Parsons sent a message from the *Enola Gay:* 'Results clear-cut. Successful in all respects. Visible effects greater than in New Mexico test.'"

"Here he comes!" shouted Serber, pointing at the radio.

The call was expensive but at that moment Oppie didn't care. "Hang on, John," he said, putting the handset on the desk and facing it toward the cloth-covered radio speaker.

"— live now from the Atlantic Ocean, President Harry S. Truman, *en route* back to the United States from the Potsdam Conference."

And then Truman's Missouri-accented voice, growing slowly in volume as the radio continued to warm up: *"A short time ago, an American airplane dropped one bomb on Hiroshima and destroyed its usefulness to the enemy. That bomb has more power than twenty thousand tons of T.N.T. The Japanese began the war from the air at Pearl Harbor. They have been repaid many fold."*

Oppie thought incongruously not of the uranium-gun bomb his team had designed but of the German V-2, "V" for *Vergeltungswaffe*—"Vengeance Weapon." He got up and paced in front of the radio.

"And the end is not yet," continued Truman. *"With this bomb we have now added a new and revolutionary increase in destruction to supplement the growing power of our armed forces. In their present form these bombs are now in production and even more powerful forms are in development."*

More powerful forms? Oppie felt his entire body sag, gravity yanking him down. Surely Truman wasn't alluding to Teller's super? Surely they were *done* now? He looked at Serber, who shrugged, apparently equally surprised by the remark.

And then, at last, the president gave the beast its name, a term first coined, as Oppie had learned from Leo Szilard, by H.G. Wells in 1913, but until this moment unknown to almost all Americans. *"It is an atomic bomb. It is a harnessing of the basic power of the universe. The force from which the sun draws its power has been loosed against those who brought war to the Far East."*

Well, thought Oppie, that wasn't quite right; Teller's hydrogen bomb would have been based on fusion, but the uranium-gun "Little Boy" design used on Hiroshima, and the plutonium-implosion Fat Man now already at the Tinian airfield south of Japan, were fission devices, the power of decay not unification. Still, either way, existing elements were transmuted into other ones; as Szilard had quipped when he'd gotten word of the Trinity test, "While the first successful alchemist was undoubtedly God, I sometimes wonder whether the second successful one may not have been the Devil himself."

Truman continued, his usually diffident voice taking on an edge: *"We are now prepared to destroy more rapidly and completely every productive enterprise the Japanese have in any city. We shall destroy their docks, their factories, and their communications. Let there be no mistake: we shall completely destroy Japan's power to make war."*

No, no, thought Oppie. The goal was to show the whole world that fighting wars was no longer tenable—that *any* conflict could escalate to Armageddon and so *all* arms should be laid down. To continue to obliterate was—

But that's *precisely* what Truman intended: *"It was to spare the Japanese people from utter destruction that the ultimatum of July the twenty-sixth was issued at Potsdam. Their leaders promptly rejected that ultimatum. If they do not now accept our terms they may expect a rain of ruin from the air the like of which has never been seen on this earth."*

But of course they would accept the terms! There was no other rational course left now. Perhaps the second bomb could be towed far out into the Pacific and detonated there, with reporters from all nations invited to watch from a safe remove. Surely there was no need for it to be dumped on Kokura or Niigata.

Truman continued: *"We have spent more than two billion dollars on the greatest scientific gamble in history—and we have won. But the greatest marvel is not the size of the enterprise, its secrecy, or its cost, but the achievement of scientific brains in making it work. It is doubtful if such another combination could be got together in the world. What has been done is the greatest achievement of organized science in history."*

Oppie had a flash of his friend I.I. Rabi, last year's Nobel laureate in physics, who had turned down Oppie's offer to become associate director here, saying he didn't want the culmination of three centuries of physics to be a tool of devastating destruction. Oppie had replied then that Hitler had given them no choice ... but Hitler had been dead now for three full months. And, with luck and good sense, in another few months the very concept of international war would also fade into history.

As Robert walked along the mesa, he passed a young man sitting in a jeep. "One down!" the fellow shouted jubilantly. But surely not one to go. Yes, two bombs had been shipped to Tinian, but now that the Little Boy had been dropped, it had to end.

Oppie had a destination in mind. It wasn't time for their usual weekly get-together—and those took place in his own office, anyway—but still: *this* was the man he had to see. Some of those he passed stopped to pump his hand or slap his back or give him a thumbs up. But Oppie could only think the same thing he'd been thinking even before the bomb had been dropped on Hiroshima: *Those poor little people.*

At last he came to Edward Teller's office. The Hungarian's door was open, so Oppie just stood there framed in the doorway until Teller at last looked up from his desk. There was nothing in front of him—no writing paper, no open journal. He'd just been staring, looking down at the battered wooden surface, lost in thought. "Edward," Oppie said when their eyes met, "how are you?"

Teller used his palms, flat against the wood, to push himself to his feet. But rather than walking over to Oppie, he headed to the window, looking out at the plateau, parched earth baking in the August heat. "I used to tell my first-year students about waves," he said, his voice as always low in pitch but now also low in volume. "You can have one coming *this* way, arriving as a crest, a high of excitement and satisfaction, and you can have another, approaching *that* way, leading with its trough, a low of sadness and ..." He paused, and Oppie wondered if he was going to say "regret," but, no, what Edward finished with was "... foreboding for what may come in the years ahead." He at last turned to face Oppenheimer. "And when two such waves meet, the interference is destructive: they cancel out, leaving only ..." He sought a word; found it: "... calm."

Oppie stepped fully into the room and Teller went on. "I put on suntan lotion at the Trinity test site, did you know that? People laughed, but it seemed a prudent thing to do. I shall never forget that sight, that fireball. Still, how many of us—a hundred, perhaps—saw that test? And, of course, we all had welder's glass or goggles. But yesterday, tens of thousands beheld such a light. And with no warning, Oppie, with no warning. The difference between them and us?" His mighty eyebrows lifted in a philosophical shrug. "We survived to tell the tale."

"But they will be the last ones, Edward. The last casualties of international war."

There was a note of hope in Teller's voice. "Has Japan surrendered?"

"Not yet, so far as I've heard. But they must." Oppie's voice cracked a bit. "They must."

"We should have warned them."

"Truman did. The Potsdam declaration—"

"No, not like that. Who could understand such a thing? You, me, other physicists, yes. But a farmer, a shopkeeper, a schoolboy? Leo was right; we should have demonstrated it. Tokyo Bay, perhaps, but not a city, not homes." At last Teller's voice took on a bit of an edge. "You should have let me circulate his petition here."

At the end of June, Szilard had sent Teller a copy of the latest petition he'd been passing around the Met Lab in Chicago, calling on the president to refrain from dropping the bomb on Japan. Of course Szilard knew, after his meeting with Robert in Washington, that Oppie wasn't likely to approve of such a thing and so he'd done an end run, asking Teller to gather signatures here on the mesa. But Teller had brought it to Oppie, seeking his permission—and Oppie had blown his stack, one of the few times during the whole project that he'd lost his temper. What, he had demanded, did Szilard or any physicist know of Japanese psychology? What did any of them know about ending a war? He'd even said a few unkind words about Szilard personally—things more typical of Groves than himself—calling him an obstructionist pest and an intellectually dishonest hypocrite; after all, Leo had been the one who had urged the previous president to create the bomb in the first place.

"Maybe," said Oppie; he certainly regretted the outburst, now more than a month in the past. But his action in barring the petition? He shrugged. "I don't know."

Teller looked out the window again, apparently accepting that.

Groves had called Oppie a little while ago. He'd said, "I think one of the wisest things I ever did was when I selected the director of Los Alamos."

Oppie had replied, "Well, I have my doubts, General Groves."

But Groves, uncharacteristically effusive, had said, "You know I've never concurred with those doubts at any time."

And it *was* a day for effusion: cheers and backslapping, flowing champagne—or spiked ginger ale masquerading as such—classes canceled and kids running loose on the mesa, the base radio blaring Vera Lynn and the Andrews Sisters. Oppie sent out word over the public-address system that there'd be a celebration in the theater later today for as many as could cram in there.

But it was also a day for reflection. Getting on two years ago, on December 30, 1943, Niels Bohr, the famed Danish physicist, winner of the 1922 Nobel, the man who had first envisioned the atom as a dense nucleus orbited by far-distant electrons, had visited them here at Los Alamos. He'd immediately asked Oppie, "Is it big enough?" *Was* the atomic bomb they were planning to build big enough to end all war? Oppie had assured him that it indeed would be, and yesterday's results must have proven that.

"Edward," Oppie said, "I think we're *done.*"

Teller turned to him again. "How do you mean?"

"Your super. It's ... excessive. I can't have anything to do with it."

"Robert, perhaps today is not the day—"

"What other day would be better? There will never be another day like this one, Edward. You know that; I know that. We can *stop.*"

"The laboratory you've created here is unique. What would you have become of Los Alamos?"

"Give it back to the Indians."

Teller looked out his window once more. The sun was growing ruddy as it slid down the sky. "There's a Hungarian proverb: *Szegény egér az, ki csak egy lyukra bízza magát.*"

Oppie frowned. One of the reasons Leo's nickname for his countrymen of "the Martians" had stuck was that Hungarian bore so little resemblance to other European languages; Oppie could make no sense of what Teller had said. "Yes?" he prodded.

"It literally means it's a poor mouse that trusts his life to only one hole. Who knows what the future is going to bring, my friend? Not you or I—and so it is always safer to have multiple options."

"Safer? I'm not sure about that."

"Preferable, then," said Teller. He turned again to face Oppie. "I do appreciate you coming by, Robert. But although your work may be over, mine has just begun."

Chapter 17

Scientists aren't responsible for the facts that are in nature. It's their job to find the facts. There's no sin connected with it—no morals. If anyone should have a sense of sin, it's God. He put the facts there.

—**Percy Bridgman**,
Oppenheimer's physics professor at Harvard

In a daze, head swimming, heart pounding, Oppie walked down the packed earth of Bathtub Row to the log-and-stone cottage at its end that had been his home for almost two and a half years now.

Log and stone: sturdy materials. The cottage had been built in 1929, he'd been told, and there was no reason to think it wouldn't be standing in 2029 or beyond. The Japanese, on the other hand, made homes mostly from thin wood and even paper; those that hadn't been blown straight to hell by the blast would have been incinerated in the fires that swept the landscape.

But here on the mesa life kept hold. The small garden Kitty had planted was back to being well tended; it had been neglected during the months she'd been away.

Oppie entered the house and caught Kitty as she was coming out of the tiny kitchen. He was used to finding her draped upon the couch, and she normally didn't get up when he arrived, but, since she was already on her feet, he closed the distance and wrapped his arms around her, pulling her toward him. She hesitated for a moment then hugged him, too.

"They ... they've dropped a second bomb," Oppie said, holding her. "Apparently Kokura was clouded over, so they ..." His voice caught; he'd intended to say "they hit Nagasaki instead," but it didn't matter, he realized; they were just names to Kitty, and to him, alien syllables.

"I'm so sorry," she said softly. Kitty was much shorter than Oppie; the words were spoken into his bony chest.

"Why didn't they surrender?" asked Oppie. "After the first one, why didn't they surrender?"

"Truman said it had to be unconditional," Kitty replied, still holding him. "Charlotte Serber thinks that's the problem." She disengaged from Oppie's embrace but took his hand and led him to the couch by the stone fireplace. "She thinks the Japs want to keep their emperor. They think he's divine; a god. She says unconditional surrender would be like asking the United States to agree to renounce Jesus."

Oppie heard the words but didn't know what to do with them, and so set them aside. "I told ... God, I told *everyone* that one bomb would be enough. Yes, we had to use it *once.* No, we couldn't do a demonstration out in a desert—they'd accuse us of having buried thousands of tons of T.N.T. beneath whatever device we showed them, saying we were lying about really having a new type of bomb. Yes, it had to be dropped on a *real* target. No, we couldn't announce *which* target in advance because they'd just move all their prisoners of war—all our boys they've captured—to wherever we said we were going to drop it, and, anyway, they'd then throw everything they had at shooting our B-29 out of the sky before it could drop its bomb." He shook his head. "But one *wasn't* enough."

"Why did they—why did *we*—only wait three days before doing it again?" asked Kitty. "I mean, communications out of Hiroshima must have been spotty at best. There was barely time for word to reach Tokyo, for anyone there to begin to comprehend ..."

"Groves said thunderstorms were forecast for the weekend. It was either now or ... well, not *never,* but, you know, next week or later ..." He shook his head once more and said so softly that Kitty had to ask him to repeat it for her: "Those poor little people."

Peer de Silva came into Hans Bethe's lab. His uniform was immaculate, but his forehead glistened with sweat from walking through the August heat. "Mr. Battle?"

Bethe suppressed a smile. Prior to the dropping of the bombs, titles such as "Doctor" and "Professor" were verboten when off the mesa, and those scientists who might have been known even then to the public were all referred to by fake names beginning with the same letters as their real ones. Few inside the barbed-wire perimeter had habitually used the conceit—few, that is, save de Silva and his ilk—and now that the whole world knew what they'd accomplished here, continuing the practice seemed silly. "Yes, captain?"

"There's a package for you." De Silva held up a cardboard box that could have contained a single encyclopedia volume. "But before I can release it, I need to know what it says."

Hans gestured with his slide rule; the box clearly had already been opened. "Surely you've looked?"

"Yes, of course." No hint of apology. "But ..."

"Well, then? Is it in German? Many in your office must be adept at reading that."

"No. It looks like code."

Hans nodded. Nothing made de Silva angrier than messages to and from the scientists in code; he'd shut down Dick Feynman's playful habit of swapping encrypted love letters with his late wife Arline while she was suffering from tuberculosis in Albuquerque. De Silva tipped the box, and five thin glass sheets slipped out, each separated from the next by a piece of tissue paper. He set them on the desktop—unlike many of the other scientists, Hans kept his working area neat and so there was plenty of room. "These lines, you see?"

Bethe's heart skipped a beat. "Ah, yes, captain. A code indeed—but not an enemy one. It is the code of nature."

De Silva frowned. "And what does it mean?"

"It means," said Hans, grinning as he studied them, "that I am right, and the irascible Mr. Tilden will have to eat his hat."

When work at Los Alamos began, General Groves had tried to enforce his compartmentalization notion: each man knowing only what he needed to in order to do his job. But from the outset Oppie had insisted on a weekly colloquium at which the senior scientists could meet for freewheeling discussions of technical issues. The strategy had succeeded: often a specialist in one area brought a useful new insight to work in another.

The task of organizing the colloquia, which were held Tuesday evenings in the base's theater, had fallen to Edward Teller. He was happy because it gave him frequent chances to shoehorn mentions of his thermonuclear dreams into whatever the topic of discussion was, and Oppie was happy because it was something actually useful that Teller could do.

Now that the bombs had been dropped on Japan, proving both the uranium-gun and plutonium-implosion designs, there weren't many big technical matters left to discuss, and attendance at the colloquia had dwindled. Most of the scientists, eager to secure jobs for the 1945-46 academic year, had already left the mesa. Still, Oppie noted, this evening the top minds had come, including Enrico Fermi, Hans Bethe, Dick Feynman, Bob Serber, and Luis Alvarez.

Teller called the group to order. "Tonight we shall speak of—"

"Let me take a wild guess," interrupted Feynman, seated in the second row. "Fusion, perchance?"

Bethe and Serber, always good-natured, both laughed, and even Teller smiled. "Yes, but perhaps some of you will be relieved to know that I plan to make no reference to the super. Rather, I wish to talk about the sun."

"With Groves as the Father and Oppie as the Holy Ghost?" quipped Feynman.

"Not the son of God," said Teller, still smiling. "The sun up in the sky."

"So much for Trinity," replied Feynman, throwing up his hands in mock frustration, and again there was some laughter.

"I have been studying solar spectra," Teller said, taking back control. "The sun, after all, is little more than a giant fusion pile. Of course, our friend Hans has also explored this area."

"I took a shine to the work," said Bethe, who was always inordinately pleased with himself when he could make a pun in English. His 1939 paper "Energy Production in Stars" was widely considered one of his best.

"Yes," continued Teller. "But Hans, who captured his solar spectra before the war, got results different from the recent plates I've been working from, which were provided by the Mount Wilson and McMath-Hulbert Observatories. I've also now checked some older plates, predating the ones Hans was working from. Have a look."

In preparation for this colloquium, Teller had gotten Oppie to have the base's photo lab make a slide showing three different sets of solar spectra. He slid it into the Kodak projector and turned it on. Everyone looked at the canvas screen hanging from the ceiling. The image showed three gray-scale horizontal bars interrupted by vertical lines of various degrees of darkness. Even at a glance, it was obvious that the top and bottom ones were pretty much the same, but the one in the middle was more complex. The top one was labeled 1929; the middle, 1938; and the bottom, this year, 1945.

There was a murmur through the room. "You're pulling our legs," said Fermi. "The one in the middle isn't our sun; it's got to be an F-class."

"Oh, yes, it *is* our sun," Bethe assured him, from the third row. "Absolutely; I took that spectrograph myself."

"But then how do you reconcile it with the ones taken before and after?" demanded Fermi. "Yours has strong carbon-absorption lines, and there's none to speak of in the upper and lower ones."

"Puzzling, isn't it?" said Teller. "Of course, we've only known what stars are made of for twenty years now." In 1925, Cecilia Payne-Gaposchkin determined that stars are composed almost entirely of hydrogen and helium; prior to that, it was assumed that, although the sun was obviously much hotter, its composition was similar to earth's, since they'd presumably both been born out of the same coalescing cloud of matter. "And of those twenty years almost no data has been added in the last six, since the war broke out in Europe." He looked out at the small group. "Now, obviously, if we are ever to reproduce fusion here on earth, we must correctly understand how it occurs in nature. I have recently developed a set of equations that I believe accurately describes the process, but they do not account for Hans's spectra, or, as I've now determined by checking with various experts, *any* solar spectrograph taken between January and April 1938. *Before* that and *after* that my proton-proton equations work but *during* that period something happened to the sun, causing it to temporarily heat up enough to undergo C-N-O-cycle fusion."

"If the sun warmed up that much, surely we'd know," said Oppie, who was seated in the front row. He turned in his wooden seat to allow those behind to see him. "There'd be an effect on earth's climate."

"And there *was,*" said Teller. "My friend Johnny von Neumann at the Institute for Advanced Study has become obsessed lately with predicting the weather. Toward that end, he's been studying past meteorological records. He says that period was indeed warmer than normal to a statistically relevant extent, although the impact was felt more in the southern hemisphere than up here."

"Which makes sense," said Alvarez, "since the southern hemisphere faces the sun more fully in our winter."

Teller nodded. "Exactly. That was also an exceptional winter for auroras. So, we have an interesting anomaly before us. The sun was feverous—running a high temperature—for a few months. The question is why?"

Oppie had the advantage of having seen both spectra before, and he'd been chewing over the issue ever since Einstein's letter had arrived. Still, it wasn't until just now, when he saw the three spectra stacked up like this, that it all went *click* in his brain. "So," he said, "the problem isn't with Teller's math."

Teller's voice was smug. "Exactly!"

"And it's not with Bethe's plates, either," continued Oppie. He had everyone's attention; still, he rose. "The problem," he said, "is with the sun. And I think I know what it is."

Silence, save for the rumbling of the room fans and a hiss from the slide projector.

"How do you mean?" asked Bob Serber at last.

Oppie gestured at the screen. "Look at it, Bob. You and I wrote the paper saying Lev Landau was wrong in proposing that the sun had a neutron core."

"Landau isn't the only one who proposed that," said Bethe. "Fritz Zwicky said the same thing, and said it first."

Oppie waved a hand dismissively—he couldn't stand Zwicky—and kept his gaze on Serber. "And we showed that such a core could make up no more than one-tenth of the sun's mass. Above that and it would be ..."

"... unstable," lisped Serber, and Oppie could see the light dawning in his old friend's eyes.

"Exactly. An instability that would require resolution—a resolution that would likely raise the temperature of the sun for a brief period."

Bethe was nodding now. "The period during which I did my spectroscopy studies and detected C-N-O fusion as the main engine powering the sun."

"Right," said Oppie. He puffed his pipe. "But that instability would die down with—"

"With the ejection of mass from the core," chimed in Teller. "The degenerate matter couldn't be maintained if the quantity of it was too little, and so it would burst forth."

"But the sun is *big,*" said Oppie. "And whatever neutron core it had—*had,* past tense—was small, maybe even as small as the one-thousandth of a solar mass that Landau would have allowed, but certainly, given that it's proven unstable, somewhere between Landau's 0.001 solar masses and Bob and my 0.1. But even at a tenth of a solar mass, if it's degenerate matter, it would be tiny—just a few kilometers across at the heart of the sun, which has a diameter of one-point-four million kilometers."

"A neutron core basically forms in an implosion," said Teller. "Like Kistiakowsky's plutonium core at the heart of a Fat Man—"

"But after the *implosion* comes a massive *explosion,*" said Serber, "and that hasn't happened."

"No?" said Oppie. "I think it *has.* Bob, you know this, but some of you others might not. My Ph.D. thesis at Göttingen was *Zur Quantentheorie kontinuierlicher Spektren"* —*On the Quantum Theory of Continuous Spectra*—"and it concentrated on the opacity of stellar surfaces to their internal radiation. The sun's visible surface is the photosphere, and what's beneath it is hidden. But if we assume the temporary temperature increase that allowed C-N-O fusion was caused by energy released by the explosion, and then calculate—"

Through all this, Hans Bethe, the world's greatest expert on solar fusion, had been quietly working his slide rule. "But if we calculate," Bethe said, speaking firmly as was his wont when the subject was physics, "the likely size of the neutron core per Zwicky's, Landau's, and Oppie's and Bob's work, and the amount of temperature increase I detected, along with your own opacity research, Oppie, we arrive at a figure for when the outwardly exploding formerly degenerate material should be able to complete traversing the bulk of the sun's body and at last hit the photosphere from behind."

"And?" asked Serber.

"Plus or minus?" said Bethe. "Give or take? I'd say ninety or so years—from when the transient solar-temperature anomaly began, that is, back in 1938. Say eighty-two or so years from now."

"Which is 2028," said Serber.

"Somewhere in there, yes: 2027, 2028, 2029," agreed Bethe.

"And how much of a kick will it have left by then?" asked Serber.

Bethe went back to his slide rule. Oppie pulled out his own. Teller started writing on the blackboard that was up on the side of the stage, next to the screen, and others began figuring with pencil and paper.

"A lot," declared Bethe, with the air of the first kid to finish the exam.

"A hell of a lot," said Oppie a moment later.

"Fuck," said Serber. "Did anyone else get an exponent of six?"

"Six, yes," called out Fermi.

Oppie felt his chest constricting. But his own slide rule was yielding confirming results. "With the sun's surface—its photosphere, the visible disc—opaque to what's happening within, that whole layer, the entire photosphere, will be pushed outward from behind and be ejected."

"Ejected ..." repeated Alvarez as if making sure he'd heard correctly.

"Exactly," said Oppie. "The photosphere has an effective temperature of 5.8 thousand Kelvin, but its expulsion will carry the surrounding corona with it, and *that* has a temperature of one million Kelvin. Now, yes, the ejected shell will cool as it expands, but it *will* be hot enough to make molten the surface of any rocky body out to ..." He moved the slide along the stock and then slid the glass cursor with its blood-red hair line until he had the answer: "... about one-point-two astronomical units."

"By definition," Alvarez said ominously, "earth is at one A.U."

"And so ..." said Fermi.

"And so," continued Oppie, "earth will be destroyed by the superheated solar ejecta; our moon, too, of course. And both inferior planets."

"Mercury and Venus," supplied Teller.

"What about Mars?" asked Bethe.

"How far out is it?" asked Alvarez. "One-point-four?"

"More like 1.5," said Oppie. "Yes, it should survive unscathed, although it'll get a lovely light show as the attenuated plasma shell crosses its orbit."

"The surfaces of Mercury, Venus, earth, and the moon all destroyed," said Teller, facing the room again, his voice tinged with shock; this was devastation on a scale vaster than even he was used to contemplating.

"Exactly," said Robert. "And our oceans boiled away, all by approximately the year 2028. After that, the sun will settle down and continue to shine steadily, as it always has, but the habitable surface of the earth will be reduced to slag."

"Venus might have life," said Bethe. "I don't imagine anything intelligent, but, still, to lose another—what's that word? Another *ecosystem.* We should send ships there, try to gather specimens."

"For Christ's sake, Hans," said Alvarez. "We're going to lose *this* ecosystem.

Bethe nodded, then turned to Robert. "But we're working largely from figures in your papers, Oppie. Are you sure about them? Your calculations—"

"Are not always correct," conceded Oppie. "I invite you all to prove me wrong. Nothing would make me happier, but ..."

He took another draw on his pipe, and so Feynman finished for him. "But if you aren't wrong, the human race has less than one hundred years, and then—"

"And then," said Oppie, his heart pounding, "the sun itself will become the destroyer of worlds."

Chapter 18

The enemy has begun to employ a new and most cruel bomb, the power of which to do damage is incalculable. Should we continue to fight, it would not only result in an ultimate collapse and obliteration of the Japanese nation but also would lead to the total extinction of human civilization.

—Hirohito

The Japanese had surrendered two weeks ago, on August 15, 1945, although the formal ceremony, to be held aboard the U.S.S. *Missouri,* was still several days away. In the end, they'd received the only thing they'd wanted since first making overtures to surrender a year ago, in the summer of 1944: Hirohito, their divine Emperor, would retain the Chrysanthemum Throne. No other solution had ever been possible: the post-war world required a functioning domestic government on the Home Islands. But Truman had continued to insist on *unconditional surrender,* not making the Hirohito concession until after the two American atomic bombs had been dropped—after the new world order had been set.

Oppie had been surprised when Edward Teller invited him to go for a walk in the late-August heat; Robert thrived in it, but the stocky Teller was built for cooler climes. Oppie's eyes needed no more shielding than the brim of his hat, but Teller had on sunglasses that were the same dark green as the material that had come to be called "trinitite," the fused-sand glass that crusted the surface of the Trinity crater.

They walked slower than Oppie normally would. It wasn't that he was that much taller than the Hungarian; rather, it was that Edward had an artificial foot, the natural one having been lost in an accident when he was twenty. Oppie had great sympathy: his own mother had been born with only the stub of a hand and wore a mechanical clamping glove throughout her adult life.

Teller wiped his wide brow with his blue shirt sleeve as they ambled down the dirt road from the technical area, then he gestured to indicate the whole mesa. "We have here the greatest collection of—yes, I'll use the word—geniuses ever assembled. What was it you called us, Oppie?"

The unherdable cats, thought Robert. But what he said was, "The Luminaries."

Teller's voice was low, like the rumble of a freight train at night. "Exactly! The Luminaries! Who better than us to solve such a problem?"

Oppie shook his head. "Solve it? The world is coming to an end. It's division by zero; there's nothing to solve."

"You were born here in the States, right?"

Oppenheimer stepped over a hole in the dirt road and frowned at the seeming *non sequitur.* "In New York City, yes."

"That makes you an aberration. Think of our colleagues here. Like so many physicists, I am from Budapest. Bethe is from Strasbourg. Fermi? Rome—and Segrè, Tivoli. Peierls hails from Berlin, and Fuchs also somewhere in Germany, I imagine."

"Yes," said Oppie. "So?"

"We are refugees, immigrants: when conditions became untenable in our homes, we *left.*"

"Left?" repeated Oppie. "Weren't you listening? There's nowhere to go. Earth will be destroyed."

"But not Mars. And there are moons of Jupiter, Saturn, Uranus, and Neptune. Did you not read that last year Kuiper spectroscopically detected an atmosphere around Titan?"

"We can no more get to Saturn's moons than our own," said Oppie.

"We have the better part of a century. Look at Germany's V-2 rockets."

"Yes?"

"Surely continued development of such technology could give us vehicles capable of leaving earth's gravity."

"Missiles rejiggered for space travel? A long shot at best."

"Well, then, how about this? Ever since Trinity, Stan Ulam has been wondering aloud whether instead of using missiles to deliver bombs one might instead use bombs to propel missiles."

"Spacecraft pushed along by atomic explosions?"

"That's what he's suggested. Regardless, one way or another, people *will* get to Mars or the moons of Jupiter or Saturn prior to the solar purge."

"Where they'd freeze to death, suffocate, or both."

"Perhaps," replied Edward, "although I've talked it over with Wigner; he's more sanguine than you. But, anyway, that issue is a mere aside. An escape into the outer solar system is, shall we say, the 'fission bomb' of solutions, the easy answer. What's perhaps called for here is the equivalent of a *fusion* bomb, a breakthrough vastly more ingenious and powerful than rocketing to Mars or Saturn—a 'super' of salvation, if you will."

"And just what form might that take?"

"Who knows? Who could have predicted before we began our work here that Neddermeyer's notion of implosion would be the key to the plutonium bomb?" The unkempt eyebrows lowered. "Certainly not *you,* Robert."

Oppie paused to light his pipe by way of response. Teller waved the smoke away. "These luminaries you have gathered will soon all disappear into academia or industry. You heard what Truman said: the great marvel was the thing our scientific brains managed to make work. As he said, it's doubtful another such combination could be gathered ever again anywhere in the world. He called it—you remember, don't you?—'The greatest achievement of organized science in history.'"

"A bomb," said Oppie bitterly, as a small lizard scampered out of their way.

"Yes, yes, a bomb—this time. But, as the magicians say, 'And now for my next trick ...'"

Oppie blew out smoke. "We're not magicians."

"No? We've already turned one element into another."

"Edward ..."

"And who knows what else we could come up with—if we stay together, that is. But we're losing people every single day. It's an exodus."

"It *is* time I let my people go," said Oppie. "They have lives to return to, careers."

"Indeed yes. But my son is almost three now, and Mici and I are trying for another child. And you, Robert, you have two children already. *We* may not live long enough to be eliminated by your photospheric purge, and, indeed, *they* might not—but our grandchildren could." He shook his head. "I love my son; if I'm so blessed, I'll surely love my eventual grandchildren. And I want more for them than ..." He trailed off.

"Yes?"

"More than what their great uncles, their great aunts, and countless others got at the hands of Hitler." Teller shrugged a bit. "It's a long time since you've had close relatives in Europe; not since your childhood, I imagine. But still, surely you must have *some* sense that this is not the way it should all end."

"The sun is a thermonuclear-fusion device," Oppie said. "How would such an ending be different from the sort of holocaust your super might cause?"

"The super is to *prevent* war; it will never be used in battle. But to be snuffed out by the sun's caprice? We—and our children—deserve better than that. Your daughter Tyke deserves better than that." Oppie had seen Teller play with his own son Paul; he'd seen him sing to the boy, play patty-cake with him. Hell, he'd seen him play patty-cake with Tyke, a huge silly grin on the Hungarian's heavy face. And Edward often had sweets in his pocket for youngsters he happened to pass while walking to his office on the mesa.

Robert had told Pat Sherr that he wasn't the "attached" kind. Peter's conception had been an accident back when he and Kitty had been having their affair. Oppie had a flashback to the summer of 1940 when he'd called Kitty's then-husband, a medical doctor she'd married less than two years previously, explaining the situation. "I suppose you'd like me to arrange for a divorce," the doctor had said without a hint of ill-will. "Yes, please," Oppie had replied, "and thank you." All so academic, so civil, so very modern.

Maybe Teller did feel things more deeply than Oppie did. But his argument was wrong—or, at least, Oppie thought, the wrong one to sway him. A species doomed, a civilization incinerated? That was a scale he could contemplate. But his actual children? Their hypothetical spawn decades hence? Please.

And yet even on the larger canvas, why should he care? "The Nazis," he said slowly, "gave the world death camps. We gave the world atomic weapons. There are no good guys." He pointed up at the bright blue sky; he and Teller knew the stars were there even if they were currently washed out in the solar glare. "Maybe this answers Enrico's question."

Teller frowned. "What question is that?"

"The absence of beings from other worlds; the fact that no extra-terrestrial entities have ever come here."

"Oh. The 'Martian problem.' It *is* perplexing, isn't it?"

Oppie sucked on his pipe as they continued along. "Maybe. Maybe not."

"You doubt more advanced civilizations exist?"

"More advanced? Perhaps not. *As* advanced as us? Yes, they probably come into existence from time to time—but they might not persist."

Teller's mouth turned downward beneath his green lenses. "Ah. You think they all eventually unleash the power of the atom and soon after destroy themselves."

Oppie felt his eyebrows going up; that notion actually hadn't occurred to him. "No, I think perhaps they *are* destroyed."

"By what?"

"Gerling says the earth and therefore the sun are 3.2 billion years old, right? And the solar anomaly we've detected had its roots in 1938, the year Otto Hahn and Lise Meitner discovered nuclear fission."

"So?"

"So it's a remarkable coincidence, isn't it, that, on a cosmic scale, essentially simultaneous with our discovery of atomic power, our sun will destroy this planet. Maybe when a planet's inhabitants begin to comprehend the true nature of the atom and all the energy it contains they become too dangerous to be allowed loose in the universe."

"Allowed?" repeated Teller as if confused by the word.

"And so perhaps the universe conspires to wipe them out."

They were approaching Bathtub Row. "You've got to stop reading all that Eastern mysticism, Oppie."

Robert smiled. "Maybe."

"Even so, there *should* be a fight," said Teller. "If the universe wishes to defeat us, we must instead defeat it. And to do that, using this group of brains you have here is the best starting point. You can lead us in this pursuit."

"I'm sorry, Edward, but no. I tried saving the world once already, and—"

"Oppie, please. This"—he waved to encompass the mesa again—"can't end here."

"For me, it already has. It may, or may not, be time for humanity to let go, but it's certainly time for me to do so." He paused, but the news would be out soon, anyway: "I sent Groves my resignation notice this morning."

A low platform lay before Fuller Lodge like an alligator basking in the autumn sun. Behind it, flags of all forty-eight states hung limply from poles in the still air. General Groves, clad in his dark brown Army Service uniform and cap, stood at the podium in front of the vast crowd, all here to say goodbye to Oppenheimer. The first few hundred people were on folding chairs. The rest stood, the craggy pine-covered Sangre de Cristo mountains behind them.

"And here's another accolade," Groves bellowed into the trio of microphones while raising a meaty hand, "on top of the Army-Navy Award of Excellence." He smiled down from the dais at Oppie. "I have here a Certificate of Appreciation from Mr. Patterson, the Secretary of War."

Oppie glazed over while Groves read the scroll aloud. He hadn't written an acceptance speech and was composing remarks in his head. He'd trusted that the right words would come in time, and perhaps they still would, but he'd slept poorly last night, his dreams haunted by the faces of Japanese children who would never grow up. There had been—there really *had* been—a point to bombing Hiroshima, damn it all, but Nagasaki was ... what? He sought a term for it but none existed in any of his six languages and so he coined one: *overkill.*

"Robert?"

He wasn't sure if that was the first or second time Groves had called for him, but Oppie snapped out of his reverie and hoisted himself from the chair. He'd meant to stride confidently to the podium but found himself shuffling, the bottoms of his too-long gray trousers touching the ground. After climbing the three steps, he took the ornate scroll from Groves and let his hand be engulfed by the general's for a firm shake. When it was free again, he raised that hand and the applause died. "It is with appreciation and gratitude," he said, leaning down toward the microphones after Groves had moved aside, "that I accept from you this scroll for the Los Alamos Laboratory, for the men and women whose work and whose hearts have made it." He gestured at the assembled group. "It is our hope," he continued, "that in years to come we may look at this scroll, and all that it signifies, with pride."

His gaze roamed over the crowd. The thousand scientists who still remained on site were all present, but so were hundreds of uniformed men and women as well as many locals, mixed between Indians and Spanish, who had worked here as domestics or general laborers. On the dais were Ken Nichols, Deak Parsons, University of California president Robert Sproul, and others.

"Today," continued Oppie, "that pride must be tempered with a profound concern. If atomic bombs are to be added as new weapons to the arsenals of a warring world, or to the arsenals of nations preparing for war, then the time will come when mankind will ..." He paused, considering whether the word that popped into his head was too much, too soon. But no: "... will *curse* the names of Los Alamos and Hiroshima."

There was a ripple through the crowd; no one had expected him to say such a thing, he supposed. But this was a unique opportunity, with the press for the first time being allowed to cover an event on the mesa, and with the brass who had accompanied Groves from Washington seated in the front row. Oppie knew he'd lost friends recently here over his support of the War Department's May-Johnson Bill, rushed before Congress two weeks ago. If passed, it would effectively give American control of atomic energy to the military rather than having it in civilian hands. But he, J. Robert Oppenheimer, already being touted as "the father of the atomic bomb," had a wider vision, and this was the perfect chance to articulate it. The inner solar system might not survive another century, but humanity wasn't going to check out early due to atomic weapons—not if he could help it. "The peoples of this world must unite or they will perish. This war that has ravaged so much of the earth has written these words. The atomic bomb has spelled them out for all men to understand."

Everyone was silent; only the rustling of aspen leaves and the occasional lonely call of a hawk could be heard.

"Other men have spoken these same words in other times, of other wars, of other weapons. They have not prevailed. There are some, misled by a false sense of history, who hold that they will not prevail today." He lifted his head, bringing his eyes out of the shadow of his porkpie's wide brim. "It is not for us to believe that. By our works we are committed—committed to a world united, before this common peril, in law and in humanity."

He stepped down from the podium as the crowd rose in a standing ovation, the people in front blocking the Sangre de Cristo, the blood of Christ at last gone from his view.

Chapter 19

I never saw a man in such an extremely nervous state as Oppenheimer. He seemed to feel that the destruction of the entire human race was imminent.

—Henry A. Wallace

"Now, *this* is a dinner party!" declared Leo Szilard. Oppie, overhearing him, looked at the short Hungarian, not sure if he meant the great spread of food that had been laid out before them here in Washington or the stellar guest list. Besides Szilard and Oppie, also present were Nobel laureates Enrico Fermi and Harold Urey as well as Ed Condon, a half-dozen United States senators, and former vice president Henry A. Wallace. Hosting was Watson Davis of the Science Service news agency.

The purpose of the dinner was to educate the senators, and although Charles Tobey, a Republican from New Hampshire, opened by saying, "It looks as if we have a nonpartisan issue," heated debate soon erupted—but among the scientists rather than the politicians. Fermi had joined Oppie in supporting the May-Johnson Bill while Urey, Condon, and, most vociferously, Szilard were against it.

The dinner—Waldorf salad, Maine lobster, and porterhouse steak—was consumed with much gusto amid spluttering, and it soon became clear to Oppie that Leo's side was winning. It didn't help that the two of them hadn't really spoken since their angry meeting in Virginia back in May. The aftertaste of that, plus Szilard's certain knowledge that Oppie had vetoed the circulation of his petition calling for a demonstration of the bomb, seemed to be giving even more force than usual to Leo's flamboyant protestations. Oppie tried his standard suave maneuvering, but the senators, perhaps sick of that from their own daily lives, were clearly warming to the excitable Hungarian.

When dinner was over Oppie sidled over to Szilard, who was standing by a window, looking at the nighttime lights of the nation's capital. "We should talk."

"We *have* talked, Robert."

"There's ... more. Which hotel are you in?"

"I always stay at the Wardman Park."

"I'll walk you back there."

"Shall we bring Urey as referee?" snapped Szilard.

Although Urey was a chemist, it was Szilard who served as a catalyst, his massive creativity sparking similarly profound insights in others. "Just you and me, Leo."

Szilard considered for a long moment then nodded. "I'll get my coat."

Oppenheimer had felt comfortable talking in low tones as he and Leo walked along Woodley Road, confident that no one would hear enough of their conversation, in German, to make sense of it. But once they reached the hotel they found the bar crowded, and so they decided to head up to Szilard's suite. Oppie noted that it was nicer than his own at the Statler; the Hungarian was known for his decadent tastes. The bathtub, he saw through the open bathroom door, was filled with steaming water; Leo must have had a standing evening order with the chambermaid.

There was a hugely padded chair by the window and an elegantly carved wooden one by the writing desk. Leo took the former leaving Oppie the latter. The curtains were drawn back and the window was open, letting in a cool October breeze.

"I've washed my hands of it myself," said Oppie, "but there's a matter you should know about."

"Oh?" said Szilard.

"Yes, it's ..." Oppie trailed off. "Funny," he said, at last. "It's an odd thing to put into words. So stark. But here it is: the world is coming to an end."

"Almost certainly," agreed Szilard, "if we let the military control atomic matters."

"No, no. It has nothing to do with the military or the bomb. It has to do with the sun. We discovered it at Los Alamos: there's an explosion working its way outward from the sun's core, which had contained a degenerate neutron mass. It will erupt through the surface in eighty-odd years, pushing the photosphere and corona outward. The total loss of solar mass will be minor, but superheated plasma will wash over the inner solar system, destroying everything out to earth's orbit."

"There must be an error."

"I wish there was. But let me go over the evidence."

Szilard sat perfectly still as Oppie recounted what was known. The Hungarian's eyes were rolled slightly up and his pupils were tracking left and right as if he were visualizing equations as Robert described them. "Are you sure?" he said at last.

"Bethe has confirmed it; so has Fermi. And Teller, too."

"My God," Leo said. "It's—my God." His normally florid cheeks had lost their color. "Have you read my friend H.G. Wells?"

"Of course."

"In the last pages of *The Time Machine,* the time traveler leaves the year 802,701 A.D. and goes many millions of years further into the future, to witness the end of our world. And that's where it's supposed to be—far, far down the road! Not something that, were I to eat right and exercise, I myself might almost live long enough to see!"

"I know," said Oppie. "I wish it wasn't true."

"Over! The whole she-bang!" Leo snapped his fingers. "Like that!"

"Like that," said Oppie softly. "But Teller thinks physicists should work together to try to find a solution."

Leo's tone calmed a bit. "It is, as you'd say, a sweet problem."

"It's not sweet," Oppie said. "It's bitter. The ashes of futility."

"Well," said Leo. "We probably won't survive that long, anyway, as I said, if we let the military control atomic matters."

"I know the May-Johnson Bill is shit—"

"That's what you said about the atomic bomb."

"— and I'll be happy if they come up with something better, but I still say politics is a matter for politicians."

"We shall never agree on that," said Leo. "But this—saving the world!—*is* a matter for intellectuals, for scientists. Not brutes, not soldiers. Everyone knew our Manhattan Project would last at most a few years. Either we would succeed or Hitler and Heisenberg would, but it was a race that was bound to be completed by 1944 or 1945. No one expects us to be working together in 1946, let alone the 1950s."

Oppie sucked on his pipe, which, out of deference to Leo, he'd let go out before they'd gotten up to his room. "We *aren't* going to be working together. I've resigned."

"Surely that was theater; your skills are needed. Humanity will—"

"— will receive its collective fate: paralyzed souls, one and all. I don't care."

"You must care *some,*" said Szilard, "or you wouldn't be bothering to tell me all this."

Oppie frowned, thinking those same words again: *Now I am become Death.* In the *Bhagavad Gita,* Vishnu, part of the Hindu trinity along with Brahma and Shiva, tries to persuade Prince Arjuna to do his duty. To impress the Prince, Vishnu takes on his multi-armed form and declares *Now I am become Death, the destroyer of worlds.* Vishnu succeeds, and Arjuna does what, as a warrior, he had been born to do.

Robert's stomach churned. He, scion of the Ethical Culture School, had *not* been born a warrior, and this was *not* his fight.

"I'm telling you, Leo, because of your ... your *passion.* I've done my bit for King and Country. Oh, I'll still work on atomic policy—Prometheus has an obligation to play fire marshal—but that's it. As for the solar photospheric ejection? Teller thinks something can be done; maybe he's right, but it's not my department."

Leo looked out at the city, countless thousands asleep. "Teller, yes. My old friend and fellow Martian. I can work with him. But ..."

"Yes?" prodded Oppie.

"The world was at war when the Manhattan Project began. We had no choice then but to crawl into bed with the army, the government. Hell, Robert, *I* was the one who got Einstein to write to Roosevelt. But we're *not* at war anymore; we don't need the military."

"If you take this on, you *will* need resources," replied Oppie. "Money, manpower. Washington can be your ally."

"Metonymy, is it? Yes, perhaps we will need friends in high places but we don't need the Pentagon, and we certainly don't need the man who built it."

"General Groves is—"

"An ignoramus. You *know* that, Robert."

"He thinks highly of you."

"As he should. I am—ah, you swap metonymy for sarcasm. Ask yourself, then: which of us is the indispensable man as we move forward, him or me?"

"The hawk or the dove, is that it?"

Szilard folded his arms in front of his sloping chest. "Answer my question."

Oppie shook his head. "I simply say there are things that the military is good at. But you've been thinking up plans to save the world for years; this is your field, not mine."

Leo had been born in 1898, and had spent much of the late 1920s and early 1930s promoting his notion of "the Bund," a society of intellectuals who would shape future civilization. He had indeed befriended H.G. Wells, a fellow utopian dreamer who had proposed a similar notion in one of his novels, and even for a time had served as Wells's agent for translated editions.

Szilard shrugged his rounded shoulders. "Did you know I'd been contemplating a switch into molecular biology? Life rather than death, you see. But now ..." He paused. "Who else knows?"

"Several at Los Alamos; I'll write up a list for you."

"But not Groves?"

"No."

"Good, good. Anyone outside of your New Mexico group?"

"Not yet." And then, offering an olive branch: "You were the only person I thought to approach."

Leo considered this then tipped his head. "I'm honored." He turned fully toward Oppie. "But there are others who must be informed at once."

"Who are you thinking of?"

"Number one has to be Einstein, of course."

"He was denied clearance to work on the atomic-bomb project," said Oppie. "His left-leaning ways."

Leo raised eyebrows at the irony. "Denying Einstein but approving you. In any event, I know Albert well; I shall head to Princeton from here—it's not far—and brief him myself." He shook his head sadly. "A better man there isn't; the government should be ashamed for having kept him in the dark during the war."

"I know," said Oppie turning toward the black night. "I swear, sometimes this country goes out of its way to vilify its most loyal servants."

Chapter 20

I don't want to see that son of a bitch in this office ever again.

—Harry S. Truman

Being uninterested in politics before Jean had come into his life, Oppenheimer hadn't voted until he was thirty-two years old. He'd cast his first ballot for the 1936 re-election of Franklin Roosevelt, whose New Deal policies had appealed to Oppie's recently kindled socialist sensibilities. He'd voted for FDR twice more: in 1940 and, in recognition of his support for the nascent United Nations, again in 1944.

And now, at last, Oppie was at the White House, having been granted a meeting with the president. But the occupant of the Oval Office was no longer FDR, a man Oppie would have loved to have met, despite some growing misgivings during the war years, but rather Harry Truman, who, in Oppie's opinion, had botched things horribly at Potsdam by failing to bring Russia into an accord for international control of atomic energy; worse, Truman had needlessly prolonged the Pacific war by insisting on unconditional surrender, instead of just letting the Japanese keep their damned Emperor in the first place.

Sure, it *was* an honor to meet the president no matter who held that title. But just as some infinities are smaller than others—there are only half as many odd numbers as integers and yet both exist in endless profusion—so certain honors were inferior to their kin. Adding to Oppie's muted mood was the fact that he was being escorted down the corridor not by Henry Stimson, the principled gentleman who had served as Secretary of War until his recent seventy-eighth birthday, but rather by his successor, Bob Patterson, in office all of a month now and bearing the same title even though the country was no longer at war.

After passing through the office of the president's secretary, Oppie and Patterson entered the Oval from a door at the north end of its major axis, facing the empty desk. Oppie had only ever seen a couple of black-and-white pictures of this place in magazines. It was smaller than he'd imagined it, but really was elliptical; he judged its eccentricity to be about zero-point-six. The presidential seal was woven into the central blue-gray rug.

Another door to the room opened and in came Truman, three inches shorter than Oppie, with a round, full face, blue eyes behind thick lenses, and hair more gray than brown. "Dr. Oppenheimer," he said, mispronouncing the surname by stretching the *O* into a long vowel. "A pleasure to meet you."

"The pleasure," replied Oppie, shaking the offered hand, "is all mine." He had flown in for this meeting; this was his third trip to Washington since the dropping of the bomb on Nagasaki, and all of them had been by plane. Without a word being said to him, the stricture against flying had been quietly lifted; even before his resignation, nine days ago, the government had decided he was no longer too valuable to risk losing in a crash.

FDR, even though he couldn't stand up, had been a towering presence, but this Truman was just a workaday Missourian chosen as a compromise running mate for Roosevelt's fourth term. Southern Democrats had objected to the flagrantly liberal Henry Wallace, who had been vice president up until this past January, and so now this man held the reins of power. More than that—Oppie had a flash of that Harvard physicist in the control bunker at Trinity—he was the one with his hand on the atomic lever, the only man in the whole world, at least so far, who had fission weapons under his command.

Really, for the task ahead, it should probably have been Szilard taking this meeting, not Oppie—but Leo had tried and failed once already to get in to see Truman, ending up with Jimmy Byrnes instead. He'd prevailed upon Oppie for this one task: perhaps the now world-famous laboratory director could succeed where Szilard had failed. Oppie had promised to report back with his assessment.

"Doctor," said Truman, "won't you and Secretary Patterson please have a seat?" There were short couches on either side of the rug. The president took the couch on the west side of the room; Oppie and Patterson sat on the other one.

"Congratulations and all that," said Truman. "Now, let's get down to it, shall we? This business of the control of nuclear weapons, right? The first thing is to define the national problem, then the international one."

A dozen replies ran through Oppie's head, none of them polite. For Pete's sake, the primary concern had to be getting international controls in place rather than all this brouhaha about whether the military or a civilian agency would manage atomic matters domestically; any fool could see that—except, apparently, *this* fool. He looked at Patterson, but the Secretary's long face was studiously neutral. "Actually, Mr. President," Oppie said slowly, "perhaps it would be best first to define the international problem."

"Well, when you get right down to it, there *is* no international problem," Truman said. "We're the only ones who've got this. You know when the Russians will have their own atom bomb?"

"As I told the House of Representatives last week, sir, no, I don't."

"Well, I do," snapped Truman. "Never."

"I assure you, Mr. President, the laws of physics are the same in Moscow as they are here; the Soviets will master this technology soon enough."

"Like the damn Nazis did? Have you seen the reports from the Alsos mission into Germany? They'd thrown up their hands; it was too much for them to fathom. No, it's like I said after we took out Hiroshima. No one but your team, and no country but America, could have made that happen."

"You are ..." But, for once, Oppie managed to intercept impolitic words on their way out; he ended instead with "... too kind, sir."

They talked for another twenty minutes, mostly about the May-Johnson Bill, the draft legislation that had been making Leo Szilard and others apoplectic. It treated nuclear matters as a state secret, rather than something the rest of the world was bound to gain access to, and threatened scientists who made even trivial violations of security with fines of $100,000 and a decade in prison.

Oppie wasn't troubled about that. Getting *any* domestic legislation in place was a beginning; it could always be tweaked after the fact. No, he was here for a more important reason. It was crucial to take the measure of this Truman, to determine if he should be made privy to the pending solar calamity.

"What's the matter, Doctor?" said Truman. "You look like you swallowed an anthill."

Oppie glanced over at the desk and noticed a little sign on it: *The buck stops here!* He turned back to Truman and said, *"Salus populi suprema lex esto."* It was the Missouri state motto—"let the welfare of the people be the supreme law"—and he'd expected Truman to recognize it, but the president just frowned. Oppie made another attempt, a trial balloon, a test: "Mr. President, I feel I have blood on my hands."

Truman reached into his breast pocket, pulled out a white silk handkerchief, and shoved it toward Oppie. "Well, why don't you wipe them, sonny boy?"

The two men locked eyes for a moment then Truman rose. "I think we're done here."

Yes, thought Oppie, rising as well. *We most certainly are.*

Chapter 21

Szilard is a fine, intelligent man who is ordinarily not given to illusions. Perhaps, like many such people, he is inclined to overestimate the significance of reason in human affairs.

—Albert Einstein

"Albert, my old friend!"

"My dear Leo. So good to see you!" Einstein, wearing a bulky plaid sweater, ushered Szilard into the small drawing room of his modest house on Mercer Street in Princeton, New Jersey.

"So," Einstein said morosely in German after he'd sat down, each word separated by a puff on his pipe, "such a thing we started."

Leo had been haunted by the same thought. If he hadn't written that letter to FDR, and if Einstein hadn't signed it, there would have been no Manhattan Project. The European war had ended of its own accord, and the Pacific war was now also over, days or weeks or maybe—just maybe—even months sooner than it otherwise would have inevitably concluded, and with the same side victorious. Perhaps American lives *had* been saved but the tally of *human* lives? More people were surely dead in Hiroshima and Nagasaki than any land invasion would have caused, and a toxic genie had been unleashed, the world forever changed.

Of the remaining chairs, Leo picked the most luxurious-looking one. "If I'd known then what I know now ..." he said, lowering himself down. He shook his head. "I naturally thought the Germans would be working on the same thing. I can't believe Heisenberg made so little progress."

"Do you know him well?" asked Einstein.

"No. Wigner and I once went to Hamburg to hear him lecture, and we spoke a bit after the talk, but that was all. But he was Teller's thesis advisor; Edward has told me stories."

"We crossed paths several times," said Einstein. "We had a lovely walk together through Göttingen in 1924, and I saw him again in Berlin in '26, and of course we were both at the Solvay Conference in '27." Einstein scraped the dottle from his pipe bowl and set about reloading it. "We disagreed on almost everything, although perhaps he's come to his senses since. Uncertainty! Nonsense."

Leo knew well of his friend's aversion to the Copenhagen interpretation of quantum mechanics; sadly, it was clear by this point—Einstein was now sixty-six—that the younger generation was passing him by. "Time will tell, Albert."

"That it will. You've heard the joke about me? Einstein is riding in a railway car. He flags down the conductor and asks, 'Does New York stop at this train?'" Einstein chuckled. "But there's an even better one about Heisenberg. Old Werner is speeding down the road. A police officer uses a bullhorn to shout at him, 'You're doing a hundred and twenty!' To which Heisenberg shouts back, 'Thanks heaps—now I'm lost!'"

Leo nodded. He liked the version that continued with Heisenberg's passenger being Erwin Schrödinger. The cop pulls them over, goes to look in the car's trunk, and calls out, "Hey, do you guys know you have a dead cat back here?" To which Schrödinger shouts back, "We do now, asshole!"

Jokes. Jokes, because all that death, all that destruction, was too much to dwell on—during the day, at least. What Szilard would give for a good night's sleep!

"I wonder if Heisenberg has heard the one about himself," continued Einstein. "He's not known for his sense of humor, but he's a fine physicist. I nominated him for the Nobel three times before he won it."

Leo nodded again. "Very kind of you."

"Oh, he deserved it, no doubt. And concerning fission matters? Heisenberg is as competent as anyone. If he had wanted to ..." Einstein drew his pipe to life but said nothing more.

"Yes?" prodded Szilard.

"I think he threw the game," said Einstein, lifting his shaggy white eyebrows. "Hitler and his monsters, what did they know of physics? A shifted decimal here, a reversed sign there. Heisenberg could have kept up a pretense of progress while making sure that those evil men were never given such power."

Leo frowned and said to Einstein what his friend had said to him at the start of all this: *"Daran habe ich gar nicht gedacht!"*

"A mere hypothesis," replied Albert with a philosophical shrug. "Perhaps we'll have evidence to test it someday." He poured brandy from a decanter on a small table and offered the snifter to Leo, who waved it away. Einstein happily kept it for himself. "At least, for the moment, the world is safe."

Szilard leaned forward. "For the moment," he replied, "but not for long."

"Leo, my boy, you are always such an alarmist!"

"Not at all. But I met with Oppenheimer a few days ago."

"Ah," said Einstein. "The man of the moment."

"He tells me he sent you some equations to check."

"Yes, that's right. Wasn't sure what it was all about but I'm always happy to help settle a bet."

"It all caused quite a stir at Los Alamos, I'm told," Leo said. "You know Oppie's pre-war work was in stellar physics, and so was Hans Bethe's. And Teller, also out there frying his brain in the desert, had devoted all his efforts for years now to fusion physics."

"Dear Edward! I hope to see him and Mici again now that the war is over."

Leo didn't own a briefcase—even now, long after his narrow escape from Germany in 1933—he limited his possessions to those that could fit in a pair of suitcases. But he'd taken the laundry bag from his Princeton hotel and had a small sheaf of papers wrapped in it. He got them out. "Oppenheimer gave me these. He, Teller, Bethe, and others have double- and triple-checked the math, as have I. Have a look. And here are the spectrographs in question from 1929, 1938, and earlier this year." He paused. "You'll need some time with these. Might I take a bath while you look them over?"

Leo waited until Einstein called out his last name. He hoisted himself out of the claw-footed tub, checked the ornately framed mirror to see that his hair was still slicked back, put on a white terry-cloth robe—rougher than he'd have liked—and returned to the drawing room.

The normally unflappable Einstein was visibly agitated. He was standing by a heavy velvet curtain, drawn against the afternoon sun. His pipe was bowl-up in an onyx ashtray and he had his fingers interlaced in front of him. "So sad," he said as if two words could encompass so much. "So sad."

Leo took the same chair as before. "Then you agree with the conclusion?"

Einstein nodded ruefully. "I guess, in the end, even if Heisenberg did refrain from helping Hitler, his gesture was meaningless. Within a century, it'll have made no difference who won the damnable war."

"Well, we still have our lives to live out, and I prefer this outcome to the other possibility," said Leo. "But, yes, the final generation to be born on earth may already be alive."

Einstein's soulful brown eyes were rimmed with red. "My younger son and I don't speak. He's in an institution, did you know that? Eduard. I haven't seen him in a dozen years."

Leo, who had no children of his own, said softly, "I'm sorry."

"I should ..." A tear found its way into one of the deep crevices on Einstein's cheek and followed the crease down. "I should make amends." His rounded, stooped shoulders moved slightly. "I was content to die with that unresolved, but somehow knowing that *he* might have *his* life cut short ..." The eyes turned to Leo now. "You should marry Trude. God knows I'm not prudish, but at least the world can end with as much peace and happiness in it as possible, no?"

"I don't dispute your utilitarian leanings, old friend, but although the world is done for, perhaps mankind is not."

"Eh?"

"As I said, I spoke at length with Oppenheimer. He is despondent—not over *this,* but over what has already happened. And he's exhausted, half-wasted away: a toothpick with a hacking cough. He needs time to recover from the war effort. But he says Teller believes there may be some way to save at least a portion of humanity; Oppenheimer says Wigner shares Teller's view. And, well, pie-in-the-sky utopian that I am, I guess I believe the same thing, too."

"You, Wigner, *and* Teller?" said Einstein. He blew his nose, rubbed his eyes, and stared into space for a time, thinking. At last he lifted liver-spotted hands, palms facing each other. "Who am I to argue with three Martians?"

Leo smiled slightly.

"All right," said Einstein. "There will be time enough for fatalism later." He adjusted his sweater so it sat properly over his paunch. "Shall we see what a fourth Martian has to say? Johnny von Neumann is here in Princeton, and he's working on something that just might prove useful."

Chapter 22

Ich bin Feuer und Flamme dafür. [I am fire and flame for it.]

—**Albert Einstein**,
on the Institute for Advanced Study

Szilard and Einstein headed out into the fall afternoon, the air chill and tart as a McIntosh fresh from the tree. Leo usually had a sprightly step, but he slowed in deference to his friend's age. They left Einstein's white clapboard house behind them as they made their way down tree-lined Mercer Street to the Institute for Advanced Study. Founded by a five-million-dollar donation by brother-and-sister retail millionaires Louis Bamberger and Carrie Fuld, the Institute boasted some of the world's top minds in physics and mathematics, as well as a smattering of equal intellects devoted to humanistic studies.

Tonight was Halloween. Last year, in Chicago, Leo had seen jack-o'-lanterns carved with Hitler's face or slanted eyes—the scariest faces then imaginable by Americans. Now, though, they were back to being goblin countenances and beneficent smiles ... or perhaps victorious grins.

"You'll see that the grounds are vast," said Einstein, still in German. "We now have over two hundred and forty hectares"—better than six hundred acres—"but the pride and joy is the Institute woods. Aspen, maple, beech, oak, birch: you name it, we've got it. There's a lovely brook and, in spring, beautiful wildflowers. I know you like to walk, Leo. The trails are soothing, and warblers and other songbirds will keep you company."

"It sounds enchanting."

"It is. Of course, we'll have snow soon enough; I don't partake myself, but I'm told the cross-country skiing is first-rate. We have our own excellent library, growing every year, but Princeton"—he clearly meant the university, not the city—"is only a short distance away, and its library is wonderful."

"Are there accommodations on site?"

"Yes. Quite luxurious, too. I prefer my house—this mile-long walk to the Institute does me good each day—but many of our members make their homes on campus. The director takes pride of place; he lives in Olden Manor, quite a charming house."

"Who else is on faculty?"

A *soupçon* of French: *"La crème de la crème."* Then back to German: "Kurt Gödel, Oswald Veblen, and Hermann Weyl have been here since the beginning, or nearly so. We also have Wolfgang Pauli—how could we exclude him?" Einstein chuckled. "Many more, as well. I tell you, Leo, the leading center for physics is no longer Göttingen or even Berkeley but right here."

They had come to the main gate. The guard waved at Einstein, and the famous man treated him to a wide smile and a friendly nod.

"And there are no teaching duties?" asked Leo.

"None. No students, no endless departmental meetings. Just the very best minds and plenty of time to think."

Szilard looked around, impressed, as they approached a sprawling three-story building of reddish-brown brick surmounted by a clock tower. "This is Fuld Hall," said Einstein, "built for us in 1939."

"Bespoke construction!" declared Leo. "I know you never saw Los Alamos—and I avoided it like death itself—but they were trying to make do with buildings originally used as a boys' school, plus Quonset huts and other such affronts to taste and comfort that could be hastily erected, all in the middle of a desert. Nobody could think straight in a place like that! I said everybody who went there would go crazy. And they did!" He recalled what Fermi had told him after one of the Italian navigator's visits to Los Alamos: *"I think those people actually* want *to build a bomb!"*

Einstein nodded sadly.

"But this place!" said Szilard. "In such a place, a man could work happily for years, for decades."

"I have no idea how many years I have left," Einstein replied, "but I intend to spend all of them here. Heaven, should such a thing turn out to exist, will doubtless be a step down." They'd entered the marble lobby of Fuld Hall now. "And speaking of a step down, Johnny's pet project has been relegated to the basement." Einstein led the way below, holding onto the wooden banister for support.

As they entered a large but mostly empty room, lit only by bare bulbs mounted in the concrete ceiling, Szilard beheld his old friend for the first time since before the war; he was hunched over a desk. Von Neumann, six years Leo's junior, was now forty-one, but Leo felt the years had been kinder to himself than to his compatriot. Johnny's hairline had retreated to the crown of his head and his cheeks had begun the slow melt into jowls. "Jancsi!" Leo called out, using the Hungarian diminutive.

Von Neumann looked up. "Szilard!" He rose, closed the distance—footfalls echoing in the vast chamber—and pumped Leo's hand. "What a pleasant surprise!" he continued in Hungarian, then he poked Leo in the belly. "I see the war still had rations of cake and pie for you!"

"The mind requires energy," replied Leo, also in their native tongue.

"What brings you here?" von Neumann asked, switching to German so that Einstein could join in. "Did you finally blow up Chicago?"

"No, no, no. I came to seek Einstein's counsel. And he said you were working on something interesting and useful."

"Ja!" replied von Neumann. "I am thinking about something much more important than bombs. I am thinking about computers."

"Ah, the old Jancsi!" said Szilard. "Always with an eye for the ladies."

"Not the women," said von Neumann. "The machines. And we intend to build the best one ever right here."

"You know," said Albert, switching for the moment to English, "I originally opposed this. So did the director, Frank Aydelotte—which was funny because, see, this thing will be able to *add a lot.*" Albert looked expectantly at Leo. "Nothing? Ah, well."

Szilard, who only ever laughed out loud at Charlie Chaplin's films, served up a weak smile, and Einstein went on in German: "This Institute is meant to be a refuge, a sanctuary for pure thought with no regard to practical applications—no more refrigerator patents for us, dear Leo! The Institute's members do theoretical work only; no experiments. But Johnny fought long to convince us we need his great electronic monstrosity to speed our figuring, and just this month he secured the funding. Me, I'm old now; haste hasn't interested me for a long while."

"There are things that a computer will be able to do that no human will ever manage with a slide rule," said von Neumann. "One project we have in mind is *perfect* weather forecasting. And, after that, maybe even control of the weather."

"Everybody talks about the weather," said Leo, "but nobody ever does anything about it—until you, Jancsi."

Von Neumann—who had been known as "Good-Time Johnny" for his love of boisterous parties back when he and Leo had been in Berlin in the 1920s—had worked here at the I.A.S. since 1933. He'd fled Hitler's rising anti-Semitism after a symbolic conversion to Catholicism had failed to prove sufficient protection. In 1943, he had taken a leave to help Oppenheimer at Los Alamos, but most of his war-related work had been on ENIAC, the world's first electronic computer, at the University of Pennsylvania. "We learned a lot from those early efforts," said von Neumann. "But the computer that will soon fill this room will use a new—" he waved a hand vaguely, seeking a term "— *architecture.* It will be the model upon which all future computers will be based, I'm sure."

"Oh?" said Leo.

Von Neumann nodded. "I designed the calculating elements used in ENIAC, and I know they are as archaic as dinosaurs compared to what we will build here." He looked up as if envisioning it. "A whole new approach."

"Well, new approaches are precisely what we're going to need," replied Szilard.

"For what?" asked von Neumann.

"Jancsi, excuse us. I need a word with Einstein." Leo put an arm around the older man's shoulders and propelled him out into the corridor. Szilard bounded up the staircase and headed out into the October sun again. He waited for Einstein to catch up, then made a gesture encompassing the vast grounds. "*This* is the place," he said firmly.

"The place for what?" asked Albert.

"To headquarter the effort to save humanity, of course. Where better? Before they all disappear into teaching posts, let's rally the very best of the great minds at Los Alamos and Chicago to come *here.* Albert, old friend, surely you have the sway, no?"

Einstein's eyebrows rose, two clouds striving to join the others serenely moving across the sky. He nodded slowly. "They *do* have a history of listening to me, Johnny's computer notwithstanding."

"Excellent. We should speak to your director, this Add-a-Lot." Leo stretched out the name, recalling Einstein's pun; the fact that he'd employed it brought a smile to the old man's face.

"Actually, Frank told me he's thinking of retiring; he turns sixty-five next year. He hasn't let the faculty know yet, but he's planning to announce it next week."

"Ah, then this wonderful place will need a new director," declared Leo, with relish. "And I know just the man!"

Chapter 23

After seeing the pictures from Hiroshima, [Oppenheimer] appeared determined that Los Alamos, the unique and outstanding laboratory he had created, should vanish.

—Edward Teller

Edward Teller had spent less than six months at the University of Chicago working with Enrico Fermi before moving in March 1943 to Los Alamos. But, despite his short stay in the Windy City, he'd made a considerable impression, and the university wanted him back—especially now that his role in the Manhattan Project had become public.

Just this week, Norris Bradbury, who had replaced Oppie as director of Los Alamos, had offered Teller the title of head of the Theoretical Division, now that Hans Bethe had departed the mesa as well. That was too little, too late, felt Teller; the job should have been his two and a half years ago. Still, it gave him a strong bargaining position today, on his return visit to the University of Chicago. He was confident that he'd be offered a tenured professorship.

"Such a place you've never seen!" exclaimed his old friend Leo Szilard, in Hungarian, as they walked the Chicago campus. He was referring to the idyllic Institute for Advanced Study in New Jersey.

"Jancsi has told me about it," replied Teller, also in their mother tongue.

"Bah! Mere words. You must take the trip with me; see it for yourself. For the work ahead, we can't remain here in Chicago." He pointed to a cluster of buildings that housed the Faculty of Arts. "We can't stay at any traditional university with a hundred irrelevant departments and endless bureaucracy."

"Jancsi says they have historians at the Institute."

"Well, yes, they do. And some others pursuing humanistic studies. Do you know what a paleographer is? I had to look it up! But it is *mostly* a place of physics, of math—and Jancsi is building the world's best computing machine there to help in those areas."

"And you see a role there for me?"

Szilard used Teller's actual two-syllable Hungarian given name, not the Anglicized version. "Ede, my boy, of course, of course! I see you as the next director!"

The November wind blowing on them had teeth. "Me?" replied Teller, genuinely surprised.

"Who else? The incumbent is retiring. You were passed over to run the T-Section at Los Alamos during the war. Here's your chance to head up something even more important: organizing the best minds in the world as we work to save the planet."

Teller drew his eyebrows together. "I had planned to continue my work on the super, either here with Fermi or back at Los Alamos."

"No, no, no," declared Leo. "Only a fool fights in a burning house. It's not just that this war is over; *all* war is over. What madness it would be to squabble over borders and resources that will boil away into nothingness in short order."

"It *would* be important work," Teller said slowly, tasting the notion.

Leo fell silent until a clutch of students, coming the other way, passed. As the young men receded behind them, Teller heard one say to his companion, "My God, that's Edward Teller!" "It would be *crucial* work," Leo continued, once they were again away from others' ears. "The *most crucial* work anyone could do."

"But why me? Surely, after his success at Los Alamos, Oppenheimer is the appropriate man."

"Oppenheimer! He vetoed circulating my petition there—you told me so yourself. I hear he told Truman he has blood on his hands—and he does! But you, dear Ede, you didn't work on those infernal bombs; you didn't focus on the short term. You had a long-term goal, and long-term thinking is what we need most now."

"There are those," Teller said, "who objected—and continue to object—to any work on fusion bombs." And then, suddenly, seeing what Szilard was getting at, his voice took on an edge: "And you would deflect me from that work, too!"

Leo smiled. "Oh, perhaps. I certainly don't wish to make the same mistake twice. Had you not driven me to Einstein's cottage, and had I not urged him there to sign the letter to Roosevelt, there would be no atomic bombs in the world today; I overestimated both the skill and resolve of the Germans and Soviets. And, yes, it's likely true, I think, that if no one of your caliber spearheads an American effort to create the super, such a weapon will never come to be."

Caliber. Spearhead. Teller frowned. Once the conversation turned to bombs, one's language became dominated by metaphors of armaments; even Leo—more lamb than lion despite his name—had succumbed. But perhaps his old friend was right. Neither Germany nor Japan would be permitted such research anymore, and who among the Soviets could possibly equal the Americans in this? Kurchatov, perhaps. Kapitsa? A stretch indeed. Still: "But this is an *administrative* job." His tone was the one researchers worldwide reserved for such positions.

"There'll be precious little administration, Ede. As Einstein told me, the ideal administrator for the Institute is a very quiet man who will not disturb people who are trying to think—and that means *you* would be free to do your *own* thinking. But, of course, the director must bring an additional ingredient to the goulash: a stature that will entice others to join our effort. I am realistic about my own reputation: I am a gadfly. Yes, yes, brilliant to those who know me, but few do. But you, Ede, will one day take a trip to Stockholm, mark my words: you, Brunauer, and Emmett, for your B-E-T formulation from before the war. A stunning accomplishment."

The sidewalk they were on forked here. Leo chose the left branch, and Teller followed. He'd never told anyone except Mici of his Nobel hopes for that work but, yes, B-E-T was highly regarded, even if, as Teller often thought, it really should be known at T-B-E; it was perhaps more significant even than his involvement with the discovery of the Teller-Jahn Effect.

"But if you continue to labor on this fusion-bomb research of yours," continued Szilard, "what's its goal?"

"Peace, of course. A weapon too terrible to ever set off."

"Exactly! But Oppenheimer's goal was to *use* his bomb. What did he say when he ordered you not to circulate my petition? No, no, no: don't answer; I read your letters to me. He told you to leave it in the hands of the policy makers, saying that scientists should stay out of such matters and trust the wiser heads in government to make sound decisions."

Teller nodded, vividly recalling that conversation: Oppie, with his usual charm, had declared he didn't think it was right for scientists to use whatever prestige they might have as a platform for political pronouncements. He spoke in luminous terms about the deep concern, thoroughness, and wisdom with which such questions were being handled in Washington. "Our fate," he had said, "is in the hands of the best, the most conscientious men of our nation—and they have information that we do not possess."

"Yes," said Edward. "I'm sorry, Leo, but he was quite persuasive."

"Ah, but did he tell you that he himself was sitting on something called the 'Scientific Panel' of the Interim Committee on Atomic Energy?"

Teller felt his heart jump. "What?"

"And did he tell you that on June sixteenth—before you'd even shown him my petition back in Los Alamos!—he'd written the report for that panel, a report which went straight to President Truman, urging that the bomb be dropped on Japan without warning."

Teller tasted acid at the back of his throat. "I didn't know any of this."

"It's true. Fermi, who was also on the Scientific Panel along with Compton and Lawrence, gave me a copy of the report, and he confirmed that Oppenheimer was its author."

There was a wooden bench ahead of them; most of the paint that had once covered it had been eroded away by the elements. Szilard sat and motioned for Teller to do the same. He then pulled a rolled-up sheaf of papers from his inside jacket pocket, flattened them, flipped to the final page, and handed the document to Teller. "Have a look at the passage I've underlined."

Teller opened his own coat long enough to remove glasses from the inside pocket of his sports jacket. He perched them on his nose, then scanned the highlighted section: *We can propose no technical demonstration likely to bring an end to the war; we see no acceptable alternates to direct military use.*

"Damn it," said Teller, re-reading the words in disbelief. "He ..."

"Lied to you," said Szilard, simply. "Or, at best, deliberately misled you."

"But why?" asked Teller.

He could see in Szilard's round face that Leo thought him naïve. "Oppenheimer was Groves's handpicked man and, from the first, Groves wanted to use this bomb. Of course Oppenheimer would play ball."

Teller tipped his head to one side. "All right, all right. There's no doubt that he went along with them—but he came to see me the day of the Hiroshima bombing. He was a wreck; I've never seen a man so ... so *anguished.* And Mici heard from Kitty that he's become even worse after Nagasaki."

"A change of heart *after* the bombing is cold comfort for those in Japan," said Leo.

"Granted, but—" And then it hit him. "This isn't about Oppenheimer," he rumbled as he pointed an accusatory finger at Szilard. "It's about General Groves! If Oppie ends up running the show at the Institute, there's no question that Groves will be in the background, pulling the strings just as he did at Los Alamos. Hell, if Oppie had had his way, we'd have all been given ranks and made to wear uniforms there! But I have only a passing acquaintance with Groves; he has no hold over me."

Leo smiled like a boy caught pulling an innocent prank. "I admit that's a bonus. But you underestimate yourself, my friend. You have connections we will need. Groves would doubtless make this an America-only effort; you saw how he treated the Tube Alloys contingent from the United Kingdom! But we will need the best minds from here in North America and from Europe, including—"

"Heisenberg," said Teller, getting it. "My thesis advisor."

"Exactly. To be honest, Niels Bohr's name had occurred to me as a potential director, but, after their falling out during the war, Heisenberg could never work under him. But you? You he would trust—as would most of the Europeans. And, of course, our fellow Martian, von Neumann, who is already at the I.A.S., would trust you, too."

"All of this is fascinating, Leo, but ..."

"But what? Destiny has called you. Besides, I looked into the details. The job of I.A.S. director pays handsomely, $20,000 a year; you are supplied with housing in Olden Manor, an eighteen-room mansion staffed by servants; and there's a generous pension. Plus, of course, a chance to focus your work on saving the world. What was it you wrote me back in the summer? 'I have no hope of clearing my conscience; the things we're working on are so terrible, nothing can save our souls.' Well, my old friend, perhaps *this* work can."

The most abstruse problems in physics made beautiful, serene sense to Teller, but this—*this*—left his head swimming. "I'll need to talk it over with Mici."

"After three years stuck in a desert? You know as well as I do that she'll welcome the luxury of the Institute." Leo extended his chubby hand. "Shall we shake on it?"

Chapter 24

Suppose Germany had developed two bombs before we had any bombs. And suppose Germany had dropped one bomb, say, on Rochester and the other on Buffalo, and then having run out of bombs she would have lost the war. Can anyone doubt that we would then have defined the dropping of atomic bombs on cities as a war crime, and that we would have sentenced the Germans who were guilty of this crime to death at Nuremberg and hanged them?

—Leo Szilard

Lieutenant General Leslie Richard Groves, Jr., was known to family and his few close friends as Dick to distinguish him from his father. Dick wasn't normally given to metaphoric thinking, but an apt analogy came to him as he got out of the car that had brought him here from the train station this bitter afternoon. It wasn't just that a November chill had come to Los Alamos, which, at 1.4 miles above sea level, would almost certainly experience another white Christmas despite its southerly location. No, more than that, the whole place seemed figuratively cold, too. The fire had gone out of it, and out of the people who remained here. Dick was reminded of taking his son and daughter to the New York World's Fair in 1939—a concentrated enclave of bustle and exhilaration—and then passing by the grounds a few months after the fair was over and finding it a decaying husk, abandoned futuristic architecture silhouetted against the setting sun.

He entered the office reserved for his visits to the mesa. Peer De Silva, whose own office was down the corridor, materialized moments later in the open doorway; well, thought Dick, he wouldn't be much of a security man if he *didn't* know when a general had arrived on site.

"Sir," said de Silva, "thank you for coming. As I said on the phone, I think something big's going on."

Dick eased himself into his swivel chair. "I'm listening."

"Per your orders, I still have everyone down to the C-level on the org chart under surveillance." The general nodded. Now that key scientists and engineers were pouring out of Chicago, Oak Ridge, and Los Alamos, precautions had to be extra-tight. The Soviets would be happy to snare leading Manhattan Project workers, especially since the U.S. had beat them to the punch by scooping up many of the best Nazi scientists, including Werner Heisenberg, who had been captured personally by Boris Pash as part of the final Alsos mission. An Edward Teller or a Hans Bethe would be a momentous prize for the Kremlin, whether enticed with riches or taken at gunpoint.

De Silva went on. "On Wednesday, October seventeenth, Oppenheimer and Leo Szilard had a private meeting in Szilard's hotel room in Washington. On Monday, October twenty-second, Szilard met with Einstein at the Institute for Advanced Study. Four days later, Edward Teller, Szilard, and Einstein met there again."

Some professors Dick knew at Princeton University enviously called the place "the Institute for Advanced Salaries"; others apparently called it "the Institute for Advanced Lunch," which would certainly appeal to that layabout Szilard. "They're all looking for the best jobs they can get."

"Granted, sir. But there's more. None of these guys were particularly circumspect during the war, even though they knew their phones were being tapped. But now the lot of them—including even Feynman—are being so careful *not* to say anything, I'm sure they're hiding something."

"Like what?"

"I don't know, General, except that it has something to do with the sun."

Groves leaned back in his seat as de Silva continued. "Back in August, a few solar-spectrum plates were sent here for Mr. Battle—Dr. Bethe, I mean—from Cornell. I delivered them to him myself, and he seemed awfully pleased. Of course, he figured I couldn't make head nor tail of them, or of what he was saying about them."

"The intellectuals' hamartia," said Groves.

"Sir?"

"My goodness, son, don't they teach the classics at West Point anymore? Their hamartia; their fatal flaw. Arrogance. They assume that anyone without a string of letters trailing behind his name like pretentious ducklings can't possibly grasp their thoughts."

"Yes, sir. Anyway, Dr. Bethe said he was going to show them to Dr. Teller. Since then, just about every book or journal they've had shipped here has been related to solar physics, stellar fusion, and the like."

"So what's your best guess?"

"I imagine it has something to do with the super, sir. Oppenheimer has come out against it, but Teller is determined to build it. If they've figured out something fundamental about how the sun does fusion, perhaps that's the breakthrough needed to get the hydrogen bomb to work."

"If they'd made a breakthrough, they would have reported it to me," Groves said.

"So one would assume, sir, but it seems like Szilard is calling the shots and, well, you know he wants to take atomic matters out of military hands. He might be thinking that the Institute for Advanced Study could make a good home for civilian atomic physics now that the war is over; they've already got Einstein there, after all."

"Szilard." Groves hissed the name then shook his head. "Okay, keep digging and keep me posted. Has Robert arrived yet?" Oppenheimer was making his first visit to the mesa since his resignation. He was scheduled to address the Association of Los Alamos Scientists, a group that had emerged in the wake of Hiroshima and Nagasaki; Groves despised its rueful acronym ALAS.

"Yes, sir."

"All right, I won't corner him until after he's done jawing tonight—and nobody jaws like Robert!—but once his speech is over, I'll get to the bottom of this."

A clear night at Los Alamos was a wondrous thing, with countless stars spangling the heavens. Tonight was not such a night; instead, a tenebrous canopy obscured almost everything, although a vague patch of brightness suggested, as though quantum effects were manifesting on a macro scale, where the moon probably was.

The rain had stopped, but the wind had a honed edge. Dick and Robert both hunched their shoulders under their coats and leaned forward, as the general walked the physicist to his guest quarters after his speech. Oppenheimer had a cigarette in one hand, the tip a flaring nova in the wind, and he alternated having his other hand in his coat pocket and reaching up to grasp the wide brim of his hat lest it take flight.

Dick was never one for small talk, but he nonetheless asked about Oppenheimer's children. Peter was now four and a half, and Toni, the nickname her parents had slowly shifted to using instead of the generic Tyke, was just shy of eleven months. "They're looking forward to Christmas," Robert said.

Dick had been surprised to discover a couple of years ago that the Oppenheimers celebrated that holiday with a tree, a gift exchange, and a turkey feast; he'd never heard of Jews doing such a thing before. But this time he merely nodded. "I'll send presents for your kids. I presume Eagle Hill is the right address?"

"Perhaps. I'll let you know."

"Still entertaining offers?"

"They *do* keep arriving," Robert conceded. "But Berkeley seems the most tempting."

"Ah," said Groves, keeping his tone flat. "I hear tell that some of the bigger names are going to that fancy place in New Jersey, what's it called ...?"

"The Institute for Advanced Study," supplied Oppenheimer.

"Right, right. You've always got your ear to the ground, Robert. Tell me: anything interesting going on there?"

"I'd imagine there always is."

"I hear you visited recently."

"You hear a lot."

"Oh, odds and ends, yes. And I know Teller is fascinated by fusion in general, but there seems to be a heightened interest among all of you in *solar* fusion."

They came to a fork in the road, hard to see in the dark. Groves led; Oppenheimer followed but said nothing. "Has there been some sort of breakthrough, Robert? I really do have a right to know."

"I told Truman I had blood on my hands," Oppenheimer replied. "I still do—no, no, I know you don't see it the same way. But there *are* things that I can wash my hands of, and this—if there *is* a 'this'—is one of them."

"So something *is* going on," said Groves.

Oppenheimer pointed at one of the Sundt apartment blocks looming ahead in the darkness. "I think I'm in this one."

Groves placed a hand on Robert's forearm to stop him, took a half step, and turned to better confront the man. "Neither of us liked it the only time I gave you an order before, Robert." Oppenheimer stiffened; having to disclose Haakon Chevalier's name was clearly a painful memory. "Don't make me do it again."

"Respectfully, General, you *can't* do it again. I resigned, remember?"

Groves thought, *Then what are you doing back on the mesa?* But he just shook his head. "All right. But, you know, there are others who *can* compel you to speak."

Oppenheimer shook his head. "I really can't imagine who might have that power." He stuck out his hand. "Good night, General."

Groves sighed and shook it. "Sleep well, Robert."

His voice was infinitely weary. "I plan to sleep"—he blew out smoke, quickly lost in the darkness—"like there's no tomorrow."

Following his speech for ALAS, Oppie returned to Berkeley and One Eagle Hill. He'd heard Haakon Chevalier was back in the Bay Area and had been thinking about whether he should reach out to his old friend but, as it turned out, he'd missed the opportunity. A letter from Hoke was waiting for him along with hundreds of others. Although there was no return address, Oppie recognized his handwriting and decided to open it first. He made himself a martini, lit a Chesterfield, moved into the living room with its redwood floor and twelve-foot-high beamed ceiling, and settled into his favorite chair, next to the stone fireplace, to read it. After the usual *Dear Opje,* Hoke declared:

I'm off to Nuremberg! It seems someone finally values my skill. As I told you, I got some work as a translator for the French delegation during the first meeting of the United Nations in San Francisco. I must have minded my "pays" and "coos" well because now our War Department has asked me to serve as a lead translator for français to anglais for the International Military Tribunal at the war-crimes trials in Germany. The hearings begin 20 November and could last many months.

We're trying something new, something I'm calling "simultaneous translation," so the proceedings won't slow down; not as complex as building your bombs but still a hellishly difficult undertaking. They also tapped me to co-author the glossary of legal terms being distributed to witnesses and others.

I plan to keep a diary of the proceedings. Nothing of moment ever happens in my own life, but the trial might make a good book—everyone loves the parry and thrust of cross-examination, eh? In any event, it shall be a time until our paths cross again, dear friend! My very best to Kitty, the children, and, of course, to you, mon cher Opje. À la prochaine!

Oppie sat, holding the lined page, not putting it down, not letting it go. They would need to have a difficult conversation at some point—Damocles had nothing on him!—but he was glad it wasn't going to happen anytime soon.

Chapter 25

[The Institute for Advanced Study at] Princeton is a madhouse: its solipsistic luminaries shining in separate & helpless desolation. Einstein is completely cuckoo. I could be of absolutely no use at such a place.

—**J. Robert Oppenheimer**,
in a 1935 letter to his brother Frank

Although the Oppenheimers did indeed decorate their house at One Eagle Hill with a Christmas tree, the actual day was nothing special: gifts had already been exchanged throughout the eight evenings of Hanukkah. Peter, closer to five now than four, sensitive and shy, had been particularly pleased with a bright red tricycle that he named Berky—his way of saying the name of the city they'd at last moved back to. Little Toni, who had just turned one, was now inseparable from the plush white rabbit that Kitty had dubbed Hoppy. And Haakon Chevalier, who had spent some previous Christmases with Oppie's family, was indeed off in Nuremberg. Since there was nothing to keep them in California over Christmas, Oppie took his family to New York City that week, and neither Kitty nor his children objected when he went off on his own on December 25.

Oppie was visiting Isidor Isaac Rabi, the previous year's Nobel laureate in physics. Rabi—not even his wife or sister ever called him by either of his I's—

had embraced his Judaism as much as Oppie had rejected his own; for every action there was an equal and opposite reaction. No Yuletide baubles adorned his home; that it was Christmas simply meant that the usually noisy Manhattan traffic was oddly subdued for a Tuesday afternoon.

Famous now and rich, thanks to the Nobel, Rabi lived with his wife and children in a posh apartment on Riverside Drive, the river in question being the majestic Hudson. The high-rise—a full ten stories tall—was near Columbia University, where he'd returned to teaching after spending most of the war years at M.I.T. working on the development of radar. It was the same Riverside Drive upon which Oppie's family had resided during Robert's youth, a short distance but a far cry from the poor, immigrant Lower East Side where Rabi had grown up. They'd known each other for sixteen years now, having first met in Leipzig in 1929.

Oppie and Rabi retreated to the latter's study, each with pipe ablaze. On Rabi's desk was a copy of the first issue of the *Bulletin of the Atomic Scientists of Chicago,* published earlier that month; Robert had read his own copy on the flight out from California. Oppie also noticed that Rabi's Nobel medal was sitting flat on a bookshelf—not framed or mounted, just sort of *there.* Although he knew many recipients, it was his first time ever seeing such a medal. He couldn't bring himself to fawn over it in Rabi's presence, but when Rabi excused himself to go to the washroom, Oppie seized the opportunity to examine it. The disc was a little over two and a half inches in diameter and had the heft that went with being made of gold. The front showed a profile of bearded, bow-tied Alfred Nobel, the inventor of dynamite.

Oppie wished the image had been facing outward; he wanted to look into the man's eyes. Nobel had received a gift few men ever did: he had learned what history would think of him. In 1888, when he was fifty-seven, six years before he actually died, a French newspaper, confusing him for his brother Ludvig who had just passed away, published an obituary for Alfred under the headline *"Le marchand de la mort est mort"* —"The merchant of death is dead." What had started for Alfred as a puzzle in chemistry had turned into the manufacture of armaments and weapons.

With this foreknowledge, Alfred had decided to change his future—and that of the world. Childless and unmarried, he revised his will, bequeathing ninety-four percent of his fortune to fund annual awards in physics, chemistry, literature, physiology or medicine, and, significantly, "to the person who shall have done the most or best work for fraternity among nations, for the abolition or reduction of standing armies, and for the holding and promotion of peace congresses."

Oppie rubbed the medal between thumb and forefinger, an atom or two of gold transferring to him, a few molecules from his body making a new home on the disk. Soon, he hoped; soon.

Prince Arjuna had questioned his duty; Alfred Nobel had changed his fate. But although the former had beheld unearthly visions and the latter had preceded Oppie as creator of the greatest man-made explosive in history, neither had stared into the very fires of hell as Oppie had. And, sure, Nobel had seen his own premature obituary, but Oppie had recently gotten advance word of the demise of the entire world, although—

"Don't bite it." Rabi's voice. "I guarantee it's real. Twenty-three carat, they tell me."

Oppie whirled around, feeling heat in his cheeks. "Sorry."

"Don't be," said Rabi, who was the better part of a foot shorter than Oppie. "Margaret wanted to take it in for show-and-tell. In the old neighborhood, not a chance. In this one? Mothers wear earrings worth more."

Oppie smiled wistfully and gently put the medal back down.

Rabi, forty-seven, looking a fair bit like Leo Szilard might if he got in shape and lost the mischievousness in his eyes, took a chair and motioned for Oppenheimer to do the same. "Where were we?"

"International control," said Oppie. "It's been two months since I met with Truman. He still thinks the Soviets will never have atomic weapons of their own, but—"

Rabi nodded. "But of course they will. Right, okay. So shall it be the United Nations?"

Despite all his weariness, such talk gave Robert a frisson of delight—which he hoped he hid better than his embarrassment of moments ago. Paying a visit to the president; dining with statesmen and captains of industry; heady talk, as now, of how to set the world straight—if those boys who had thrown him with painted genitals into the icebox; if Patrick Blackett, who'd avoided Robert's apple and had since moved from Cambridge to Manchester; if *Jean* could see him now ...

Well, all but Jean would. His picture had been in newspapers worldwide; his name daily on a hundred thousand tongues. He'd known that riches material and reputational would accrue to whoever succeeded in creating an atomic bomb. That's why he'd maneuvered for the position: to satiate Kitty's appetites and, yes, even his own. But when Hitler, with Soviet troops a mere two blocks from the *Reichskanzlei,* had put a Luger shot through his own skull, Oppie had felt those rewards slipping away even as the Allies held victory parades.

Yesterday, Christmas Eve, had been twenty weeks to the day since their Little Boy had obliterated Hiroshima: a hundred and forty nights of tossing and turning; a hundred and forty morning newspapers and evening radio reports—startling how quickly finding one's own name in the news could turn you into an avid follower of the fourth estate. He'd even seen speculation that he'd be *Time*'s Man of the Year, following Ike, who'd taken that honor last year, and George, who'd earned it the year before.

Ike.

George.

It wasn't an affectation; it really wasn't. That's how he thought of them, how he knew them: General Dwight D. Eisenhower; Army Chief of Staff George Marshall.

And now here he was, sitting with a Nobel laureate, planning a new world order—and, unlike Hitler's mad designs, a benign one. Last month, the Association of Atomic Scientists had come into being, and Oppie was already working on his essay for their proposed book, *One World or None.* He and Rabi, Szilard and Wigner, Bohr and Bethe, plus so many others, had quickly agreed that the only path that would avoid an insane arms race would be to put control of atomic matters into the hands of an international body, and the nascent United Nations, all of two months old, did appear to be the most likely prospect.

"Yes," said Oppie, after relighting his pipe. "The U.N. seems the proper choice. The General Assembly will have its first meeting in—what?—sixteen days."

"We'll have to convince the right people to put the idea forward," said Rabi. "I hear Dean Acheson is likely to ask David Lilienthal to head the committee advising the president."

Oppie nodded. "I've never met Lilienthal, but I spoke to Dean late in September. I told him most of us on the Manhattan Project were strongly disinclined to continue weapons work, told him it was against the dictates of both our hearts and spirits."

"Most," said Rabi, emphasizing, rather than questioning, Oppie's word.

"Well, there's Teller, of course, and—"

"Teller." Rabi almost spat the name. "I'll never understand his position."

"Nor I," replied Oppie. He heard a distant buzzing sound and raised his eyebrows questioningly at Rabi.

"Helen will get it," his host said and then he took a draw on his own pipe. Apparently it was empty, so he rose and headed over to his desk to refill it from an ornate tobacco jar. On his way back, he paused by the large window, and Robert saw him bathed in amber light. "Oh, Oppie, come see!"

Robert got up and went to stand next to Rabi. The sun was setting, and the ice floes on the Hudson were no longer white but flamingo pink and canary yellow. Of course, to Rabi the sun was merely a celestial artist, painting the landscape; he knew nothing of the impending solar crisis. To Robert, the chromatic transformation was the work of a trickster, a cosmic cheat.

Rabi's handsome face had taken on the same tint as Alfred Nobel's stamped on the medal; he looked beatific as he gazed at the wide river.

"One approach would be to denature uranium all over the world," Oppie said.

Rabi gestured at the spectacle before them and sounded annoyed. "You spoil a beautiful moment. And, besides, even if you *could* contaminate the world's entire supply of uranium so that it wasn't suitable for fission, surely it could be, well, 'renatured' and—"

There was a knock at the study's door, then after a couple of seconds, the door opened, and Helen, Rabi's brunette wife, stuck her head in. "Boys, you'll never guess who's come for a visit!" She stepped aside, and Oppie felt his jaw drop.

"Hydroxyl, hydroxyl, hydroxyl!" said the elderly, paunchy white-haired man with a twinkle in his eyes.

Rabi got it first: "And HO, HO, HO to you!" And then, in German, *"Mein Gott,* what brings you here?"

"The train from Princeton," replied Einstein. "And I want to catch the last one back tonight." He stepped fully into the room, and Helen smiled and withdrew, closing the door behind her. "Maja"—Einstein's sister, who had lived with him since 1939—"is waiting for me in a little deli down the street. Thank God for us Jews, eh? Almost nothing was open today!"

The great physicist must have already doffed his coat, although there was still a rosiness to his craggy cheeks—it was a bitterly cold day. He was wearing a cranberry sweater and beige slacks. "May I sit? We have much to talk about!"

Rabi kept a neat house, Oppie had observed, but, like every academic, he had books and papers piled on unused chairs. He quickly relocated the stack from the last remaining seat in the study onto the floor, and took that chair for himself, gesturing for Einstein to claim the more comfortable one he'd vacated.

"I heard you were out this way," Einstein said, looking at Robert. "I imagine your house is bugged—by the F.B.I., at least, if not the Soviets. Mine is, too, of course. But, so far as I've been able to determine, Rabi hasn't attracted that *schmuck* Hoover's special attention. I'm hoping we can speak freely here."

"About what?" asked Rabi.

Einstein looked at Oppie, then at Rabi, then back at Oppie. "You haven't told him? About the fate of the world!"

Rabi said, "We've been working on a solution to take to—"

"No," Oppenheimer said, interrupting. "That's not what he's talking about."

It was Rabi's turn to shift his gaze from face to face. "What then?"

"You discovered it, or so Szilard told me," said Einstein, looking at Oppie. "You tell him."

Oppie hesitated. He trusted Rabi wholeheartedly—even as much as he trusted his own beloved brother. And in the almost two months since General Groves had tried to get him to disclose what was going on, Oppie had succeeded most of the time in putting it out of his conscious mind, locking it away next to other largely banished thoughts, including the horrific pictures Serber and Morrison had brought back from their visit to Hiroshima and Nagasaki. He looked over at the window; the sun had set. Out of sight, out of mind.

"All right," said Robert. "Rabi, you were at the Trinity test. Did you meet William Lawrence?"

"The science guy from the *New York Times?*"

"That's him. He was with us for quite some time—promised an exclusive in exchange for keeping things secret until we gave the okay. Anyway, he taught me something we academics never seem to know: don't bury the lead with long-winded explanations of context. Just go straight to the punch, and so ..." Oppie took a deep breath. "And so, as *Herr Doktor* Einstein will confirm, here it is. The sun is struggling with an internal instability that will cause a photospheric ejection within eighty-odd years; the world is doomed."

"Das ist wahr," said Einstein, his hair a bobbing white cloud, and then he repeated it in English: "It's true."

Rabi's jaw slackened, lengthening his squarish face for a moment. He removed his glasses and pulled out a handkerchief to polish the lenses—a habitual move, a grasp at the ordinary, as he let it sink in.

"And Earth won't recover?" asked Rabi.

"The atmosphere will be blown away," said Oppie. "The oceans? Probably boiled off."

"And I don't suppose surface habitats under, say, protective domes, or maybe subterranean cities could survive?"

"Not a chance," said Oppie.

Rabi was quiet, staring out the window. It was so dark the Hudson might as well have been the Styx. Oppie and Einstein had both absorbed the same awful news earlier; they knew better than to rush him. After a time, Rabi turned back to face them, all color gone from his cheeks, his eyes looking unfocused, his mouth downturned. "Well, then," he said. After another moment he slowly began asking a series of technical questions, which Oppie answered with occasional additions from Einstein. Shock gave way, as the clock hands moved along, to grim acceptance. Understanding it all was, as Sherlock Holmes might have had it, a three-pipe problem—three apiece, that is—but at last, the younger Nobel laureate knew as much on the topic as the older one did, and almost as much as Oppie himself.

"All right," said Rabi. Some pink had begun to return to his face. "But what in God's name do we do about it?"

"I'm going to do nothing," Oppie replied flatly. "First, because I doubt anything *can* be done. And, second, because I've seen how it takes hold of minds—Szilard's for one. It becomes an obsession that causes people to ignore the real problems of the here and now. If we don't prevent a nuclear arms race, it won't matter a tinker's damn what'll happen in a hundred years because there will be nobody left by then."

"But someone has to direct the effort, co-ordinate it ..." said Rabi.

"Szilard has all but anointed Teller," said Einstein.

"Teller!" exclaimed Rabi. "You can't be serious."

Einstein replied: "Of course, no one at the Institute for Advanced Study—that's where Szilard proposes the effort should be centered—wants Teller; he wouldn't even be considered for a position there." Oppie had been to the I.A.S. once, a decade ago, before the war, before the bomb—a simpler time. Then, the idyllic spot had seemed unreal, a luxurious retreat from reality. But now? Just last month, the 1945 Nobel in physics had gone to Wolfgang Pauli; although many who had been recruited by the Institute over the years were already Nobel laureates, that was the first time someone had received the prize while at the I.A.S.

Einstein went on. "No, Teller will never do. I've been asking around; we're going to need a new director anyway, since the incumbent is retiring, and everyone agrees on who it should be."

"Ah," said Oppie. "Yes, of course. Rabi, you'd be perfect. You know I wanted you as associate director back at Los Alamos, and with that nifty coin"—he pointed at the Nobel medal, back on the shelf—"you certainly have the necessary prestige now, if you didn't already before. Plus—"

"Nein," said Einstein. *"Nein, nein.* Not Rabi—with due respect—but rather you, Robert."

"I don't want the job."

"But you are the best qualified for it."

"I doubt many will think so."

"Wouldn't have thought so, perhaps, when you began at Los Alamos," said Einstein. "But now? There can be no doubt: you are the finest scientific administrator in the world."

To be praised thus by Einstein! Oppie fought to keep from beaming. "Nonsense. It was the quality of the team; anyone could have succeeded with such men beneath him."

"Robert," said Rabi, "modesty was never your strong suit. Dr. Einstein is right. You. You're the man. It has to be. Remember what Truman said of your last job: 'The greatest achievement of organized science in history.' And *you* were the organizer."

"Come, Robert," said Einstein, "it's almost New Year's. Time for a resolution: resolve to do *this.*"

They'd been sitting for a long time. Oppie got up and looked out the window. Night in Manhattan was nothing like night on the war-time mesa. Lamps blazed at street corners and in windows; if the stars were out, one couldn't tell through the glare.

He thought about Teller, about his strange love for ever bigger explosions, about that day he had come into Teller's office, the day that all of this solar madness had begun. On the blackboard had been Teller's chart of weapon ideas, the final row showing a delivery method of "Backyard." A man obsessed with destruction on a planetary scale could hardly be in charge of preventing such a thing from happening.

And Oppie thought about Trinity, here, befitting the holiday, fleetingly of the Christian version of God the Father, the Son, and the Holy Ghost, and, of course, about the Hindu one, the *Trimurti* of Brahma the creator, Vishnu the preserver, and Shiva the destroyer. And he thought about the three of them in this room—if not an actual Holy Trinity of physicists, three wise men for Christmas, at least. And, most of all, he thought about the Trinity test, the first time the sun had touched the surface of the earth. He recalled the thought that had come into his mind then, the words that four-armed Vishnu had used to persuade the reluctant prince Arjuna to do his duty, to discharge his obligation, to take upon himself the role he'd been born to.

Now ...

Now I ...

Now I am ...

Oppie shook his head slightly and looked out the window again, its borders veined with frost.

No, not *I.* Not alone.

And not *Death.* Not this time.

Behind him, out of sight but *not* out of mind, the greatest physicist since Isaac Newton, and the trusted friend Oppie had turned to for counsel so many times before.

His heart pounded. He turned around, faced them, faced himself, faced the future. All right, then. All right.

He spoke firmly, with conviction and—yes, damn it, yes; he was going to be in the center again—with elation. "Now we are become Life, the saviors of the world."

Chapter 26

Mrs. Oppenheimer impressed me as a strong woman with strong convictions. It requires a very strong person to be a real Communist.

—**John Lansdale**,
head of Manhattan Project security

"No. Damn it, no. *Not again.* I won't go."

Kitty Oppenheimer stood framed in the Manhattan hotel suite's master-bedroom doorway. While Oppie had been meeting with Rabi—and unexpectedly with Einstein—Kitty and the children had been enjoying a Christmas holiday. Today, though, Kitty's mother, who had come in by train from Pennsylvania, was off with the children seeing the dinosaurs at the American Museum of Natural History. Kitty's legs were spread to give her balance but she still swayed. Oppie had hoped when they'd descended from the mesa, dropping 7,000 feet, that booze wouldn't have continued to hit his wife quite so hard. Oh, she could handle it—she could handle just about *anything*—but life would have been easier for them both if she were just a little less tipsy most of the time.

Unlike many others, she hadn't minded the climate at Los Alamos—they'd vacationed for years in nearby Perro Caliente, after all. But Olden Manor at the I.A.S. would be a big step up from Bathtub Row, or even from their villa with the red-tiled roof and whitewashed walls back on Eagle Hill in Berkeley.

Kitty's tone was fierce. "I'm a scientist, too, damn it."

Oppie held his tongue. She'd been *becoming* a scientist, true, and had been a lab assistant for a biology professor before the war, but she still had no Ph.D. Of course, the years they'd spent at Los Alamos had afforded no opportunity for her to continue work toward that degree. But her science was ...

"Botany," Robert said.

"Yes, damn it. Botany. It's as much a science as physics—more, actually, if you count the unsolved mysteries. How life began—plants came before animals, remember. How genetic information is encoded and passed from one generation to the next. Precisely how plants turn sunlight into food. I *wish* botany could be reduced to a handful of particles and a few laws."

"All right," said Oppie. "Point taken. But the I.A.S. has no department devoted to any sort of natural history."

"I don't care. I suffered through Los Alamos without knowing what the fuck was going on. If we're moving to this vaunted Institute of yours—if we're going down this goddamn road again—then I *demand* to be in the know. You tell me *everything,* and *I* have an active role. Back on the mesa, you made Charlotte Serber a group leader, for Christ's sake."

That was true. Charlotte had been the only female one, by virtue of her position as site librarian. She'd had no special qualification for that job; Oppie could have as easily given it to Kitty, but he'd wanted Kitty to take the—to him—even more important public role of director's wife.

"I spent three damn years on that hilltop," Kitty continued. Oppie's first thought was that it had only been thirty-one months. His second was that out of those, she'd disappeared for three months after Toni had been born, meaning, for her, it was closer to two years than three. But he said nothing. There weren't going to be any more babies—they'd agreed on that and, unlike before their marriage, were now taking precautions—so hopefully depression would never hit her so hard again.

He thought once more of *Casablanca.* They'd sat together at that screening in the Los Alamos camp theater, holding hands after they'd finished the slightly burnt popcorn. She was part of his work, the thing that kept him going. And, unlike Rick and Ilsa, where he was going she *could* follow—and what he had to do she *could* be part of.

"All right," he said. "All right. I'll tell you all of it; everything."

Her mica-dark eyes went wide as if she hadn't expected to win this fight. "Well, then," she said, moving over to the hotel-room's couch and sitting with arms crossed in front of her chest, "go ahead."

Oppie nodded. "Give me a minute. I'm going to need a drink, too."

Three martinis later, she knew everything he did. He'd paced and smoked while telling her; she'd been on the couch the whole time, letting him refill glasses as necessary.

"And *this* is what you want to devote years to?" she asked. "Some fool's errand? How can you possibly succeed?"

Oppie finally sat down on the sofa, but there was a distance between them. "I don't know. I have no idea. But it's a sweet problem, isn't it? If there were a straightforward solution, it ..."

He stopped himself, realizing he was echoing what Edward Teller had said back in the summer of '42 at that first meeting of the Luminaries: "An atomic-fission bomb," he'd announced, "is straightforward; your grad students could make one. But a bomb based on nuclear fusion? *That* is a challenge worthy of *us.*"

But no. Building a fusion bomb wasn't worthy then and it wasn't now. But *this*—this!—was. Rabi had said years ago that he didn't want the culmination of three centuries of physics to be a bomb. But outwitting the sun, outwitting nature, outwitting God himself, surely that *was* fitting. He lifted his shoulders slightly. "I'm going to do this."

"But why?"

"'O Arjuna, perform your duty with equipoise. The sacrifice made as a matter of duty by those who desire no reward is of the nature of goodness.'"

"The fucking *Gita,* again? Robert, we're talking about your—*our*—future."

He looked up. "Yes. Yes, we are. And our son's, and our daughter's, and their children's, too."

Kitty seemed to consider this and, when she spoke again, her voice was calmer. "True. And ... and maybe I ..."

She said nothing more, but Oppie could read it in her face: *Maybe I* do *owe them something.* She couldn't give Peter or Toni love or affection—neither could he, really—but she *could* help give them a future. "All right," she said. "I'm in."

Oppie was surprised at how good this felt. "Excellent. And, I promise, you *will* fully participate."

Kitty took a sip of her drink and stared out the hotel room's window at a chiaroscuro Manhattan. But when she turned her eyes back to Oppie she startled him; she'd obviously been recalling the same night at the movies he'd been thinking about a while ago. "Louie," she said, "I think this is the beginning of a beautiful friendship."

Chapter 27

Hell, this is a mecca for intellectuals, and we were reading in the New York Times every day that Oppenheimer was the greatest intellectual in the world. Of course we wanted him—then.

—Anonymous I.A.S. faculty member

In the 1939-1940 academic year, I.I. Rabi had been a visiting professor at the Institute for Advanced Study, so he knew the place better than Oppenheimer did. At Einstein's behest, he'd come to Princeton now to help Oppie get oriented, although Rabi intended to keep his home base at Columbia, an hour and a half away.

Frank Aydelotte had originally intended to stay on as I.A.S. director until June 30, 1946, the magic date that would entitle him to a full pension. But he'd been persuaded to step down sooner in exchange for a guarantee that his retirement stipend wouldn't be reduced; as Einstein had said, they couldn't let a prize replacement such as Oppenheimer slip through their fingers by delaying. Even so, Aydelotte would not be out of the actual director's office until January 31. Until then, Oppenheimer was situated in room 118 and didn't have a secretary, and so, with no warning except a perfunctory knock, his door swung wide open.

"General!" exclaimed Oppie, his face splitting in an affectionate grin. "What are you doing here?" He and Rabi had been talking, pipes aglow, while standing by the small room's single window, gazing out at the snow-covered grounds.

"Oh, Washington isn't that far," said Groves, shouldering his way into the room, followed by Ken Nichols. Both were wearing civilian clothes. "And I heard you were here." He looked at the other man. "Dr. Rabi," he said, mispronouncing the name as if it were the word for a Jewish cleric rather than a homonym of Robby. They'd met only a few times, when their infrequent visits to Los Alamos happened to coincide—most significantly five and a half months ago for the Trinity test. "Perhaps you know my assistant, Colonel Nichols?"

Rabi nodded at the younger man. "Colonel, good morning. And good morning to you, General." Oppenheimer noticed that the professor's tone was wary. Rabi clearly suspected that Groves had an ulterior motive—a thought that hadn't even occurred to Oppie. There *was* some antipathy between the two men: Rabi along with Bob Bacher had convinced Oppenheimer that Groves's notion of making Los Alamos a military laboratory, with scientists commissioned and given ranks, would never work since too many good men would refuse to participate under such circumstances.

"Dr. Rabi," the general said, "I'm counting on your discretion. You're still subject to the same security oath you took for your work on radar and that pertained when you visited Site Y." Groves, chilled from being outdoors, rubbed his hands together. "Let's have seats." There were three chairs in the room: two bare-bones wooden ones and a leather-padded executive's chair. Groves helped himself to the latter and swiveled it to face the scientists, who took the other two. Nichols stood near Groves, his bespectacled face impassive.

"I'm sure you remember," Groves said to Robert, "how Richard Feynman liked to pick safes at Los Alamos, and how he took delight in slipping out through the perimeter fence and then startling the gate guards by coming back in without ever having logged out. Made it look like we were quite incompetent in matters of security, no? Except we weren't—and we aren't. If you'll forgive the expression, gentlemen, we have it down to a science. I won't say that I know everything that's going on, but Colonel Nichols and I have got a very good idea now."

"Have you bugged my apartment?" demanded Rabi, his face reddening. "I know that the F.B.I. is playing foolish games these days, but if you've done it, General, by God, I'll go straight to the president and—"

"Relax, Doctor. No, we haven't. We have no reason to. Oh, you had a brief flirtation with socialist ideas in your youth, but unlike our friend here, you had the good sense to stay clear of all that Commie garbage for decades now." Groves looked at Robert. "You, on the other hand, have attracted a lot of attention. Did you know that J. Edgar Hoover sent a summary of your file to the president and the secretary of state on November fifteenth? Thank God I was alerted and so the bugging of your hotel room in Manhattan was handled by my office instead of Hoover's. So far, only Colonel Nichols, myself, and two others at the M.E.D. have heard the tapes or read the transcripts, and Hoover knows nothing of ..." Groves paused; he was clearly aware that both Robert and Rabi were wondering exactly how much he had sussed out. "... of the impending photospheric ejection and the subsequent destruction of our planet."

Oppie exhaled a giant cloud of smoke. Christ, he'd told Kitty *everything* in that hotel suite. And, of course, Groves would have understood even the technical matters. As he'd famously said to Szilard three years ago, "That'd be the equivalent of about *two* Ph.D.'s, wouldn't it?"

"General," said Rabi, "for all the same reasons I articulated in 1943, this *can't* be a military undertaking."

"Relax. I've no intention of putting people in uniform, not now that the war is over. But you're going to need me and everything I have access to. For instance, Dr. Rabi, there's no reason you should have heard about them, but were you aware of the Alsos missions?"

Rabi sounded irritated. "No."

Groves leaned back in the swivel chair. Oppie, feeling a need to pace, got up and returned to the window, coolness radiating from the glass, the view outside framed with ice. "There were three of them," Groves said. "They followed right behind our Allied troops. The first went into Italy; the second, France; and the third, at last, into Germany itself. Their purpose was to determine how far along the Nazis were in developing an atomic bomb of their own."

"Ah," said Rabi.

"Do you know what 'Alsos' means?"

Oppie spoke up even though Groves was still looking at Rabi. "It's Greek for 'grove.'"

The General turned to him. "Exactly. I didn't choose the name—G-2 did—

and I didn't like it, but it was indeed a reference to me. I was in charge of the missions, and your friend Boris Pash led them."

Pash. It'd been over two years since the lieutenant colonel had grilled Oppie at Berkeley about who George Eltenton's intermediary had been. Robert knew the third Alsos mission had entered Germany late in February of this year, but he'd been too busy racing to get the bomb finished to pay much attention. He'd had only a vague awareness when the mission was underway and no idea that Pash had gone overseas.

Groves made a gesture toward Nichols who reached into the inside pocket of his civilian suit jacket and pulled out a piece of beige paper; Oppie recognized the general's handwriting with its tall ascenders. Nichols handed the sheet to Groves.

"Do Jews make Christmas lists?" the general asked. "No, I don't suppose they do. Well, they're lists of things you might like to receive as presents, see? Let's just say I took the liberty of drawing one up for you, Robert. A little late, I know, but still." Groves held up the paper and Oppie strode over to take it. It consisted of ten surnames, one per line:

Bagge
Diebner
Gerlach
Hahn
Harteck
Heisenberg
Korsching
von Laue
von Weizsäcker
Wirtz

German physicists. Two he knew personally from his time at Göttingen: Werner Heisenberg, who'd gone on to win the 1932 Nobel Prize for the creation of quantum mechanics, and Otto Hahn, who had been named the 1944 winner of the chemistry Nobel for his discovery of the fission of heavy atomic nuclei.

"What about them?" said Oppie, handing the list to the still-seated Rabi so he could have a look, too.

"We have them," said Groves. "We have them all. Oh, they're in England right now, at a place called Farm Hall, but they're under my jurisdiction—and they will be for another five days. On January third, they're to be repatriated, part of the post-war reconstruction of Germany. Unless ..."

"Yes?" said Rabi.

"Unless you want any of them." He looked at one scientist and then the other. "We don't have time to debate this, gentlemen. Our window is closing. Once they're back in Germany, they're lost for good." He crossed his arms in front of his giant chest. "*This* is why you need the government, the military, *me.* Take your pick. As long as they're still in custody, I can order them sent anywhere I want—anywhere *you* want."

"My God," said Oppie. He turned to Rabi.

I.I. turned both eyes on the general. "You're serious?"

But before Groves could answer, Oppie chimed in. "He's *always* serious."

"Well, goodness," said Rabi, "I mean, of course we could use Heisenberg. And—heavens!—imagine having Otto Hahn!"

"Carl von Weizsäcker, too," said Oppie. Groves looked at him questioningly. "He's an expert on stellar fusion. Before the war, he was collaborating with Hans Bethe on that very topic. If we've got any hope of preventing the photospheric purge, or even just pinning down precisely when it will occur, we need him."

"Done, done, and done," said Groves, a satisfied smirk on his face. He took the sheet back from Rabi, swiveled to face the nearby desk, and, with a fountain pen retrieved from his pocket, put bold check marks next to the three names. "Anyone else you want?"

"Not especially from that list," said Oppie. He looked at Rabi, who nodded his concurrence.

"From anywhere—well, at least anywhere outside Russia or China."

"George Volkoff," replied Oppie. His own interest in astrophysics had been kindled by a talk Volkoff had given entitled "The Source of Stellar Energy" at Berkeley in 1937.

"He's at the Montreal laboratory," supplied Nichols.

"I *know* that," snapped Groves. "Get the R.C.A.F. to fly him down here."

"And," said Oppie, "we should try again for Subrahmanyan Chandrasekhar."

"Who?" asked Nichols, who was now jotting things into a small notebook.

"An Indian-born physicist," said Oppie. "Been at the University of Chicago since '37. Everyone calls him Chandra for short—well, everyone but his students; they have to graduate before he lets them do that. Anyway, just write that: C-H-A-N-D-R-A."

"Is he with you at the Met Lab?" asked Nichols, looking at Rabi.

But it was Groves who answered. "No. Robert wanted him out at Los Alamos, but he refused to work either place."

"Chandra's an atheist," Oppie said, "but he was raised Hindu. He found our goal ... unpalatable. But now perhaps he'll feel differently." He'd seen Groves frown at the mention of atheism. "He really *is* one of us: 'Subrahmanyan' is Sanskrit for 'Luminary.'"

"And he's a world-leading expert on stellar physics," added Rabi. "The Oppenheimer-Volkoff limit is a lovely companion to the Chandrasekhar limit: the former gives the maximum possible size of a neutron star; the latter, the maximum for a white dwarf."

"All right," said the general. "We'll get him."

Oppie looked at Nichols, then Rabi, then Groves. "And speaking of people from Chicago—"

"Fermi," said Groves, bunching his chins together as he nodded. "No problem. If we can't arm-twist the University of Chicago to cover his salary, I still have an open budget at the M.E.D. Anyone else from there?"

"Wigner, too," said Rabi, indicating that Nichols should write down that name as well.

"And ..." began Oppie.

Groves looked at him. "Yes?"

"And Szilard."

"For God's sake, Robert."

"He's already in this," Oppie said. "Hell, he's the reason we're getting to headquarter everything here in Princeton. Plus, no one has a more nimble interdisciplinary mind. And no one is more committed to saving the world."

"And no one is a bigger pain in the butt," said Groves.

"And yet—"

"And yet nothing, Robert. No Szilard—no way, no how. Not ever."

Chapter 28

The physicist has become a military asset of such value that only with the assurance of peace will society permit him to pursue in his own quiet way the scientific knowledge which inspires, elevates, and entertains his fellow men.

—I.I. Rabi

"They're squeezing me out," said Edward Teller, and then with a bitterness he rarely gave voice to, he added, *"again."*

Mici Teller sat beside her husband on the threadbare couch in their Los Alamos home. They'd never rated a place on Bathtub Row, although with so many people abandoning the mesa, Mici had suggested they put in their name for one of the inevitable vacancies. But Edward could be the very embodiment of inertia; he simply didn't want to move. "Who is?" she asked.

He passed her the yellow telegram sheet, which Peer de Silva had delivered a few moments ago.

> BOARD UNANIMOUSLY NAMES OPPENHEIMER MY SUCCESSOR. APOLOGIES FOR CONFUSION. CONFIDENT YOU WILL LAND ON FEET. BEST WISHES FOR NEW YEAR. AYDELOTTE.

"I'm sure they'd still like to have you as part of the team," Mici said. She placed the sheet on the coffee table and ran her fingers through his thick dark hair.

"Under Oppenheimer again?" Edward shook his head. "First he shoved fusion research out of the center; then he put Bethe in charge of the Technical Division instead of me. No, I don't want to work for him again."

"We can stay here, then. I've grown used to it."

Teller's shoulders went up and down as he laughed. "You've always been a terrible liar, my love." He pointed at the tiny kitchen. "Our pipes are frozen, and—damn it!—my piano is already *en route* to Princeton."

"We can get it back. I'm sure the I.A.S. will pay the freight under the circumstances."

"Perhaps. But even if they are flush, money here is growing tight. Norris Bradbury says the military has only guaranteed six more months of funding for Los Alamos. And he's made it damn clear that all future work to be done here will be simply refining the plutonium fission bomb, rather than anything to do with the super."

"Well, didn't Mulliken say he'd like to have you return to Chicago?"

"Hah! Our pipes might freeze *there*, too!" He shook his head. "But, yes, I could surely get my old professorship back. I hear Fermi will be dividing his time between Chicago and the new Princeton group, so there might be good positioning for someone who can be in Chicago full-time."

"Well, then," said Mici, "perhaps that's the answer."

His shoulders rose again. "Maybe. But what I really need is a laboratory of my own, a place devoted to the super. God only knows whether Oppenheimer and his gang can save the whole world from the sun's fury, but I at least can save this country from man's folly. With the super, no one will dare attack us."

A sudden crash from the kitchen. Edward and Mici got up and hurried the short distance. Their son Paul, almost three, was sitting surrounded by wooden blocks. Whatever he'd built had come tumbling down around him; Edward knew how he felt. But the boy was good-natured and had already started piling up blocks again. "That's another reason to go back east," said Mici. "Not many playmates left here for Paul, although ..."

"Well, he'll always have me." Edward bent low. "Come along, little man!" Paul gleefully scrambled onto his father's broad back and was treated to a piggyback ride around the living room.

Mici smiled. "I think he's going to have even more company by the end of next summer."

Edward had finished his second circumnavigation of the living room, and he returned the boy to the kitchen and his blocks, tousling the little guy's hair after he'd climbed down. "What do you mean?"

"I'm late," Mici said.

Edward lifted his eyebrows. "Late for what?"

She shook her head fondly. "For a genius, sweetness, you can be awfully thick." She smiled. *"Late.* So, you see, maybe we *do* need the extra room of a place on Bathtub Row."

Beaming, Edward closed the distance between them and swept his wife into his arms.

"But for God's sake," demanded Robert Oppenheimer, "how in hell do we break this news to the world?"

The meeting in his temporary I.A.S. office was well into its third hour. In deference to Groves's dislike of smoking, Oppie had pushed up the window, dislodging icicles from the slight brick overhang; they'd fallen like failed rockets, piercing the snow. He stood in the cold draft, sending walnut clouds outside; most of it just came right back in. I.I. Rabi, much less addicted, stayed in his seat and simply refrained.

Groves was still in the swivel chair, but Colonel Nichols, apparently having given up on ever getting an "At ease" from his superior, had finally gone ahead and perched himself on the edge of the mahogany desk.

The general rubbed his graying temples as if trying to massage away a headache. "Break the news?" he repeated. "This isn't news—and we *never* break security."

Rabi sounded appalled. "You can't seriously be proposing that we keep secret that our whole damn world is going to be annihilated?"

"If it's going to be, no good can come from telling everyone," replied Groves. "But the point of this undertaking we're embarking on is to *prevent* that, and mindless panic along the way will just impede us."

"Granted," said Rabi, "but the public still has a right to be told."

"Rights aren't my department," said Groves. "I work on a need-to-know basis, and John Q. Public simply doesn't need to know." He raised a large hand. "Yes, yes, you academics are all about openness. But take a step back. Would the public even *want* to know? Is it in their best interest to tell them?"

Groves turned his eyes on Oppie. "I hear the Wall Street crash of 1929 sailed by without you being aware of it, Robert; that was nice, I'm sure. But I remember it vividly. There was mass hysteria, people jumping out windows, riots in the streets. Of course, now that we're past all that, the reaction seems overblown—but then? The desperate response to the headlines was utterly predictable." His expression became even more dour than usual. "And now we've just finished a world war. The property damage is incalculable. It will take decades to rebuild everything that's been destroyed in Europe."

"And in Japan," said Oppie.

"Yes, in Japan, too," said Groves, who had the decency not to sound irritated at Robert's interjection. "Do you think all that will go on in earnest if we tell people that the world is likely doomed anyway? They'll wonder, quite rightly, what the point of it all is."

"Until the end comes," said Oppie, *"if it comes,* people will still require places to live, places to work, infrastructure."

"Exactly," said Groves. "Pressing, immediate concerns—and we need people to focus solely on them."

"If they can focus on anything," said Rabi. "Jews worldwide are mourning our dead, and everyone of every faith who lives anywhere in Europe or Russia or, yes, Japan or China, surely knows someone who was killed."

"Indeed they do," said Groves as if Rabi were making his point for him. "We're still tallying the figures, but it looks like more than fifty million people were killed worldwide. You really want to tell everybody that those fifty million were just a drop in the bucket? That, if we fail, billions more will follow them into a mass grave?"

Oppie's pipe had gone out. As he refilled it, he said simply, "Everyone dies."

"Yes, yes," said Groves. "But not all at once. Robert, I know you're wringing your hands over what we did in Japan. I'm not; I have a clear conscience. It was war, and American lives were saved, period. And Japan has survivors, far more than it has dead. In the scenario you've outlined, this solar purge, everyone dies in a matter of—what? Seconds, minutes? A day at most? Telling people who are still burying their dead or, perhaps worse, living with the false hope that someone missing since the war might turn up alive—telling them that we're all going to die, with not a single person left alive to grieve, would be downright cruel."

"But it won't happen until the late 2020s," said Oppie. "That's far enough in the future that it won't change people's behavior."

"Oh?" snapped Groves. "You know that for a fact, do you?"

"Well, no. But it's like finding out another ice age is coming in a century or so. Or the opposite: that the polar caps are going to melt, and we'll have coastal flooding and insane hurricanes. What would we do about it? Nothing. Just go on squabbling as usual."

"You lived for years near San Francisco," said Groves, "a city that will surely be destroyed—again!—by an earthquake in the next hundred-odd years. Not everyone is quite as good at ignoring risks as you."

Isidor Rabi pulled his wooden chair around so he could better face Oppie. "The general may be right. Early on, Fermi was talking about the possibility of nuclear chain reactions in public lectures. Szilard and I thought he should keep that idea secret. When I told Enrico, he said, 'Nuts!' He felt there was only a remote possibility such a thing could occur, so why hide it? I asked him what he meant by 'a remote possibility,' and he said, 'Ten percent.' I said ten percent *isn't* remote in matters of life and death. If I have pneumonia and the doctor tells me there's a ten percent chance I'm going to die of it, I get excited."

"Bingo," said Groves. "This is Pandora's box. Once the information is out, there's no way to ever make it secret again, so we'd need a very good, very specific reason—not just some highfalutin moral talk—to justify letting the cat out of the bag."

Mentioning both a box and a cat made Oppie think of Schrödinger, of course. But telling people what the sun was going to do wouldn't force one or the other possibility to be the truth: humanity would still be in superposition, possibly alive, possibly dead, depending on what the scientists here would or would not accomplish in time.

The general went on. "Your vaunted Szilard wanted to warn the Japanese, remember? A demonstration of the bomb. There were all sorts of sound reasons why we were never going to do that, but number one was that we had no way to predict *how* they'd react to a demonstration. Would they lay down their arms, as Szilard thought, or would they redouble their efforts, deciding if they were going to go out it might as well be in a blaze of glory, taking as many of us with them as they could? Or, if we merely demonstrated the bomb, would they have then believed we didn't actually have the spine to ever use it on a city, and so go on fighting even harder?" He made a dismissive gesture. "That was tiny compared to this. Telling all 2.3 billion humans that the planet is doomed would be tantamount to conducting the biggest psychological experiment in history."

"There have been doomsayers before," said Oppie, "and civilization has ... has *soldiered* on."

"Sure," said Groves with a curt nod. "But they've all been crackpots." He waved a finger between Oppie and Rabi. "Not the world's top scientists." Then he turned the finger toward himself. "And not the United States government." Groves looked at each physicist in turn. "Can you predict the result of letting people know, Dr. Rabi? Can you, Dr. Oppenheimer?"

He gave them a second to respond, but neither did, so the general went on. "Say you tell me that only ten percent of humanity might react negatively—to use the figure you said Fermi proposed for the likelihood of a chain reaction. Fine, but how big are your error bars? If, as that popinjay Szilard would have it, your guess is correct within a factor of ten, then even at best we'd need to deal with twenty-three million people panicking, and at worst with *everyone* panicking. Robert, I know how hard you're pushing for international control of atomic energy. Maybe you'll get that, maybe you won't. But we've entered a new era, gentlemen, thanks to Robert and me: the atomic era. Soon enough, just *one* panicking person will be able to set off an escalation that will kill us as surely as your solar purge. I, for one, don't want to give anybody with that power another reason to be on edge."

"He's got a point," said Rabi, looking at Oppenheimer. "And remember, we have no idea what percentage of humanity, if any, we'll be able to save. If getting people off this planet really is the answer, we might be able to move thousands but not millions, let alone billions. There will be riots as soon as we announce who gets to live and who gets left behind to die."

Groves nodded sharply. "Precisely. You remember—what was it, seven years ago? That Orson Welles broadcast?"

"The War of the Worlds," supplied Colonel Nichols.

"That's it," said Groves. "Remember the panic it caused?"

Oppie hadn't been aware of the radio drama at the time, but the putative site of the first Martian landing was just four miles southeast of here, in Grover's Mill; Einstein had taken great pleasure in pointing it out to him when they'd gone on a drive together.

"That panic had been over a single one-hour broadcast on one network in one country saying the world was coming to an end," continued Groves. "Imagine what a constant barrage of such coverage everywhere on the planet for weeks or months would do."

"But this *does* affect the whole world," said Oppie, "and we could use help from the whole world, or, at least, the whole *scientific* world."

Groves shifted his weight. "I'm getting you the best Germans," he said. "But even if I thought those in Russia, say, or China, had anything to offer us—and that I doubt—that's not the issue. It's not a question of competence; it's a question, as I said, of secrecy. And not just for the sake of preventing panic. For the sake of *getting things done.* Robert, you think we'd have gotten to use Los Alamos as a base of operations if Congress had known? The jockeying for political pork—for it to be in *this* district or *that* one, irrespective of whether it suited *our* needs—would have consumed months if not years." He set his gaze on Rabi. "And you, Dr. Rabi, you mentioned Enrico Fermi. Do you think for one second that he'd have been allowed to build his first atomic pile under Stagg Field—at the University of Chicago, for crying out loud!—if there'd been public oversight? Hell, he didn't even tell the university's president! If something went wrong, he might have poisoned or blown up the entire city."

"Yes, but he—"

"No buts, Robert. Did you let the world know when Edward Teller said, back at your Berkeley Luminaries meeting in '42, that setting off an atomic bomb might ignite the entire atmosphere? Did we tell the world just before the Trinity test that Fermi was taking bets on whether that was indeed true? On whether we'd only wipe New Mexico off the map or destroy the whole planet? The governor of New Mexico only found out just before we set off the bomb there because I myself told him, and the vice president didn't know a thing about any of our efforts until *after* he'd replaced FDR."

"I had a meeting with Truman," said Oppie. "He is not ... gifted."

"Well, you've certainly got no influence left with him," said Groves. "I do, but you don't, not after your last visit. 'Blood on my hands,' I believe you said. In case you haven't heard, that did *not* go over well."

The cold was getting too much for Oppie. He pulled the window back down, the wooden frame creaking as he did so, and returned to the chair he'd vacated. Rabi rotated his own seat so that both of them were facing the general again. Groves lifted his eyebrows; Oppie suspected he was thinking that this is the closest he'd ever get to having scientists standing at attention.

"We spent two billion dollars on the atomic-bomb effort," said Groves. "*Two billion.* And, Dr. Rabi, over at M.I.T., your people spent 1.5 billion on radar, a project almost as secret. Those kinds of funds were available because the projects *didn't* have to come up before the House or the Senate. I can move mountains as long as we avoid congressional committees, senate debates, and, most of all, a fickle public. Tell the voters you're spending millions, let alone billions, on *anything*, and they start screaming it should instead be used to eliminate poverty, or on new highways, or on symphony orchestras, or God only knows what else."

Groves rose from his padded throne, forcing Oppenheimer and Rabi to look up at him. "Hear this, gentlemen: I got Robert unfettered access to the deepest coffers in the world before and I can do it again—but *only* if we keep this whole thing under wraps. Agreed?"

Oppenheimer glanced at Rabi, who was frowning. "Yes, damn it all," Oppie said. "Agreed."

"All right," said Rabi, looking up at Groves. "All right." Oppie watched as his friend shifted his gaze even higher. "But may God have mercy on our souls."

Chapter 29

As a direct result of Oppenheimer's work, we now know that black holes have played and are playing a decisive part in the evolution of the universe. He lived for twenty-seven years after the discovery, never spoke about it, and never came back to work on it. Several times, I asked him why he did not come back to it. He never answered my question, but always changed the conversation to some other subject.

—Freeman Dyson

Oppenheimer had experience dealing with squabbling children: Peter was five and a half now and Toni, thirteen months. But, for God's sake, Leslie Groves was fifty and Leo Szilard would turn forty-nine in February. Oppie, at forty-two, was a good piece younger than either of them, and he had no desire to serve *in loco parentis,* mediating between the general and the genius, the soldier and the scientist, the militarist and the Martian. But just as they needed Groves, Oppie was still convinced, despite his own conflicts with the man, that they also needed Leo's insights and inventiveness.

Teller had once told Oppie that the Hungarian word *szilárd* could be translated as "rather stubborn," and Groves, as his surname suggested, was as rigid as clusters of tree trunks. The two men repelled each other like protons itching to burst a nucleus apart, and—*pace* Pauli—it seemed they couldn't both be in the same place at the same time.

If Groves had been a habitual drinker, or Szilard more than a social one, perhaps having both over to Olden Manor, getting them drunk, and letting a bond form over their shared love of rich desserts might have worked. After all, as Oppie said to Kitty, if he genuinely believed he could help bring Russia and the United States, with a combined population of 238 million, onto the same page about arms control, surely he could broker a peace between just two men.

But any notion of a carefully orchestrated reunion evaporated as Groves, Oppie, and Nichols were finally leaving Oppie's temporary office—and who should they run into heading toward them in the ground-floor corridor of Fuld Hull but Leo Szilard, his winter jacket unbuttoned to reveal a three-piece suit.

"Good God," muttered Groves.

"Not quite," replied Szilard, closing the distance.

Isidor Rabi had departed for New York an hour ago, while Groves and Oppenheimer had continued to work, hammering out financial matters. "Leo, what are you doing here?" asked Oppie.

Szilard pointed stubby fingers at a room on the opposite side of the corridor: von Neumann's office. "I've come to see Jancsi. I have some ideas about this computing machine of his."

At that moment, the door to room 113 opened, and von Neumann's secretary emerged. "Oh, Dr. Szilard! You're early. The professor is down in the basement. Do you know the way?"

"Yes, thank you." Leo made a half turn, but then, apparently unable to resist, reversed the maneuver and faced Groves, who now had his own winter jacket back on. "So," said Szilard, looking him up and down, "you got everything you wanted."

"We got peace," said the general, simply.

"For now."

"That's all one can ever ask."

"Is it? With a world government we could have peace for all time."

Oppie eyed both men warily, a mongoose and a cobra, each capable of killing the other.

"You're a dreamer," Groves said dismissively.

"I prefer my dreams to nuclear nightmares. You military types—"

"Leo," said Oppie, gently.

"— see everything in such simplistic terms. If you and your ilk would—"

"Halt." Groves barked it as if it were an order. Szilard just stared. "It was us 'military types' who brought the world to peace. And it was you, *Mister* Szilard, and *your* ilk who were nothing but an impediment to everything we worked for during the war."

Leo spluttered. "An impediment? Need I remind you that it was *I* who conceived of the chain reaction in the first place? That it was *I* who got Einstein to write Roosevelt, and—"

"And that's another thing!" said Groves, his voice starting to boil with fury. "There is a chain of command. Maybe—*maybe*—back in 1939 you didn't know any better, but once the M.E.D. was up and running, you had no business even *trying* to get to see the commander in chief."

Oppenheimer saw a couple of other people at the far end of the hallway—Gödel and Weyl, it looked like—but they disappeared into Aydelotte's office. "General Groves, Leo," said Oppie. "Please."

"I'm not a soldier," Szilard said. "I'm a citizen."

"For all of two years now!"

Szilard was clearly trying to keep his tone even. "I was not aware that there are degrees of citizenship. In any event, I'm a—"

"A what?" sneered Groves. "A professor? Show me your students. An academic? Show me your published papers."

"I am attached to the University of Chicago and—"

"And even in the ivory tower, there are chains of command. You report to Arthur Compton—and Compton reports to *me.* If you had an ounce—"

"A brass hat such as you will never understand academia. Unlike in the military, we don't kowtow—"

"Kowtow! We *earn* our position in the hierarchy!"

"Like you earned the rank of general?"

Groves's face was turning red. "I never wanted this job; I wanted to go overseas—see some action—not spend the war herding obstinate goats!"

Oppie looked at Nichols for help, but the colonel simply stood at attention, staring at a blank spot on the corridor wall.

"Some hardship!" said Szilard. "You're the world-famous atomic general now—and you owe *that* to *me.* Without me, there'd be no atomic bomb."

"And your days of having anything to do with it are *over.* After that petition stunt—"

"Which *you* had classified 'secret' so I couldn't release it to the journal *Science*—"

"Damn right I blocked it!"

"Yes, because it might be, and I quote, 'injurious to the prestige of government activity'—hardly what Congress had in mind when they passed the Espionage Act!"

"That's not the reason at all. God, how I hate pushy Jews like you!"

"Meine lieben Herren!"

It was the one voice they both had to heed. Groves, swinging around, popped a string of Ps like gunfire: "P-P-P-Professor Einstein, I—"

For his part, Leo immediately affected a relieved tone. *"Albert, so schön, dich zu sehen!"*

"This is my home," said Einstein sharply in English. "My sanctuary." His office was just down the corridor. He'd emerged from it wearing a green cardigan, his white hair even more askew than usual. "Leo, I acceded to your request to bring this madness here, but it is at the sufferance of the long-established faculty. There will be peace—and there will be quiet!" He looked at Groves and then Szilard. "I don't know if either of you can save the world, but *I* can and will save this intellectual refuge."

"Of course," said Groves. "Professor Einstein, sir, I hope you didn't think I included yourself when—"

The soulful eyes locked on Groves and, to Oppie's surprise, the general closed his mouth and looked contritely at the polished stone floor. Einstein then turned to Szilard. "You, Leo, why are you here?"

"I was just heading downstairs to speak to von Neumann."

Einstein stretched out his right arm, pointing at the nearest staircase. "Go!"

Leo nodded and shuffled away.

"And you?" demanded Einstein of the general.

Oppie spoke up. "We've been working on organizational matters, but are heading over to Olden Manor. Time for a bite to eat."

"Off with you, then!" declared Einstein. "Be gone, the lot of you! There's thinking to be done here!"

Olden Manor had three extra bedrooms, and as their discussions wore on, it was decided that General Groves and Colonel Nichols would stay the night. After the military men had gone to bed, Oppie and Kitty went to their own room and talked until almost 2:00 a.m.

"Is Groves insane?" asked Kitty, propping herself up on an elbow. "He expects you to work under another goddamn shroud of secrecy?"

Oppie stared up at the ceiling, a rectangle of darkness. "We've argued it back and forth, but—yes. Yes, that's what we're going to do. Better that than the panic that would ensue if we had to announce prematurely that only a small fraction of humanity might be saved."

"Jesus," said Kitty.

"I know it's not easy," Oppie said, "for any of us. And, well, especially now not for me."

"Why?"

"Keeping others from stumbling onto the solar instability will mean making sure that the underlying research that led to its discovery isn't brought into the spotlight."

"Can it be classified?"

"No, no, it's too late. It's already been published ... by me."

Kitty made a questioning sound, and Robert went on. "That trio of papers I did in 1938 and '39, with Serber, Volkoff, and Snyder. They're out there for anyone anywhere to see, in the *Physical Review.* And any decent physicist who has access to those papers, and understands what they imply, and also has access to solar spectra taken during the period when Hans Bethe thought the sun routinely underwent C-N-O fusion will make the connection."

"But those papers ... Robert, they're key to you winning the Nobel prize."

He felt a tickle in his throat on top of the one usually there. "I know," he said softly.

Words in the dark: "You deserve that prize, damn it."

"Yes," said Oppie, even more softly. "I do, but ..."

"But what? You can't just bury the papers, for God's sake. You said it yourself: they're already out there."

"Yes, they are. And so we're going to have to ..." He sighed, letting go of air, letting go of a dream. "We're going to have to obfuscate them."

"What the hell does that mean?"

"At least the name will live on: the 'Oppenheimer-Volkoff limit.' That's what it's called: the maximum upper mass of a neutron core. George and I calculated it at 0.7 solar masses—which allowed the sun to indeed have the sort of hidden neutron core Lev Landau postulated. But we also figured out, as a concomitant of that, the lower limit for a stable neutron core, and that was 0.1 solar masses. So we'll get some people to plant articles in journals, suggesting more oomph for the strong nuclear force at the heart of stars, so that the upper cut-off, the Oppenheimer-Volkoff limit, will seem higher—1.4, 1.5, or more. That, in turn, will pull the minimum stable mass out of the solar range. It'll make sure that gung-ho post-docs don't stumble on what's really going to happen anytime soon."

"And what about you? Your Nobel? The medal? The fame? Hell, the money?"

Robert closed his eyes and recited from the *Gita* once more:

> *"Vanquish enemies at arms ...*
> *"Gain mastery of the sciences*
> *"And varied arts ...*
> *"You may do all this, but karma's force*
> *"Alone prevents what is not destined*
> *"And compels what is to be."*

Kitty rolled over on her side, her back now to Robert. She let out a long, whispery sigh, the last sound she made that night.

Chapter 30

We had known the sin of pride. We had the pride of thinking we knew what was good for man. This is not the natural business of the scientist.

—J. Robert Oppenheimer

"God damn it, Oppenheimer, I said no!"

Oppie was taken aback. He'd never heard Groves swear before, and the general had never previously failed to precede his last name with either "Doctor" or "Professor."

Oppie tried for a calming tone. "There *is* a need for the sort of blue-skying Szilard specializes in. If we're going to solve this, it'll demand fresh ideas and new approaches, and nobody is better at coming up with those than him. Suppose—suppose I make sure you'll only rarely have to deal with him?"

"How?" demanded Groves.

At that moment, the cook appeared from the kitchen, with more coffee. Kitty was off with the kids and Colonel Nichols was in Princeton, running errands for the general. "Suppose I give Leo his own private department, housed here at the Institute, but not in Fuld Hall? He and a few other ... 'oddballs,' shall we say? They'll be left alone to bounce ideas off each other. If they come up with nothing, well ..." He smiled at Groves, who had occasionally chided Oppie about his one area of ignorance, namely sports. "No harm, no foul."

Oppie saw the mustachioed upper lip twitch as the general noted the athletic metaphor. But the levity didn't last. "Szilard is a menace."

"I know you think so," said Oppie. They were seated in the living room of Olden Manor, which, like most of the interior, was painted bright white and had creaky oak-plank flooring. A van Gogh sunset, formerly part of his father's collection, hung above the marble fireplace. Prior to being acquired by the I.A.S., this mansion had been the residence of the governor of New Jersey. Although Frank Aydelotte was still wrapping up his administrative duties, he and his wife had already vacated in favor of an apartment in Princeton near the Quaker church they attended.

"I understand," continued Oppie, "that about a year ago you asked Conant at Harvard to hire Szilard away from the Manhattan Project." Groves brought his eyebrows together, the look of a man who felt a confidence had been breached. The way Oppie had heard it, the general had even offered to have the government cover Szilard's salary just to get Harvard to take him.

"Then you also know," said Groves, "that Dr. Conant laughed in my face and said I couldn't pay him enough to assume the headache named Szilard—and he doubted any other university would want him, either."

"But *I* want him," said Oppie. "Here, with all his peripatetic thinking, at the Institute for Advance Study. Honestly, on these grounds—and I mean that both figuratively and literally—he's a better fit than either you or me. And he already knows what we're working on, and you've made it abundantly clear you want that kept secret. Surely having him nearby is much better from a security point of view than having him at large."

Groves held up an admonishing finger. "Not one penny of any salary or expenses for him is to come from the United States government."

"No, no. Anyone I assign to his group will be financed out of my director's fund here."

"And what are you going to call the group?" asked Groves. "The loony bin?"

Oppie smiled slightly. "Well, I was rather taken by that British code name, 'Tube Alloys.' How about 'Compact Cement'?" He closed his eyes and recited two lines from "An Anatomy of the World," the poem John

Donne, Jean's favorite poet, had written about a young woman who had died much too soon:

> *"The cement which did faithfully compact*
> *"And glue all virtues, now resolv'd, and slack'd."*

Although he didn't elaborate on it with Groves, the 335-year-old poem's imagery resonated in this era of Einsteinian relativity:

> *Alas, we scarce live long enough to try*
> *Whether a true-made clock run right, or lie.*

That stanza was followed closely by another:

> *And as in lasting, so in length is man*
> *Contracted to an inch, who was a span.*

And, indeed, Donne's pleas were apropos of the work to be tackled:

> *Thou might'st have better spar'd the sun, or man ...*

"'Compact Cement,'" repeated Groves, trying the name on for size, then, in good military fashion, immediately reducing it to initials: "CC." He nodded. "All right; it'll do. Who else are you going to assign to CC?"

"Kurt Gödel, if he's willing. "They call him *Herr Warum*—'Mr. Why'—because of his insatiable curiosity. And he and Einstein are very close; even the director here doesn't have any authority over Einstein, as you saw, but if Gödel is part of CC, I'm sure the great man will"—Oppie paused for a brief smile—"gravitate toward it."

Groves harrumphed his assent. "Who else?"

"Maybe Dick Feynman? A truly original thinker. As Wigner says of him, 'He's a second Dirac—only this time human.'"

"Yes, good. Keep that jackass away from anything sensitive." The general considered. "And you're going to let Szilard run the show there?"

"No," said Robert. "He's not an administrator. We need somebody with absolute discretion, a head for details, and so forth."

"That's certainly not Feynman, either," said Groves. "Gödel, then?"

"I asked him, but he doesn't want to be burdened with oversight. But I have someone else in mind."

"Who?"

"Kitty."

"Mrs. Oppenheimer?" Groves's head shook slightly. "Robert, I—"

"She's brilliant, scientifically literate, and fluent in both English and German, which will help with some of the people you're sending us from over there."

"She's a Communist,"

"She *was* a Communist. But she hasn't been for years."

"And she's related to a high-ranking Nazi."

Oppie nodded. "Wilhelm Keitel, chief of the *Oberkommando der Wehrmacht.* He's being tried before the International Military Tribunal at Nuremberg even as we speak. But they're estranged. Seriously, General, she's no more of a security risk than I am. I wouldn't try to put her in charge of Nobel laureates, but so far we have none of those assigned to CC."

"But if she's doing that, who will look after your kids?"

"Peter will be old enough for kindergarten next fall; I'm hoping to send him to the Ethical Culture School in New York, my *alma mater.* As for Toni, we'll get a governess. I hear Rubby Sherr is taking a job at Princeton, so maybe his wife Pat will be interested in the job. She looked after Toni for us while Kitty was away from Los Alamos."

"You've really thought this through, haven't you?"

"Yes, I have. Kitty will handle the leadership task well."

Groves blew out air noisily. "As you wish."

"Thank you."

"All right," the general said. "You've got your Department of Wild Ideas. What about more practical concerns—if any of this can be termed 'practical.'" He looked about to see if the cook was within earshot, then, in a lowered voice, continued, "What about trying to fix the sun or develop some kind of solar shield?"

"One group should handle both of those," replied Oppie, "since either way, they'll need to figure out the same physics. Bethe should be in charge, of course; I'm sure you'll agree he did a fabulous job running the T-Section at Los Alamos. And Chandrasekhar, if he does indeed agree to join us, obviously belongs in this group. Plus Volkoff. And my own expertise is in solar physics, as you know, so if there's any time left for me beyond my director's chores—and I'm hoping this time there *will* be—I'll work with Bethe's group."

"And I suppose you have a clever code name for that group, too?"

"'Patient Power,'" said Oppie. "It's from *Prometheus Unbound,* but people will figure it's just another of the countless atomic-energy efforts that are springing up everywhere—Patient Power being sort of the opposite of Rapid Rupture, you see?"

"And what about getting folks off the planet—to Mars, or wherever?"

Oppie knew the general didn't take kindly to people referring to something as "mere engineering," but it really was just that, at least if somewhere in the solar system was the goal. "Freeman Dyson has said he wants in on that."

"He's just a kid."

Robert nodded. "He just turned twenty-two. A great age for doing first-rate physics. But, yes, Rabi's already agreed to head up that group; he understands for it to be taken seriously it needs a Nobelist like him at the top. And, of course, he's the pre-eminent American experimental physicist, and his division is the one most likely to conduct practical experiments. We'd considered 'Exodus' as the designation for his group, but that's too obvious. He's proposed calling it 'Names,' because in the Hebrew bible, the Book of Exodus is known as *Shemot*—'Names'—after its opening line, 'These are the names—'"

"'—of the sons of Israel,'" finished Groves, the chaplain's child. He shook his head. "Don't you people ever have *simple* thoughts?"

Given his outburst earlier, Oppie wasn't sure if by "you people," the general meant Jews or geniuses, but he decided to believe it was the latter. Smiling, he said, "Not if we can help it."

Groves considered. "Well, Dyson and Rabi are excellent scientists, of course—and I knew it even before Rabi got his Nobel. The work he did on radar was tremendous. Good, practical work, too, just like what we were doing: things actually built that changed the world. But to go to Mars?" Groves shook his head. "That's going to take a lot of hardware."

"True," said Oppie. "Teller thinks the template is the V-2." He shook his head. "Too bad von Braun wasn't on that list of Germans you could get for us."

"There's a reason for that, Robert."

"Oh, of course, of course. Our alliance with Russia may have fallen apart, but we're still friends with Great Britain, and I suspect the British want to string von Braun up in Piccadilly Circus. Have you seen the photos of the damage his rockets did to London?"

"Yes."

"Incredible machines. I'm sure Teller is right that we'll need something like them."

"We have them," said Groves, matter-of-factly.

"What?"

"We have, as complete rockets or components that could be assembled into them, about a hundred V-2s."

"Where? Here? In the United States?" Oppie was stunned.

"Yes. At Fort Bliss in Texas."

"My God. And you've got people studying them? Figuring out how they work?"

"Oh, no need for that," said Groves, a smile lifting his jowls a bit.

"Huh?"

"Wernher von Braun is in Texas; has been since October. He's being co-operative, plus we've also recovered a giant trove of his working papers from a German mine they were hidden in. And by the end of next month, more than a hundred of his German rocketeers will have joined him at Fort Bliss."

"Jesus Christ," said Oppie, absolutely flabbergasted.

"Now, now," cautioned the general. "But, yes. You said we needed to get people off this planet. Well, by gum, now you've got a head start: the world's best rockets *and* the people who made them!"

Chapter 31

1946

I believe that interplanetary travel is now (with the release of atomic energy) a definite possibility.

—**Richard Feynman**,
December 5, 1945

Oppie began the new year with his three divisions established: Hans Bethe's Patient Power struggling with solar physics; Kitty and Szilard's Compact Cement wrestling with unconventional ideas; and I.I. Rabi's Names group desperately trying to find ways to get humans off the planet.

Actually, at Rabi's suggestion, his division had quickly transitioned from being just "Names" to "New Names," matching the alliterative appellations for the other two. Although surprisingly few of the emigré scientists who'd worked on the Manhattan Project had done it, changing one's name when moving to a new land was common, and so there was still a hint of relocation about the code term without its scope being obvious.

But the overall effort—the totality of what they were doing—still lacked a title. Something as nondescript as the Manhattan Project was called for although the obvious, the Princeton Project, would likely draw complaints from the nearby university, should word of it ever go public.

After mulling it over, Oppie decided that the umbrella would be "the Arbor Project." Most assumed he'd chosen the Latin word for tree in honor of the Institute's famed woods. Szilard, always alert to obscure symbolism, wondered if it was after "The Arbor," the final play by the Czech Jewish playwright Hermann Unger; Oppie did not disabuse him. But, in fact, he'd picked the term as a quiet memorial to his beloved Jean Tatlock, who'd been born in Ann Arbor, Michigan, and whose thirty-first birthday would have been January 4, 1946, the same day Oppie announced the name.

The Institute really was an excellent headquarters for the Arbor Project. Besides providing pleasant on-site accommodations and the treed neighborhoods of Princeton for those, such as Einstein, who chose not to live on the actual grounds, it was also centrally located for other team members who would visit weekly or monthly while carrying out research at their own facilities. For Rabi, at Columbia, it was a ninety-minute drive. For Groves in Washington, it was a three-hour drive. Feynman, at Cornell, enjoyed the opportunity to barrel along the country roads for four hours with Hans Bethe riding shotgun, and Fermi could fly in easily enough from Chicago. Only von Braun, 2,100 miles away at Fort Bliss, found it arduous to get here.

Now that Frank Aydelotte had fully retired, Oppie had at last taken possession of the spacious office of the Institute's director, with a lovely view of the woods and a pond. Among its advantages were privacy: no one could barge in without first passing through the secretary's room. It also was as far away as one could get from Einstein's office while still being on the first floor of Fuld Hall, meaning another heated discussion shouldn't rouse the Grand Old Man from his lair.

Today, Rabi, Groves, Feynman, and Fermi were in Oppie's office, along with Szilard, who had moved into a room at the Nassau Inn, a half-hour walk northeast of the Institute, and Kitty, who was relishing her new role. One might have expected it to be cramped, but the first renovation Oppie had ordered to this, room 107, was the removal of all bookcases so that larger groups could be accommodated with comfortable chairs.

"Before the war," said Kitty, seated against the long, blank west wall, "there were 2.3 billion people. Of course, it went down some during the war—but I wouldn't be surprised to see a post-war baby boom." She'd spent time yesterday researching this in the Princeton University library. "It's difficult to map a trend, though. There was very steep worldwide population growth between 1650 and 1900; it's been less rapid since. But, even so, by the time the solar purge hits, by 2028 or 2030, we might well have tripled or quadrupled the current population to—"

"Seven or nine billion," said Groves, stuffed into a chair by the north-facing window.

Kitty nodded. "That ballpark, yes."

"And how many of those can we save?" asked the general.

Oppie, behind his director's desk, crossed then uncrossed his legs. He was still getting used to the sounds of his new office. The creaking of steam pipes; deeper creaking as floorboards responded to shifting furniture; the ticking of the wall clock; through the closed door, the clacking of his secretary's typing. And today, the ragged wheeze of Groves's breathing. Those sounds continued uninterrupted, nobody volunteering an answer to the question hanging in the air.

Even though it was Oppie's office, he wasn't smoking, and nor were the others—not even Kitty. Fermi detested the habit, Groves disapproved of it, Feynman had kept his promise to his late wife that he'd quit, and Oppie had never seen Szilard with a pipe or cigarette. Still, Oppie could play with his accessories—frayed tobacco pouch, silver lighter, glass ashtray—and he did so, repeatedly rearranging their order on his desk. "Well," he said at last, "as many as possible."

"And how many is that?" snapped Groves. "Are we talking about saving billions, millions, thousands—or just one new Adam and one new Eve?"

Oppie looked at the swirling grain in his desktop, a vortex of tan and beige. He'd spent these last few years so concerned with how many could be killed, his mind was resisting switching gears to how many could be saved.

Robert had done cold-blooded calculus at Los Alamos, telling Fermi that an alternative plan, to poison the German food supply with radioactive fission products, would only be worth pursuing if it could guarantee half a million enemy dead. He'd been surprised at how easily that number had come to him—no dithering with a slide rule, no back-of-an-envelope figuring. It had popped out of his mouth, flat, uninflected, just one in a countless string of questions he'd had to answer every day.

But now, this: how many to save?

Oppie had recently heard Groves shout down a college student who had sat out the war. "What about all the dead in Hiroshima and Nagasaki?" he'd demanded.

Groves had shot back, "I wish all of you who kept bringing that up could take a trip to Pearl Harbor, see the graves of all the American boys there. We shortened the war; we *saved* lives."

And maybe they had—thousands or even tens of thousands of American troops that might otherwise have died during an invasion of Japan. But those numbers—the indisputably dead at both atomic targets versus the hypothetical Allied casualties who had lived instead—were paltry. A hundred-thousandth part, or so, of the planet's population. Could they evacuate *billions* to Mars? If a man weighed 200 pounds, and you could somehow get even a ten-to-one ratio of rocket propellant to payload, you'd still need a ton of fuel per person—an inconceivable two billion tons to move everyone alive today.

Oppie found himself shaking his head and he brought a pair of fingers up to rub his forehead. Moving billions was out of the question. But millions? Surely they could do millions? He lifted his gaze, hoping to see optimism on the faces of the other scientists, but there was none. "I think," he said at last, "that a statistically relevant population could be preserved."

That vagueness loosened other tongues. "Thousands, certainly," said Fermi, who was leaning against the door to the secretary's office, even though there was an empty chair.

"Tens of thousands," said Szilard, seated as far from Groves as possible. "Perhaps hundreds of thousands."

Groves frowned deeply and looked like he was about to speak; Oppie had heard of his outburst in Chicago all those years ago about wedding caterers when Szilard had similarly mentioned a figure whose accuracy was within a factor of ten. "General," said Oppie, "I know you want precision, but when one has no idea *how* you're going to do something, it's very difficult to try to come up with good numbers."

Groves astonished him by nodding his jowly head vigorously. "Of course. Which is why I wanted to get this out on the table right at the beginning. You academic types can be so impractical—no offense. The reality is that we'll almost certainly have to leave far, far more people behind than we'll be able to rescue. Robert, I know this place is famous for its physicists, but I think you have some social scientists here, too, yes?"

Oppie nodded.

"Might be worth getting them to chew on the problem of selection criteria."

"*International* selection criteria," said Szilard. "I have some ideas. I attempted years ago to create an organization I called the Bund, and—"

"Good, good," said Oppie before Groves came to a boil. "You can spearhead that, then."

But Groves fixed his eyes on Leo. "And don't forget that we have to keep everything secret," he said. "Let people enjoy their lives; that's fine. But if it gets out that we can only skim off the cream of humanity to save, there will be riots. Even if the solar purge is too far off to affect many of those currently alive, you can bet they'll be fighting for their children or grandchildren to be selected."

Oppie looked again at the faces around him. Szilard was a bachelor and Feynman, a widower for seven months now, was childless. But he and the others had kids.

Memories swirled like the grain in the wood.

Would you like to adopt her?

Jesus, Robert. She has two perfectly good parents already. Why would you even ask such a thing?

Because I can't love her.

And he couldn't: neither Tyke nor Peter, at least not in any normal, human way. Daughter, son—it made no difference; he truly was not the attached kind. Not then, when death was the task, and not even now, when life was. Oh, he cared for them, after a fashion, but not in the way Teller clearly loved his already-born son Paul or the second child Szilard had said was on its way. He cared for Kitty, too, with what he supposed was a kind of love—a passionate rapport, even—but it was nothing compared to his feelings for Jean. He'd failed to kill Patrick Blackett, but Blackett had surely killed something within him, something that, through an unknowable necromancy, only Jean had ever managed to resuscitate.

Still, for dealing with vast anonymous death—death on the scale the super would afford—Teller was better suited than Oppie. But making decisions about individuals, about which people, or what sort of persons, might live and which, by being omitted from the list, would die, was something Oppie *could* do. He had a talent for choosing others' futures, a knack born when he'd confronted the unbearability of a universe in which both he and Patrick Blackett—the spurned and the spurner—existed, a skill polished to a bright-red apple sheen on the mesa when he'd sought to give up his daughter for adoption.

"I'll help you with that, Leo," Oppie said. "And, yes, General, we'll bring in some of the humanist-studies experts here—telling them it's purely a hypothetical problem, of course."

Szilard shook his head. "Another black day for mankind," he said, looking at each person, even Groves, in turn. "The day upon which we decided to abandon most of our own kind to the flames."

Chapter 32

There can be no question about the existence of at least the most conspicuous of them [the canals of Mars]. Some can be seen in telescopes of moderate size and a few have been photographed. We find clear evidence of changes taking place which we can only attribute to the growth of vegetation.

—**Sir Harold Spencer Jones**, Astronomer Royal, in his *Life on Other Worlds*, various printings through 1959

The next day, Oppie met in his office with the New Names group, I.I. Rabi's team that was supposed to, somehow, get humans off earth before the end came. Besides Rabi, members Luis Alvarez and Freeman Dyson were also present, as well as General Leslie Groves, clad in a business suit, and Oppie's old friend Deak Parsons, who, as associate director, had been second in command at Los Alamos, and who, as a navy captain, had crawled into the *Enola Gay*'s bomb bay in flight and armed Little Boy. Following the war, Deak had been promoted to rear admiral, and Groves had soon brought him up to speed on the Arbor Project, letting Deak pull strings behind the scenes with the navy just as Groves did with the army.

"So," said the general, "as we've discussed before, our initial thought is Mars, right? But let's take a moment to consider if that really is the best choice."

Groves, Oppie knew, was stinging from public criticism, rampant since the Manhattan Project literally blew its cover five months ago. Groves's insistence on selecting a uranium-enrichment method quickly, before a thorough study of the practicalities had been completed, had possibly delayed the atomic bomb's development by as much as a year. If Groves *had* waited until all the facts had been in, it would have been obvious that centrifugal separation instead of his pick of gaseous diffusion would have been faster and more efficient—and the first strategic use of an atomic bomb might well have been on Berlin rather than Hiroshima.

"Mars is damn near the only choice," said tall, blond Luis Alvarez, now thirty-four, a sharp-tongued San Franciscan, who was leaning against the wall.

"True," said Oppie, seated at his desk. "Of course, a man couldn't easily live there."

"Are we sure of that?" asked Deak Parsons, a decade older than Alvarez with graying temples and the frontline of his hair in retreat against his advancing forehead.

"Yes," said Oppie.

"No," said Alvarez.

"Depends who you ask," added Rabi, seated by the back window.

"Apparently," said Groves. "We're asking *you*—the gentlemen in this room."

"Problem is, there are no recent studies, really," said Oppie. When he'd lived in California, he'd closely followed the work done at the Mount Wilson observatory near Pasadena. "From time to time—every 780 days, to be precise—the sun, earth, and Mars line up perfectly. Mars is in 'opposition' then, since it's directly opposite the sun from earth's point of view. Obviously, that's a good time for observing, because it means when Mars is up in the sky at any given place on earth the sun is down, and vice versa.

"But not all such oppositions are created equal. You hear that earth has an elliptical orbit; that's technically true, but it's got very little eccentricity—it's almost circular. The same *isn't* true for Mars, though, so sometimes when an opposition occurs, Mars is significantly closer to us than at other times. Truly favorable oppositions, when Mars also happens to be at perihelion—as close as it gets to both us and the sun—only happen once every fifteen or seventeen years. At such an opposition, Mars is almost twice as wide in our telescope eyepieces as it is at an unfavorable one, letting us make out much more surface detail. The last favorable opposition was in 1939. Before that, 1924. But that one, 1924, was pretty much a dud; a Martian dust storm obscured most of the planet's surface then."

Groves frowned. "And the next—what did you call it? Favorable opposition?"

"Not for a decade. September 1956—they always occur in August or September, by the way."

A dozen large Mars maps and photographs were piled on Oppie's desk. Topmost was a pen-and-ink map made by Gerard de Vaucouleurs based on observations by himself and four other astronomers during the favorable opposition of 1939 and the ordinary one of 1941; it was the most-recent map of Mars anybody had produced. "What about the canals?" Groves asked, standing now and waving a thick finger over three dotted north-south lines near the center labeled "Phison," "Euphrates," and "Hiddekel." Similar lines appeared elsewhere.

"Good question," said Oppie. "No one knows. They were discovered in 1877 by Giovanni Schiaparelli, but he called them *canali*—Italian for 'channels.' The idea that they might be artificial canals comes from Percival Lowell two decades later. Of course, even Lowell had to admit that the visible lines are unlikely to be watercourses *per se;* the narrowest objects we can perceive on the Martian surface are a mile wide, and in the thin Martian atmosphere, shallow water would quickly evaporate away through that much surface area. But they *could* be narrower waterways bordered on either side by wide swaths of vegetation; in that case, it would be the accompanying green banks that we're actually seeing."

Groves pointed at the pile. "Show me a photo of them."

Oppie, on the other side of the desk, raised thin shoulders. "That's a problem. Oh, there *are* a few photographs that seem to show the canals but most of the pictures we have of them are drawings."

"Why on—on Mars—would that be?"

"Well, see, the difficulty is the lengthy exposure times needed for taking astronomical photos: the longer you keep the lens uncovered, the more the rippling of earth's own atmosphere blurs things. Lots of observers have seen the canals, myself included. We can see things in the night sky that film simply can't record."

"We also are prone to optical illusions," said Rabi, rather derisively, "as well as optical *delusions.*"

Oppie turned his torso to face Rabi. "Granted. Lowell was the biggest advocate of the canals, but he's been dead for thirty years. But there are still many—Earl Slipher at Lowell's observatory, for instance—who are adamant they're real."

Rabi made a dismissive sound. "He'd hardly be the first scientist to champion a mentor's cause long after it had been discarded by most others working in the same field."

"But there *are* areas on Mars that seem to grow and shrink with the seasons," said Luis Alvarez. "And they *are* green."

"True," said young Freeman Dyson, seated against the west wall. He had a British accent, an intense unblinking stare, and a long face. "Of course, the obvious thought is vegetation."

"So," said Admiral Parsons, summing up, "there might or might not be canals; there might or might not be plants."

"But there *are* definitely polar caps," said Oppie. "And they're at least partially water ice. Sunlight reflecting off water ice and dry ice look the same bright white in visible light, but water ice appears black in infrared whereas dry ice stays white. The Martian ice caps turn black beyond a wavelength of 15,000 ångstroms. The ice caps can't be very thick, though."

"Why do you say that?" asked Groves.

"You're from Albany, New York, right?" asked Oppie. "You know how piles of snow stick around long after the ambient temperature has risen above freezing? That's because there's so much of it, and the inside of the piles hasn't warmed up yet. But on Mars, the caps shrink and grow almost instantly in response to temperature changes; they might be only millimeters thick."

"I'm hearing an awful lot of mights and maybes," said Groves. He took out a Hershey bar and broke off a square.

"A lot of what we know about Mars dates back to the 1890s," said Oppie. "We just haven't put much money into astronomy this century. The biggest telescope in the world—the Hooker, the one I've used at Mount Wilson—went into service in 1917, and nothing has beat it since."

"Two World Wars ago," grumbled Groves.

"Exactly."

"What about Mars's atmosphere? You said it's thin?"

"Very—maybe one percent as dense as ours."

"What's it made of? Any oxygen? Water vapor?"

"Spectrograms taken from the surface of earth *will* show lines for oxygen and water vapor, even on the moon, which has no atmosphere at all, because they're in *our* atmosphere. But at quadrature—"

"What?"

I.I. Rabi, the radar expert, spoke up. "When a line drawn between the earth and the sun and a line drawn between the earth and Mars intercept at a right angle: that's quadrature. And at those times Mars is moving fast enough relative to earth that its spectral lines undergo Doppler shifts, which *would* separate Martian oxygen and water vapor from the tellurian lines—the earth-originating ones—*if* there were any appreciable amount in Mars's atmosphere. But no shifted lines for either O_2 or H_2O appear, so if either is present, it's just trace quantities."

"In the atmosphere, that is," offered Alvarez. "The red color of Mars almost certainly comes from rust—iron oxide. And God alone knows how much water there is locked up in the ground as permafrost or below the surface in aquifers."

"True," said Oppie. "Of course, someday we'll put telescopes in orbit; those will get us much clearer pictures and unpolluted spectrograms. But until then?" He raised both hands in a "what can you do?" gesture.

"Still, we're talking about a world with an unbreathable atmosphere and no guaranteed source of water," said Groves. "With conditions like that, we can't just transport people to Mars."

"No," agreed Oppie. "They'd need self-contained habitats with air and water—submarines writ large."

"Okay, then," said the general. "Well, Professor Rabi, why don't you take a stab at picking target landing sites—I know it's premature, but let's assume that nearer to canals is better than farther, and closer to the equator, where it's warmer, is a plus." He turned to Oppie. "Remember all that hand-wringing over target selection in Japan? At least this time we won't have to worry about Henry Stimson vetoing the best ones."

Oppie managed a small smile.

"Now," said Groves, "back to my first question: what about prospects *other* than Mars?"

"In our solar system?" asked Alvarez. He'd gotten up and was pacing back and forth along the west wall. "The big four outer planets are gas giants; forget about them. Pluto probably *is* rocky, but it was only discovered—what?—sixteen years ago. We just don't know much of anything about it, except that it must be damned cold. At closest approach, it's still thirty times farther away from the sun than we are."

"What about other moons?" asked Groves, lowering himself back into a chair.

"There are a few that are quite large," said Alvarez. "Jupiter's moon Ganymede and Saturn's moon Titan are both bigger than the planet Mercury, but we know very little about them, except that Titan, at least, has some sort of atmosphere."

"All right," said Groves, breaking off more chocolate. "Given how little we know about the other moons, do we agree to aim for Mars right out of the starting gate? I've got to give von Braun and his boys *some* idea of how far away the target they should be working toward is."

"Mars is the closest possibility that will survive," said Rabi. "I vote for it."

Dyson nodded. "Mars."

"Yeah," said Alvarez. "Of course, we should continue to consider other candidates in the solar system, but it may be that we also want to try even farther afield. There just might not be anything suitable here."

"Another—what would you call it? Another star system?" said Groves, frowning.

"No," said Oppie. "I mean, *yes,* that's what you'd call it, since 'solar' refers specifically to our sun. But I don't think Louis has the right idea. If there's no suitable home in the solar system, then we should *make one* here. It's far more likely that within eighty years we could build a massive free-floating space colony—maybe even in the asteroid belt, where low-gravity mining will be cheap and easy—than to talk about ... about 'star ships.' The sun *will* calm down after the photospheric belch. If someday we do want to venture to other stars, we can always put engines on whatever refuge we build, but that's for centuries or millennia down the road. For now, we *can* plausibly build structures in solar space; we *can* harvest the sun's virtually inexhaustible energy; we *can* mine the asteroids. Within eighty years, all of that is easily doable. Rabi, I think your team should be looking at both those possibilities—Mars, and a habitat orbiting the sun outside the danger zone." Oppie paused. "I mean, look, if someone said we should put a man on the moon within a decade, I'd balk. But men—and women and children—on Mars, within eight decades? A massive space habitat far enough from the sun to survive the photospheric purge within the same timeframe? Easy." He looked from face to face, collecting nods of agreement, then turned back to the general, favoring the military man with a wide smile.

Groves heaved himself to his feet, looking pleased. "Gentlemen," he said, "we have just taken a quantum leap into *Buck Rogers.*"

Oppie smirked. Some objected to that metaphor because quantum leaps are infinitesimally microscopic, but, as most fussbudgets do, they were missing the point. A quantum leap goes from *here* to *there* instantaneously, bypassing the steps in between, and this was certainly that. With von Braun's rockets—and von Braun himself!—the U.S. was suddenly well on its way into outer space, a realm that otherwise might have remained unexplored until the twenty-first century if not the twenty-second.

Oppie thought back to his meeting in the Oval Office, and Truman's painted-glass desktop sign with its walnut base, and he couldn't help himself. "Yes," he said, "I guess the Buck *starts* here."

On January 24, 1946, following months of negotiations, the United States, the Soviet Union, and several other countries agreed to establish the United Nations Atomic Energy Commission. That pleased Oppie, of course, but he was even more delighted when Truman established a special committee to prepare a concrete proposal for the international control of atomic weapons—and he was downright thrilled when that committee's chairman, Dean Acheson, decided there should be a board of consultants for the committee.

David Lilienthal was named A.E.C. chairman, and he quickly added Oppie as one of the five members of the consulting board. The public transition, at least on this issue, was finally complete: J. Robert Oppenheimer was no longer a scientist devoid of moral responsibility; he was involved directly in policy making, and at the highest levels.

Positive steps indeed. But, as Oppie remarked one night, although Kitty's divorce from her penultimate husband had been clean and simple even with her being pregnant with Oppie's child, the breaking up of the war-time alliance between the United States and the Soviet Union was proving to be anything but. On March 5, Winston Churchill, no longer prime minister but rather leader of His Majesty's Loyal Opposition, gave a speech in the gymnasium of Westminster College, which, despite a name that echoed the famed British abbey, was in Fulton, Missouri; his audience there included President Truman. Churchill thundered out:

> *"It is my duty to place before you certain facts about the present position in Europe. From Stettin in the Baltic to Trieste in the Adriatic an iron curtain has descended across the Continent ..."*

Oppie had been hoping for increasing access to Soviet scientists; he was sure the expertise of some of them would be useful to the Arbor Project—Kurchatov, certainly, who had been Robert's opposite number during the war in the Russian atomic-bomb effort. God only knew who else; little scientific information came out of Russia, although they surely had first-rate minds there. But this "iron curtain"—a catchy name, thought Oppie—would make accessing them even harder.

Still, he was pleasantly surprised at how smoothly the first half of the new year went. Those who came from New Mexico to New Jersey seemed to settle in well. And, except for that time Einstein had blown up, the work of the Arboreals, as Szilard had dubbed them, seemed to continue apace without significantly disturbing the Institute's established faculty.

Rabi's New Names group was indeed focusing on the engineering problems of getting to Mars, with the assumption that all the same principles would apply to any undertaking within the outer solar system.

Bethe's Patient Power team had confirmed in multiple ways the reality of the impending photospheric purge, but they were having trouble pinning down precisely when it would occur, since the timing, they'd discovered, would be affected by the solar sunspot cycle. Such cycles had been tracked since 1755, with the one beginning that year designated as Solar Cycle 1; the current cycle, number 18, started in February 1944.

Each cycle begins and ends at a *solar minimum,* when sunspots have almost or entirely disappeared. In the middle of a cycle there's a *solar maximum,* the time of the most sunspots—as well as huge solar flares and vastly increased auroral displays on earth. Various calculations showed the inevitable photospheric purge was most likely to happen during the solar maximum of cycle 25.

But although cycles averaged 11.1 years, ones as short as 9.0 years and as long as 13.6 years had been recorded. If the average prevailed, cycle 25 would begin in the fall of 2021, and the solar maximum, when the purge would be unleashed, would occur around the spring of 2027. But the figure really couldn't be pinned down until cycle 25 began, decades from now.

As for the Compact Cement team, housed a quarter-mile away from Fuld Hall, well, they were out of sight—and quite possibly out of their minds. While the other two teams had ordered truckloads of back numbers of scientific journals, the CC crew had bought up complete runs of several science-fiction magazines, including *Amazing Stories, Astounding Stories,* and *Startling Stories.* If one walked by, the sound of Dick Feynman's bongos was often heard, and, in all weather, Leo Szilard could be spotted wandering apparently aimlessly around the Institute grounds. Kitty, however, assured Oppie every night that the CC discussions, although "untethered," as she called them, were spirited and productive.

Oppie expressed his surprise at how well it was all going over lunch one day with Hans Bethe. The blue-eyed Strasbourgian shook his head. "Don't you see, Oppie? For most of us, Los Alamos was the best time of our lives. Oh, sure, the conditions were appalling, but we were *alive.* Pursuing a goal! Pure science; pure engineering—no distractions. None of us would say it out loud, but many were sorry when the war was over. Back to teaching? Yes, a noble calling to be sure, but not our true passion. Back to the real world of mundane neighbors and throngs of stupid people, of small talk and popular music? Such vacuity! We were cast out of heaven when the bombs fell—and you've given us a new ascension. We should call the Institute's main entrance the Pearly Gates and you, sir, should be known as Saint Peter!"

Oppie smiled. A server came by with a bowl of fruit, a treat here in winter: apples, oranges, pears, bananas. An apple was out of the question, of course, but he selected an orange, and slowly peeled off the rind, revealing the acidic yet soft interior.

Chapter 33

Do what we may, by your unfathomable folly, you and I are linked together in a cloudy legend, which nothing, no fact, no explanation, no truth will ever unmake or unravel.

—Haakon Chevalier

"Hoke!" said Oppenheimer warmly. "So good to see you! And Barb, you look lovely!"

"Thank you," Haakon Chevalier replied, but Oppie detected a subtle edge in his old friend's voice. Although the Oppenheimers' principal residence had been at the I.A.S. for eight months now, Robert had come back to Berkeley ostensibly to confer with Ernest Lawrence, and Kitty had tagged along while Pat Sherr, back in Princeton, looked after Peter and Toni. Kitty and Oppie had decided to keep this house on Eagle Hill for just such trips, and today they were throwing a party there in order to see their Bay Area friends.

Barb gave Oppie a hug and a peck on the cheek, and she and Kitty headed off to the living room. They'd asked the Chevaliers to come over an hour before the festivities were to begin so they could have a little private time together. But, as usual, the Chevaliers were late.

"I'm willing to bet," Oppie said, "that you haven't had a martini as good as mine since 1943. Let me fix you one." He headed for the kitchen, and Hoke followed, but as soon as the door was closed behind them, he put a hand on Robert's arm. "My God, Opje, the F.B.I. hauled me into their offices. They grilled me for six hours!"

Robert's heart jumped, and he had a flash of memory from this very room three and a half years previously: him, Hoke, the cocktail shaker, more. He held up a silencing finger and motioned for Haakon to follow him. They walked through the Spanish-style villa and came out the rear entrance—and words from that earlier meeting flashed into Oppie's mind: *"I do* not *feel friendly to the idea of moving information out the back door."* After passing through the garden—Kitty paid for it to be tended when they were not here—they entered a wooded area with ground covered by ivy and oak leaves. "Sorry," said Oppie. Of course he couldn't tell Chevalier about the Arbor Project, but there was no doubt that his clandestine activities, despite everyone's best efforts, were attracting attention. "I suspect the house is bugged."

"The Russians?" asked Haakon, eyes wide.

"Hoover."

"Well, the F.B.I. is definitely concerned about *something.* They hauled me in, as I said. While I was there, the agents kept phoning somebody else—I couldn't figure out who. But I recently ran into George Eltenton—you know, the chemical engineer from Shell Development—and I'll be damned if he hadn't been interrogated by F.B.I. agents the same day I was, and the agents *he* was with kept taking calls. We figured they were phoning each other to see if my story jibed with his."

Oppie looked back at the garden flowers, everything neatly arranged. "And did it?"

"Yes, of course."

"And"—there was still a shred of hope—"what was that story about?"

"Oh, with all you've been up to—all that stuff in New Mexico—I doubt you'd even remember, but ..."

"Try me."

"Well, just before you left Berkeley for there, I was—well, I was *here.*" He pointed back at the whitewashed villa. "Your going-away party. I asked if you happened to know Eltenton and I, well, I passed on his suggestion—his, notion, really; just a thought—that you might, you know, see your way clear to sharing some information with the Russians."

Oppie closed his eyes and nodded. "Yes, I remember."

"Well, of course, I wasn't keen on mentioning my conversation with Eltenton, but the agents kept pressing, and so I told them."

Oppie's heart jumped. "I see."

"And then they brought up *your* name, and, well, I had to admit I'd let you know—that is, that I'd reported to you—the idea Eltenton had mooted."

"You told the F.B.I. that?"

"Yes. I'm sorry if—"

Oppie took a deep breath. Overhead, birds were circling. "No, no. It was the right thing to do, surely."

"Well, good. But they just wouldn't let up. Hour after hour. Mountain out of a molehill, if you ask me."

Robert frowned. "I had to report that conversation we'd had in my kitchen, you know. I mean, the sort of thing Eltenton was suggesting ... well, it might have had serious implications."

"I was just keeping you informed," said Hoke, his tone innocent.

"Still. Of course, I kept your name out of things."

Haakon tilted his head as if weighing this. "Funny, though. They kept insisting I'd approached three—"

"Robert!" Kitty was calling to him; she'd come out to the edge of the garden. Oppie looked back at her, scowling. "Darling," she shouted, "the other guests are arriving! You'd better come in!"

"In a minute!" he snapped and turned back to Chevalier.

Hoke went on: "As I was saying, they kept insisting I'd approached *three* scientists, not just one."

Oppie swallowed. "Really?"

"Said they had affidavits from all three of them."

Robert was taken aback. "Did you see the affidavits?"

"Well, no."

"Ah."

Hoke's voice was tentative. "But you say you kept my name out of things?"

"Yes, yes," replied Oppie. "For many months, but ..."

"But what?"

"Well, eventually my old boss—General Groves, you must have heard his name in the news—he ordered me to tell him who it was who had approached me, and so—"

"Jesus, Robert! And you didn't think I should know you'd done that?"

"All mail to and from the mesa—from our lab—was censored. I couldn't possibly get word out about a sensitive matter."

"I wrote *you,*" Haakon said. "I told you I couldn't get a job because of some security bullshit. Did you get *that* letter?"

"Sure," said Oppie simply.

"I didn't have any on-going work until the Nuremberg trials, and only then because they were desperate for translators."

"Yes, that must have been fascinating! I wanted to ask you—"

"And, for fuck's sake, now that I'm back here, Berkeley has denied me tenure."

"I'm—"

"Robert!" Kitty again. "You really must come in now! All the guests have arrived!"

Oppie was aware that his voice had taken on a sharp edge. "I'll be in shortly!"

"Really, it's rude to—"

"Christ's sake, you miserable bitch, I said I'll be in soon! Just mind your own goddamn fucking business!"

Even at this distance, Kitty's shocked expression was obvious. She'd closed the door behind herself before calling out, so hopefully none of the guests had heard him just now. Oppie turned to Chevalier, but Haakon, red in the face, just shook his head and headed back toward the house.

Oppenheimer stood alone among the trees, their perfectly vertical trunks living monuments to rectitude. He patted his pockets, looking for his pipe, hoping to calm himself, but he'd left the damn thing inside.

Chapter 34

The history of science is rich in the example of the fruitfulness of bringing two sets of techniques, two sets of ideas, developed in separate contexts for the pursuit of new truth, into touch with one another.

—J. Robert Oppenheimer

No matter where he was, Oppie often found himself thinking of Jean. Being here in Berkeley, though—his old haunts now haunted by her—brought his lost love to mind even more frequently. Her father, the now seventy-year-old Chaucerian scholar, had retired at the end of this academic year, so there was less chance of running into him on the U.C.B. campus than on previous trips, thank God. Oppie hadn't spoken to him in the two and half years since Jean killed herself and he had no desire to speak to him now. According to Mary Ellen, Robert's old landlady, John Strong Perry Tatlock, after breaking into his daughter's apartment through a window and discovering her dead in the bathroom, had found and burned much of her received correspondence. Whether any of it had been from Oppie, or had been about Oppie from others—*He's married, you know; his work will always come first; for God's sake, Jean, he's a Jew!*—he chose not to learn.

He'd done everything he could for her, and yet she was dead—a funeral without him present, a grave marker somewhere he'd yet to visit. And therefore, *de facto,* Q.E.D., *everything* had not been enough.

The Arbor Project, in her honor.

The Arbor Project, to save those who could still be saved.

Even so, whatever solution they found—if they found any at all—would change things for her not one iota, one jot, one atom.

Oppie paced the house on Eagle Hill, encountering his own clouds of pipe smoke each time he reversed course at the end of the main corridor. He should apologize to Kitty for his outburst; he knew that. But now that the party guests were gone, Kitty was upstairs, lying on the bed, finding comfort in booze—more succor than he could ever provide.

What Haakon had said was disturbing, distressing. The war was *over,* for fuck's sake. Couldn't this—this "Chevalier affair"—be buried along with all the other dead? *So what* if an overture had been made? Who the hell cared now?

Oppie had already made the phone call he needed to make; the rendezvous was set. Was it madness that he'd chosen the same location he'd been observed at before? No, no. It was genius, surely. Let them think it a pilgrimage, a sad, empty man's need to sit where he'd sat before and listen to the echoes of laughter from years gone by. Surely it was better to meet across the bridge, across the bay, in San Francisco, anyway? Neither his home nor ...

Yes, yes, it made sense. And it was time to go.

"Kitty!" he shouted, from the bottom of the staircase, *"I'll be back!"*

She replied but he couldn't make out the words. Too soft, too slurred.

He sighed. There was no need for a coat in August, and so he simply walked out the front door, got into his car, and drove, fast, as was his wont, toward the bridge. It was all just physics, after all. Acceleration, vectors, friction. Timidity was for English majors.

The Xochimilco Café at 787 Broadway in San Francisco was as he remembered it from his visits there with Jean, including that final night they'd spent together, even—yes, yes, it *was* him—even the nut-brown mustachioed bartender was the same. This time of day the joint wasn't crowded, and the booth he wanted was free: the one where he'd sat that last night with Jean as they drank and flirted and prepared to repair to her lair.

Yellow walls, red tablecloth, leather cushions fixed up here and there with strapping tape, an open area where, later, people would dance. He inhaled the scents of garlic, cumin, cinnamon, and chilies, and ordered a tequila from the boyish Chicana waitress who came floating by in her colorful Mexican skirt.

Oppie waited, passing the time with thoughts of Jean, of that night, and the nights before it, of her laugh and her voice, and her deep, unfathomable sadness, of his successes at comforting her, and his failures, too.

Each time the outside door opened, he looked up. Someone asking to use the washroom. A guy delivering peppers to the kitchen. A hooker who looked a question at Oppie, which he replied to with a shake of the head; she sat on a stool and chatted with the barkeep, waiting for a better prospect.

And then, at last, the person he'd come here to meet.

He was tall and thin, and Oppie knew he was forty-one. He had a receding chin, a heavy lower lip, a long nose, large ears, and blond hair frosting over to white. It had been—what?—five years since he'd last seen him, at the FAECT union-organizing meeting at One Eagle Hill, and Oppie had to admit the years had been kinder to this man than they had been to himself. He rose and waved a beckoning arm.

Long strides closed the distance. "Hello, Robert," the man said, a tad stiffly, in a clipped Manchester accent.

"Hello," Oppie replied, taking the single outstretched hand in both of his, skeletal fingers wrapping around normal ones. "So good of you to come." He sat back down, and George Eltenton, chemical engineer for Shell Development, sat opposite him.

"Haakon Chevalier tells me he's been denied tenure," said Eltenton without preamble.

"I know," said Oppie. "I know, and it's awful. I'll speak to President Sproul on his behalf, but ..." He shrugged a little. "My power is limited since I left the Berkeley faculty."

"They grilled us, you know. Government agents."

"Yes. I'm sorry for that, too." The waitress came and took Eltenton's order, a bottle of Coca-Cola. She disappeared, and Oppie said, "Have you faced similar ..." He didn't want to overstate things but there was no better word: "... repercussions?"

"Besides being harassed by the bloody Federal Bureau of Investigation, you mean?"

"Yes," said Oppie, conceding with a nod that that was no small thing. "Besides."

Eltenton lifted his hands off the table. "No. Shell is more than content with my work. But they have offices worldwide, and, unlike poor Hoke, I'm not an American. I've just put in for a transfer back to England. My daughter Anya is thirteen now, and we think we can get her into Sadler's Wells Ballet School."

Anya. He didn't make any effort to hide his fondness for all things Russian. "Very good," said Oppie. Eltenton's drink was deposited and the waitress disappeared again. "I'm glad you're landing on your feet."

"Unlike Haakon." Just enough bitterness.

"Yes," said Oppie.

"Anyway," said Eltenton, "I'm here. What was it you wanted to talk about?"

Oppie looked around the decrepit room, making sure no one could overhear them. "When you had Haakon reach out to me, he suggested that you had an entrée to the Soviet embassy."

"What is this, Oppenheimer? Entrapment? Is there a tape recorder somewhere?"

"No! Goodness, no. You can ..." But he trailed off, realizing there was no point in saying, "You can trust me."

"Then what?" asked Eltenton, his Coke hissing next to him.

Oppie took a deep breath. "I'd like to make contact with the Soviets."

It was Eltenton's turn to peer around, making sure they had privacy. "Look, the war is over and although I think it's bollocks, one can no longer really think of the Russians and the Americans as allies."

"But you knew—or you knew someone who knew—how to get material to Russian physicists."

"And if I did?"

"Do you still have those connections?"

"Why? You want to give the Russians the atomic bomb *now?*"

"No, no. That's not for me to decide."

"Then what?"

"I need to ... consult ... with their best physicists. I need to talk to Igor Kurchatov."

"I'm not familiar with that name."

"Your contacts will be."

Eltenton just stared at him.

"Please," said Oppie. "It's a matter of life, *not* death. Can you arrange it?"

At last, Eltenton lifted his bottle and took a sip. "It won't be easy."

"And I wouldn't ask if, honestly, a great many lives—including countless Soviet lives—didn't depend upon it."

The thick lower lip was thrust out farther as he thought; it made the man even look Russian. "All right," he said at last. "I'll see what I can do."

Chapter 35

Haakon, Haakon, believe me, I am serious, I have real reason to believe, and I cannot tell you why, but I assure you I have real reason to change my mind about Russia. They are not what you believe them to be. You must not continue your trust, your blind faith, in the policies of the U.S.S.R.

—J. Robert Oppenheimer

"Julius Robert Oppenheimer, what a pleasure, at last!"

Oppie looked around before taking the outstretched hand. He knew Russians liked to use all three of a person's names; the man he was greeting had already introduced himself as Stepan Zakharovich Apresyan.

They were in an open area of grass bordered by trees, and although the park was crowded this August day no one else was nearby. "Actually," Oppie said, as he released his grip, "the J doesn't stand for anything."

"Ah," said Apresyan, in the knowing tone of one used to keeping secrets. "No. Of course it doesn't."

Oppie was sure that Apresyan—the Russian-born son of an Armenian priest, youthful and eager at thirty-two—doubtless had reviewed a full dossier on him, just as Oppie had gotten Groves to provide him with the file on physicist Igor Kurchatov, Oppie's equivalent in the Russian atomic-bomb program.

"We've had our eye on you for a long time," Apresyan said, looking him up and down as if he were a mythical beast at last sighted in the wild. "You appear, if I may, thin. Are you well?"

Oppie shrugged—and he could feel how bony his shoulders were as he did so, feel how much of a scarecrow figure he was. The weight he'd lost in wartime was not coming back.

"I'm fine," he said, pleased that no cough followed the words. His throat was always raw, but being here, in the company of this man, the vice consul from the Soviet Consulate General in San Francisco, had made it as dry as the sands back on *La Jornada del Muerto.*

The two of them were walking west in Golden Gate Park on a sunny afternoon, heading toward Ocean Beach and the Pacific. They quite likely were being shadowed by both the F.B.I. and the N.K.G.B., or whatever they were calling it now, but the park was three miles long, and the air was filled with the sounds of boisterous kids and exasperated parents calling out to them. Like the best of children, Oppie thought, he and Apresyan might be seen but they wouldn't be heard.

Continuing along, they came to the California Academy of Sciences, which had been located in the park since 1916 and now consisted of three buildings: the North American Hall of Birds and Mammals, the Steinhart Aquarium, and the Simson African Hall. Nature in all her splendor surrounded here by even more nature.

The Academy dealt solely with what they called *natural* sciences: the old-fashioned gentlemanly pursuits of stargazing and weather-forecasting, of studying plants and animals, of collecting rocks and fossils. Physics didn't fall under its mandate; his field was, Oppie mused, therefore an *unnatural* science. Perverse. Not in accordance with accepted standards of right and wrong.

And this—*this*—was an unnatural meeting, or certainly would be thought such by many he had to deal with. The J-for-nothing Robert Oppenheimer who had spurned Haakon Chevalier's overture on behalf of George Eltenton, who had severed his ties with Communist-front organizations, who had counseled his former students to do the same, walking—fucking *strolling*—along with a Soviet official whose job title everyone knew was simply a congenial public shield for espionage work.

"Your English is impeccable," said Oppie.

Apresyan was handsome with deep-set eyes and full lips. He tilted his head. "Languages are my thing," he replied, and Oppie smiled at the ostentatious use of Yankee slang, a move worthy of himself. "I speak thirteen of them. Russian, English, Turkish, Arabic ..."

Oppie could *read* nine languages, but the pool of ones he could converse in was smaller. "Dutch?" Oppie asked, picking a tongue any random eavesdropper would be unlikely to know.

"Ja inderdaad," replied Apresyan.

"Good," replied Oppie, also in Dutch. "Let's speak that then."

Apresyan nodded his assent. "I'm pleased you reached out. It's been a while since you've been a party member."

Even in Dutch, Oppie felt the need to issue a denial. "I've never been a member of the Communist Party."

"No? Weren't you, Professor Chevalier, and, oh, many others, including that history professor, Gordon Griffiths, for one? Weren't you all members of the Berkeley faculty Communist club before the U.S. entered the war?"

"Je vergist je," said Oppie. *You're mistaken.*

"Of course, of course," replied Apresyan; the knowing tone was the same in Dutch as English. "I must have heard wrong."

They walked a few dozen yards along the path, birds hopping out of their way. Oppie was wearing his usual hat, but he could feel the afternoon sun on the back of his hand.

"Still," said the vice consul, "there *are* benefits to being in the Party. And for you there'd be *special* benefits, including membership in the Soviet Academy of Sciences. If 'Comrade Oppenheimer' doesn't sit well on the tongue, perhaps 'Academician Oppenheimer' does?"

Oppie's heart was racing. "I'm not looking to defect."

"Surely 'emigrate' is a less-problematic word? And surely, as you yourself have often said, the world would be a safer place if atomic secrets were more evenly distributed. Right now, not only is America the sole country to *have* the bomb, it's proven that it'll *use* it, too. There need to be checks and balances. The threat of retaliation is what will *keep* the bomb from ever being used again. And no one would want a repeat of the horrors of the past, would they?"

When Oppie thought of Russia, he thought of ballet, of careful choreography, of performers hitting their marks. And this lithe Russian certainly knew how to hit *his.* The path turned, and there, in front of them, was one of Golden Gate Park's great attractions: the Oriental Tea Garden, or, as it had been known until the war, the Japanese Tea Garden. Created for the 1894 World's Fair, the garden had transitioned from temporary exhibit to permanent installation. A Japanese horticulturalist named Makoto Hagiwara had moved into the house here with his family to serve as custodians. Makoto-san died in 1925, but his daughter Takano took over the work. Kitty, who had often visited here when they lived in Berkeley, had admired Takano's arrangements—until she and her children were evicted in 1942 and forced into one of General Groves's internment camps.

Oppie had never been to Japan. Bob Serber and Phil Morrison had gone shortly after the destruction of Hiroshima, after the annihilation of Nagasaki, to glean what knowledge they could from the devastation, but Oppie had stayed home. He couldn't face the aftermath, but here, suddenly, in front of him, risen ghosts: a five-tiered pagoda, a meticulous rock garden, bonsai trees, and Buddhist and Shinto sculptures. Fountains and little waterfalls mocked him with aqueous laughter.

Those poor little people.

"We can offer you a lot," said Apresyan. "A beautiful home in Moscow. The best laboratories. The best equipment. Unlimited funds. And you'd work right alongside Kurchatov."

"I've no interest in making bombs anymore," said Oppie. "Even my interest in controlling their use is secondary now. I want to talk to Kurchatov, and to others—others who he will know but I'm not even aware of. Your best minds in physics, especially ..." He paused as a young couple holding hands came down the garden steps, waiting until they were out of earshot; Dutch and English weren't that different when it came to technical terms: "... *de fysica van fusie.*" The physics of fusion.

"Ah, then America *is* proceeding with a hydrogen bomb," said Apresyan, as calmly as if remarking on the weather.

"I didn't say that. You've researched my past; you know that before the war my field was stellar physics—the fusion that powers stars and what happens at the ends of their lives. There are ... problems ... in that realm that we—that *I*—need help with."

They passed the arching Drum Bridge, a wooden semi-circle over a stream with climbing slats instead of stairs, and continued through the elegant landscaping, scarlet and salmon-pink flowers punctuating the green. A serene Buddha, eyes closed, ignored them.

"Well," said Apresyan, "Dr. Kurchatov's energies remain focused, naturally, until the current imbalance of power can be resolved. If you could help him with that, I'm sure the Academy would welcome him turning to more arcane matters." Oppie said nothing, and after a time, the Russian went on: "And, speaking of power imbalances, the West really does owe us a first-rate physicist since Gamow left."

At the last Solvay Conference, in 1933, George Gamow had defected from the Soviet Union. A year later, he was teaching at George Washington University; it was he who had recruited Edward Teller to the United States from London. Although Gamow had declined to work on the Manhattan Project, his areas of interest of late were astrophysics and cosmology; Oppie hoped to bring him on to the Arbor Project's Patient Power solar-research team.

"I simply want to open a conduit," said Oppie. "A channel of communication between those of us working on ... on certain problems here in the United States and those in Russia who might have valuable insights. A two-way street, as it were."

They were well out of the Oriental Garden now; indeed, they were past Crossover Drive. "We've held receptions at the consulate before with visiting Soviet scientists," Apresyan said. "But, although I assure you that Dr. Kurchatov is most happy in Russia, after the unfortunate loss of Gamow, you can surely understand that our top minds cannot be brought to the very shadow of the Presidio."

A large striped ball about the size of a desktop globe went bouncing across their path, and a trio of boys chased after it. Oppie lit his pipe and smoked it in silence. As they got farther west, he could smell dung from the bison paddock and, soon, salt air as seagulls wheeled overhead.

And then they came to the end of the park, and, Oppie had assumed, the end of their business. The Dutch Windmill, no longer used for park irrigation and falling into disrepair, was to their right, and in front of them was the road that separated the park from the sands of Ocean Beach. Beyond that, the Pacific—"the peaceful," earth's own sea of tranquility—stretched to the horizon, azure meeting cerulean.

Oppie was about to quip something along the lines of them likely being the only ones to pass by the Dutch windmill today who were actually speaking Dutch when Stepan Zakharovich Apresyan pointed just past the shoreline. "See that small boat? The red one?"

Oppie tilted his head down a bit so his porkpie brim would better shield against the afternoon sun. *"Ja."*

"It's a speedboat, manned and ready to go. There's a Russian trawler, the *Krylov,* in international waters. Just cross the road, board the boat, and ..."

Oppie waited for him to say more. When he didn't, Oppie said, "I have a wife."

"A wife who has run off on you repeatedly," replied the vice consul. "A wife who, to be honest, wasn't the woman you really wanted to marry. But if you wish, she can easily be collected, too."

"And two children."

"Yes, including a daughter you offered up for adoption."

Oppie's eyes went wide, and Apresyan shrugged amiably. "We were only searching for certain information, but you know the saying: a wide net catches many fish. He gestured out at the ocean. "That boat has an anchor, but do you? New York, Cambridge, Göttingen, Leiden, Berkeley, Los Alamos, Princeton." He turned to Oppie. *"Jij bent niet het type dat een band vormt."*

The most direct translation was, "You're not the type to form bonds," but ...

His heart fluttered.

But, yes, it could also be rendered as, "You're not the 'attached' kind."

Oh, Robert. Robert, Robert.

"There's a new life waiting," Apresyan said. "A rewarding one, a wealthy one."

If only ..., Oppie thought. Somewhere fresh; a place where no one would care, anymore at least, about what had happened with Haakon Chevalier. Somewhere far from Jean's ghost; far from Trinity's ashes.

But he couldn't go. There was work to be done. There was a world to be saved.

"I'm sorry," said Oppie and he could hear the wistful regret in his own voice. "I can't. But, please, I implore you, let Kurchatov contact me; let him and me talk." He switched at last back to English. "Good day, Mr. Vice Consul." Robert turned and headed back into Golden Gate Park.

From behind him, fading into the distance, over the sounds of traffic and gently crashing waves, he heard Apresyan say, *"Dosvedanya, comrade,"* but Oppie didn't turn around.

Chapter 36

1947

Not included among the dossiers is one for rocket scientist Wernher von Braun. It was never transferred to N.A.R.A.

—U.S. National Archives and Records Administration

Dick Feynman had the old itch again.

He'd been trying to keep it in check, leafing through the Institute's copy of the June 1947 *Bulletin of the Atomic Scientists.* They'd dropped the *of Chicago* from the name since he'd last looked at an issue. More interestingly, this issue debuted something called "the doomsday clock," a stylized and stark black-and-white clock face—or, to be precise, the upper-left quarter of one—sprawled across a solid flame-orange cover. The clock was set at seven minutes to midnight, an indication of the editorial board's assessment of how close the world was to nuclear Armageddon; the plan was to move the minute hand closer to or farther from the vertical in subsequent issues as conditions warranted.

Dick put the journal down. It was late and the library was empty; heck, most of Fuld Hall was empty. He could amble back to his guest room, but ...

But.

That damned itch.

Oh, things weren't as bad here at the Institute for Advanced Study as they'd been at Los Alamos. There were no military police, no barbed wire, and no sworn security oaths.

But, still, there were locks on doors.

And combinations to safes.

And things being kept secret.

Dick didn't like that the people of the world weren't being told about the impending disaster, but he'd agreed to abide by the will of the majority. Still, there were other things being kept under wraps not to avoid panic or to protect American interests but merely because, for some self-important types, secrecy was an obsessive kink. And, well, such folk really did need to have their noses tweaked now and then.

Dick had gotten along well enough with the *other* Dick, General Leslie R. Groves, at Los Alamos, but he could understand Leo Szilard's perspective on the man. Physically, Groves was a Zeppelin, but instead of hydrogen or helium he was pumped up by swagger and bluster.

The general had annexed room 212 on the second floor of Fuld Hall as his office here, next to Gödel's and directly above the one for von Neumann's secretary, but he spent most of his time in Washington. Groves was off-site tonight, and Feynman amused himself by picking the lock to the general's door. The I.A.S. had been built without any particular regard for security, and Dick found the mechanism disappointingly easy to defeat; he was inside in a matter of seconds.

But then it was a different story. Groves had a standalone safe about the size of a refrigerator; he'd likely have preferred a built-in one, lest those Commies he suspected were lurking around every corner haul it away. It was a type Feynman had never seen before, with a brass combination dial set in the middle of its burgundy door. Perfect: a challenge.

Of course, Dick first looked in the obvious places where people frequently wrote down combinations, and he tried a few numbers he'd dug up associated with Groves, including birth date, anniversary, and phone numbers. No success—and no problem, either. Dick rubbed the tips of his thumbs against each of his other fingers. You could crack a safe by carefully listening but it took more expertise to do it entirely by feel. Being unfamiliar with the model, Feynman didn't know how many tumblers would have to fall into place, but the usual count was three. He looked at his watch—half the fun was seeing how long it took—then got to work. At first he just spun the dial at various speeds, getting used to its clicking and the ever-so-slight changes in resistance as the pointer passed over various numbers. Then, once he had the feel of the mechanism, he gave the dial a big spin to reset everything so he could start clean.

In the end, it took him twenty-three minutes and eighteen seconds to get the safe's door open, a quite respectable time. His intention had been just to leave a gift for Groves—a little something to surprise the general the next time he opened this vault. Feynman collected Walking Liberty fifty-cent pieces from 1918, the year he'd been born, to leave as calling cards—after all, who could be angry at getting a free half buck?—and he fished one out of the front pocket of his beige slacks. But as he went to place it on the top file folder, the words on the tab caught his eye. In block letters, someone had written "Project Overcast."

Feynman had enjoyed many conversations with Johnny von Neumann when visiting here and knew about his plan to use his computer to accurately predict the weather months or even years in advance. Dick wasn't sure that would ever be possible. At Los Alamos, much of his own work had been on the gaseous diffusion method of separating Uranium-235 from U-238, work that was vexed by the drunken-walk meandering of particles known as Brownian motion. He suspected that such randomness would always befuddle meteorological soothsayers as they tried to read cirrus entrails. Still, he *was* intrigued—he liked to describe himself as a curious character in both senses of the word—and so he picked up the manila folder. It was thick; he almost spilled the contents onto the floor as he hefted it.

He decided he might as well just leaf through it here, rather than take it back to the library. Groves was fat but he wasn't slovenly: his desk was tidy and there was plenty of room to spread out papers. Dick lowered himself into the padded chair, wondering if it was relieved to be taking a much lighter burden for a change, and he began to read.

And read.

And read.

Despite the name, Project Overcast had nothing to do with the weather. The first document in the file was a memo stamped "Classified" and dated just over two years ago—July 6, 1945—with the subject heading "Exploitation of German Specialists in Science and Technology in the United States." It outlined "principles and procedures" under which Overcast was to operate, one of which was set off in its own paragraph:

> *No known or alleged war criminals should be brought to the United States. If any specialists who are brought to this country are subsequently found to be listed as alleged war criminals, they should be returned to Europe for trial.*

The second sentence had been underlined in blue ink, and the letters "WVB" had been jotted in the margin.

WVB. Dick's first thought was "women's volleyball," a game he always enjoyed watching.

But his second thought was Wernher von Braun.

He started riffling through the rest of the documents in the folder. As with so much in his approach to problem solving, he wasn't sure what he was looking for—but he was confident he'd recognize it when he found it.

And find it he did, although it was couched in the usual military alphabet soup. The deputy director of "JIOA" said that "negative OMGUS reports" were preventing "SD" from approving immigration for key "OPC" assets. Dick had to hunt around in other documents to find out what the initials stood for. "JIOA" turned out to be the Joint Intelligence Objectives Agency, which had put together more than a thousand dossiers on Nazi medical doctors, scientists, engineers, and technicians who might be useful to the American military. "OPC"—Operation Paperclip—was the new name for what had originally been called Operation Overcast, apparently because those Nazis desired by the U.S. military had their dossiers flagged with a paperclip. "OMGUS" was the Office of the Military Government, United States—the U.S. authority in the American-occupied part of Germany. And "SD," it eventually dawned on Dick, was the U.S. Department of State.

The memo concluded, "It is not considered advisable to submit any of the enclosed dossiers to the Departments of State and Justice at this time."

Presumably there had originally been several dossiers included, but Groves had brought only one of them here to the I.A.S. The cover note on it said, "OMGUS indicates that he is regarded as a potential security threat to the United States and he will be wanted for denazification trial in view of his party membership." And the dossier itself was that of Herr Doktor Professor Wernher von Braun.

Dick imagined von Braun was considered a war criminal simply because he was the father of the V-2 rocket, explosions of which had killed 2,700 civilians in London and injured another 6,500; by the same standards, as Leo Szilard had observed, Dick himself would have been named a war criminal had the Japanese won.

But, as Feynman worked his way through the papers about von Braun, he found his stomach knotting. There was no easy way to make a copy of the relevant pages, and so he read them over and over again, committing every word to memory.

When he at last departed Groves's office, he left no fifty-cent piece or any other sign that he'd been there. It was after 3:00 a.m. as he exited Fuld Hall to walk in the chill to his visitor's quarters. There was no moon, just a vaulting canopy of stars; Dick figured there had to be at least six million of them.

Chapter 37

I aim at the stars.
—Wernher von Braun

But sometimes he hits London.
—Mort Sahl

"You know what they're calling me and my staff in Washington?" Wernher von Braun asked in his thick accent as he and Oppenheimer walked along the dirt road through the Texas heat. He didn't wait for Oppie's guess. "'Intellectual reparations,'" von Braun declared and then he bellowed a laugh. "I like that." The cloudless summer sky was the silver of sardine scales; the sun shimmered against it. "Better than what we'd dubbed ourselves: 'Prisoners of peace.'" He looked around the desolate grounds. "Speaking of names, this has to be a euphemism, right? Fort Bliss? Fort Piss is more like it." They were speaking German, but von Braun had switched to English for the last few words.

"Actually," said Oppie, as a Jeep passed them heading the other way, "it's named for William Bliss. He was the son-in-law of an American president." Oppie normally paid little attention to military history, but the story of Bliss had caught his eye: he'd been a child math prodigy who'd grown up to be a decorated soldier as well as a mathematics professor.

"Ha!" barked von Braun. "The new world and the old—not so different, eh? Nepotism everywhere!"

"Oh, there are many differences," said Oppie.

"True, true," agreed von Braun amiably. "To a European, a hundred miles is a big journey; to an American, a hundred years is a long time."

A long time. Yes, it was useful to have Europeans on this project. They could bring the sense of urgency it so desperately needed and that Oppie had been having trouble instilling in American scientists. A hundred years could pass very quickly indeed, eighty-odd years even more rapidly.

Oppie knew that his own feet stuck out as he walked; for his part, Wernher von Braun had a commanding strut. The two of them must have been an odd sight for the various soldiers milling around the base: one duck-footed, the other practically goose-stepping. Wernher put a friendly arm around Oppie's narrow shoulders and said, "You and I are cut from the same cloth. If it were not for that pesky war, we would have been friends long before this."

Oppie was taken aback. Although as tall as von Braun, the stocky German outweighed him by over a hundred pounds and was eight years younger. They were at opposite ends of the political spectrum, too—not to mention that von Braun probably had never had many friends with names like "Oppenheimer" even before becoming a born-again Christian last year here in Texas. "How do you mean?"

Wernher spread his arms as if it were obvious. "Both of us the brains behind massive technological efforts. Each with his sometimes benighted military supervisor—you with Groves, me with Dornberger. Both now celebrated for our war-time accomplishments. And both with a larger purpose, science—" Von Braun stopped, but the lilt of his voice suggested he'd originally intended to utter more. Oppie suspected the rocketeer had halted before the words *"über alles"* could pass his lips.

Oppie didn't mind the typical Germanic bravado; he'd gotten used to it during his years at Göttingen. Nor could he fault anyone who hadn't personally started it for being on the losing side of a war. And although the idea had failed to fly, Oppie would indeed have been proud to wear an American service uniform at Los Alamos. But there was a world of difference between U.S. Army green and Nazi S.S. black; he'd seen the photos that had emerged of *Schutzstaffel Sturmbannführer* von Braun peacocking about in that fetishistic garb.

"It's been brought to my attention that there were ..." Oppie began and then paused as he sought a politic word: "... *oddities*, shall we say, about the V-2 production facility at Dora."

"At Mittelwerk," corrected von Braun. Mittelwerk—the Middle Works, named for its central location in Germany—was an innocuous and soulless moniker, the kind of banality that a civil servant in any bureaucracy would have been proud of. The transcripts about Dora from the Nuremberg war-crimes trials had been suddenly classified; apparently the American government wanted nothing to call public attention to the backgrounds of the 115 German rocket scientists now here at Fort Bliss. But Oppie had received a full briefing, courtesy of Dick Feynman's prodigious memory of a secret file he'd seen, about what had gone on in the 7.5 miles of dank and stinking underground tunnels that composed the hidden factory. Even Albert Speer had called the conditions barbarous. Cumulatively 60,000 prisoners had toiled there, a third of whom had died, literally worked to death. That statistic was staggering: more people perished building von Braun's V-2 rockets than were killed by them as weapons.

Hitler had vowed in December 1941 to exterminate all Jews within Germany's reach, so by the time Mittelwerk completed its first batch of V-2s, on New Year's Eve 1943, there were few Jews left at the Dora concentration camp, the facility that fed Mittelwerk's voracious appetite for slave labor. Oppie had never felt a close connection to European Jewry, but Leo Szilard and I.I. Rabi did. They'd brought the deprivations at Dora to his attention after Szilard had heard about them from Feynman. To their credit, Szilard and Rabi's outrage abated not at all when they found out that von Braun's slaves were mostly Christian prisoners of war from Poland, France, Belgium, and Italy. "We cannot be in bed with this man," Szilard had said, and "Even war has rules of decency," insisted Rabi.

That was true—and the distinction von Braun was making was disingenuous. The Dora camp and the Mittelwerk complex were adjacent facilities; you couldn't visit one without being aware of the other. Von Braun claimed to have only rarely entered the subterranean factory himself but, as he'd said, he and Oppie were of a kind: administrators of giant technological undertakings. And although Oppie had thrown a single sheet of paper at his assistant in 1943, shouting, "Here's your damned organization chart!," he *did* know where every one of the 8,200 residents of his Los Alamos facility had come from and what they did; you couldn't *not* know and still administer such a place effectively. He knew, and von Braun had to have known, too.

"Very well," said Oppie. "At Mittelwerk, if you prefer." There was a sour taste in his mouth. "But slave laborers in the tunnels. The horrific environment. Prisoners flogged and hanged."

Oppie liked people who took their time before replying; to him, silence meant thoughtfulness. But von Braun was not reflective, and there was no careful consideration before he spoke. "Oppie, you had a war to win and so did I. As it happened, neither of us succeeded. Your bomb wasn't ready to use against us, and my rockets were not enough to subdue the Allies. And perhaps there *were* deaths: you say there were some at Mittelwerk; I remind you of the tens of thousands in Hiroshima and Nagasaki."

"Yes, but ..." said Oppie, falling into that very trap of beginning to speak before he'd composed his own thoughts. He sought a distinction—a *principled* distinction—between what he had facilitated and what this robust German had done. But the words that came to mind were the same ones that had haunted him so often since August of two years ago. *Those poor little people.* He closed his mouth and they walked on in silence.

Silence, however, didn't appeal to the boisterous engineer. As they approached the PX, the big man gave Oppie a good-natured slap on the back, which damn near sent him face-first into the dirt. "All sins forgiven, eh, Oppie? Come, let me buy you a drink!"

Nineteen Forty-Seven was coming to a close. The first babies of Kitty's predicted post-war boom were beginning to walk, and the Arbor Project was starting to bear fruit. Although the recovered V-2 rockets were of obvious benefit to the New Names effort, fascinating discoveries about how to build long-term sealed habitats had also been made examining German U-boats, particularly of Type XXI, the original *Elektroboot,* the first submarines to operate submerged most of the time instead of only performing short emergency dives. Under the terms of surrender, all U-boats in home waters had sailed to the British submarine base at Harwich. Freeman Dyson, always happy for a trip back to England, spent weeks there and returned to Princeton with reports of useful technology that could be applied to building space ships. Oppie loved the historical resonance: Harwich was almost certainly where the *Mayflower* had set sail to bring Pilgrims to the figurative new world; secrets uncovered there would now aid in the transportation of refugees to a literal one.

He was still upset, though, by his meeting with von Braun, three months ago now. Much of the information about him was still classified, but there *were* public accounts. Von Braun was of Junker stock, the Prussian landed aristocracy, well known for producing high-ranking civil servants and military officers. Still, wearing blinders wasn't his birthright. And Oppie had certainly met many an intellectual of his stripe: lacking in empathy and sharply focused on a narrow area of interest. But the sheer *callousness* of the man grated.

On November 25, Oppie gave a public lecture at M.I.T. entitled "Physics in the Contemporary World." As with so many of his speeches, it was partially from notes and partially extemporaneous. This was the annual Arthur D. Little Memorial Lecture, a big deal, but Oppie was confident the right words would spill forth from his mouth. And, for the most part, they did. He lamented the derailing of pure-science research because of the war but spoke soaringly about the turnaround since: "It has been an exciting and an inspiring sight to watch the recovery—a recovery testifying to extraordinary vitality and vigor in this human activity. Today, barely two years after the end of hostilities, physics is booming." The audience members—a mix of students, academics, and the social elite of Cambridge, Massachusetts—were clearly with him, and he was happy to stoke their excitement for a new renaissance in his field.

But ...

But it wasn't really a time for just pure research—not that this audience, or anyone in the general public, would ever know. Now there was another demand on physicists and, for all the distance between them, von Braun's Ph.D. *was* in physics, with his 1934 dissertation focused tightly on his personal obsession: *Konstruktive, theoretische und experimentelle Beiträge zu dem Problem der Flüssigkeitsrakete*—"Constructive, Theoretical, and Experimental Contributions to the Problem of the Liquid-Fueled Rocket." The thesis had been quickly classified secret by the Nazis, but now that it could at last be freely read, von Braun was eager to have people do so, and he'd pressed a copy of it onto Oppie when he'd visited Fort Bliss. Oppie had duly turned it over to Rabi's NN team.

And, as all members of the Arbor Project—von Braun included, even if he was off in Texas—set about to do their research, it seemed to Oppie that they *had* to reflect on the moral questions.

He looked out at his audience in the M.I.T. auditorium. The room was darkened but light from the stage bounced off spectacles in the blackness, round disks, hundreds of full moons in an ebony sky. And he let the words come: "Despite the vision and far-seeing wisdom of our war-time heads of state, the physicists have felt the peculiarly intimate responsibility for suggesting, for supporting, and in the end, in large measure, for achieving the realization of atomic weapons."

He could hear the rustling of the audience and a few surprised whispers. It was, indeed, an apparent *non sequitur*, a veering off from the direction he had previously been headed. But von Braun, even if he wasn't there, needed to hear this; the *world* needed to hear this. He went on, the words spoken aloud the moment they bloomed in his mind: "In some sort of crude sense," he said, looking out, "which no ..."

He sought a word.

"Vulgarity ..."

He shook his head slightly, tried again: "... no humor ..."

All eyes on him. The speech would be widely reported, and M.I.T. would transcribe it for the archives. He would make sure von Braun got a copy.

"... no overstatement can quite extinguish ..."

He was doing it again, he knew, saying more than he should, but he couldn't help himself; the words were a chain reaction, one rebounding off another and setting a new one free, and it had to run its course: "... the physicists have known sin." He took a deep breath, a pause. *All sins forgiven, my ass.*

There was no turning back, no regaining the garden, no reclaiming innocence in either sense of the word.

"And this," he said with finality, "is a knowledge which they cannot lose."

The great hall was silent, but Oppie's own pulse thundered applause in his ears.

Chapter 38

1948

I would see people building a bridge, or they'd be making a new road, and I thought, they're crazy, they just don't understand, they don't understand. Why are they making new things? It's so useless.

—Richard Feynman

Dick Feynman's talk at the Pocono conference had been a disaster. He'd driven the three hours back to Ithaca without saying a word, Charlie Parker and Dizzy Gillespie on the radio when they could get reception, while Hans Bethe alternately snoozed in the passenger seat and stared out at the springtime countryside of Pennsylvania and upstate New York. Dick dropped Hans at his house, then, without going home himself, he headed straight to his favorite bar, three blocks from the Cornell campus. It was a Saturday night; *something* had to be going on.

I adore you, sweetheart. I know how much you like to hear that—but I don't only write it because you like it—I write it because it makes me warm all over inside to write it to you.

"You've been ignoring me all evening," said the blonde in the form-fitting silvery dress as she slipped onto the barstool next to him.

Feynman had a taste of his beer. "Not all evening," he said, looking off in the distance. "You came in here at 9:44."

"So you did notice!"

It was a little after midnight now. "And you've been with five guys since."

"Only four!" Her blue irises rolled up a bit as she mentally counted. "No, you're right. Five." She gave him a half smile. "But not you."

"Each of them bought you a drink," he said. "I'm not going to."

She swiveled her hips on the stool, facing him more closely. "Why not?"

He pointed up at the ceiling fan with its trio of light bulbs, each in a tulip-shaped holder, each casting a conical beam in the smoky air.

"You know," he said as if it had been the topic of conversation all along, "you could argue that light is the hardest-working thing in the universe. After all, it goes faster than anything else—almost seven hundred thousand miles an hour. But it's actually lazy. It does it by taking the easiest possible path. That's something called the principle of least effort. I subscribe to that, and so all you're getting for free is that one physics lesson."

Her nose wrinkled as she studied him. "You're a physics student?"

Feynman often answered yes to that question—there was another week before his thirtieth birthday, and he looked younger than his age. Undergrads were far more likely to let him pick them up if they thought he was still a student. But, after the humiliation of the Pocono conference, he felt an urge to assert his status. "No, I'm a physics *professor.*"

She twisted her mouth sideways as she studied his face, presumably for wrinkles. "Maybe," she said at last.

> *It is such a terribly long time since I last wrote to you—almost two years—but I know you'll excuse me because you understand how I am, stubborn and realistic; and I thought there was no sense to writing.*

"In fact," said Dick, looking the blonde full in the face for the first time, "I worked on the atomic bomb."

"Now I know you're kidding. That was Hans Bethe, and, one, that's a New York accent you've got there, not a German one, and, two, you aren't nearly old enough to be him."

Feynman felt a rueful smile creasing his features. Yes, here in Ithaca, Bethe was the famous physicist, formerly head of the Technical Division at Los Alamos. But Dick had come to think of Hans and the others who'd been at the Pocono conference, including Bohr, Dirac, Oppenheimer, Rabi, Teller, and Feynman's old doctoral supervisor, John Archibald Wheeler, as peers, as colleagues—as though he were now their equal. But Edward Teller had challenged him at Pocono almost as soon as Dick had started to explain his new method for diagramming particle interactions under quantum electrodynamics.

"What about the exclusion principle?" Teller had demanded.

Dick had shaken his head. *"It doesn't make any differ—"*

"How do you know?" roared the Hungarian.

"I know. I worked from a—"

"Neh!" exclaimed Teller. *"How could it be!"*

Dick had tried to go on, tried to explain the *simplicity*, the *clarity* of his new method, but the assembled geniuses just weren't getting it. He turned to look at the girl next to him. She was somewhere between pretty and beautiful, twenty, twenty-one, with a sort of Dutch air to her. He hadn't asked her name and certainly wasn't about to proffer his own if it was inevitably going to be greeted with a "never heard of you," so he decided to mentally call her Heidi.

> *But now I know my darling wife that it is right to do what I have delayed in doing, and that I have done so much in the past. I want to tell you I love you. I want to love you. I always will love you.*

"Do you know who Paul Dirac is?" Dick asked, expecting and receiving a shake of Heidi's lovely head. "Well, he won the Nobel prize in physics. Among many things, he's responsible for the concept of anti-matter."

"Oh, really?" Heidi said. "I'm pro-matter myself." She winked. "It's better than nothing."

The girl was clever! He laughed, and she took that as a sign of encouragement, rotating slightly on her stool to bring her right knee, in that silky dress, into contact with his left, covered by his jeans.

"Anti-matter is like regular matter," Dick said, "except it has the opposite charge."

There was a pile of white paper napkins on the bar counter; it was almost as if this place were *meant* for doing physics. Dick grabbed one and took a beat-up fountain pen out of his breast pocket. He printed a lower-case *e* in the lower left of the napkin, the indigo ink spreading to mostly fill in the enclosed part of the letter, then he drew a superscripted minus sign next to it. "That's an electron—negative, see?" In the lower right, he printed another little *e* but gave this one a superscripted plus sign. "But this guy, he's got the same mass but the opposite charge. He's an anti-electron, or, if you prefer, a positron."

He drew lines diagonally upward from each one converging in the center of the napkin.

"A collision!" said Heidi. "Opposites attract."

He looked at her and thought, *Indeed they do.*

> *When you were sick you worried because you could not give me something that you wanted to and thought I needed. You needn't have worried. Just as I told you then there was no real need because I loved you in so many ways so much. And now it is clearly even more true—you can give me nothing now, yet I love you so that you stand in my way of loving anyone else—but I want you to stand there. You, dead, are so much better than anyone else alive.*

"But I left out a couple of things," Dick said, and he pulled the napkin toward himself and began marking it up some more. "A graph needs axes. This one, going up—the *y*-axis—is time, and this one, across, is space." She nodded, but her gaze was wandering a bit, presumably scanning the bar for a better prospect. "Oh, and of course there are directions of movement." He drew a little arrowhead pointing diagonally upward in the middle of the diagonal line coming from the electron—and one pointing diagonally *downward* in the line connected to the positron. "See what I did there?"

She glanced at the napkin and shook her head.

"Make you a deal," he said. "You see what's interesting there, and I *will* buy you a drink."

He was violating the rule a bartender back in Albuquerque had taught him in 1946. Never give girls you want to sleep with anything, never buy them anything. When everyone else *is,* they'll become obsessed with the guy who *isn't.* But Dick figured he was making a safe bet, and—

"Wait a minute," said Heidi. "You said time was going from the bottom to the top, right?"

His heart jumped. "Right."

"And so the electron is going forward in time—as well as moving to the right in space."

"Correct again."

"But you've got the anti-electron, the—what did you call it?"

"The positron."

"Going left across the page and *down.* You've got it going *backward* in time. That can't be right!"

Feynman may not have known the girl's name but he knew the bartender's well enough. "Mike?"

The lanky guy came over. "Another one?"

"For me, yes—and whatever she'd like for the lady."

"A martini, please," said Heidi.

> *I'll bet you are surprised that I don't even have a girlfriend (except you, sweetheart) after two years. But you can't help it, darling, nor can I—I don't understand it, for I have met many girls and very nice ones and I don't want to remain alone—but in two or three meetings they all seem ashes. You only are left to me. You are real.*

A martini. Which, of course, brought Oppenheimer—the master—to mind, and took Dick right back to the humiliation in the Poconos.

"That's what I put on the chalkboard during a conference I was just at," Dick said. "A positron going back in time. And Dirac—Mr. Anti-Matter himself!—leaps to his feet and says what you just said: 'That can't be right.' To which I say, no, it *is* right—a positron is nothing more than an electron moving backward in time. And, of course, he brings up causality—that you can't have an effect happening before its cause—and I say who says so? And he calls out, 'Is it unitary?' And I didn't know what the hell that means. The Brits use that term more than we do, apparently; turns out it means, do the probabilities all added together equal one. But I didn't know that, so I simply said, 'I'll explain it to you, so you can see how it works. Then *you* can tell *me* if it's unitary.'" Dick took a sip of his old beer and nodded thanks at the bartender who had delivered a new one along with Heidi's martini. "The whole thing was a fiasco."

"What a wonderful notion, though!" Heidi said, after her first sip. "If you could go back in time, what would you change?"

> *My darling wife, I do adore you. I love my wife. My wife is dead.*

What would he change? Well, for one, he'd have prepared a better introduction to his new way of diagramming quantum-electrodynamical interactions for that conference! And—

And—he wouldn't have hit on Professor Smith's wife, especially not while being his house guest.

And he wouldn't have gotten those two girls—the waitress and the student—pregnant last year.

And, yes, he might have refused to work on the atomic bomb.

But he still would have married Arline, married her even though he knew she was dying of tuberculosis. Their marriage had been the happiest, and, true, the saddest, time of his life, but oh so worth it.

> *P.S.: Please excuse my not mailing this—but I don't know your new address.*

When she'd finished her martini, the young lady held out her hand. "Susan," she said.

He had signed that unsent letter, penned a year and a half ago, "Rich," but that was the short form he saved solely for her, for his darling Arline, for his Putzie, for his wife. "Dick," he said, shaking Susan's hand.

"Well, Dick, it's getting late. Walk me home?"

There was no turning back time, no changing what was always going to be. He rose and offered her his arm, and they made their tipsy way out, blackness overhead, and he knew he'd do what he'd done so often since Arline's passing: try once again to fill the ravenous void.

Work continued apace on the Arbor Project for the rest of 1948, the various teams separately pursuing their assigned lines of research. Although he was still fond of management by walking around, Oppie rarely visited the Compact Cement division where Feynman, Gödel, and Szilard did what they did best: thinking up wild ideas—"botching," as Leo called it. Partly it was so he wouldn't be seen as undermining Kitty's authority as head of that group, and partly it was because they were housed in a separate building, far from Fuld Hall.

Still, Leo Szilard was as given as ever to perambulation, and running into him as Robert made his way from Olden Manor to his own office was a common enough occurrence.

"Guten Tag!" declared Leo as he approached. He preferred to speak German with those who knew that language.

Oppie replied in the same tongue. "How are you?"

"Good, good. Did you hear the news? Blackett won the Nobel."

Oppie's heart kicked his sternum. *"Patrick* Blackett?"

"Yes," said Szilard. "For his work on cloud chambers and cosmic rays. I'd kind of thought it would go to Yukawa for his prediction of the pi meson, but I suppose it's too soon after the war for even the neutral Swedes to honor a Japanese, and ..."

Leo went on, but Oppie ceased to listen.

Patrick Blackett.

His old tutor from the Cavendish back in 1925.

His old unrequited love.

The man he'd tried to poison with a deadly apple.

This year's Nobel laureate.

"Robert?" said Szilard, touching the sleeve of Oppie's jacket. "What's the matter? You look like you've seen a ghost."

"No," said Oppie. "Not a ghost." He blinked a few times. "I'm happy for him."

"Who?" said Leo. His chatter had apparently veered off in another direction while Oppie had been lost in his own thoughts, and so he had to give voice to the name again, a name he hadn't spoken in two decades. "Blackett."

"Ah, yes!" declared Leo. "May we all be so lucky some day, eh, Robert?"

Oppie looked down at his feet, splayed left and right like clock hands at ten and two. "He had his chance."

Leo's tone was puzzled. "Now, now, Oppie. After all, you were just on the cover of *Time!* Glory enough for us all."

Oppie gave Leo a curt *"auf Wiedersehen"* and began walking off, his mind thousands of miles away and decades in the past.

Chapter 39

1949

[Oppenheimer] certainly did not suffer fools gladly—and there are lots of fools. He could be extremely cutting and he was especially cutting to people in high positions whom he considered fools.

—Hans Bethe

After staring into an atomic fireball, Oppie mused, *you'd think flashbulbs wouldn't bother me.* But they did, each little explosion stinging his eyes and leaving an afterimage that lingered like guilt.

Robert strode into the massive, marble-walled caucus room on the second floor of the senate office building, six Corinthian columns along each of its long sides, feeling alive and important. He smiled at or shook hands with a phalanx of reporters, many of whom had previously written fawning pieces about him.

At the front of the room there were six long mahogany tables forming three sides of a square. The five members of the Atomic Energy Commission sat at the middle table, ordered, it amused Oppie to notice, left to right by increasing degree of baldness and right to left by seated height. At the far right was Lewis Strauss, and that positioning tickled him, too.

Oppie's world-line intersected frequently with that of the fifty-three-year-old Strauss. In addition to his role as an A.E.C. member, Strauss was also one of the trustees of the Institute for Advanced Study. In November 1945, Truman bestowed upon him the rank of rear admiral in the Navy Reserve—essentially an honorific now that the war was over—and, in the months soon following, Strauss had supported Einstein's suggestion of Oppenheimer for the I.A.S.'s directorship, perhaps thinking that Oppie in peacetime would follow an admiral's instructions as obediently as he'd followed a general's during the war. But Robert had firmly rejected Strauss's meddling for two and a half years now—partly because Strauss wasn't privy to the Arbor Project, and partly because Oppie found the pompous, thin-skinned businessman irritating.

Even his name irked Oppie. Robert had met many a Strauss during his time in Göttingen, but the admiral, born in Charleston, had a Southern drawl that elongated his surname to "Straws," any hint of the Teutonic buried under hominy and huckleberry. Each time Oppie heard him say it, he winced.

As a teenager, Oppie knew, Strauss had wanted to become a physicist, but he'd managed only a high-school diploma before his father put him on the road selling shoes. During World War I, though, Lewis ingratiated himself into a position as an aide to future-president Herbert Hoover, and, after the war, with Hoover's help, he landed a job at a New York investment-banking firm. Ever the opportunist, Strauss married the daughter of one of the partners, and come the year of the great crash—the one that had originally sailed by Oppie unnoticed—he was a partner himself, raking in more than a million dollars annually. Strauss had his claws firmly dug into business *and* government, equally at home on Wall Street and in the West Wing.

But it was the Southerner's efforts to play in the arena he'd never actually gotten around to studying—physics—that truly made Robert angry. Lewis Strauss was the sole member of the Atomic Energy Commission who opposed the exporting of radioisotopes produced by U.S. reactors to friendly powers for use in medical and industrial applications. As Oppie understood it, Strauss felt that, by definition, an atheist nation such as Russia couldn't possibly be moral, and any isotopes that left U.S. control were bound to eventually end up in Soviet clutches.

Of course, the U.S. didn't export U-235 or any plutonium, but iron isotopes such as Fe-59? There was no sane reason to withhold them from allies.

Still, Strauss had taken his fight against exports to the press, which was out in force today, and also to Republican Senator Bourke Hickenlooper, an Iowan who looked like Central Casting's notion of an accountant.

Hickenlooper was immediate past chairman of the Joint Committee on Atomic Energy, the body that oversaw the A.E.C., and he was jealous that Joe McCarthy, a senator from the neighboring state of Wisconsin, was getting so much press attention for *his* hearings. After being coached by the admiral, Hick—as his constituents called him—accused the rest of the A.E.C. of "incredible mismanagement" for having let some two thousand shipments of isotopes go overseas. In response, the new chair of the Joint Committee, Brien McMahon, called precisely the sort of public hearing Hick wanted—and, to best McCarthy, *this* hearing was open to the public, with klieg lights blazing to aid the newsreel cameras.

Today, Oppie had been summoned to provide his expert opinion. Although not a member of the A.E.C., he was chairman of its group of scientific consultants, the General Advisory Committee; the other members had sneakily voted him chair at their first meeting while he himself had been stuck in traffic, thanks to a snowstorm.

Oppie took a seat at another one of the mahogany tables, next to the A.E.C.'s general counsel, a wavy-haired New Yorker in his early thirties called Joe "The Fox" Volpe. After a bit of preliminary material, Hick looked over at Strauss, and Oppie noted a smug little nod pass between them. The senator called Oppie to the settee reserved for those speaking. A carved eagle was perched on its backrest, poised to pounce on anyone wavering from the patriotic good.

Admiral Strauss was president of the Reform temple Emanu-El in Manhattan, the same synagogue that Felix Adler had abandoned to found his Ethical Culture Society and its primary and secondary school at which Oppie had been a student. Adler's position—and Oppie's own—was the opposite of Strauss's: morality could indeed be established without any recourse to theology. McMahon wasn't requiring the swearing of oaths, although in this case, Oppie thought, the *Rubber Bible,* that giant compendium of chemistry and physics data, would have served admirably as scripture: facts, after all, are facts. He might defer to Lewis on picking a pair of *shoes,* but when it came to science, the businessman really needed to shut the hell up.

"When we furnish isotopes to other nations," said Hickenlooper, rising to face Oppie, thumbs hitched into suspenders, "we are embarking on a program which I believe is inimical to our national defense." He fixed his eyes on Robert as if to make sure the scientist understood what he was supposed to say, then asked his question: "Dr. Oppenheimer, on this matter of exporting isotopes, surely you agree with Admiral Strauss here"—he said the name the way Lewis himself did as he indicated the man, who was leaning forward earnestly, chin supported on arms held up by the polished wood in front of him—"that there's *some* possibility of them being used *not* for peaceful manufacturing or medicine but for atomic processes—first, atomic energy, and then, possibly, atomic bombs. Surely that objection is well-founded, sir, wouldn't you say?"

Oppie looked out at the faces, the crowd, the *audience,* and spread his arms wide, palms up, an imploring Christ. "No one can force me to say that you cannot use these isotopes for atomic energy," he said. He paused, making sure every eye was on him. "You can use a shovel for atomic energy; in fact you do." There were a few laughs. "You can use a bottle of beer for atomic energy; in fact, you do." More laughter, the holdouts from a moment earlier now emboldened. "But to get some perspective, the fact is that during the war and after the war these materials have played no significant part and, in my knowledge, no part at all."

He had them, Oppie knew, had them in his thrall. "My own rating of the importance of isotopes in this broad sense is that they are far less important than, oh, electronic devices but far more important than, let us say ..." He made a show of seeking a word, then delivered it like a punch line: "... *vitamins.*" Open guffaws. To milk the moment, he added with dancing eyebrows, "Somewhere in between."

Hick was frowning and his face had grown red. He dismissed Oppie, and Robert strode across the room. "Well, Joe," he said, grinning, as he sat back down in his previous seat, "how did I do?"

Volpe shook his head left and right, left and right, oscillating in anguished discomfort. "Too well," he said. "*Much* too well." The lawyer cast his gaze across the room at Lewis Strauss, and Oppie turned to look in that direction.

Robert's throat constricted. He'd faced down rattlesnakes on the mesa, coyotes in the scrub, buzzards in the desert. He knew the expression of something that wanted you dead. But Lewis Strauss's face, red with rage, taut with humiliation, was worse than that, a look Oppie had only ever seen once before, a look telegraphing not just wanting him dead—of that there was no doubt—but of wanting to see him suffer first, to have Oppie *know* who it was who had destroyed him. He knew the look because he'd seen it himself, years ago at the Cavendish, as he glared in the shaving mirror, straight razor scraping flesh, on the day he'd tried to kill Patrick Blackett with a poisoned apple.

Oppie shuddered, turned away, and more bulbs exploded in his face.

Chapter 40

Four Years Later: 1953

I have to put a stop to it. Ike has to know what's really going on. This is the biggest mistake the United States could make!

—Admiral William "Deak" Parsons,
on hearing that President Eisenhower had ordered Oppenheimer cut off from classified information; Parsons died the next day of a heart attack before speaking to the president

"Ah, Robert, thank you for coming by."

"Sure," said Oppie. "Glad to."

The Atomic Energy Commission boardroom in Washington was octagonal, with a long wooden table so highly polished that one could use its surface as a mirror. Lewis Strauss had risen from the head of the table as Oppie entered. Ken Nichols, squinty-eyed and now sporting a pencil-thin mustache, was also there, standing by the window. The slats of the Venetian blinds were open, and the sun was already low on this, the shortest day of the year.

"Did you hear about Admiral Parsons?" said Strauss, shaking Oppie's hand with an unpleasant lack of pressure.

Oppie nodded. "Deak? Yes. So sad. Just fifty-two; far too young. Kitty sent Martha some of her best orchids and a card." Bill Parsons—"Deak," short for "Deacon," a pun on his last name—had proved, as Groves had said he would, an invaluable Navy liaison for the Arbor Project, often visiting the Oppenheimers at Olden Manor. He had recently written Oppie about the McCarthyism hysteria sweeping the nation, opining that "the anti-intellectualism of recent months may have passed its peak." Robert hoped that was true.

"General Nichols," said Oppie, eyeing the man who had been Leslie Groves's assistant during the war years. Oppie recognized the look on Nichols's face, the same naked hatred he'd seen that day they'd met for the first time eleven years ago, when Groves had humiliated the doctorate-holding district engineer by dispatching him to do his dry cleaning. Hundreds of others must have witnessed Groves treat Nichols poorly, but those others would have been fellow soldiers, uniformed men and women who understood that some Dicks were dicks, and that you took orders—*sir, yes, sir!*—no matter what. But Oppie was a *civilian* and, if not an actual card-carrying Communist, close enough in Nichols's simplistic world-view.

"Doctor," said Nichols, by way of greeting: a title they were both entitled to use, but Nichols made it sound like a diminutive, dismissing snot-nosed Bobby out of hand.

"So, listen," drawled Strauss, "we've got a thorny problem here related to your security clearance. You've got a Q level"—access to all nuclear-weapons information—"and that's raising some eyebrows. President Eisenhower has issued an executive order requiring re-evaluation of all individuals whose files contain derogatory information, and, well ..."

"And my file is bursting with just that," said Oppie good-naturedly, "if viewed in the wrong light."

"If viewed in *any* light," snapped Nichols, but Strauss shot him a look.

"And, unfortunately," continued Strauss, "we have to move yours to the top of the heap. A former government official has submitted a letter that suggests, well, it ..."

"It says," Nichols supplied with relish, "'that more probably than not, J. Robert Oppenheimer is an agent of the Soviet Union.'"

Oppie felt his jaw slacken. "But that's absurd!" Had he been seen all those years ago meeting with Stepan Zakharovich Apresyan? If so, why wait until now to make such a wild claim?

"Of course, of course," said Strauss as if waving away a trifle. "Still, I'm afraid the letter caught the president's eye, and so ..." Strauss paused dramatically, and Oppie got the solid impression the older man was enjoying himself mightily. "... and so the A.E.C. has prepared its own letter." He hefted a document and riffled its many pages as if he himself were shocked at how lengthy it was. "Naturally," he said, "this is just a draft. It will require General Nichols's signature, as general manager of the commission, but he hasn't signed it yet."

"Yet?" repeated Oppenheimer.

"Here," said Strauss, handing it over. "Have a look." He gestured for Oppie to take a seat at the mirror-like table; Robert did so. As was his habit with lengthy correspondence, he went straight to the end, which said:

> ... *in view of these allegations which, until disproved, raise questions as to your veracity, conduct and even your loyalty, your employment on Atomic Energy Commission work and your eligibility for access to restricted data are hereby suspended, effective immediately.*

"This is contemptible," Oppie said, looking up.

"'Comprehensive' would be a better word, I think," said Nichols. "Twenty-four charges, I believe."

Oppie went back to the first page and started reading—quickly as always; he could absorb a paragraph at a glance. "Well," he said, "some of this I simply deny." He flipped the page. "And some is flat-out wrong." Flip. Flip. Flip. "But I suppose bits of this do fall into the category of *nolo contendere.*"

Neither Strauss nor Nichols had any Latin, apparently, or any legal training; both were frowning at him. "That is," Oppie said, "I would choose not to contest some of these—" he hated the word Nichols had used; a summary of a man's life is not the same thing as a list of charges "— points."

"That would be wise," said Nichols. "There is extensive documentation for each one."

Oppie had reached the last page again and he pointed to the space for Nichols's signature. "But, as you said, it hasn't been signed."

"No," agreed Strauss, frowning—but the frown looked like a smirk in the reflection from below. "And, of course, it doesn't have to be. I mean, there's no need for a full investigation unless ..."

"Unless I want to keep my security clearance and my consulting position."

Strauss smiled—a vile, reptilian rictus—and leaned over, tapping a part of the final page. "In which case, I believe this paragraph applies." Oppie read it:

> *To assist in the resolution of this matter, you have the privilege of appearing before an Atomic Energy Commission personnel security board. To avail yourself of Atomic Energy Commission hearing procedures, you must, within 30 days following receipt of this letter, submit to me, in writing, your reply to the information outlined above and request the opportunity of appearing before the personnel security board.*

"So, if I go quietly ...?" said Oppie. "If I resign ...?"

"Then we burn that letter of charges, and General Nichols doesn't have to autograph anything."

"But I have the ..." he paused, then spit out the word, "*'privilege'* of defending myself in a hearing, if I choose to fight?"

"Those are indeed the alternatives," said Strauss, "but we—*they*—did take the liberty of drawing up a letter of resignation for you." He took a sheet off his desk and pulled a Mont Blanc fountain pen from his jacket pocket. "Sign *this* one, and no one will ever have to see *that* one again. But if you don't—well, there'd have to be an investigation into each one of the—how many did you say, Nick?"

"Twenty-four."

The West Virginian frowned again as if the number were bigger than he'd remembered. "They'd have to investigate each of the twenty-four charges. Review all the available documents, question witnesses—colleagues, family, friends. A trial, as it were." Strauss adopted an avuncular tone. "So much bother, really; hardly worth it."

Oppie wasn't smoking but he did blow out air. "Boy, you guys really play for keeps, don't you?"

Strauss had a wry smile now. "Yes, Dr. Oppenheimer. Of course we play for keeps."

"Do hey know about this up on Capitol Hill?"

A twitch of the mouth. "Not yet."

"How long do I have to decide?"

"Oh, there's no rush," said Strauss, now the soul of magnanimity. "Take your time. I'll be home at eight tonight. Why not call me then with your answer?"

"Tonight?" Oppie felt his eyes widening. "It's already"—he looked at his Timex "— almost four. I ..." He swallowed then found some strength. "I need to talk to my lawyer."

"Of course, of course," said Strauss. "You took the train in from Princeton, I imagine. Do you need a lift? I'll ask my chauffeur to drive you wherever you wish."

Would he? thought Oppie. Would he drive me all the way to Perro Caliente? Drive me far, far away from all this madness? Drive me to somewhere peaceful and calm?

"Thank you," Oppie said stiffly as he rose. "That's very kind of you." He reached for the letter of charges, but Strauss put a hand on Oppie's forearm.

"Oh, I'm afraid we can't let you have that. Wouldn't do to have an unsigned version floating around—could cause all sorts of confusion."

"So I'm to go by my memory when discussing this with counsel?"

"Doctor, a man of your intellect? You must remember every little thing, no?"

No, thought Oppie, looking at Strauss. *But apparently* you *do.*

Kitty had come to Washington with Robert. That evening, he rendezvoused with her at the home of his lawyer, Herbert Marks, in Georgetown; Herb's wife Anne had been Oppie's secretary back on the mesa.

"It's bullshit, is what it is," Herb said. "You *saved* this country, and now some frothing megalomaniac is trying to bring you down."

"You can't just give in," said Kitty. Herb and Anne were not privy to the Arbor Project, so Kitty added vaguely and yet pointedly, "Not with everything that's at stake."

Anne agreed. "You're half the reason there *are* atomic secrets to begin with! Without what we accomplished under you at Los Alamos, there'd be no atomic bombs." They were seated around a small table with folding legs, the kind used for playing bridge. Oppie was in the east position. Anne, at north, put a hand on his forearm. "Resigning would be just plain wrong. Eisenhower has far too many warmongers whispering in his ear; he *needs* to hear your voice."

"I don't know," Oppie said, sounding bone-weary even to himself. Words that were familiar to him, but not anyone else at the table, bubbled up and out, a phrase from Jean's suicide note of years ago: "I am disgusted with everything."

"It's all right," said Herb. "We'll draft a response, let them know that you want—hell, demand!—a hearing. No one sweeps J. Robert Oppenheimer aside!"

Oppie tried to lift his lips in a smile, but he doubted he succeeded. Still, Strauss could stew by his phone all night; the reply would be delivered, in writing, tomorrow.

It took hours to craft it. Oppie felt increasingly disoriented, so Kitty took charge, vetoing anything that was wishy-washy legalese. He would refuse to resign, and Strauss and Nichols—nasty, conniving bastards, the pair of them—would know why. "Take this down," Kitty said to Anne, who was skilled at shorthand: "'I have thought most earnestly of the alternative suggested. Under the circumstances this course of action would mean that I believe—'"

"'Accept and concur,'" proffered Herb.

"Yes, yes," said Kitty: "'... that I accept and concur that I am not fit to serve this government that I have now served for some ...' Robert?"

He managed to get the figure out: "Twelve years."

"'—for some twelve years. This I *cannot* do.'"

"Exactly," said Anne as she wrote. "Fuck them."

Kitty nodded and went on. "'If I *were* thus unworthy I could hardly have served our country as I have tried—'"

"'Or been director of—'" said Herb.

"Right," said Kitty. "'... or been the director of our Institute in Princeton, or have spoken, as on more than one occasion I have found myself speaking, in the name of science.'"

"'And our country?'" suggested Anne.

"Yes!" said Kitty. "Perfect. '... in the name of our science and our country.'"

"Oppie?" asked Herb. "Does all that sound good to you?"

I wanted to live ... and to give ... and I got paralyzed somehow.

Robert rose. "I'm dead," he said. They'd already arranged to spend the night. He summoned what little strength he still had and trudged up to the guest bedroom.

Kitty was in the Marks's kitchen, pouring herself another glass of wine, when she heard the crash. She raced to the stairs and beat Anne and Herbert to the top. The guest room was empty, but the adjacent bathroom had its door closed.

"Robert!" Kitty called, rapping knuckles on the white-painted wood. "Robert!"

There was no reply. She tried to open the door, and at first thought he'd locked it—but no. Something was blocking it. *Oh, God!* It was Robert's body. He had fallen or collapsed.

With Anne and Herb's help, she managed to push the door—and her husband!—enough that she could slip inside. Robert was a heap of long limbs on the floor, but, yes, he *was* breathing. They'd all been drinking, Robert even more than usual, and—*shit!*—there, open and—*fuck!*—empty: Kitty's bottle of prescription sleeping pills.

"Call a doctor!" she shouted. "Quickly!"

Anne ran off to do that, and Kitty and Herb got Robert to his feet. They walked him to the short leather couch in the guest room and got him to sit up on it. He soon roused a little but was mumbling, his words almost impossible to make out. Kitty thought she heard "ease" or maybe "appease" and "your awful pain" and something crazy like "you gaunt terrible bleeding Jesus." But she couldn't be sure.

Chapter 41

The trouble with Oppenheimer is that he loves a woman who doesn't love him—the United States government.

—Albert Einstein

A shabby room, thought Oppie, for a shabby bit of business. The hearing was being held on the second floor of a building simply called T-3, one of a flock of dilapidated temporary structure slapped together early in the war on the National Mall between the Washington Monument and the Lincoln Memorial.

Gordon Gray, the president of the University of North Carolina, was chairing the security-clearance review board. At forty-four, Gray was five years younger than Oppie. He rapped a wooden gavel against its circular stand. "The hearing will now resume. I should like to ask Dr. Oppenheimer whether he wishes to testify under oath in this proceeding?"

Oppie nodded. "Surely."

"You are not required to do so," said Gray.

"I think it best," said Oppie, rising.

"J. Robert Oppenheimer, do you swear that the testimony you are to give the board shall be the truth, the whole truth, and nothing but the truth, so help you God?"

God, he suspected, probably didn't feel He owed Prometheus any favors—but Robert supposed it couldn't hurt to ask. "I do."

Roger Robb, lead counsel for the Atomic Energy Commission, was a sharp-featured forty-six-year-old with slicked-back dark hair. When he smiled, it looked pained, like he'd just taken a football to the gut. "Doctor," he said, "let me ask you a blunt question. Don't you know, and didn't you know certainly by 1943, that the Communist Party was an instrument of espionage in this country?"

Gray and the other two board members sat at a baize-covered mahogany table, black binders full of classified documents piled in front of them. Two more tables, pushed together along their short edges ran down the middle of the room, with Oppie's lawyers and Kitty on one side, and, on the other, Roger Robb plus squinty-eyed C. Arthur Rolander, the A.E.C.'s deputy director of security, who had helped prepare the case against Oppenheimer.

Oppie tried for a conversational tone. "I wasn't clear about it."

Robb rose and moved close to Oppie. "Didn't you suspect it?"

A small shake of the head. "No."

"What did you know about George Eltenton's background in 1943 when this Eltenton-Chevalier episode occurred?"

Oppie ticked off facts on long fingers, starting with the tobacco-stained index one and working his way toward the pinkie, with its charred tip, the effect of his habitually using it to brush ash off his burning cigarettes: "That he was an Englishman; that he was a chemical engineer; that he had spent some time in the Soviet Union; that he was employed, I think, at Shell Development Company."

"How did you know all those things?"

Oppie lit his pipe. "Well, about the Shell Development Company, I suppose he or someone else working there told me. As for the background in Russia, I don't remember. That he was an Englishman was obvious."

"Why?"

"His accent."

"You were fairly well acquainted with him, were you not?"

"No. I think we probably saw each other no more than four or five times."

Or six.

"When did you first mention your conversation with Chevalier to any security officer?"

"I didn't do it that way. I first mentioned Eltenton."

"Yes?"

"On a visit to Berkeley."

"Was that to Lieutenant Johnson?"

"I don't remember, but it was to a security officer there."

"If the record shows that it was to Lieutenant Lyall Johnson on August 25, 1943, you would accept that?"

"I would accept that."

"I think your first interview with Johnson was quite brief, was it not?"

"That's right. I think I said little more than that Eltenton was somebody to worry about."

"Yes."

"Then I was asked: why did I say this?" He waited for Robb to prod him to go on, but the—the *prosecutor;* he was that in all but title—simply stood, waiting for Robert to continue. And, at last, an acidic taste in his mouth, cramps in his stomach, he did so. "Then I invented a ..." Damn it, damn it, damn it. He exhaled, inhaled, and finished the thought: "... a cock-and-bull story."

Robb nodded, but there was a restrained glee in his eyes, the kind he might have shown when someone agreed to sell him an item for five dollars that he knew was worth fifty. "You were interviewed the next day by Colonel Pash, were you not?"

"That's right."

"That was quite a lengthy interview, was it not?"

"I didn't think it was that long."

"Did you tell Pash the truth about this thing?"

The room was arranged—no doubt at Robb's urging—so that from Oppie's point of view there was a window behind the tribunal; the background was brighter than the foreground, and it was giving Robert a headache. Perhaps, under better circumstances, he'd have found a way to give nuance to his response. But all he did was utter, "No."

"You *lied* to him?" said Robb, in a mock perish-the-thought tone.

Misled, perhaps; misinformed, like Rick had been about the waters in Casablanca. But *lied?* Such a bald label. Oppie tipped his head. "Yes."

"What did you tell Pash that was not true?"

Another inhalation, then: "That Eltenton had attempted to approach three members of the project through intermediaries."

"*Three* members of the project?"

"Through intermediaries."

"Intermediar*ies?*"

"Through *an* intermediary."

"So that we may be clear, did you disclose to Pash the identity of Chevalier?"

"No."

"Let us refer, then, for the time being, to Chevalier as X."

"All right."

"Did you tell Pash that X had approached three persons on the project?"

Oppie crossed his legs one way, then the other. "I am not clear whether I said there were three Xs or ... or that X approached three people."

"Didn't you say that X had approached three people?"

Oppie looked down. "Probably."

"Why did you do that, Doctor?"

Why did he do that?

That was indeed the question.

Why?

All those years ago—damn near thirty!—he'd been hauled into the office of the head of the Cavendish Laboratory, accompanied by his parents, who had been visiting Cambridge. His father brought along the latest acquisition for his art collection, a Renoir portrait of a young girl purchased from a London gallery ("a little something for above the lab's fireplace," Julius had said with a wink, as he handed it over). Robert had been asked to explain why, oh, why he'd coated the apple meant for his tutor, Patrick Blackett, with cyanide.

But he *couldn't* explain—not then, not in front of his parents. He couldn't tell them how his heart, and other parts, yearned for Blackett, how, as Pauli had recently been saying, the universe would not allow both of them to occupy the same space, and so—don't you see?—one *had* to go. Instead, he'd offered an answer that belied his intellect, thus denying his defining characteristic, but left private matters private.

And now, here, in Washington, he took a deep breath and repeated his reply from back then, verbatim, in a low, diffident tone. "Because," he said, "I was ... an idiot."

Robb made a sound in his throat. "Is that your only explanation, Doctor?"

Oppie roused a little. "I was ... reluctant to mention Chevalier."

"Yes."

"No doubt somewhat reluctant to mention myself."

"Yes. But why would you tell him that Chevalier had gone to *three* people?"

It had worked at the Cavendish, damn it all. Soon enough he'd been on his way, briefly into the care of Freud's disciple Ernest Jones and then off to Göttingen. But you can't change one, let alone many, experimental parameters and expect the same result. "I have no explanation for that," Robert said, his voice still soft, "except the one already offered."

"Didn't that make it all the worse for Chevalier?"

"I didn't mention Chevalier."

"No, but X."

Robert frowned, considering this, then tilted his head in agreement. "It would have."

"Certainly! In other words, if X had gone to three people that would have shown, would it not—"

"— that he was deeply involved."

"That he was deeply involved! That it was *not* just a casual conversation."

"Right."

"And you knew that, didn't you?"

Knew? Could have reasoned out, perhaps. Might have hypothesized. But *knew?* Oppie shrugged a little. "Yes."

Robb was brandishing a transcript. "Did you tell Colonel Pash that X had told you that the information would be transmitted through someone at the Russian consulate?" Oppie, feeling nauseated, said nothing. *"Did you?"*

"I would have said not, but I clearly see that I must have."

"If X had said that, that would have shown conclusively that it was a criminal conspiracy, would it not?"

If ... If ... "That's right."

"Did Pash ask you for the name of X?"

"I imagine he did."

"Don't you know whether he did?"

"Sure."

"Did he tell you *why* he wanted it?"

"In order to stop the business."

"He told you that it was a very serious matter, didn't he?"

"I don't recollect that, but he certainly would have."

"You *knew* that he wanted to investigate it, did you not?"

"That's right."

"And didn't you know, Doctor, that by refusing to give the name of X you were impeding the investigation?"

He looked at Kitty, impassive next to Lloyd Garrison, Oppie's lead attorney, then back at Robb, practically a silhouette, looming in front of him. "I must have known that."

"You knew, Doctor, that Colonel Pash and his organization would move heaven and earth to find those three people, didn't you?"

"It makes sense."

"And you knew that they would move heaven and earth to find out the identity of X, didn't you?"

"Yes."

"And yet you wouldn't tell them?"

Except for the upward lilt, it wasn't a question, but, as the silence grew, Oppie replied, "That is true."

"How long had you known this man Chevalier in 1943?"

"Perhaps five years. Five or six, probably."

"How had you known him?"

"As a quite close friend."

"He followed the Party line pretty closely, didn't he?"

"Yes, I imagine he did."

"Did you have any reason to suspect he was a member of the Communist Party?"

"No."

"You knew he was quite a Red, didn't you?"

"I would say quite Pink."

"Not Red?"

"I won't quibble."

"You say in your answer that you *still* consider him a friend."

"I do."

"Doctor, I would like to go back with you, if I may, to your interview with Colonel Pash on August twenty-sixth, 1943. Is there any doubt now that you *did* mention to Pash a man attached to the Soviet consul?"

"I had completely forgotten it. I can only rely on the transcript."

"Doctor, for your information, I might say we have a record of your voice."

Jesus fucking Christ. "Sure."

"Do you have any doubt you said that?"

"No."

"Was that true? Had there been a mention of a man connected with the Soviet consul?"

"I am fairly certain not."

"Dr. Oppenheimer, don't you think you told a story in great detail that was fabricated?"

Oppie exhaled noisily. His pipe had gone out, but he passed it nervously from hand to hand. "I certainly did."

"Why did you go into great circumstantial detail about this thing if you were telling a"—Robb made quotation marks with his fingers—"'cock-and-bull' story?"

Oppie could feel his heart hammering. He shook his head slightly, not in negation but as if trying to get loose components to fall back into place. His tone had become defensive, high-pitched. "I fear that this whole thing is a piece of idiocy. I'm afraid I can't explain why there was a consul, why there were three people approached on the project, why two of them were supposedly at Los Alamos. All of that seems wholly false to me."

"You will agree, would you not, sir, that if the story you told to Colonel Pash was true, it made things look very bad for Mr. Chevalier?"

Oppie coughed. "For anyone involved in it, yes, sir."

"Including you?"

"Right."

"Isn't it a fair statement today, Dr. Oppenheimer, that, according to your testimony now, you told not one lie to Colonel Pash but a whole fabrication and tissue of lies?"

It wasn't a criminal proceeding, Oppie knew; it wasn't even a trial. If only it *had* been. *No person shall be compelled in any criminal case to be a witness against himself.* Ah, but apparently the Fifth was for tax frauds and grifters, not those who had won wars.

He closed his eyes, closed them tight, closed them as if against a blinding, piercing explosion. "Right," he said, the word all but lost to the wind.

Chapter 42

I go to my office at the Institute solely for the privilege of walking home with Kurt Gödel.

—Albert Einstein

On his visits to the I.A.S., Dick Feynman had observed the ritual often enough to discern its pattern. Kurt Gödel's office was in room 210 of Fuld Hall, directly above Johnny von Neumann's. Albert Einstein was seventy-five now, and his hearing was failing, but Helen Dukas, his secretary, apparently knew the distinctive echo Gödel's footfalls made as he descended the east staircase, and she would alert Albert as soon as they'd begun. By the time Gödel, who would turn forty-eight at the end of this month, was making his way along the first-floor hallway, Helen would have gotten Einstein into his jacket.

Oppenheimer wasn't at the I.A.S. currently—he was in Washington, dealing with that security-hearing bullshit—and so there was no one here today to play policeman, meaning, as far as Dick was concerned, this was the perfect opportunity.

When visiting the Institute, Feynman normally worked in the east library on the second floor. At just thirty-six, he was fleeter of foot than either the arthritic Einstein or the valetudinarian Gödel, and he'd started moving as soon as he'd heard Gödel emerge from his office across the hall. Dick was down the central staircase and out the main doors before the east door had debouched either of the older physicists.

When they did emerge—Gödel in something parka-like against imaginary cold, Einstein with just a light jacket over a cardigan that protruded below the jacket's hem—Dick boldly strode over to them. "Why, Professor Einstein! Dr. Gödel! What a pleasant surprise!"

Einstein's hooded eyes focused on him, and it was clear he was trying to place the face.

"Dick Feynman. I work with Hans Bethe at Cornell."

That merited a nod.

"And John Wheeler was my thesis supervisor."

"Ah, Wheeler!" said Einstein, clearly pleased. Interest in general relativity had waned during the thirties and forties, but Wheeler had done much of late to revive it.

Gödel, peering imploringly through round glasses, had said nothing but was clearly counting on Einstein to dispense with this interloper. Everyone knew that the Einstein-Gödel walks were sacrosanct.

Dick was indeed conscious that he was intruding. True, he was known for not being intimidated by great men—Niels Bohr prized his company precisely because he was perfectly willing to shoot down the Nobelist's ideas. But, damn it all, a chance to talk with the greatest physicist of all time *and* the greatest logician since Aristotle was not to be passed up. And one or the other of them just might have the answer he needed.

It was a little before 2:00 p.m.—neither of the older men kept long office hours—and Dick rubbed his hands together appreciatively. "Such a beautiful day for a walk. May I join you?"

The habitually taciturn Gödel was wearing a white linen fedora. "Actually ..."

Dick knew in this case he *would* have to offer a present up front if he was going to get what he wanted. "Dr. Gödel, I'm fascinated by your concept of a rotating universe. Won't you explain it to me?"

To his delight, Einstein added, "*Ja, Kurt!* See if you can make it make sense to *him.*" The wizened face turned to Feynman. "I don't understand it myself."

Feynman started walking backward, facing the other two. He knew where they were going, of course—the mile-long journey to Einstein's house at 112

Mercer Street, after which Gödel would continue alone to his own abode, 1.6 miles farther on, at 145 Linden Lane.

Gödel wasn't yet convinced. "You're not a spy?" he said in his thick German accent.

Feynman tried not to laugh. Gödel's paranoia was almost as legendary as his hypochondria. "No, sir. I'm part of the Arbor Project. I'm working with Kitty Oppenheimer and Leo Szilard."

"The death of humanity," said Gödel, with no apparent regret. "It was inevitable."

"Not if we can help it," said Dick.

"You could still be a spy. Klaus Fuchs was."

Dick knew this wasn't the time to mention that he and Klaus had, in fact, been pals at Los Alamos. "I play the bongos. No one trying to be inconspicuous would do that."

"There, you see!" crowed Einstein, delighted. "Logic, Kurt!"

"All right, all right," said Gödel, holding up his hands. "Rotating universes, is it? Very well."

Dick turned around and fell in next to Gödel—he didn't have the *chutzpah* to try to take the place between Gödel and Einstein. Most of quantum physics had left these two behind—"we are museum pieces!" Einstein was said to have exclaimed recently—and they rarely spoke to any other scientists anymore.

"Albert thinks the universe is immortal and immutable, and he has added his 'cosmological constant' to relativity to ensure that," said Gödel. "To make the universe beautiful, he says, because he thinks aesthetics are important! But me? I'm a simple man—I love the pink flamingo on my lawn, which Albert dismisses as *kitsch*—and I will force nothing to *be* a certain way just so that it is more appealing to the mind's eye. We can dispense with the cosmological constant if we are willing to assume either an expanding universe—"

"Such nonsense!" declared Einstein.

"— or," continued Gödel, "if we allow for one that rotates." They turned left on Olden Lane. Einstein, frowning, lit his pipe. "And one that rotates does produce an exact solution to Albert's field equations."

"And in such a universe," Feynman provided, to show he was following along, "the centrifugal force caused by the rotation of the universe would keep everything from collapsing under the force of gravity."

"But to propose a universe so finely tuned!" said Einstein. "Nonsense."

"Maybe," said Gödel, amiably. "Or maybe we'll find someday that *any* universe that can support cohesive matter, complex chemistry, and eventually life must be finely tuned. Eternity is the concert, but you must tune your violin before you begin to play it, Albert."

"Except you don't believe in eternity," declared Einstein.

And this, Feynman knew, was the key point. Gödel's rotating universe allowed for what he called closed time-like curves, in which paths through space-time loop back on themselves, permitting, as his paper on the topic said, "travel into any region of the past, present, and future, and back again." Indeed, his theory had such curves passing through every four-dimensional point: regardless of where or when you were, you were on a closed time-like curve and theoretically able to follow the loop backward or forward. That meant there was nothing special about the future as opposed to the past—or about the present.

Einstein was happy to accept that there was no one "present"—no "now" universally shared by all; that notion was one of the cornerstone breakthroughs of relativity. But he also held nonetheless that for any individual the past was both *done* (immutably fixed) and *gone* (no longer existed in any material sense). Conversely, he contended the future didn't yet exist, and therefore was uncertain and malleable. In contrast, the closed time-like curves Gödel was postulating gave no special character to any class of moments—none were irretrievably gone, nothing was forever written in stone, everything was up for grabs.

"An assault on the very nature of time!" Einstein declared as they came to the intersection of Olden Lane and Mercer Street. Appropriately, they did not meet orthogonally, but rather obliquely to their right and acutely to their left. In curved space-time, no true right angles really existed.

They continued to argue as they walked along Mercer. The shade was intermittent; many trees were still acquiring their spring wigs of leaves.

"Besides," continued Einstein, "we clearly do *not* live in a rotating universe. Such a universe would not appear like, say, a geologist's solid-rock core sample when spun, in which everything would seem to rotate at the same speed. No, general relativity demands in such a universe that far-away galaxies should be seen rotating slowly around us—and they aren't."

"Oh, I know, I know," said Gödel. "I don't argue for one second that my metric describes *our* universe—merely one that *your* equations make possible."

"But, you know," Dick said, "we *should* be living in a rotating universe. There are an infinite number of possible rotating universes, including one degree clockwise per day, two degrees clockwise per day, and so on, plus the equally infinite counter-clockwise versions. But there's only *one* non-rotating possibility: zero degrees in either direction. And I distrust anything that is a special case."

"As one should," said Einstein. "But the observational evidence is clear."

Einstein's white-clad house was just a block and a half up Mercer from where they'd turned, and soon enough they were upon it. The three now stood outside its small wrought-iron gate, and Dick hoped briefly that Einstein would invite them in. But instead he said, "A pleasure, young man. And Kurt, although I don't believe in closed time-like curves, I *do* look forward to reversing our course tomorrow morning."

Gödel tipped his fedora at his friend, and Einstein made his slow way through the gate and up the four steps to his front door. Feynman and Gödel stood there, and it was clear by his fidgeting that Gödel wished Dick would go off in a separate direction now—that damned paranoia again. And so, since it was make-or-break, Dick dived in. "But what if our universe *is* rotating in a way that would make it seem like it *isn't?*"

"You mean a very slow rotational speed?"

"No. But you know what John Wheeler proposed: that maybe there's only one electron in the entire universe, and it just keeps moving backward and forward in time so that there seem to be a gazillion of them?"

"Ah, yes. *Furchtbar herzig.* A charming conceit."

"But what John didn't take into account is that an electron moving backward in time is a positron. My diagrams—"

"Oh!" interrupted Gödel. *"That's* who you are! The young man with the squiggles."

Feynman grinned. "Guilty as charged. Anyway, of course, if an object containing an electron moving into the future happens to be rotating clockwise, it can be considered just as validly as that same object containing a positron rotating counter-clockwise."

Gödel's eyes closed for a longer-than-normal blink as he visualized this. "Right, yes. Of course, this isn't Uhlenbeck's electron spin, but—"

"No. Electrons and positrons spin in the same direction. I'm talking about the gross physical rotation of whatever object the electron or the positron happens to be part of. If something is corkscrewing right as it goes into the future, it'll be corkscrewing left as it moves into the past."

Gödel nodded.

"Well," continued Dick, "suppose our universe flickers back and forth, almost instantaneously, between being matter and anti-matter, with electrons changing into positrons and back again as if they were ..." Dick waved his hand vaguely.

"Sort of ... oscillating?" offered Gödel. "No one has ever suggested such a thing for fundamental particles before."

"I know but think about it. If the universe oscillates quickly between matter and anti-matter—between being made of matter particles moving forward in time within a universe rotating clockwise and being made of anti-matter particles going backward in time as part of a universe rotating counter-clockwise—the net effect would be zero overall *apparent* rotation."

"And then even *our* own, actual universe could be permeated by closed time-like curves!" declared Gödel. "What an interesting thought! Of course, there'd be some jittering—"

"Like Brownian motion or the saccades of the eye, only orders of magnitude more rapid."

"Right," said Gödel. "Quite beyond the ability of any of our current instruments to detect—but, in theory, experimentally testable and falsifiable." He looked Feynman up and down, apparently assessing the risks, and, to Dick's delight, he said, "Won't you walk me the rest of the way home? Let's talk this through!"

Chapter 43

What a pity that they attacked him and not some nice guy like Bethe. Now we have all to be on Oppenheimer's side!

—Enrico Fermi

Roger Robb rose again from his chair and looked at Oppie. The sun wasn't behind the lawyer, and Oppie could for once clearly see his carnivorous, sharp-featured face. "Doctor, may we again refer to your written submission to this board, please, sir? On page four: 'In the spring of 1936, I had been introduced by a friend to Jean Tatlock, the daughter of a noted professor of English at the university, and, in the autumn, I began to court her. We were at least twice close enough to marriage to think of ourselves as engaged.'" Oppie nodded and Robb went on. "However, Doctor, between 1939 and 1944, as I understand it, your acquaintance with Miss Tatlock had become fairly casual. Is that right?"

In the afternoon light, Oppie could also see Kitty. She had fallen recently, breaking her leg, which was now in a cast; a pair of crutches leaned against the wall behind her, birch sentinels. Her face was a study in composure, but she was gripping the wooden arms of her chair, red painted nails stark against fingers drained of blood.

"I don't think it would be right to say that our acquaintance was 'casual,'" Oppie replied slowly. "We had been very much involved with one another, and there was still very deep ..." He looked at Kitty again. "... feeling when we saw each other."

Robb nodded. "How many times would you say you saw her between 1939 and 1944?"

"That's five years. Would ten times be a good guess?"

"What were the occasions for your seeing her?"

"Of course, sometimes we saw each other socially with other people. I remember visiting her around New Year's of 1941."

"Where?"

"I went to her house or to the hospital she worked at, I don't know which, and we went out for a drink at the Top of the Mark. I remember that she came more than once to visit our home in Berkeley."

Robb swung to face Kitty. "Visit you and Mrs. Oppenheimer?"

"Right," said Oppie. "Her father lived around the corner from us in Berkeley. I visited her there once. And ... I visited her, as I think I said earlier, in June or July of 1943."

"I believe you said, in connection with that, that you 'had to see her.'"

Oppie forced his eyes not to go back to Kitty. "Yes."

"Why did you have to see her?"

"She had indicated a great desire to see me before we left for Los Alamos. At that time I couldn't go. For one thing, I wasn't supposed to say where we were going." Robb looked like he was about to prod for more, so Oppie went on. "I felt that she *had* to see me. She was undergoing psychiatric treatment. She was ... extremely unhappy."

"Did you find out why she had to see you?"

Eyes straight ahead. "Because she was still in love with me."

"Where did you see her?"

"At her home on Telegraph Hill."

"When did you see her after that?"

"She took me to the airport, and I never saw her again."

"That was 1943?"

"Yes."

"Was she a Communist at that time?"

"We didn't even talk about it. I doubt it."

"You have said in your written answer that you knew she had been a Communist."

"Yes. I knew that in the fall of 1936."

"Was there any reason for you to believe that she *wasn't* still a Communist in 1943?"

Oppie uncrossed his legs. "No."

"You spent the night with her, didn't you?"

He struggled to keep the syllable even, natural, uninflected. "Yes."

A sharp intake of breath from Kitty.

Robb's voice took on a note of incredulity. "That is when you were working on a secret war project?"

Again: even. Steady as she goes. "Yes."

"Did you think that consistent with good security?"

And now, rallying somewhat: "It *was,* as a matter of fact. Not a word—" But he could see Robb's feigned astonishment, and, worse, the real shock on the faces of the three members of the board who would decide his fate. He dropped his gaze to the floor and lowered his voice. "It was not good practice."

When Robb finally finished at half past four, Chairman Gray called an adjournment. Oppie got up from the couch and quickly moved to fetch Kitty's crutches for her, but Lloyd Garrison beat him to it. She moved purposely, the twin supports swinging like the pendulums of grandfather clocks. "Kitty," he said in a low voice, as he pulled up next to her, "I'm sorry."

She kept her eyes straight ahead. "Yes," she said, in a savage whisper. "You certainly are."

It was an ordeal getting downstairs from room 2022, and Kitty pointedly let Garrison, not Oppie, carry her crutches as she hopped down backward, one hand gripping the only banister.

When they were out on the National Mall again, Oppie took stock; Kitty, he noted, was doing the same thing. The fury she'd been radiating moments ago had shifted, and he saw in her eyes the same look she'd had when they'd closed up One Eagle Hill for the move to Olden Manor, the wistfulness that went with being unsure if they'd ever return.

This morning, when they'd arrived for the day's proceedings, it hadn't seemed such a long walk from here to the White House, due north of the temporary office building. But now? Now it looked impossibly distant. And off to the east, the Capitol Dome might as well have been on another continent, another world. Not visible from here but hitherto just a short drive across the Potomac, the Pentagon, too, he knew was almost certainly out of his reach now. Edwin Hubble had been right: the universe was expanding—and all the corridors of power, all the places where Oppie had once held sway, were receding from him.

Wednesday, April 21, 1954, was the day before Oppie's fiftieth birthday. Instead of lead counsel Lloyd Garrison, who had proven ineffective, Robert's long-standing personal attorney Herb Marks—he of the night of the sleeping-pills overdose—was asking the questions this session. That gave Oppie some confidence. Buoying him even more was that the questions were being asked of the formidable Isidor Isaac Rabi.

"Dr. Rabi," said Herb, "have you spoken to Chairman Lewis Strauss of the Atomic Energy Commission on behalf of Dr. Oppenheimer?" Marks stretched the chairman's name into Lewis's idiosyncratic pronunciation.

"Absolutely," declared Rabi. When he wasn't testifying, Oppie was relegated to a shopworn couch behind the witness stand. That meant that he couldn't see the witness's face, but he suspected Rabi's eyes—almost as sad and wise as Einstein's—were fixed not on Herb Marks, who, after all, was merely a means to an end, but on Gordon Gray, chairman of the security board. "I never hid my opinion from Mr. Strauss that I thought the suspension of Dr. Oppenheimer's clearance was a very unfortunate thing and should not have been done."

Rabi had an impassioned way of speaking that Oppie enjoyed even under mundane circumstances. But today, the Nobel laureate was on fire. "In other words, there he was: he was a consultant, and if you don't want to consult the guy, you don't consult him, period!" A shake of the head, and then, in a disgusted tone: "Why you have to then proceed to suspend clearance and go through all this ..." He spread his arms, encompassing the room, then, with a world-weary sense of unfairness, added, "It didn't seem called for against a man who had accomplished what Dr. Oppenheimer has accomplished."

Herb Marks looked like he was going to interrupt. *God, no!* thought Oppie. Let Rabi go on!

And the Nobelist did just that, leaning forward in the witness chair. "There is a real, positive record. We have an A-bomb and a whole series of it, and we have a whole series of super bombs." He lifted his arms in exasperation. "What more do you want, mermaids? This is just a tremendous achievement! If the end of that road is this kind of hearing, which can't help but be humiliating"—again, a shake of the mighty head—"I think it's a pretty bad show."

Oppie clamped his pipe stem between his teeth and folded his arms across his chest. He even allowed himself a moment of amusement as Roger Robb rose for cross-examination: Robb was about to question Rabi about Robert. But his smile soon faded.

"Dr. Rabi," said Robb with that kicked-in-the-gut smile of his, "getting back to the Chevalier incident, if you had been put in that position, you of course would have told the whole truth about it, wouldn't you?"

"I am," said Rabi genially, "naturally a truthful person."

"You would not have lied about it?"

"Look," said Rabi, "I take a serious view of that incident, but I don't think it's crucial."

Robb's tone dripped with be-that-as-it-may scorn. "Of course, Doctor, you don't know what Dr. Oppenheimer's testimony before this board about that incident may have been, do you?"

Rabi crammed all four syllables of *irrelevant* into one prim "No."

"So," said Robb, sharply, "the board may be in a better position to judge than you."

"It may be," conceded Rabi. But Oppie was pleased that his old friend wasn't giving up: "On the other hand, *I* am in possession of a long experience with this man, going back to *1929,* which is *twenty-five years.* There is a kind of seat-of-the-pants feeling upon which I myself lay great weight."

"Of course," said Robb dismissively. "But as a scientist evaluating, say, an explosion, you perhaps would be in a better position having witnessed it than somebody who had not, is that right?"

Rabi lifted his arms in exasperation. "I am not fencing with you. I really don't know what you are getting at."

The prosecutor's tone was unctuous. "I am not fencing with you, either."

The Columbia professor replied, "If you are saying that an eyewitness to something can give a better account of it than a historian, that I don't know. Historians would deny it." He waved a hand. "It's a semantic question."

"Let me get back again to the concrete," said Robb. "Would you agree, Doctor, that in evaluating the Chevalier incident one should consider what Dr. Oppenheimer *says* happened together with the testimony of persons such as yourself?"

"Wait a minute. I didn't testify to that incident. I have only heard about it."

"Fine. But one who had *heard* Dr. Oppenheimer describe the incident would be in a better position to evaluate it than one who had not, is that correct?"

To Oppie's delight, Rabi was having none of it. "I reserve the right to my own opinion. I am in possession of a long period of association, with keen observation of all sorts of minute reactions. I have seen his mind work. I have seen his sentiments develop. And I will still stick to my right to have my own opinion."

Robb evidently realized he was fighting a losing battle. "Thank you, Doctor." He returned to his seat.

Gordon Gray looked at the other table. "Do you have any more questions?"

Lloyd Garrison nodded at Herb Marks, and Marks rose. "I think I better ask one more question, if the board will indulge me."

Gray nodded.

"Dr. Rabi, in the course of questioning Dr. Oppenheimer, about these circumstances, counsel for the board put the question to him whether the story that he had told the security officers wasn't a fabrication and a tissue of lies, and to this Oppenheimer responded, 'Right.' He accepted counsel's characterization."

Rabi half turned as if to catch a glimpse of Oppie, but they really couldn't make eye contact. Marks went on. "I ask you, Dr. Rabi, whether this leads you to wish to express any further comment?"

Rabi turned fully forward and Oppie suspected he again had his gaze fixed on the seated board rather than Marks. "Look," he said, "there were very strong personal loyalties there, and I take it in mentioning Eltenton he felt he had discharged his full obligation. Yes, anything else was a very foolish action, but I would *not* put a sinister implication to it."

"Are you confident, Dr. Rabi, that Dr. Oppenheimer would not make that kind of mistake again?"

In a *Time* magazine cover story about him, Robert had described his childhood self as an "unctuous, repulsively good little boy." In the 1940s, I.I. Rabi—or so Oppie had heard—had called the adult Robert "a rich spoiled Jewish brat from New York." But if Prince Arjuna could come to accept his responsibilities, apparently so could one Bob Oppenheimer.

"I certainly am," said Rabi. "He is a man who learns with extraordinary rapidity." He held his hands out, palms up, the very scales of justice. "I think he is just a much more mature person than he was then."

Oppie smiled and leaned back on the couch. It was 3:25 p.m., and Gray called a recess until tomorrow. Rabi rose, turned around, and walked toward Oppie, who was rising himself. Robert finally got to see his old friend's face, which, while not beaming, showed the satisfaction of a job well done.

"Thank you," Robert said, taking Rabi's hand. "Thank you."

"Such *tsuris!*" Rabi declared. "Let's hope they got the message. Who's left to testify?"

Kitty, her leg still in a cast, managed to make it over to them by this point. Rabi kissed her on the cheek as she, too, thanked him for his testimony. "Goodness, woman," he said, "what happened to you?"

"Damn stairs at Olden Manor," Kitty replied with a vague gesture. "Took a tumble."

Rabi's expression had just a hint of skepticism, as though he were thinking, *Took a tumbler, you mean.* He turned back to Robert. "Sorry, what were you saying?"

"You asked who was left to testify."

"Oh, right," said Rabi. "And ...?"

Oppie gestured for them to start moving. "Edward Teller."

Rabi instantly froze. "Oh, shit."

Chapter 44

I do really feel it would have been a better world without Teller. I think he is an enemy of humanity.

—I.I. Rabi

"Dr. Teller," said prosecutor Roger Robb, standing in front of the ursine physicist, "may I ask you, sir, at the outset, are you appearing as a witness here today because you want to be here?"

Teller's voice was its usual thickly accented rumble. "I appear because I have been asked to and because I consider it my duty upon request to say what I think in the matter." He shifted in the witness chair, and his artificial foot made a *clack* against the floorboards. "I would have preferred not to appear."

"I believe, sir, that you stated to me some time ago that anything you had to say, you wished to say in the presence of Dr. Oppenheimer?"

"That is correct."

"Is it your intention to suggest that Dr. Oppenheimer is disloyal to the United States?"

From his couch at the rear of the room, Robert saw the back of the head move left and right. "I do not want to suggest anything of the kind." He paused, and Oppie wondered if he was finished, but the Hungarian soon went on. "I know Oppenheimer as an intellectually most alert and very complicated person, and I think it would be presumptuous and wrong on my part if I would try in any way to analyze his motives. But I have always assumed, and I now assume, that he is loyal to the United States. I believe this and I *shall* believe it until I see *very* conclusive proof to the opposite."

Robb nodded curtly. "Now, a question which is the corollary of that. Do you or do you not believe that Dr. Oppenheimer is a security risk?"

There was silence in the courtroom, although through the window, in the distance, a tour guide with a bullhorn was lecturing visitors about the white spire dedicated to the president who couldn't tell a lie.

Teller took a deep breath, the broad shoulders rising. "In a great number of cases I have seen Dr. Oppenheimer act—I understood that Dr. Oppenheimer acted—in a way which for me was exceedingly hard to understand." He shook his head and Oppie imagined him drawing his great shaggy eyebrows together. "I thoroughly disagreed with him in numerous issues and his actions frankly appeared to me confused and ..." He paused as if hoping for a better adjective but concluded with one he'd used before: "... complicated."

Numerous issues. They disagreed about the super—that one thing. Yes, you could divide it into dozens of subtopics, but the gulf between them hadn't been *that* large ... or so Oppie had thought.

"To this extent," Teller continued, "I feel that I would like to see the vital interests of this country in hands which I understand better and therefore trust more. In this very limited sense I would feel personally more secure if public matters would rest in other hands."

Oppie's heart sank. He felt ... he felt like Chevalier must have when he'd learned Robert had named him to the authorities. There was bile in his throat.

Surely that was enough. Surely Robb now had everything he needed. But no. The bastard was insatiable. "Doctor, I would like to ask for your expert opinion again. In your opinion, if Dr. Oppenheimer should go fishing for the rest of his life, what would be the effect upon the atomic-energy and the thermonuclear programs?"

Jesus Christ, thought Oppie. *For fuck's sake.*

"You mean from now on?" asked Teller.

"Yes, sir."

Teller shifted his bulk again. "In that case I should like to say two things.

Within the A.E.C., I should say that whole committees could go fishing without affecting the work of those who are actively engaged in the work." Oppie saw the three members of the board look startled. "In particular, however, the general recommendations that I know have come from Oppenheimer were more frequently—and I mean not only and not even particularly the thermonuclear case but other cases—more frequently a hindrance than a help, and therefore I think that further work of Dr. Oppenheimer on committees would not be helpful."

Robb looked like he was going to speak again, but Chairman Gray held up a hand. "Do you feel that it would endanger the common defense and security to grant clearance to Dr. Oppenheimer?" he asked.

Teller was silent for a time and when he at last spoke there was a note, Oppie thought, of contrition in the husky voice as if his old colleague realized he might have gone too far. "I believe—and that is merely a question of belief and there is no expertness, no real information behind it—that Dr. Oppenheimer's character is such that he would not knowingly and willingly do anything that is designed to endanger the safety of this country. To the extent, therefore, that your question is directed toward intent, I would say I do not see any reason to deny clearance."

Oppie hadn't been aware that he was holding his breath, but it suddenly exploded from him in a relieved sigh.

But Teller wasn't done, damn it all. "But if it is a question of wisdom and judgment, as demonstrated by actions since 1945, then I would say one *would* be wiser *not* to grant clearance." He fell silent for a long moment then added, almost plaintively, "May I limit myself to these comments?"

Gray said yes and dismissed Teller. Oppie had seen the man stand up countless times before. It was always a bit of an ordeal, as Teller had no feeling in his artificial foot. But at last he was erect. Oppie expected him to simply head toward the door, but Edward startled him by turning around and walking toward him. He loomed over Oppie and looked down with pale irises, hooded lids, and unkempt eyebrows. "I'm sorry," he said, offering his hand.

Oppie stared at the hand, so much meatier than his own. But it was his character that was being judged here, and the only thing to do was take it. "After what you've just said," Robert replied softly, "I don't know what you mean."

Teller released his grip, turned, and shuffled toward the exit.

Chapter 45

There is a story behind my story. If a reporter digs deep enough he will find that it is a bigger story than my suspension.

—J. Robert Oppenheimer

There was nothing to do now but go back to Princeton and wait for the security board's verdict. Oppenheimer was in no mood for administrative trivia. He went straight to the second-floor corner office in Building A, which was being used by Rabi's Patient Power group, hoping for some distraction.

"Well," said Luis Alvarez as he paced the hypotenuse between the north and west windows and back again, "if we're hoping to shield the earth from the photospheric purge, we want something that will stay stationary in between the earth and the sun so that the shield is in permanent conjunction from earth's point of view."

"There's no such orbit," said Oppie, with a bit of the old glee he used to employ in shooting down students. "Or, to put it more precisely, there's *only* one such orbit: the only orbit that goes around the sun in precisely 365 and one-quarter days is *this* one, the one occupied by earth."

"What about the Lagrange points?" asked Rabi, seated at the one desk in the room.

Oppie, leaning back in a wooden chair, nodded. In any system in which a small body is under the gravitational influence of two large ones, there are five points at which the small body will theoretically be retained by the gravity of the larger ones, although only two of those points are stable in the long term. In the earth-moon system, the two stable ones are at the points of equilateral triangles that have the earth and the moon at the other vertices.

"L1 is the point that's correctly positioned between the sun and the earth," said Oppie. "That's where any shield should go, but it's not stable. An object at L4 or L5 *would* stay in place—but at 400,000 kilometers ahead or behind the earth's position in its orbit around the sun. No good for a shield."

"Okay, okay," said Alvarez. "But suppose, as we get closer to the actual solar purge, we have bigger and bigger fusion bombs—which, if Teller gets his way, we surely will. And suppose by appropriately rocketing such bombs into the sun itself we could subtly alter the purge date, fine-tuning it a bit, until it landed on a day in which there's naturally a large body shielding the earth from the sun."

"A solar eclipse!" declared Rabi.

"Right," said Alvarez. "If we can't stop the purge, maybe we can regulate to some degree precisely when it occurs. And if we can get it to happen during a total solar eclipse, the moon could take the brunt of the blast, possibly shielding earth."

"The swath of totality is very narrow," said Oppie, "and that's pretty much the same thing as the part of the earth that would be shielded. For the total eclipse coming up next month, it'll only be ninety-five miles wide."

"That's better than nothing," said Alvarez.

"The timing is impossible," Rabi said. "The maximum length of totality in even the best solar eclipse is what—seven minutes? Volkoff is still crunching the numbers to figure out what the duration of the photospheric purge will be—how long from when its leading edge touches the earth until the trailing one does—but it's going to be way longer than seven minutes. As soon as a point on earth moves out of the umbra, it'll be obliterated."

"And," said Oppie, "you're assuming the moon is solid enough to shield earth from the blast."

"Right," said Alvarez. "The whole lunar surface might turn molten, but the actual astronomical body could survive."

"But the moon is very lightweight and not very dense," said Rabi. "I suspect the purge will simply vaporize it."

"We still need to do the math," said Alvarez.

"Oh, we will, we will," said Rabi. "But even if we could get the sun to basically hold its nose until we tell it that it can sneeze—and that's one hell of a tall order—I still don't think it'll work. We need something *dense*—something that could have its outer volatile layers burned away but still leave behind a solid core to shield us."

"An *iron* core," said Oppie. "Like the one the earth has."

Rabi nodded. "Yes. But you can't use the earth to shield itself, obviously."

"No, no!" said Oppie. "But you might be able to use the earth to shield the moon!"

"What do you mean?" asked Alvarez.

"A total *lunar* eclipse: the sun, the earth, and the moon all in a straight line. As I said, the earth's core is probably iron, right? Dense as hell. So, sure the oceans will be boiled off, and the crust burned away, but that iron core *might* survive, and, everything in the core's lee will be shielded from the onslaught. Under the specific geometry of a lunar eclipse, we still lose the earth, but we could, perhaps, see the moon spared. And even if the moon's nearside still gets hammered—the ancient maria running liquid again—the far side might come through unscathed."

"*If* we can control the timing of the purge so that it coincides with a lunar eclipse," said Rabi.

"Yes," agreed Oppie. "A slim chance, to be sure, but it would be a *lot* easier to move large numbers of humans to the far side of the moon than it would be to Mars."

"But we're *sure* that Mars will survive, regardless," said Alvarez. "It's only the slimmest of chances that we could arrange for the earth to shield the moon."

"True," said Oppie. "Mars should still be the primary target, if we can't find some other way to prevent the purge or shield the earth." He looked at the wall clock, Roman numerals orbiting its nucleus. "I'm bushed. These last few weeks have been murder on me. I'll see you tomorrow."

In the end, the verdict in the matter of J. Robert Oppenheimer was delivered in writing. Oppie had just returned home to Olden Manor when the letter arrived, but it was Kitty who, in her cast, had hobbled to the door and dealt with the messenger. She came into the living room bearing the envelope. "It's here."

Oppie looked up from his place on the couch and Kitty sat next to him. She used a silver letter opener to slit the flap then pulled out the pages, holding them so both she and he could read them simultaneously. Although they were laid out as unadorned paragraphs, never, thought Oppie, had the term "bullet list" been more appropriate:

> *We have come to a clear conclusion that he is a loyal citizen. We have, however, been unable to arrive at the conclusion that it would be clearly consistent with the security interests of the United States to reinstate Dr. Oppenheimer's clearance and therefore do not so recommend.*
>
> *We find that Dr. Oppenheimer's continuing conduct and associations have reflected a serious disregard for the requirements of the security system.*
>
> *We find his conduct in the hydrogen bomb program sufficiently disturbing as to raise a doubt as to whether his future participation would be clearly consistent with the best interests of security.*
>
> *We have regretfully concluded that Dr. Oppenheimer has been less than candid in several instances in his testimony before this Board.*

"Well," Oppie said, sagging into the upholstery. "That's that." His breathing was ragged. "Not with a bang but a whimper."

Kitty pulled him close, and he rested his head on her shoulder. "Assholes," she said, and he nodded, his cheek stubble catching as it slid over the silk of her blouse. "Bad enough to put you through all that," she continued, "but to humiliate me! Goddamned assholes."

To humiliate *her.* Yes, yes, what they had done was as unforgivable as what *he* had done. Pushing him about his relationship with Jean while his wife was sitting right there—right there! Barbarians.

Kitty's pain at having all of that paraded out was bad enough but even worse, he knew, was her realization that her prominence, her access to power, was over now, too.

He closed his eyes, but ghosts are visible even thus, and Jean's specter fluttered across his field of vision, sad and wan and lonely.

Chapter 46

Our failure to clear Dr. Oppenheimer will be a black mark on the escutcheon of our country.

—**Ward Evans,** in his dissenting opinion as a member of Oppenheimer's security board

Edward Teller took a deep breath of the mountain air. There was nothing like the dry, floral-tinged scent of the Los Alamos mesa in summer, especially after the long flight from San Francisco and the dusty drive from Santa Fe. Oh, his house in Livermore, where he worked now, was so much nicer than the apartment he and Mici had shared here, but, still, for three intellectually invigorating years, *this* had been his home, and he was returning to it with joy. Mici had come along, too, leaving Paul, now eleven, and Wendy, a precocious seven, with Ernest Lawrence's family. So many of the old gang had come back for this meeting! He'd never get to attend a high-school reunion in Budapest, but this gathering, nine years after the summer of Trinity, felt like a triumphant homecoming.

They were staying in a guesthouse; their war-time quarters here were occupied by someone else now. A picnic was to be held on the eastern terrace of Fuller Lodge today, and he was eager to see his old friends.

The sky was the luminous unblemished blue that came with high altitudes. Long tables were set up under awnings with bowls of Mexican-style salads and platters of dainty desserts. A couple of young men Edward didn't know were manning a barbecue, serving up hamburgers and hot dogs. Well, there were many faces, after all these years, that he didn't know, although he imagined most of these people knew who he was. He was certainly aware that his eyebrows were ... distinctive.

Ah, but there was Robert Christy, a Canadian theoretician—the fellow who had confirmed Edward's suggestion that the core of the implosion bomb should be a solid ball rather than the hollow sphere originally proposed. Shortly after the war, when housing was hard to find, Christy and his wife had shared a home in Chicago with Edward and Mici.

Edward moved quickly toward him. "Bob!"

Christy, who had a long thin face, a nose worthy of the same adjectives, full lips, and a cleft chin, was, at thirty-eight, eight years younger than Edward. He turned his attention toward Teller, and their eyes engaged for a moment. Edward extended his right hand, and—

—and, without a word, Christy pivoted on his heel and walked away.

Edward felt his mouth drop open, and Mici, who had now caught up with her husband, said, "How rude!" She plucked at Edward's sleeve, aiming him toward I.I. Rabi, who was standing nearby.

But a frown creased Rabi's broad face, as Edward again proffered his hand. "I won't shake your hand either, Edward," he said.

"Rabi," asked Mici, "what's going on?"

Edward saw the Nobel laureate's face soften as he looked at Mici. "Don't you read the papers, Mrs. Teller?"

She didn't respond, and Rabi turned back to Edward. "You've got a lot of nerve showing up here."

Edward looked around. Other people—old friends and colleagues as well as strangers—were looking at them now with expressions ranging from stone-faced to downright angry. He blew out air, any restorative effect the mountain scents had had earlier having dissipated.

"Let's go," Mici said softly.

He found himself standing there, stunned, for several heartbeats—he could hear each one, pounding in his ears. His bowel roiled; the ulcerative colitis that had been plaguing him these last few years did not take kindly to stress. But soon he felt Mici's small hand in his, gently pulling him. At last, Edward's good foot moved, followed by his metal one, and they walked back toward the guesthouse. He kept his gaze down, looking at yellow-brown dirt. A snake slithered across the path in front of them; he brought them to a halt as they waited for it to disappear.

"I had to tell the truth," he said at last, as much to himself as to Mici, in Hungarian.

"Of course you did, Ede."

"The evening before I was to appear as a witness, Roger Robb had called me in. He showed me Oppenheimer's testimony about this man Chevalier. The lies, the deceit, the fabrication Oppenheimer himself called 'a cock-and-bull story.'"

"Yes," said Mici, although Edward was aware that this was all new to her.

"I *had* to say what I felt. Who could trust such a man in light of all that?" Mici nodded as they walked on. "And his constant obstructionism on the hydrogen bomb! You've seen Oppenheimer with his kids; he's indifferent to their future. But I want our Paul and Wendy to grow up in a world safe from Communism."

Mici's grip tightened lovingly, reassuringly.

"I had no choice," said Edward.

"None at all," Mici replied.

They'd come to the guesthouse. Edward opened the door, then held it until Mici was inside. He stood there on the threshold for a long moment, wishing his much-traveled piano was back here on the mesa, wishing he could drown out the anger and betrayal swirling in his head with Mozart, with Beethoven.

"There's no point in staying for the meeting," Edward said, his voice even lower than usual. "Pack your things. We're leaving."

Oppie was glad to be back in his office at the Institute for Advanced Study. He'd been terrified that Lewis Strauss—who was still on the I.A.S.'s board of directors—would push for his removal from this post, too, but perhaps the Southerner subscribed to the theory that one should keep one's friends close and one's enemies even closer. Or maybe Strauss simply feared the wrath of Einstein. In any event, there seemed to be no sign that Oppie's position here was any less solid than it had been before the nightmare of the security-board hearing had begun.

Leo Szilard dropped by, bringing Oppie a pastry with rich yellow-white icing. Oppie thanked him but simply put it on his desk. "Well," declared Leo, "if you're not going to eat it, I shall"—and he promptly retrieved the treat and disposed of it in a trio of bites. Then he said, "Come, it's a beautiful day. Help me walk this off."

Robert grabbed his hat, and they headed out the back door of Fuld Hall into the sunshine. Oppie's inclination was to stick to well-worn paths, but Leo struck out across the lawn, heading toward the Institute woods. Oppie followed.

"A terrible business," Szilard said. "It never should have happened."

Robert nodded. "At least the ordeal is over, and at least I won't have to keep taking trips to Washington."

"Yes, yes, but it's not just the end of *your* government career," said Szilard, shaking his head. "Don't you see? It's the end of the new world order."

Oppie's long legs had taken him two yards ahead of the stout Hungarian. He slowed. "What do you mean?"

"The period following World War II was the first time ever that scientists—not science, but specific, nameable scientists—had been seen as responsible for a turning point in history. Before that, there was precisely one famous living scientist, my dear friend Albert, and even he would admit that he was famed more for his eccentricity and hairdo than anything the masses could actually articulate. But following the war, there were scientists who were world famous. You were on the cover of *Time* magazine!"

"I could have done without the most-recent appearance."

"Ah, Americans love nothing more than to see a once-powerful person torn down. But don't you understand? Since the war, we scientists were embraced as public intellectuals. What we said about policy was given as much weight as what we said about physics. We were *heard.* But this travesty of a security board? It's shown that if a scientist speaks up—if he does anything but toe the party line—then he will be shut out. The verdict in your trial was—did you hear what Edward said?"

"Oh, yes."

"I don't mean *at* the trial. But before?"

Oppie shook his head.

"He wanted you defrocked, you and all the 'Oppenheimer men,' the whole 'Oppenheimer machine.' By which he meant all of us who dared to question the power of the military to dictate policy. Men like Teller and Lawrence, they'll gladly give the hawks whatever they wish—and they'll go to any lengths to shut up those who would challenge that."

Oppie resumed walking, and Leo did his best to keep up. "But it's madness," Robert said at last. "Teller *knows* about the photospheric purge."

"Yes, and about our project here to preserve humanity that he intended to run until *you* replaced him."

"True, and I suppose being rejected hurt. But, still, he *must* think about the future."

Szilard put a hand on Robert's arm, and they stopped again. "Oppie, Oppie, you are, if you'll forgive me, naïve. Me, I'm something different—impractical, perhaps. But you simply don't see what's in front of your eyes. Most men in power care only about *preserving* that power. I've read a dozen articles calling you a twentieth-century Faust, but they're wrong, wrong, wrong. You have made no bargain with the devil; *they* have—the warmongers who see that now, after Hiroshima, the sky's the limit—the Eagle will shower them with money. They have accepted earthly pleasures—power, prestige, wealth—in the present, and, even if those few who know our truth believe it to be only for a finite time and that in the end they will be engulfed in flames, at least *everyone* will meet the same fate. So why not be on top until then?"

Szilard frowned and went on. "'Trinity.' Such an odd name for a Jew to choose. But it was apt, Oppie, so apt. The apotheosis of the scientist; the physicist as Messiah, able to preach to the multitudes." He shook his head. "But the savior has been nailed to the cross—and all his ilk, too." He began to walk again, and Oppie did, as well. "And there won't be a resurrection; even an atomic bomb couldn't now shift the stone that has entombed liberal science. 'The Oppenheimer machine?' There never was such a thing! But the *war* machine? It is supreme now, with high priests named Edward Teller, Ernest Lawrence, and Lewis Strauss."

Oppie pulled his pipe from his pocket and set about filling it with his favorite walnut blend.

"When Groves insisted on keeping the solar purge secret, I balked," continued Leo. "The military mind! Bah. He was surely wrong then—but circumstances have changed; your hearing was the turning point. No far-off-future concern matters to those in charge, and they'll shoot down anyone who tries to deflect them from their here-and-now. Overnight, scientists have gone from being unbridled intellectuals, with our views on any topic commanding attention, to hyperspecialists, permitted to speak only about tiny areas and, even within those bounds, our thoughts are to be expressed in a tongue as obscure and rarely understood as—"

"As Hungarian?" said Oppie.

Szilard smiled. "Exactly. In the end, you weren't tried for your past associations; the first twenty-three charges were stage dressing. But that final charge—that you, a scientist, might oppose the policy of those in power, standing in the way of the thermonuclear hydrogen bomb!" They stopped walking again, and Leo scraped the sole of his shoe against a rock as if to dislodge something unpleasant stuck to it. "No, it's clear that if we are to save them, we must indeed do it in secret." He looked up at Oppie. "Whether we *should* save them the way things are now—that's a question I'll leave for others to answer."

Chapter 47

One usually reads that dying men confess their sins to the living. It has always seemed to me that it would be much more logical the other way about. So I confessed my sins to Fermi. None but he, apart from the Deity, if there is one, knows what I then told him.

—Edward Teller

When Laura Fermi had called, asking Edward Teller to fly to Illinois, she'd warned him what to expect, but it was still horrifying. Teller stood in the doorway to the private room at the University of Chicago's Billings Hospital, looking at his old friend. Enrico hadn't noticed his arrival yet.

Except, God damn it, he wasn't an *old* friend—he was young, just fifty-three, far, far too young to be dying.

Time seemed to be on Enrico's mind, too. Clad in pale yellow hospital pajamas, his head leaning against a pillow, he was holding what looked like a pocket watch. A feeding tube ran directly into his stomach, making him resemble an oversized—and horribly malnourished—fetus. Edward had thought Oppenheimer had looked skeletal during the hearing, but he'd been positively robust compared with what was left of Fermi.

Laura, standing next to her husband, caught sight of Teller first. She had a lovely, broad face and short, wavy blonde hair. “Ed!” she exclaimed. “Thank you so much for coming!” She moved over, hugged him, kissed him on the cheek, and ushered him into the room.

Enrico, whose smile was restrained at the best of times, managed a small grin. He turned the timepiece around, revealing it to be a stopwatch. “Checking the flow of nutrients,” he said. His voice had lost much of its strength, but none of its Roman accent. Teller noted that Enrico’s ivory slide rule was sitting within easy reach; the Nobel winner clearly still had an active mind even if his body was betraying him. After spending the past summer in Europe, Enrico had returned to Chicago complaining of digestive difficulties. Exploratory surgery two weeks ago, on October 9, 1954, had revealed pervasive stomach cancer that had already metastasized. The diagnosis was terminal, with only weeks or months of life left.

Laura led Edward over to the bed, and Enrico lifted his right arm. “Don’t worry, my friend,” he said. “I, at least, am willing to shake your hand.”

Edward took the offered appendage—bone and tendon loosely wrapped in onion skin—and squeezed it gently. “Thank you,” he said because he didn’t know what else to say.

Laura smiled. “I’ll go now,” she said. “Leave you two alone to catch up.” She kissed Enrico’s forehead and left.

Fermi stared wistfully after her. “You have no idea how beautiful she was as a teenager. I was the envy of every other boy.” He looked up at Teller. “Don’t be so glum, old friend. *I’m* the one who’s dying.”

The two physicists had known each other since the summer of 1932—twenty-two years now—through peace and war and peace again. Edward tried to smile, and Fermi went on. “I’ve now been blessed by a Catholic priest, a Protestant minister, and a Jewish rabbi. Each came and asked if he had my permission to bless me—and I hadn’t even sneezed!” His smile emphasized his skull. “It pleased them, and it did me no harm, so why not?”

“Well, you *are* the Pope,” Teller said; Fermi had earned that nickname decades ago for his infallibility in matters of physics. “You can perform your own benediction, maybe even your own canonization.”

“‘Saint Enrico,’” Fermi said, but he shook his head. “Sounds too much like ‘Satan Rico.’”

Edward gestured at his friend's sunken torso. "Do you suppose it was radiation?" Fermi—the Italian navigator himself—had been present during almost all the early runs of the first atomic pile beneath Stagg Field, and, at both Los Alamos and here in Chicago, he'd always been a hands-on experimentalist.

"Who knows?" said Enrico. "If so, it's played a dirty trick on me."

Teller's eyes were stinging. "It's a dirty trick on your friends."

Enrico shrugged philosophically, gaunt shoulders sliding up to touch the bottom of his pillow. "If the cancer was caused by radiation, well, I suppose Oppie would say it was—what's that Hindu term he likes?"

"Karma," said Edward. The word felt heavy in his mouth.

"Yes. And speaking of ..." Enrico paused; Edward expected him to finish with "... karma," but instead he said, "Oppenheimer." Fermi's downturned brown eyes at the best of times gave him a melancholy air, but here, as he fastened his gaze on Teller, they seemed to convey not just sadness but disappointment. "Look, Ed, I know as well as anyone that Oppenheimer can be difficult to take. People of his ilk, born with money, often are. Arrogant, condescending. But ..."

He trailed off, and Edward wasn't sure if it was because his illness had robbed him of further wind or because he was simply gathering his thoughts. At last, though, he went on. "But the things you said at his security-board hearing." Fermi shook his head again, hair rubbing against the drool-stained pillowcase. "They were ..." Teller braced himself for a mild rebuke; he wasn't prepared for the term now tossed at him: "... reprehensible."

"Enrico, please."

"No?" said Fermi. "What word would you use? He brought you to Los Alamos; he gave you free reign to work on the super when everyone else was concentrating on the fission bomb. The stature you have now, and the fact that the super exists *at all*, you owe to him."

"We would have had the super years earlier if he'd shifted our focus to it immediately."

"And what would we have done with it? Wipe the entire nation of Japan off the map? Or Germany, if we'd gotten finished even sooner? Japan, at least, has no neighbors that share its borders, but Germany? My God! Denmark, Poland, Czechoslovakia, Austria, Switzerland, France, Belgium, and the Netherlands all touch it, and my Italy is just to the south and your Hungary to the east. You couldn't use a hydrogen bomb in Europe."

"The foes now are gigantic," said Teller. "Russia, China. There *are* suitable targets deep inland."

"*Now,* perhaps. But Oppie had to deal with the situation as it was *then*—and he pampered you at Los Alamos."

"By promoting Bethe over me?"

"Ed ..."

"Fine, fine." Teller waved dismissively. "But since the war, you have to agree he's been obstructionist."

"Because he spoke against the fusion bomb? Because he held to his carefully considered opinions? Because he didn't agree with *you?* For *that,* you'd destroy him?"

"He can still teach, if he wishes." *And if anyone will have him.*

"For a man like Oppenheimer, a man who has had years of a life at the very heart of things, to be cut off from the halls of power is devastating. You know that."

"He still has the Institute for Advanced Study—taken from me, I might add—and everything that's going on there."

Fermi lifted his eyebrows, and that just made his eyes look even sadder. "And you and I are among the few who *do* know what he's working on and how important it is."

Teller glanced out the window: autumn maples, like mushroom clouds, their caps afire. "I'm not to blame, Enrico. He destroyed himself. He lied to the security officials. The night before I testified, Roger Robb showed me the transcripts, and—"

"And you would posture now that those transcripts altered your feelings? That it wasn't until you saw them that you'd decided to push Oppie into the path of a speeding ..."

Enrico paused. They were both speaking English, the language they shared, and Teller had mentally completed the sentence—*in the path of a speeding train?*—before the Italian went on. When he did, he surprised Edward: "... a speeding streetcar?"

The Nobelist *did* know him. Teller rarely spoke of the injury that had cost him his right foot. A foolish stunt, an act of youthful bravado and stupidity. At seventeen, in Karlsruhe, having missed his stop, he'd jumped off the front of a moving trolley car, lost his balance, and fallen. The trolley's rear wheel ran over his ankle, shearing off his foot.

"We've all made stupid mistakes," Enrico continued. "At least Oppenheimer's was made to protect a friend, no? This Chevalier?"

"Friend," said Edward. The word sounded bitter, even to him. "I've lost so many over this. And—" *And now I'm going to lose you, too.*

"If I were you," said Enrico, his voice growing ever more raw, "I'd lay low for a time. Disappear from public view. Memories fade. And if you can make some amends—"

"I'm entitled to *my* opinions, too. And I *do* think the vital interests of this country are now in safer hands with Oppenheimer out of things."

Fermi looked like he was going to object, but to save his dying friend some breath—and to save himself from hearing the objection—Teller went on: "But I *have* taken a conciliatory step as far as the super is concerned to counter the ... misconception."

A brief popular-history book entitled *The Hydrogen Bomb: The Men, the Menace, the Mechanism* by two *Time-Life* correspondents had recently been published. It portrayed Teller as a visionary genius and the sole creator of the super, whereas Oppenheimer was relegated to the role of villain and even spy. Moreover, the book said the super had been developed at the Livermore Lab, founded two years ago in northern California by Teller and Ernest Lawrence, not as it actually was at Los Alamos. That infuriated Oppenheimer's successor there, Norris Bradbury—and, Edward supposed, very likely Oppie himself.

"I wrote this," said Edward. He produced a typescript from his inside jacket pocket and passed it to Fermi, who needed the strength of both arms to hold up the dozen sheets.

"'The Work of Many Hands,'" said Enrico, reading the title out loud. "What is this?"

"A correct account of the development of the super. But I don't know if I should publish it. Lewis Strauss says it'll just make things worse."

Fermi skimmed the article. "Why *wouldn't* you publish this? It *was* the work of many hands. You'd do well to be seen sharing the credit." He continued leafing through, then went back to the beginning, and quickly scanned the pages again. "There's no mention of Stanislaw Ulam."

Teller felt his abdominal muscles clench. Enrico was not the first person to note that lack. "Ulam contributed nothing! He didn't believe it would work!"

"The latter doesn't imply the former. I saw his equations."

"Yes, but—"

"Ed, you are trying to rehabilitate your reputation. Be magnanimous."

Teller harrumphed. "I suppose I could insert a mention."

"Good," said Enrico. He made a feeble imitation of the hand sign of papal benediction. "The Pope approves."

Edward was weary of—of *everything.* He looked around the small, ugly room and spotted an appropriately small, ugly chair, which he dragged across the tiles with a chalk-on-slate sound. When it was abreast of Fermi, he lowered himself onto it and let loose a heavy sigh. "There is something I have to get off my chest."

"It's a rare soul who gets to give confession directly to the Pope," said Enrico, smiling his weak smile.

Edward shifted his bulk on the wooden seat. His prosthetic foot banged against the metal side railing of the hospital bed, but he felt nothing.

"I *want* to use the bomb," he said at last. "I want to see every last Communist gone. If there *is* a hope of saving humanity—of a fresh start on Mars or elsewhere—then we need to begin *clean.*"

"You're advocating preventive war against Russia?"

"I'm not the only one," said Teller, and he hated the defensiveness in his voice. "John von Neumann agrees. He says 'If you say why not bomb them tomorrow, I say why not today? If you say today at five o'clock, I say why not one o'clock?'"

"Von Neumann puts way too much stock in his theory of games. The Russian people are no different from anyone else."

"I *hate* the Communists," Teller said.

"Ed, Ed, even Hitler only killed six million. Would you really wipe out all of the Soviet Union?"

"Not just them. China, now, too. It would take only a handful of supers to eliminate all the Communists, to give mankind a clean start, a world free of the cancer—"

He stopped, shocked at his own choice of metaphor. "Forgive me, Enrico."

"Ego te absolvo," intoned Fermi. "For that—but for what you're proposing? Edward, it's inhuman."

Teller rapped his artificial foot against the bed frame again, deliberately this time. "I'm something a bit less than that. The super can *cleanse.* Besides, consider how much it will cost to relocate what's left of humanity before the photospheric purge. Billions, maybe even trillions, of dollars. Eliminate the enemy *now* and we'll avoid the financially ruinous arms race everyone fears is coming. All that money can go into funding the—"

"Exodus?" offered Fermi.

"Exactly."

But Fermi shook his head. "Old Testament; not my department—and certainly not something I'll live to see."

"You *will* be remembered," said Teller.

"Will I?" Fermi seemed to consider this. "Perhaps. For the Chicago pile, maybe. But you know what Leo Szilard said when we finally got it running? 'This will go down as a dark day in the history of mankind.' Enrico tilted his skull. "Perhaps he was right, after all."

"An opportunity like this—a time when we have a clear superiority in weaponry—may never come again. It's now or never."

"Then, for the love of the God neither of us believes in, Ed, let it be never. Let this notion of yours die with me."

"But—"

"Your word, Edward. A dying man's final request. No preventive war; no pre-emptive first strike." Fermi held out his hand again.

Teller stared at it then, at last, shook it gently.

Chapter 48

1958

It may be possible to propel a vehicle weighing several thousand tons to velocities several times earth escape velocities. A circular disk of material, which is called the pusher, is connected through a shock-absorbing mechanism to the ship proper, which is above the pusher-shock-absorber assembly. Nuclear bombs, which are stored in the ship, are fired periodically below the pusher. Each bomb is surrounded by a mass of propellant. As a result of each explosion, the propellant strikes the pusher and drives it upward into the shock absorbers, which then deliver a structurally tolerable impulse to the ship.

—***Feasibility Study of a Nuclear-Bomb-Propelled Space Vehicle***,
contract between the United States Air Force and General Atomic,
June 30, 1958

"You, there! Big man! Wait!" Leo Szilard moved quickly to catch up with the broad-shouldered fellow.

"Yes?" The voice was accented and higher pitched than one might have expected based on his size.

"Sprechen Sie Deutsch?"

"Ja."

"Ah, sehr gut," said Szilard, and he continued on in German. "Then you must indeed be him!" He put his hands on hips. "Well, well, well! Wernher von Braun, at last!"

The "big man," although stocky, had nowhere near Szilard's girth, but he was a head taller than the Hungarian. "And who might you be?"

Leo was surprised. "I'm Szilard, that's who! Surely you know!"

"Oh," said von Braun, sounding unimpressed. "What are you doing here in San Diego?"

"One might ask the same of you. I heard you were in Texas with your rockets."

They were out front of the circular technical library that was at the heart of the new General Atomic facility in Torrey Pines. "Oppenheimer had mentioned what they were working on here," von Braun said. "Of course, I'd seen Ulam and Everett's report back in 1955, but I hadn't realized anyone had taken it seriously."

Leo knew that report well: he and his Compact Cement teammates back in Princeton had spent a lot of time discussing it. Although its title was *On a Method of Propulsion of Projectiles by Means of External Nuclear Explosions,* and although it made no mention of manned space travel, the applicability of the proposed technique for that goal was obvious. The work being done here—dubbed Project *Orion*—had grown from Stanislaw Ulam's idea, first put forth right after the Trinity test, of using exploding bombs to propel spaceships.

"Oh, they take it very seriously indeed," said Szilard. "Freeman Dyson has come out here from the Institute for Advanced Study as our Arbor Project emissary; he'll be part of *Orion* for at least this academic year."

"Dyson, yes. A sharp mind, that one." Von Braun looked down on Szilard, and perhaps not just literally; Leo knew the German, essentially an engineer, had little use for the kind of *luftmensch* thinking Szilard was famous for. "And you are here why?"

"Not to stay, I assure you," said Leo. "Well, not to stay *here* at General Atomic, although they have engaged me as a consultant." G.A. was the division of General Dynamics devoted to "harnessing the power of nuclear technologies for the benefit of mankind." "But I could see making a home in La Jolla. Jonas Salk and I have plans to create an institute for biological studies, and I'm going to suggest we build it there. Such a beautiful area!"

"Biological studies?" said von Braun in a tone that suggested Szilard had uttered the equivalent of astrology.

"Yes—the science of life! *Getting* humans off this earth is only one part of the solution; *making* mankind more suitable for space travel and for living on other worlds surely is a key component, too."

"Ah," said von Braun. The summer sky had cirrus graffiti scrawled across it, and there was a tang of salt in the ocean air. "So, then, what do you think?"

"Of Project *Orion?*" Leo raised his eyebrows. "It has gumption, I'll give it that." He pointed at the two-story library, looking like a giant white checkers piece. "Ted Taylor tells me that this building is a hundred and thirty-five feet in diameter, precisely what they envision for their 4,000-ton spaceship design. That's five times as wide as your biggest planned rocket, no? The thing they intend to build is gigantic!"

"Girth," said von Braun, "isn't everything."

Leo chuckled. "Perhaps not. But their propulsion scheme? Popping an endless string of small fusion bombs out a trapdoor like seeds from a watermelon, and exploding them to push a space vessel ahead. Visionary." He put a hand on his chest. "I contributed one idea myself. Have you ever used a Coca-Cola machine?"

"Of course."

"So efficient: you select what you want, and a mechanism neatly delivers the bottle. I said *that's* how they should move their bombs from storage aboard the space ship to the trap door, selecting from a variety of bomb sizes depending on the propulsive need. Dyson loved the notion; he tells me engineers from Coca-Cola in Atlanta will be here next week to show them how it's done."

The taller man's eyes narrowed. "I hear you have Oppenheimer's ear. Will you tell him you favor this project?"

"Over your rockets? Come now. You yourself must know that *Orion* is far more efficient."

"But rocketry is proven technology!" declared von Braun. "This is moonshine."

Szilard smiled. "Rutherford used the same word to describe getting lots of energy by splitting the atom, but we did that. I used the same word to describe H.G. Wells's notion of atomic bombs, and then we built one."

"Of course it was built. It was simple, straight-forward engineering, just like my rockets—"

"Your rockets!" Leo made an exasperated sound. "You want everyone to believe that all you ever cared about was building rockets for space travel—don't deny it! But what you were actually building—what you were *charged* with building—were *missiles* to fly just a thousand kilometers from Germany to Britain. Yes, sure, *that's* something chemically fueled rockets *are* good for—tiny hops! But such things are all but useless for making trips to other planets."

"You need to read my novel *Project Mars.* I can send you the manuscript or—"

"I know your ideas for manned space flight, but—"

"They will work! They will all work!"

"Sure, but on a scale wholly inappropriate to our task. Even you must agree! Dyson walked me through it all. Chemical rockets have exhaust velocities of about three kilometers per second, and to increase velocity, you need to use *stages*—big fuel tanks that are dumped, in order from bottom to top, once emptied. I've seen your designs; that's precisely what you propose. And you need *n* stages for every velocity increment of 3*n* kilometers per second, right?"

"Ja."

"Getting to low earth orbit takes two rocket stages; high earth orbit, three stages; just going to the moon, four; and a lunar round-trip, as many as five!"

"Yes, but—"

"But what? It's really a simple geometric progression, roughly speaking, in terms of how much of one of your rockets can be anything *but* fuel. In a chemical rocket, the ratio of fuel to payload is about four to the *n*th power, so the ratio of fuel to payload is sixteen pounds to one pound for low earth orbit, right? And sixty-four to one for high earth orbit, no? Then 256-to-one to go one way to the moon, and a whopping 1,024-to-one for a lunar round-trip. To put a hundred pounds of payload on the moon—a very small man, much thinner than me and much shorter than you!—and bring him safely back to the earth, you'd need roughly *one hundred thousand* pounds of chemical fuel."

"Yes, yes," said von Braun. He looked around, making sure no one else was near enough to overhear, then added, "But we're in luck—if you can call it that—because we're *not* planning round-trip missions. We're talking about an exodus; we're talking about colonization ships."

"All right," said Szilard. "Still, the farther you want to go from good old *terra firma,* the more rocket fuel you'll need. On the other hand, with this *Orion* notion, exhaust velocity will be *thousands* of kilometers per second instead of just three, you only need *one* stage, and the ratio between fuel mass and payload stays pretty much constant no matter how far you go. Whether you just want to make it into orbit or trek all the way to Alpha Centauri, more than one-tenth of your ship's mass can be payload."

"*If* their mad scheme works. I, for one, prefer the tried-and-true instead of something cobbled together out of soft-drink-vending machines and giant springs."

"Dyson says *Orion* will be ready to take people to Mars by 1965—and to the moons of Saturn by 1970. Can you do that with your vengeance weapons?"

Vengeance. The "V" in V-2. "Ah, I see why you are so riled up," said von Braun, nodding as if a conspiracy had at last been revealed. "You had friends in London, yes?"

And that just made Leo angrier. Sure, he'd lived in London; it was there, at an intersection on Southampton Road in 1933, that he'd first conceived of the nuclear chain reaction. But he'd balked when Jimmy Byrnes had suggested Leo's opposition to atomic bombs was because he worried about his native Hungary, and he didn't like this hulking Junker implying that a selfish impulse drove him now.

"I'm looking for the best solution for all mankind," Leo said. "You—you are looking for the best solution for von Braun!"

"Well," said the German, "time will tell—and may the best machine win."

Chapter 49

Compare Oppenheimer to Teller? You can't compare their character any more than you can compare an orchid to a dandelion. An orchid is more finely designed and built and delicate and subtle and aromatic. And a dandelion is something you kick up with the heel of your shoe if it's going to take over your grass.

—**Dorothy McKibbin,** who ran the Manhattan Project's office at 109 East Palace in Santa Fe

Oppie shook his head in amazement as he walked around the spacious grounds, more than a mile on a side. Although the theoretical physics community had largely turned its back on Edward Teller, the government clearly adored the Hungarian, giving him everything he'd been dreaming of: his own richly funded lab, here in Livermore, California, an hour southeast of Berkeley. Once the Soviets tested their first fission bomb, back in 1949, based in part on secrets stolen from Oppie's mesa by Klaus Fuchs, Washington was desperate for something even more destructive, and Teller was happy to lead the way.

Teller and Ernest Lawrence had founded this facility in 1952. Herbert York had served as director for the first six years, and now Teller himself was in his second year as director of the lab, which currently employed 3,000 people and had an annual budget of $65 million. And, unlike at Los Alamos—a compound that still existed but was very much in the shadow now of this newer one—at Teller's facility, fusion-bomb research held center stage.

Oppenheimer made his way into the main building and found Teller's office. His secretary had Oppie wait in a wooden chair, and he whiled away the time looking at the latest issue of *The Magnet,* the lab's employee newsletter. At last, the secretary said, "Dr. Teller is ready for you."

Oppie rose, swallowed, and headed into the inner sanctum. He'd seen Teller occasionally since the security-board hearings, but not alone, not one-on-one. As he entered the wood-paneled office, he tried to sound warm. "Edward! So good to see you!"

Teller rose and made his way around from behind his wide, cluttered desk. "Robert," he said. Not Oppie. Robert. "You're well?"

He coughed. "Yes."

"And Kitty?"

Oppie dropped his gaze. He and Kitty had had a fight before his trip out here. In a drunken rage, she'd accused him of wanting to take a trip to Livermore not because he needed to see Teller but to see *her*—"her" being Jean, who had lived nearby. But Jean had been dead for fourteen years now. When Oppie had, gently, he'd thought, pointed that out to Kitty, she'd thrown her drink glass at him.

"She's fine," Oppie said. "And Mici?"

"She's doing well. She sends her love, of course." *Of course.*

"Very kind of her."

Silence. Teller looked him up and down, then: "And now that the pleasantries are properly discharged, Robert, what in the hell do you want?"

"So, if I may try to sum up," said Teller, in his ponderous, deep voice, each syllable a rumble, "you feel the best way to get humans from earth to Mars is *not* by using von Braun's chemical rockets but rather through this *Orion* design?"

"Yes," replied Oppenheimer.

"And *Orion* requires fusion bombs be ejected from its rear, and uses the explosive force of them pressing against a metal plate for propulsion?"

"Yes."

"And it will take thousands of fusion bombs to propel the ship over interplanetary distances?"

"That's right."

"So the key to saving humanity is ..."

"Yes?" said Oppie, waiting for the Hungarian to finish.

"No, I prefer for *you* to fill in the blank. The key to saving humanity is ..."

Oppie blinked. "... is the fusion bomb."

"Also known as ...?"

Oppie crossed and uncrossed his legs. "The thermonuclear hydrogen bomb."

"Or, you know, more colloquially ...?"

"The super."

"The super!" agreed Teller. "The same bomb you told me after Hiroshima that you could never work on. The same bomb whose development you did everything you possibly could to slow for over a decade now. The same bomb I have devoted my career to perfecting."

Oppie took a long pull on his pipe then let the smoke escape from his lungs. "The irony isn't lost on me, Ed."

"Irony!" The word exploded from Teller's mouth. "Irony, is it? I've been shunned for four years now, ever since your god-damned security trial!"

"*I* shook your hand, Ed."

"You did—but not Christy! Not Rabi! Not dozens of others. *You* lie to the government and are—what? Martyred? But *I* tell the truth and am ostracized."

"I understand how you—"

"Don't!" snapped Teller. "Don't you dare say you understand how I feel. You couldn't possibly. Born rich and safe here in the United States? I've been exiled three times! When I was eighteen—a boy, a boy with one foot!—I had to run from my home in Hungary because there was no hope of a university career for a Jew. And when I was thirty-three, I had to flee Germany, the Nazis, Hitler. All that time you were sitting pretty, dabbling with Communism and sleeping with other people's wives. And then, because *you* demanded a security-board hearing even though you knew that you'd lied repeatedly, *I* end up being exiled from most of the physics community!"

"Edward, you're being—"

"Unfair? Tell me, Oppie, how does that taste? Irony, indeed, eh? And now you want my help!"

"The world wants—needs!—your help. And, come on, you owe ..."

"What?"

"No, nothing."

"Say it."

Oppie sat silently.

"Say it!" roared Teller.

"All right, damn it. The last time the world was in danger—the Second World War—you sat it out. We needed the A-bomb, and you wouldn't help. I coddled you at Los Alamos, letting you pursue your own project and—"

"And now that project is the key to mankind's salvation, eh? Right?"

Oppie took a deep breath and exhaled noisily. "Right," he said meekly.

"Well, then," Teller said, "for me to function, you must rehabilitate my reputation."

"Ed, you know I have no power left."

"Ah, but you do! What did you create in honor of Einstein's seventieth birthday?"

Oppie nodded, understanding dawning. "The Einstein Award." Bestowed by the Institute for Advanced Study, it went to a recipient chosen by a committee Oppie chaired. The award had been given twice so far: jointly to Kurt Gödel and Julian Schwinger in 1951 and to Dick Feynman in 1954; that year, the *New York Times* had declared the award "next only to the Nobel Prize" in prestige.

"So," said Teller, folding arms in front of his chest, "it's been four years since the last laureate. Time for another."

Ironically—how much that word applied today!—the gold medal and $15,000 in prize money were provided by a memorial foundation named for Lewis Strauss's parents. The award was always given on Einstein's birthday, which was March 14; this year's recipient would be the first since the great man had passed away.

Oppie frowned. They'd planned to give the award to Willard Libby, a Manhattan Project alumnus whose development of radiocarbon dating had revolutionized archaeology and palaeontology. "It isn't just me on the committee," he said.

"It wasn't just you at Los Alamos," replied Teller, "but your way prevailed. It wasn't just you on the board of consultants for the international control of atomic energy, but we all know that the Acheson-Lilienthal Report was virtually dictated by you. Even now, where you go, for good or ill, others follow."

"All right, Edward. All right. I'll make it happen; you'll get the medal."

"Good," declared the Hungarian. He paused, then nodded in satisfaction. "Now, there is work to be done. To the stars by H-bomb, eh? Let's get to it!"

Chapter 50

1959

[With Project Orion,*] we could get a colony of several thousand people to Alpha Centauri, about four light-years away, in about 150 years [of travel time]. These numbers represent the absolute lower limit of what could be done with our present resources and technology if we were forced by some astronomical catastrophe to send a Noah's ark out of the wreckage of the solar system.*

—Freeman Dyson

"Hydrogen bombs are the only way we know to burn the cheapest fuel we have, deuterium," said Freeman Dyson. He was at the podium in the lecture hall of the circular library that shared a diameter with the planned *Orion* vessel. "Now," he continued, the usual twinkle in his unblinking blue eyes, "I do not know exactly how efficient hydrogen bombs are, and, if I *did* know, I wouldn't tell you." All fifty General Atomic employees working on Project *Orion* were there, and just about every one of them laughed. "So, as we proceed, I'll put upper and lower limits on the number we're not supposed to know exactly ..."

It was Dyson's farewell lecture; he was heading back shortly to Princeton and the Institute for Advanced Study. But he was leaving behind feasibility studies that could, as promised, get manned *Orion* spaceships to Mars within the next six years, by 1965, and to the moons of Jupiter just five years later. If any of those were to be the new home for humanity, the *Orion* team would be ready, and well before von Braun's chemical rockets might be able to put humans on the dead—and soon to be even deader—terrestrial moon.

Dick Feynman, holding a scientific journal, came into Oppie's office. "Forget about humanity going to Europa," he announced.

Oppie had been working on budgets. He finished tallying the figures in front of him and used a fountain pen to jot down the seven-digit total. Leslie Groves had left the army to take a vice president's role at computer-maker and military-contractor Sperry Rand but still managed to keep the black-money spigot open. "Why?" Robert asked, at last looking up at Feynman, who was now leaning against the doorjamb.

"Too much radiation."

Oppie tapped out his pipe into an ashtray. "Are you talking about Burke and Franklin?" Four years ago, in 1955, those two had discovered decametric radio emissions coming from Jupiter, extending up to forty megahertz. "Their work implied a powerful magnetic field—"

"Yes, yes," said Feynman. "Perhaps even exceeding ten gauss. And last year, *Explorer* discovered the Van Allen radiation belts."

The whole world knew *Sputnik,* the first artificial satellite, which went up in October 1957. Already forgotten by most was *Explorer 1,* the first *American* satellite, launched just 119 days later. But *Explorer 1* had made an astounding discovery: earth's Van Allen radiation belts. In the nine months since then, physicists had determined that the toroidal belts, which trapped highly charged particles from the solar wind, were key to our planet retaining its atmosphere; without them, the solar wind would have scoured most of it off long ago. They were also vital to protecting those on the surface from harmful radiation.

"Highly charged particles *around earth,*" stressed Oppie.

"Sure. But if earth's magnetic field gives us such radiation belts, *any* planet with a strong bipolar magnetic field is likely to have them—and Jupiter's field is gigantic, at least ten or twenty times earth's."

"But if there's only decametric radiation coming from the planet itself—"

"Yeah, that wouldn't be so bad." Feynman held up the latest *Astronomical Journal*, dated October 1959. "But Frank Drake's got a note in here. He found decimetric radiation coming from Jupiter. Deci, not deca; DIM, not DAM."

Oppie frowned. "So, a hundred times shorter than the earlier discovery, which—shit. That would mean it's—"

"Bingo. Synchrotron radiation, emitted by electrons hurtling at relativistic speeds in the Jovian counterpart of the Van Allen belts. Radiation a million times more intense than that in our own belts. And, before you ask, I already worked it out: Jupiter's moons Io, Europa, Ganymede, and even Callisto, probably, orbit *within* Jupiter's Van Allen belts. Maybe Europa *does* have an ocean, as some have suggested, but its surface has to be uninhabitable. We might as well try to relocate humanity inside nuclear piles."

Oppie gestured for Feynman to hand him the journal. Dick had placed a slip of paper in it to mark the page, but Robert was momentarily confused. There were *two* notes from Frank Drake published in this issue, one after the other. The first was irrelevant, but the second—"Non-thermal microwave radiation from Jupiter"—was the one Feynman was concerned about. It actually had a co-author, which the journal listed as S. Hvatum. Oppie figured the initial was a typo; he knew the first name of Drake's colleague at the National Radio Astronomy Observatory in Greenbank was Hein. Sadly, the rest of the brief piece—just three paragraphs, taking up much less than a full page—was harder to find fault with. Drake was a good empirical research scientist: steady, reputable, occasionally brilliant. His conclusion, presented in the usual dispassionate passive voice of such things—"a total number of particles 10^6 times greater than in the terrestrial system will suffice to explain the observations"—meant that Feynman was right. There was no way any biological molecules could long survive on the surface of Europa or the other major Jovian moons. Oh, Oppie supposed, Europa might have deep-sea life, shielded by many tens or hundreds of meters of water, *if* life exists at all beyond earth and *if* Europa actually has an ocean. But as a second home for humanity? Impossible.

"Well, then," said Oppie, closing the journal, "that's that. If we're going to any solid body in the solar system, it just has to be Mars."

"Or one of Saturn's moons. Titan, for instance."

"Right, true. But I'm still putting my money on the red planet. Thank goodness it, at least, appears somewhat hospitable."

Feynman shrugged philosophically and said, "Where there is life, there is hope."

A week later, I.I. Rabi came into Oppie's office holding a chipped Masonite clipboard with some papers clamped to. "Would you like to fly out and see the latest *Orion* test?" He glanced at the topmost page. "It'll be at Point Loma on the Pacific coast near San Diego next Saturday."

Still, after all these years, mention of a trip to California brought Jean to mind, even if San Diego was about as far as one could get from San Francisco and still be in that state.

"I suppose it'd be a good idea," replied Oppie. "Get a real sense of the damn thing."

"I should warn you, though," said Rabi, holding up the clipboard, which presumably contained the news. "Rolander might be there."

Oppie's stomach clenched. C. Arthur Rolander, who'd sat next to Roger Robb during Oppenheimer's trial, had been the A.E.C.'s security weasel who had helped stack the deck against him. "What in hell would he be doing there?"

Rabi shook his head. "Would you believe it? He's vice president of General Atomic now."

"For fuck's sake," said Oppie. "I was planning on the next time I saw him being when I piss on his grave." He shook his head. "No, I'll stay here. But Szilard's often out that way. Ask him to attend, would you?"

"Three!"

It amused Leo Szilard, standing on the warm hillside covered with cacti and flowering shrubs overlooking the Pacific, that they were starting things with a countdown. It was a German invention to have such a thing before a rocket launch, but it wasn't the work of Wernher von Braun, or even of von Braun's great predecessor, Hermann Oberth, but rather of the screenwriter Thea von Harbou who wrote Fritz Lang's 1929 science-fiction movie *Frau im Mond.*

"Two!"

Indeed, science-fiction influences were ubiquitous this day. The meter-long test-flight model *Orion* looked for all the world like the ship described in Jules Verne's 1865 novel *De la terre à la lune*—a stubby bullet shape—and plans for the full vessel involved clever shock absorbers, just as Verne's own vessel did.

"One!"

Even the propulsive methods had an explosive commonality. Verne's ship was impelled by one giant kick from a gargantuan ground-based canon. A full-scale *Orion* would employ myriad thermonuclear-bomb detonations, and this test vehicle, nicknamed *Putt-Putt,* would use grapefruit-sized balls of C-4, ejected through a hole in its pusher plate.

"Zero!"

The first explosion was—

Mein Gott!

Leo thought for sure the test model must have been blown to bits. But no! There! Just above the great cloud of black smoke: the U.S.S. *Putt-Putt,* its fiberglass hull intact, and—

Another explosion!

Another black cloud.

And, again, triumphantly, the projectile-shaped craft emerging from the top of the cloud.

Blam!

And again, the little ship going higher and higher still, climbing toward the sky.

It seemed to fly on forever, although, as Leo later learned, the actual ascent had only lasted twenty-three seconds. In that time, though, *Putt-Putt* had risen up fifty-six meters, more than fifty times its own height.

When the chain of explosions ended, Leo applauded with the others as a parachute was deployed. *Putt-Putt* descended slowly from the heavens, an angel of mercy coming down to save mankind.

Chapter 51

Four Years Later: 1963

We were a bunch of crazies, in a certain way, and it was an unusual time when crazy people were actually given a chance to do their stuff.

—Freeman Dyson

Eighteen years, thought Oppie. Time enough for a boy to become a man. Oh, the anniversary wasn't technically until tomorrow, but that was only an error of 0.015 percent—good enough, as the saying went, for government work. But the coincidence of dates was too tasty a morsel for any newscaster to pass up: eighteen years between August 6, 1945, when *Enola Gay* had dropped the first Little Boy bomb on Hiroshima, and today, August 5, 1963, when, at last, the leaders of the United States, the Soviet Union, and the United Kingdom became the initial signatories to the world's first nuclear treaty—with, it was hoped, all other nations soon following suit. U.S. Secretary of State Dean Rusk was in Moscow right now, putting the eight letters of his name on the document, signing next to Foreign Minister Andrei Gromyko and Foreign Secretary Alexander Douglas-Home.

Oppie knew he should be elated. Since Day One, since Hiroshima burned, he had pushed and fought for nuclear-arms control, for rational men and women to pledge never again to use the weapons he'd made possible. And now, at last, it was here—a treaty! Oh, there was much, much more to be done before the world would be safe from nuclear bombs—as President Kennedy said in announcing the treaty, "According to the ancient Chinese proverb, 'A journey of a thousand miles must begin with a single step.' And if that journey is a thousand miles, or even more, let history record that we, in this land, at this time, took the first step."

Yes, he should be thrilled for this—this *thing* that the news-readers were variously referring to as the Limited Test-Ban Treaty and the Partial Nuclear Test-Ban Treaty, all because its full title had more syllables than the American public would sit still for: *Treaty Banning Nuclear Weapons Tests in the Atmosphere, in Outer Space and Under Water.* Without a Q clearance, Oppie had gotten wind only of the title long before he'd had a chance, along with the rest of the general public, to see the full text, and he'd hoped for a loophole. Yes, *tests* would be outlawed, but *practical uses* might still be permitted. But, in fact, article one of the treaty explicitly dashed that hope: "Each of the Parties to this Treaty undertakes to prohibit, to prevent, and not to carry out any nuclear weapon test explosion, *or any other nuclear explosion,* at any place under its jurisdiction or control in the atmosphere; beyond its limits, including outer space; or under water, including territorial waters or high seas."

And that, as the saying went, was that. Oppie thought again of his favorite poet, T.S. Eliot, who had been a visiting artist at the Institute for Advanced Study for thirteen months starting in October 1947; of Eliot's master work, "The Hollow Men;" and of its concluding stanza:

This is the way the world ends
This is the way the world ends
This is the way the world ends
Not with a bang but a whimper.

No, not with a single explosive bang, and not with the tens of thousands of nuclear blasts that would have propelled a spaceship full of refugees to humanity's new home. With a trio of autographs, two in the Roman alphabet and one in Cyrillic, Project *Orion* had inadvertently been killed.

Although Princeton never got as hot as Los Alamos in summer, it attained much greater levels of humidity, and, as Oppie walked along the grounds of the Institute, he felt sweat beneath the brim of his hat.

He hadn't been paying much attention to what was up ahead; his gaze was mostly downward at the earth, a prisoner of gravity whose escape tunnel, carved out a spoonful at a time, had collapsed. And so he was startled when suddenly Leo Szilard, in a three-piece blue suit and a jaunty fedora, was in front of him.

"Why so glum, Robert?"

"Oh, hi, Leo." He told him about the impact the test-ban treaty would have on *Orion.*

Leo surprised him by not seeming concerned. The Hungarian had been wandering aimlessly about the grounds, as usual, and reversed his course, falling in next to Oppie and walking beside him. "Bah, it never would have flown anyway," he said.

"Why not?" asked Oppie. "You saw the test yourself, and as far as I could tell the physics was elegant."

"It never would have flown anyway," Szilard repeated, "because you killed it years before it even got started."

Oppie raised his eyebrows, astonished. "Me? How?"

"That closed-door Senate hearing, remember? Not long after Hiroshima, back in 1946."

"What about it?"

"You were asked if three or four men could smuggle atomic bombs into New York and blow up the whole city, remember? And what did you say?"

"I said, sure, of course it could be done."

"And when a senator asked you what instrument you'd use to detect an atomic bomb somewhere in a city, what did you say to that?"

Oppie smiled slightly. "A screwdriver, to pry open each and every suitcase."

"There, you see!" crowed Szilard. "You were talking about tiny bombs thirteen years ago—and those were fission bombs, atomic bombs. But *Orion* would have used thousands—millions!—of tiny fusion super bombs. Tiny, delivered by a souped-up Coca-Cola machine! Von Braun isn't going to lose an entire rocket, but the *Orion* people, keeping track of countless bombs? If a handful of them, or even one, ended up in the hands of a crazy individual or the next Hitler—*ka-boom!*"

Oppie felt his smile slip into a frown. Leo was right. In fact, after that Senate session, at Oppie's recommendation, physicists Robert Hofstadter and Wolfgang Panofsky were commissioned to prepare a study, inevitably nicknamed the "Screwdriver Report," enumerating methods to prevent such an act of atomic terrorism. At least up until when Oppie had lost his Q clearance, that report had still been classified—because, of course, it had shown there were *no* effective ways.

Szilard continued: "No matter how important *Orion* might have been to getting humans off earth in the next century, we never would have survived even to the end of *this* century if we started cranking out tiny supers. Someone, somewhere, somehow would have gotten his hands on them and that, my friend, would have been the end of us all."

Dick Feynman picked up the magazine on the table in Oppie's secretary's office. It was the October 1963 edition of the *Bulletin of the Atomic Scientists,* just out. As it often did, the cover depicted the doomsday clock, showing how close humanity was to nuclear annihilation. The clock face was dusty rose this issue, a shade Dick knew well from Los Alamos sunsets. As always, there were no numerals on the face, and no minutes and only four hours were marked, each by a black circle: nine, ten, eleven, and twelve. But, unusually, there were *three* hands on the clock: a short black hour one pointing, as it always did, at midnight; a longer white minute hand aimed at the forty-eight spot—in other words, at twelve minutes to midnight; and also a black outline of a minute hand, filled with the same color as the rest of the clock, pointing at seven minutes to midnight.

Dick snorted slightly. You'd think the inventor of the Feynman diagrams, a system that could explicate any reaction in quantum electrodynamics, could figure out what such a simple graphic was trying to convey but, for the life of him, he couldn't. He opened the cover and there was the explanation, beginning right on page two. The editorial began:

> *Conclusion of a limited test-ban treaty is an encouraging event. It strengthens the slim hope that mankind will escape destruction in a nuclear war, and justifies the moving of the Bulletin's clock a few minutes back from the hour of doom.*

The lord giveth, Feynman the atheist thought, and, as he knew all too well, *the lord taketh away.* Of course, the treaty was an important breakthrough, but it *had* killed Project *Orion.* In any event, the *Bulletin*'s graphic designer could certainly take a lesson from Feynman diagrams. A simple arrowhead going counter-clockwise from the outlined minute hand to the solid white one would have made the intended meaning clear: that we'd backed off five more minutes from midnight.

Apparently, the clock had last been reset, with its hands positioned at seven to midnight, in 1960. The *Bulletin*'s Science and Security Board met only twice a year to assess whether fiddling with the minute hand was appropriate, and so the Cuban Missile Crisis of a year ago, for all that the hand probably should have jumped to one minute before doom, began and ended in its entirety between two board meetings and therefore had had no effect on the clock.

Dick hated serving on committees but the one that set the clock intrigued him. What an interesting notion, that we didn't know what time it is until we had a group consensus. And what of the dissenters? Just as—who was it now? That guy who'd sent him to the dictionary to look up "escutcheon." Ward Evans, that was it: just as Ward Evans had dissented at Oppenheimer's security-board show trial those many years ago, what if the majority of the *Bulletin*'s committee voted for, say, three minutes to midnight, but the remainder felt two minutes was the more appropriate setting?

It was somewhat like the observation phenomenon in quantum physics—the cat alive *and* dead until someone checked on the poor beast's health—but, instead of the first observer creating a reality all subsequent ones were stuck with, the minority view meant that, although for most it was *this* time, for some it could instead be *that* time, and—

And, Jesus H. Christ, where the H doubtless stood for Heisenberg, that was it! That was *exactly* what was needed: an experiment, a device, an instrument, a *machine* that collapsed not into one reality but into *two,* being both *this* and *that,* or, more precisely, more importantly, more powerfully, being both *now* and *then*, simultaneously the present and the past.

A buzzer sounded from Verna Hobson's black phone and she picked up the handset. When she'd put it down again, she turned to Feynman and said, "Dr. Oppenheimer will see you now."

Dick got to his feet but headed not toward the inner door that led to the director's office but to the one that led out into the ground floor of Fuld Hall. "No," said Feynman, "he'll see me then!" And he sprinted into the corridor and up the stairs, heading for Kurt Gödel's office.

Chapter 52

From Dallas, Texas, the flash apparently official: President Kennedy died at 1:00 p.m. Central Standard Time—two o'clock Eastern Standard Time—some thirty-eight minutes ago.

—Walter Cronkite

Vindication at last! Oppie sat at his desk in Fuld Hall, drafting his acceptance speech. Teller might have extorted the Einstein Award, and, yes, it had been Teller himself who had also received this honor last year. But now, finally, it was Robert's turn: next week, he'd receive the Enrico Fermi Award, named for the Italian navigator who had passed away nine years ago. That it came with a tax-free $50,000 check was nice. The news announced just this morning, that President Kennedy would personally present the award to him, was definitely sweet. And the gold medal with Fermi's likeness, looking down and to the left with that slight, shy smile Oppie remembered so fondly, would certainly be a keepsake.

But what mattered most was the organization that was sponsoring the award. The A.E.C., the goddamned Atomic Energy Commission, the same body that had stripped Oppie of his security clearance nine years ago, had now done a complete one-eighty and was about to bestow its highest honor, its prize for lifetime achievement, on J. Robert Oppenheimer! He'd be back in the canon of nuclear giants along with the previous recipients: Fermi himself (the only posthumous laureate), then von Neumann, Lawrence, Wigner, Seaborg, Bethe, and, yes, Teller.

Glenn Seaborg, who had shared the Nobel Prize for the discovery of plutonium, was the current A.E.C. chair, and Oppie had no doubt that it was he, along with Oppie's White House supporters including Dean Rusk, McGeorge Bundy, and Arthur Schlesinger, Jr., who had ensured Oppie would be this year's recipient: a full, public, presidential acknowledgement that the commission had been wrong, wrong, so-fucking-wrong in stripping him of his Q clearance. Seaborg had told Oppie that, when he informed his predecessor, Lewis Strauss, about the upcoming award, Strauss had looked like Seaborg had punched him in the face.

Verna was out, and she'd left the inner door to Oppie's office open, but Oppie heard a knock on the outer door and, without looking up from the blue-lined pad he was writing on, he called out, "Come in!"

"Dad ..."

He saw his son Peter, now twenty-two, tall and lean, a look of pure shock on his face. Oppie pushed back his chair, got up, and strode into the secretarial office. "Is Kitty—"

Peter raised a hand. "She's fine. Dad, I just heard it on my car radio. President Kennedy has been shot."

Robert felt as if a bullet were tearing into his own flesh. He averted his gaze and took hold of the edge of Verna's desk to steady himself. "I—I need a drink. Peter?"

"God, yes."

He staggered into the walk-in closet where a few bottles were always kept, and—

A bullet. A single bullet. History didn't turn on atom bombs; it pivoted on shots from guns, whether it was the assassination of Archduke Ferdinand beginning the First World War, or Hitler's own bullet to the brain ending the Second in Europe, or, now, with the person who'd challenged the nation to put a man on the moon by the decade's close, who'd stared down Khrushchev during the Cuban Missile Crisis when the world was truly at the brink of nuclear annihilation: shot, fate unknown. Alive; dead. Schrödinger's cat, with the future hanging in the balance.

"Dad ...?" said Peter. Oppie heard him but still just stood there, staring at the bottles arranged on the top of a small safe, glass rockets poised for launch.

"It's okay, Dad," said Peter again. "Never mind, then." Oppie felt his son's hand on his forearm leading him out of the closet into the room and helping him find a seat.

Verna came running in. "My God, did you hear?"

Oppie raised his head but he sounded far-off even to himself. "Peter says the president's been shot."

"Not just shot," said Verna, her voice breaking. "They just announced it. He's dead."

Oppie sat for a moment listening to the barrage of his own pulse. "Well, then," he said, his head swimming. "Well, then." He was quiet for a time but at last rallied some strength. "Verna, can you knock on all the office doors? Tell everyone to go home, be with their families."

She nodded and left.

"And, Peter, maybe ... maybe you can drive me home?"

"Of course, Dad."

But Oppie continued to just sit there, face propped up by his hands, bony elbows on the chair's arms. "Now," he said softly, "things are going to come apart very fast."

The choice of Oppie was controversial among die-hard McCarthyites, and Senator Bourke Hickenlooper publicly turned down the invitation to the award ceremony, sniffing that it was "unthinkable" that the medal go to Oppenheimer. But miraculously, Kennedy's successor, Lyndon B. Johnson, stayed the course, personally presenting the Fermi Award to Oppie at a gala in the cabinet room of the White House. The ceremony was held on December second, the twenty-first anniversary of Fermi's original sustained nuclear reaction beneath the bleachers at Stagg Field in Chicago.

Kitty and their children—son Peter and their daughter Toni, almost twenty—were beaming with pride. So were General Groves, who was now sixty-seven, retired from Sperry Rand and slipping into frailty, and Isidor

Isaac Rabi, going strong at sixty-five. Leo Szilard, also sixty-five, had lost much of his bulk during his recent self-directed radiation therapy for bladder cancer, but his smile was as angelic as ever. Last year's Fermi Prize winner, though, stood alone by a floor-to-ceiling black velvet curtain, his face as dead as his artificial foot.

Oppie stared for several seconds at the plaque Johnson handed him. "I think it is just possible, Mr. President," he said, appearing, he knew, feeble and scrawny next to the ruddy six-foot-three Texan, "that it has taken some charity and some courage for you to make this award today." Robert paused and looked out at the faces: scientists and politicians, humanitarians and statesmen, the best and the brightest. "That would seem to me a good augury," he concluded, "for all our futures."

Chapter 53

Two Years Later: 1965

"Who's interested in the Mars atmosphere or the initial thrust of a satellite? The story lacks a girl!"

—**Wernher von Braun**, summarizing the eighteen editors who rejected his novel *Project Mars*

While other ex-Nazis were trying to slide quietly into anonymous post-war life, Wernher von Braun was reveling in his new-found celebrity. Between 1954 and 1956, *Collier's* published a wildly popular series of cover stories about exploring the solar system featuring commentary by him. Subsequent appearances on Walt Disney's television show, accompanied by his trademark models of futuristic rocket ships and a wheel-shaped space station, made his eager face and thick, high-pitched accent well-known.

Wernher had been named chief architect of the *Saturn V*, the giant rocket that, if all went well, would put the first man on the moon, but, to him, that was just one small step. His real goal had always been Mars. And so, of course, he'd arranged to be at the Jet Propulsion Laboratory in Pasadena for the unveiling of the first-ever close-up photographs of the red planet.

The initial attempt to get such things had been a bust. The unmanned probe *Mariner III* had failed just eight hours after launch, its solar panels never deploying, but its twin, *Mariner IV*, had successfully completed the seven-

and-a-half-month journey to Mars. The probe's black-and-white television camera took twenty-two still pictures, covering, in total, about one percent of the planet's surface. Yesterday—August 4, 1965—the images, finally decoded from raw numerical data, had been revealed at J.P.L., and today, with glossy eight-by-ten prints of each one, Wernher arrived at the Institute for Advanced Study to share the news.

A representative from each of the three divisions of the Arbor Project came to meet him. I.I. Rabi, who had turned sixty-seven last week, was there from the New Names group, charged with evacuating the planet. Kitty Oppenheimer, who would turn fifty-five next week, represented the Compact Cement far-out ideas team. And Robert Oppenheimer, now sixty-two but looking older, was there on behalf of Patient Power, the group trying to either fix the sun or shield the earth. They all gathered to meet von Braun in room 108 of Fuld Hall, adjacent to, and accessible directly from, Oppie's office. It had four windows set in a semi-circular bay giving spectacular views of the wide south lawn, the pond, and the woods. But all eyes were on the photographic prints, each one curling slightly upward. They were spread out, along with several Mars maps, on a long mahogany table.

"Let's skip the appetizers and get down to the giblets," said von Braun, still boyish at fifty-three. "The key photo is this one, number eleven." He moved it to the table's center, and the other scientists craned to look at it. Oppie felt his heart jump. He heard Rabi suck in his breath, and Kitty muttered, "Shit."

"That was taken at a distance of seventy-eight-hundred miles," said von Braun, who stepped back now so the others could see the photo better. "East to west, it covers a hundred and seventy miles. North-south, one-fifty."

"Where?" demanded Oppie. "What co-ordinates?"

Von Braun consulted a series of stapled sheets he had brought with him. "It's centered on thirty-one degrees south and one-niner-seven degrees east."

Oppie turned his attention to the giant 1962 Air Force map of Mars, flattening out its creases with his palm. He quickly found the spot. On the map, a canal cut diagonally across the middle of that area starting in the southwest and running up to the northeast as if flowing from Mare Cimmerium to Mare Sirenum.

And in the *Mariner* photo, maybe, just maybe, if he really, really, *really* willed himself to see it, there was a diagonal line, although at a less steep angle, running ... no, not into a sea, or even a plain, but into—

There was nothing else it could be, was there?

—into a *crater.* Only one-half of its rim was clearly visible, like the bowed part of a capital D, but it dominated most of the frame. And the bloody thing wasn't alone. Oppie quickly counted seven—no, eight!—other craters in photo eleven. Given the size of the area being portrayed, the D crater was perhaps eighty miles across, the one adjacent to it was maybe thirty, two were twenty, and the rest were ten down to as little as five.

Oppie knew that Mare Cimmerium was named in honor of the Cimmerians, a people Homer mentioned in the *Odyssey* who lived in perpetual darkness. And after three and a half centuries of looking at the red planet through telescopes, that darkness had finally lifted, and mankind was at last seeing the true face of its celestial neighbor.

It was heartbreaking.

It was like looking at the goddamned moon.

In photo eleven, there were small craters within large craters, and some craters overlapped and obliterated parts of others. And, once you'd seen them in this, the sharpest of the pictures, you couldn't help seeing them in the other photos, too. Craters everywhere.

But no sign of water.

No sign of water *erosion.*

Just dusty death.

Even worse than that. *Death* implied there'd once been life, but this planet's surface looked ancient, untouched for millions or billions of years. Barren, sterile.

With von Braun's guidance, Oppie next located the spot on the Air Force map captured by picture eight. That area was bisected by Erinnys, one of Percival Lowell's more prominent canals, which, according to him, flowed from the west end of Mare Sirenum to Titanum Sinus in Memnonia. But this photo, too, depicted nothing but craters, albeit none as large as the one that dominated picture eleven.

"And there's more," said von Braun.

"Oh, joy," said Kitty.

"*Mariner IV* didn't go into orbit," said von Braun. "It was a fly-by mission. Still, it *did* pass behind Mars from earth's point of view, and just before it did so—and just after it emerged on the other side—its S-band radio, beaming toward earth at twenty-three hundred megahertz, passed through the Martian atmosphere. There was no specific occultation experiment aboard, but we can make some reliable conclusions thanks to the amplitude and phase changes that were detected. Based on them, we were able to confirm that the Martian atmosphere is almost entirely carbon dioxide. That, of course, suggests that, despite our best hopes, the polar caps don't contain any appreciable amount of frozen water—which could have been melted for drinking or irrigation, or electrolyzed into hydrogen and oxygen for fuel—but are almost exclusively dry ice."

"Which is fun at a kid's birthday party or to shatter a goldfish," said Rabi, "but otherwise pretty damn useless."

"Yes," said von Braun, nodding. "And the occultation also let us get a handle on the density of the Martian atmosphere. It's *thin*—even thinner than we'd thought. Somewhere between four and six millibars." Earth's was roughly a thousand millibars, one bar originally having been defined as earth's sea-level atmospheric pressure. The red planet had an atmosphere about one-half of one percent as dense as earth's—and what little of it there was consisted of poisonous CO_2. Oppenheimer felt light-headed.

"The bad news isn't over yet," said von Braun. "*Mariner IV* had a helium magnetometer aboard. As it approached Mars, we expected it to detect the planet's magnetic field. The sooner it detected it—that is, the farther from Mars *Mariner* found it—the stronger the field must be. We knew Mars couldn't have as strong a field as earth. But based on the planet's mass and rate of rotation, we figured it might have a magnetic field about one-tenth as powerful as earth's, and so we expected *Mariner* to encounter the shock front many hours before making its closest approach to the planet. Now, I won't say we didn't find *anything.* There was one little hiccup slightly after closest approach that *might* have been the shock front. If it *was,* well, then Mars has a magnetic moment 0.03 percent of earth's—and if it *wasn't,* then it's even less, or perhaps totally nonexistent."

Oppie found a chair and collapsed into it, stunned. With such a minuscule magnetic field, Mars couldn't possibly have anything akin to earth's Van Allen belts. That lack helped explain the incredibly tenuous Martian atmosphere *Mariner IV* had detected—nothing to deflect the ever-present solar wind from stripping it away. But it also meant that any life on the surface—be it native lichen or refugee humans—would be pelted by long-range alpha particles that were always spewing out of the sun. The surface of Mars wasn't just sterile; it was constantly being *sterilized.*

Oppenheimer looked from person to person. Von Braun's eyebrows and arms were lifted in the classic don't-shoot-the-messenger plea. Rabi, frowning deeply, was chewing at the edge of his thumbnail. Kitty was shaking her head slowly left to right.

"Well," said Oppie, when he could at last find his voice again, "that's just devastating."

"It's bullshit is what it is," said Kitty. "Jesus Christ." She pointed at the big Mars map Oppie had been consulting. "How old is that thing?"

"Three years," Robert replied.

"Three years ago, the best map ever made still showed canals! But in reality—"

"In reality," said Rabi, "it's a dead world. There's no way any but a tiny number of humans could ever live on Mars, and even then they'd have to be in some sort of sealed habitat."

"Or maybe underground," said Kitty, "to shield against the radiation. *Shit.* It'd be impossible to sustain anything more than a tiny colony there, and then only in what might as well be catacombs."

"So what now?" asked Oppie. He felt bone-weary, as ancient as the surface in the photographs.

Rabi was pacing. "We can't go to any of the moons of Jupiter: the radiation it puts out, plus its strong magnetic field concentrating that radiation in the orbital paths of the largest moons, make them uninhabitable. And now, pretty much the opposite problem: Mars has too little of a magnetic field, meaning solar radiation showers down upon it unchecked."

"And so we can't go there, either," said Kitty.

"I hate to agree," said von Braun, "but yes. Mars doesn't seem to hold our answer."

"There has to be another possibility," said Rabi. "There has to be something we haven't thought of."

But Kitty was back to shaking her head. "You want my considered opinion?" She waited until all eyes were on her then said, "We're pretty much fucked."

Chapter 54

Two Years Later: 1967

What does such a man think, confronted with death, a man with his head so full of ideas, so wise in so many directions? What goes on behind those eyes that were once so brilliantly blue, now rather bleary with pain?

—David Lilienthal,
chairman, Atomic Energy Commission

At least *they* died quickly.

It had been three weeks since Oppie's doctors had told him that the radiation therapy was no longer working—and it had been a full year now since he'd first been diagnosed with throat cancer.

The irony was not lost on him: the very fact that such a thing as nuclear medicine existed was largely his doing, and the isotopes that had initially kept the tumors in check were precisely the sort Lewis Strauss had wanted to ban exports of—God, was it really eighteen years ago?

Isotopes are far less important than electronic devices but far more important than vitamins. Somewhere in between.

Somewhere in between.

Of course, Oppie had been talking then about their potential for use in weaponry, not in holding the insatiable crab at bay. For that, they had been, until recently, *the* most important thing. Now that they'd stopped working for him, they would try chemotherapy, but the prospects, he knew, were meager; physics trumps chemistry any day.

Oppie wasn't the first Manhattan Project scientist to benefit from radioisotopes. Leo Szilard had gone down this path already, organizing his own experimental treatment for bladder cancer at Sloan-Kettering in 1960. Six weeks of radiation bought him years of remission; he'd lasted until 1964, passing away at the age of sixty-six. The year the treatments began, Szilard's turn for the Einstein Award had come. Trude, finally his wife, had remarked on how impressive the list of previous winners was, and Leo, from his hospital bed, had quipped, "Yes, and it is getting better and better!"

Oppie missed flamboyant Leo, and Einstein the eccentric, gone a dozen years now, and the taciturn Fermi, who had passed five months before Einstein. Intellects vast and cool but oh so sympathetic, born in the last years of the nineteenth century—or, in Enrico's case, the first of the twentieth—intelligences greater than the common man's and yet as mortal as ...

... as his own.

If the battle for life had truly been a game of chess with Death—akin to that Bergman film—Oppie had no doubt that his departed friends would have won; Death was evil, and evil, he was convinced, was *stupid.* Then again, so, it turned out, was smoking. Way back at Leiden—four decades ago now!—Paul Ehrenfest had droned on incessantly about the dangers of tobacco. Oppie had finally kicked his four-pack-a-day cigarette habit three years ago, although he still smoked a pipe. But even doing that was hard now. Just breathing hurt his throat. Day after day of decline, week after week of decay, month after month of agony.

The thought came to him again: at least they died quickly.

They were the three *Apollo 1* astronauts. Chaffee, White, and ... what was it, now? Griffin? No—Grissom. Gus Grissom. Yesterday, January 26, 1967, they'd been incinerated in their space capsule—not on re-entry, which had always been a valid fear, but in a routine ground test before they'd even gone up.

"Flame!"

"We've got a fire in the cockpit!"

"Open her up!"

And a scream.

Oh, yes, it had been painful, but it had been over in minutes if not seconds. By the time the ground crew got the command module's door open, all three men were dead, the nylon spacesuits melted into their bodies, skin flayed from bone. He hadn't seen pictures yet—and the public never would—but von Braun, director of the Marshall Space Flight Center, thoroughly American now in all but accent, was his conduit to NASA information. The corpses, he'd said, looked like—

—like the corpses in Hiroshima, in Nagasaki.

A spark inside the capsule, yards of flammable Velcro stuck to every bare surface, and a foolishly ill-conceived test of a pure-oxygen high-pressure atmosphere.

God only knew how long this disaster would delay *Apollo.*

Oppie was sitting in his living room at Olden Manor; Kitty was in the attached greenhouse he'd had built for her as a birthday present, tending her orchids. For fuck's sake, he thought, there should have been greenhouses—and humans!—on Mars by now. If only they hadn't canceled *Orion.*

He looked down at the little table next to his chair, and the circular glass ashtray, filled with pipe dottle and Kitty's butts. If only he hadn't smoked himself to death.

The sun shone through the brown curtains, a thousand pinpricks where its rays found holes in the weave. If only even one of their mad schemes to shield the earth had panned out.

In the bookcase next to him sat his copy of *Les Fleurs du mal,* Baudelaire's astringent verse illustrated with etchings by Tony-George Roux. He reached for the book, even such a small effort almost too much for him now. It fell open in his lap to pages 204 and 205, the poem *"Une Martyre"* and the picture that reminded him so much of ... of ...

He snapped the fifty-year-old book shut. If only he'd been there for Jean the night everything had proven too much for her.

In the same bookcase, but on the bottom shelf, at the far left, politics trumping alphabetical order, were two volumes by his erstwhile friend Haakon Chevalier: the clumsy *roman à clef* from 1959 called *The Man Who Would Be God* and the more on-the-nose work of nonfiction—or so Hoke would have it—from just two years ago, *Oppenheimer: The Story of a Friendship.*

If only he'd turned Chevalier in immediately upon that approach in the kitchen at Eagle Hill—or, he supposed, if only he'd never mentioned Chevalier at all. Odd, he reflected, that the options occurred to him now in that order. It seemed part of him still was that unctuous, repulsively good little boy he'd been during his sheltered New York childhood, a childhood that hadn't prepared him for a world full of cruel and bitter things. It had given him, as he'd told *Time* magazine two decades ago, no normal, healthy way to be a bastard.

If only.

If only.

At the end of a life, Oppie supposed, that's all there was: regret.

Of course, he'd left his mark. No trip to Stockholm, no Nobel, but he'd changed the world more than most of the laureates—including the Peace Prize ones—ever had, changed it even more than Alfred Nobel had with his invention of dynamite. Still, if sheer destructive power were the measure of greatness, it'd be Teller whose name would live on.

Live on for whatever little time earth had left.

Oh, maybe one of his Arbor Project teams would find a solution. *Orion* had looked so promising, but there was no point persevering to save the world from a natural catastrophe less than six decades hence if human folly would have destroyed it sooner. It had been the right decision to ban atmospheric nuclear tests, to bar nukes from space, to take at least one small step back from the precipice.

Still, if only they had succeeded. If only—

The doorbell rang. Robert knew from long experience that Kitty couldn't hear it in the odd glass acoustics of her greenhouse. He slipped Baudelaire back onto the shelf and, using his two twig-like arms, managed to get himself to his feet. It was a painful shuffle to the foyer and an effort even to turn the brass knob. The door creaked open.

And there, with the magnificent trees of the Institute for Advanced Study as a wall behind them, stood gangly Richard Feynman. Next to him was much-shorter Kurt Gödel, his wide-spaced eyes behind horn-rim glasses, bundled up against a February cold that he imagined should be present although Robert felt no chill in the air.

"My whole life I've wanted to say this," said Feynman, a grin stretching his mouth, "and I figured you deserved to hear it."

"Yes?" said Oppie.

"Eureka!" exclaimed Feynman. "Or," he said, draping a friendly arm around Gödel's narrow shoulders, "more precisely, *we* have found it."

"Found what?"

Gödel, ordinarily reticent, spoke up. "For God's sake, Robert, let us in. We'll catch our deaths out here!"

Oppie stepped aside and gestured for the two men to enter. Automatically, he offered, "Drinks?"

"Absolutely," said Feynman. "This calls for your best bottle of champagne!"

Chapter 55

Each observer has his own set of "nows," and none of these various systems of layers can claim the prerogative of representing the objective lapse of time.

—Kurt Gödel

"Where's Kitty?" asked Gödel.

"In the greenhouse," replied Oppie. "Why?"

Feynman smiled. "Kitty is our group leader at Compact Cement, you know. She should hear this first—or, at least, at the same time you do."

Oppie nodded and started shuffling toward the back of Olden Manor. But apparently his slow pace, the best he could manage these days, was not sprightly enough for his impatient visitors, who clearly didn't want to wait for him to get Kitty and return; they fell in behind him, Feynman giving a lupine "Hey, there!" as they passed the Oppenheimers' pretty maid.

There was a door going from near the kitchen into the greenhouse. Oppie led the way in, the warm, muggy air a sweltering contrast to the dry coolness of the mansion proper. Kitty was there, clad in blue trousers and a loose-fitting white blouse with the sleeves rolled up. She was using a hose to water beds of plants.

Neither Gödel nor Feynman had been in the greenhouse before, and Dick immediately went over to look at a long metal box filled with plants sprouting around a packing mixture of pearlescent beads. "What's this?"

"Hydroponics," replied Kitty, shutting off her hose. "That's what I've been working on in my spare time: plants that we could grow on Mars or aboard a space habitat without soil. The ones I keep out here need a lot of sunlight, but I've got more in the basement that are getting by with just dim bulbs." She smiled. "And speaking of dim bulbs, what brings you two here?"

Gödel merely blinked behind his thick glasses, but Dick laughed. "Well, you know what Kurt and I have been fiddling around with," he said.

"Yes, of course," replied Kitty. "Don't tell me something's actually come of it!"

"Yes," said Dick. "I didn't believe the numbers being spit out by Johnny von Neumann's computer at first, but I had two of our younger members—that bright boy and girl you brought in from Stanford last month, Oppie—double and triple check everything, and it's solid."

"That's amazing," said Kitty.

"Wait a minute," said Robert. "Guys, *she* may know what you've been working on, but *I* don't."

"True!" said Dick. "You will, but not yet—that damned linearity of time, eh, Kurt?" He nudged the shorter man.

"Except it's *not* linear," Gödel said. "It forms hoops—closed time-like curves."

"That's what *he* calls them," said Dick. "But, as far as quantum electrodynamics is concerned, there's no 'like' about it: they *are* loops in time—and we can, at least in theory, move material objects along a single loop, or through an interconnected series of them, to any point in the past."

"So?" said Oppie. "I've read all of Kurt's papers. He's been saying that for eighteen years now."

Kurt nodded. "It was my present to Einstein for his seventieth birthday: a novel solution to the field equations of general relativity."

"Which," Feynman said, a twinkle in his eye, "made Einstein doubt general relativity—his own creation!"

"Yes," said Gödel. "But he would not doubt it now. Feynman and I have cobbled together a machine that will actually displace objects to any point along a closed time-like curve."

"Seriously?" asked Kitty.

"Seriously," said Feynman. His flippant voice wasn't really up to giving credence to that word, but Oppie decided to take it at face value.

"You mean you can dial up, say, October fourth, 1957, and *go* there?" asked Robert, pulling the date the Space Age had begun out of the air. He sat down on the edge of a large planter, his mind racing even as his cancer-ridden body continued to fail him.

"The device works with relative rather than absolute dates," said Gödel, "so that would be coded as negative nine years five months, but yes: you could go there."

"Have you—my God, have you tested it?" asked Robert, and "Jesus, does it work?" Kitty asked at the same time.

"It *seems* to work," said Gödel. "We tried putting some innocuous things into it—stones from deep in the Institute woods, and so on—and they did indeed disappear, but that doesn't prove they actually traveled in time."

"Did you send them forward or backward?"

"Backward," said Feynman. "We haven't figured out how to send anything forward. Of course, if time *is* circular, you should be able to send things back so far that they wrap around to the future, but we've got nowhere near the energy required for that."

"That's incredible," said Kitty. "I'm—wow, I'm just flummoxed. But that's amazing. Good work, boys!"

"It *is* amazing," allowed Oppie, "but I don't see how it's applicable to the solar-purge problem."

Feynman laughed. "Spoken like a true administrator. 'Dammit, Smathers, I sent you to Ford's Theatre to review a play—what's all this crap about the president being assassinated?'"

"It's the answer to everything," said Gödel. "But, come, can we get out of all this humidity? We're going to catch something, I'm sure."

Feynman moved toward the door that led back into the house. "We'll be happy to explain," he said, stepping inside. "And maybe you can get that cute maid of yours to bring us that champagne?"

Chapter 56

Quite independently from her drinking I have found Kitty the most despicable female I have ever known, because of her cruelty. To an outsider like me, Oppenheimer's family life looked like hell on earth.

—**Abraham Pais**,
I.A.S. physicist

Robert had flown to Berkeley for the experiment. He still owned the home at One Eagle Hill and it seemed the perfect base of operations for Feynman and company to set up their equipment, away from the prying eyes of institute professors who were not part of the Arbor Project. Gödel, as afraid of flying as he was of just about everything else, stayed back in Princeton, but I.I. Rabi, who would soon succeed Oppie as project head, was already out there, as were Feynman and five of the newer crop of physicists, two of whom were women; the times were indeed a-changin'.

Oppie had asked Kitty to come along, but she'd refused. She needed him to be either alive or dead, she said, not somehow weirdly both. Where he was going she wouldn't follow; what he had to do she wouldn't be any part of. After Oppie had quietly slipped away from Princeton, she had, he'd heard, locked the door to the bedroom he had been resting in these past few weeks and told well-wishers who came by that he wasn't up to seeing visitors and that she herself simply couldn't bear to enter it.

At last, everything was ready on Eagle Hill. Oppie, as always, hoped the right words would come to him in the moment. He was fond for many reasons of Oscar Wilde, and particularly so for the quip sometimes purported to have been his final words: "Either these curtains go or I do!" But although Robert's next utterance would be his last in linear time, it would not, he profoundly hoped, be his true final pronouncement. With the best smile he could muster, and to a round of applause from the small group of scientists, he said: "The American navigator is about to arrive in the old world."

The countdown, conducted with gusto by Feynman, was brief: "Five, four, three, two, one," and then—

Inside the clear acrylic containment bubble, Oppie found his skin tingling and what wisps of white hair he still had seemed charged with electricity. His sense of balance disappeared; fortunately, he was, in good H.G. Wells fashion, seated on the complicated contraption's saddle. It seemed as though he were briefly watching a movie in reverse, with Dick counting up instead of down, the monosyllables of "one, two, three, four, five" in bizarre retrograde, like a rewinding tape. During the counting up, one of the young male scientists walked backward from his control console; smoke was sucked into the bowl of Rabi's pipe; and a young female physicist rose from her chair without having to push up on its arms.

But soon everything accelerated into a greenish-gray blur with odd spectral flashes at the peripheries of his vision. That lasted—subjectively, of course—perhaps half a minute, and then the same basement room he had been in solidified around him. But no one else was there, although his attention was immediately caught by things that he and Kitty hadn't bothered to ship to Los Alamos but had subsequently disposed of, including Peter's stroller and crib. The light, coming in from the high-up windows, had changed both direction and appearance; he'd arrived late, apparently, on a sunny afternoon.

Oppie just sat for a while, letting his stomach settle and his sense of balance return—and allowing his racing heart to calm at least a little.

He was *here* and it was *now*, and, of all the nows he could have chosen—one in which he might have prevented the dropping of either of the atomic bombs anywhere, another in which he could have facilitated Leo Szilard's request for a demonstration, a third in which he'd turned down General Groves's offer to run the damn project—*this* was the only one that made sense to him, the only one of those he desired that wouldn't produce expanding ripples resulting in large-scale changes to the history yet to come, that looming future that he'd at last made his uneasy peace with, the forthcoming past that he knew had to be.

When he finally felt ready to do so, Oppie dismounted and exited from the sphere. The machine would return to its origin after twenty-odd minutes—the maximum they could hold this rickety prototype in another time with its modest power supply. Something akin to the spooky action at a distance that Einstein so deplored kept it linked to the base station that would be built in this very basement in 1967, and it would soon be pulled back to then. He figured his old friend Rabi had guessed that it would come back empty, but the others, doubtless, would be shocked.

Oppie managed the staircase out of the cellar, slowly, a step at a time, and shuffled his way to the room where he kept the mineralogical specimens from his youth. He removed a wooden tray from a cabinet. The tray had a glass window in its hinged lid and twenty-four small compartments within. But this particular tray, labeled "Poconos, September 1916," only had twenty-one specimens in it, that being the number that had passed young Robert's exacting standards of collectability. Oppie reached into his pocket and pulled out a translucent green cobble about the size of a large grape. He placed it in one of the empty squares, then closed the lid and put the tray back in the cabinet.

Before he'd traveled back, Oppie and Feynman had looked in the same case, still kept at Eagle Hill, confirming that it only contained the original twenty-one specimens, but now—then, back, ahead, in 1967—after Oppie's disappearance, Dick would check again and this time he would find the piece of trinitite, the fused glass created—or that would be created—by the Trinity blast, a year and a half from Robert's current now.

Each piece of trinitite was unique, containing distinctive patterns of bubbles and even tiny bits of the actual plutonium bomb or its support tower; there was no way this pebble of it could be mistaken for any other. But when Feynman tested this one, whose exact point of collection was precisely documented, he would find that its radioactive decay had started *not* twenty-two years ago, as one would expect for trinitite in 1967, but *forty-five* years ago, reflecting the fact that it had passed through much of the forties, all of the fifties, and most of the sixties *twice,* thereby proving that this, the initial test of the time machine with a human passenger, had been a success.

Robert had volunteered to be the guinea pig: the first chronic argonaut, to use Wells's lovely coinage. His days were numbered, anyway; three, four, surely no more than five. And although he never did get his Nobel, this contribution was one he *could* still make, ensuring, when the truth eventually came out, that he'd go down in history for, well, going down in history.

After putting the specimen tray away, Oppie took a cab to Telegraph Hill in San Francisco, having the driver drop him by a wooden telephone booth. It took most of Oppie's strength to push the folding door open. Before he'd traveled back, he and his secretary Verna had gone scrounging for coins dated 1944 or earlier; he had a bunch with him now, along with a small wad of similarly old dollar bills. He fished out an Indian-head nickel and deposited it into the pay phone's slot. When the operator came on, he said, "Atwater 3-4-1-8, please," and waited. After three jangling rings, the voice he hadn't heard for a quarter of a century came on. "Hello?"

He'd contemplated various openings, ranging from the poetic to the cloying, but in the end settled on a simple, "Hello, Jean."

"Hello?" she said again. "Who's this?"

He coughed, cleared his throat, and tried to put some strength behind the words. "It's Robert," and then, since the only reply was crackling static, he added his last name.

"God," said Jean. "What's wrong with your voice?"

"I'm, ah, a bit under the weather." The understatement of the year. "I'm just down the street from your place. May I come over?"

"You're here in San Francisco? My God, yes, yes."

"I'm on my way." He hung up then found another five-cent piece, fed the slot, and made a quick, second call. He didn't expect his voice to be recognized this time, and it wasn't. But the startled and anxious man agreed to his request. Oppie hung up again and set out.

The two blocks were excruciating even with his cane, and they were made worse by the steep San Francisco incline. But at last he reached 1405

Montgomery Street. Jean, in a sky-blue robe over a white nightgown, was standing in the narrow doorway. She didn't seem to realize that this shambling figure was the person she was waiting for until he was only yards away.

There was a lamp attached to the wall next to the doorway, and its harsh lighting, Oppie was sure, accentuated the crags and sags of his face. "Jean," he said, between wheezes.

She peered at him. "Are you—are you Julius?"

She meant Oppie's father—and Oppie realized with a start that his dad had died at age sixty-six; he was going to fall short of that figure by four years. "He's dead, Jean." A pause for breath, then: "He died in 1939. You know that."

"But ... then who?"

"It's me, Jean. Robert. Oppie. Bob. It's me."

"No. No, Robert is—"

"Young. And I'm old. Twenty-three years older, to be precise." His breathing was returning to its ragged norm. "I'm old, and I'm dying. I'm the one who is supposed to die soon, not you."

She narrowed her eyes, the green irises luminous in the lamp glow. "What—what are you talking about?"

"Please," he said, pointing to the staircase just behind her. "May we?"

She hesitated a moment, her expression one of utter bafflement, but then she beckoned him forward and helped him up first one flight and then another to her cramped third-floor studio apartment. She then aided him in sitting on the short couch and brought him a glass of water.

"It *is* you, isn't it?" Jean said, pulling over a wooden chair and sitting facing him.

"Yes."

"But what happened?"

"Age. Illness."

"Age? I don't ..."

Oppie tried to cross his legs but it was too painful. He thought about bringing up H.G. Wells, but perhaps the science-fiction writer was too pedestrian for her tastes: Wells, who had predicted, and named, the atomic bomb; Wells, who even earlier, had predicted, and named, time machines. "I've come back to see you," he said. "Come back from 1967."

"But ... how?"

She was staggeringly bright, he knew, but, still, to even begin to explain would take precious hours—hours he didn't have. "Physics," he said simply.

"You have to prove it to me," she said. "You have to prove you're who you say you are."

He closed his eyes and recited the words:

"Is even this
"Not enough to appease your awful pain
"You gaunt terrible bleeding Jesus"

And she, the author, the woman who had penned those words when she was just sixteen, added the final French line of that stanza: *"Fils de Dieu."* Son of God. She shook her head. "I never shared that poem with anyone but ..."

"But *me.*"

She studied his face some more, her eyes darting left and right, trying to see beyond the wrinkles and folds. Her mouth hung slightly open and her head oscillated in disbelief. But at last she nodded and, in an astonished voice, agreed, "With anyone but you."

He smiled warmly. "It's so good to see you, Jean." And then a small, affectionate laugh. "But I really should have been here eleven days ago."

"Why?"

"Then I could've properly played the role of the Ghost of Christmas Yet to Come."

He'd hoped for her wan, shy smile but received nothing. "I know the years have not been kind to me." He coughed three times then paused as if waiting for a fourth before going on. "And not just the years. Smoking." He gestured at an overflowing ashtray and a crumpled package of Chesterfields. "Oh, Jean, I beg you to quit. I can't reveal much about the future, but it will be proven in the early 1960s that cigarette smoking causes lung cancer." He paused and waited for the breath his habit had cost him to return. "Funny thing: it's like the bomb. The Brits were working on this first, too; they announced—will announce—the link between smoking and cancer in 1962. That'll finally get the Americans going. Our surgeon general will issue a report in 1964."

"I'm not worried about the future," said Jean.

He reached out, took her hand—young, smooth flesh, warm and vibrant. "I know," he said softly. "Shall I recite something else?" She looked at him quizzically, and he took that as leave to go on: "'I wanted to live and to give and I got paralyzed somehow.'" Her eyes went wide, and he continued: "'I think I would have been a liability all my life. At least I could take away the burden of a paralyzed soul from a fighting world.'"

She was silent.

"Recognize the words?"

"I—I haven't ..."

"Haven't written them yet. No, but you were planning to—them, or something like them; you've doubtless been mulling over what to say. You were going to write that down tonight, after you took the pills."

She shook her head. "This is ..." She was a psychiatrist; she had a whole lexicon of lunacy at her disposal. But after a moment she finished with: "... unnerving."

"For both of us. But I've come, my love, to stop you from taking those pills, from writing that letter."

She looked down at the scuffed floorboards. "I just want to be *done,* Robert. I want all the pain, all the confusion, to be over."

He tilted his head slightly. "I don't think pain and confusion ever end entirely. But they *do* abate. I've tried to kill myself, too—once, as I told you years ago, when I was even younger than you are now, after my horrid year at the Cavendish, and again ..." He closed his eyes, remembering that night—both thirteen years ago and a decade from now—in the bathroom of Herb and Anne Marks, after Lewis Strauss had hit him with that foul letter of charges. "You're not finished," he said softly. "There are stanzas yet to write."

"Everything is so hard, and you—you've been so far away."

"I know." He coughed again, and she squeezed his hand as if she could pump the cancer out of him. "You're just twenty-nine," he said, marveling at it. "God, to be twenty-nine again!" He'd been that age in 1933, the middle of the easy-going pre-war years at Berkeley and Caltech. So long ago. The Paleozoic. He looked her in the eyes, painfully conscious that the mesmerizing power his gaze used to have was gone. "Promise me, Jean. Hold on until—let's see—hold on seven more weeks. Can you do that? Until February twenty-first, until your birthday—for me. At least *taste* being thirty."

She considered this but then shook her head. "Even if I were to do that, where will you be in *six* weeks? That'll be—yes—Valentine's Day. Where will you be? Not *this* you, but the younger one, the one of this time? Where will *he* be that night?"

Yes, the younger one: the other him, the one that also existed. She *was* sharp. "You know I'm working on a secret project."

"Something *so* important? So desperately important?" She looked at him with imploring eyes. "What is it, then? What *is* this damn thing that matters more than me?"

Oppie thought back—thought ahead—to April of 1954 and prosecutor Roger Robb looming over him.

> *"You spent the night with her, didn't you?"*
> *"Yes."*
> *"That is when you were working on a secret war project?"*
> *"Yes."*
> *"Did you think that consistent with good security?"*
> *"It was, as a matter of fact. Not a word—"*

And indeed not a word had been spoken about any classified matter. He had always been loyal, always kept secrets, never compromised security, never jeopardized the Manhattan Project. An unctuous, repulsively good little boy.

But they were going to throw him into the trash anyway. In the most public, most humiliating way possible, the government he had served so well for so long was going to strip him of his security clearance, turning him from a national hero into a national joke. And, if one were going to be punished regardless, one might as well do the crime, right?

Jean looked at him, jade eyes pleading, the woman who had been planning tonight to become *une martyre.*

A woman who loved him.

A woman he loved.

But, damn it all, he happened to love this country, too.

"I'm sorry," he said. "I can't. But if you can hold on"—he closed his eyes, did the math—"five hundred and seventy-eight days ... no, this is a leap year, isn't it? Five hundred and seventy-*nine* days, I promise you'll know." *The whole world will know.*

"That's so far in the future."

He smiled sadly. "I was just thinking that's so long ago. August sixth, 1945." He shook his head.

She got up off her wooden chair and sat next to him on the couch. "And if I wait that long, will we be together?"

He felt his heart kick. There was indeed another Robert Oppenheimer, right now, toiling away in Los Alamos, a young, energetic Oppie who, less than a month ago, had finally given Haakon Chevalier's name to General Groves. *That* Oppie would be the one who would be looking to build a post-war life. What choice would he—that other he—make if he had an option? After Kitty had run out on him, leaving behind Tyke, who—God!—wouldn't be born for another eleven months? He—this Oppie—hadn't had any choice to make once Japan surrendered; Jean had been long gone for him. But if she *had* held on, if she'd still been alive when that other Oppie *could* depart the mesa for good?

Yes, things would change after that point. But the solar instability had been uncovered *before* then—and doubtless an effort would still be mounted to save some portion of the human species.

He turned and hugged her as tightly as he was able, but it was barely enough to compress the fabric of her blouse where it billowed out.

There are no secrets about the world of nature, he'd told—would tell—broadcaster Edward R. Murrow. *There are only secrets about the thoughts and intentions of men.*

"Please hang on," he said, thinking, *Lord, these affairs are hard on the heart.* "Just hang on. A year and a half. And then, if you're free and you're still interested, yes, I'm sure we'll be together."

"Forever?" she asked, burying her head in his bony shoulder.

He nodded slightly. "Until the end of the world."

Chapter 57

Well—yes. In modern times, of course.

—J. Robert Oppenheimer,
when asked if the Trinity atomic bomb
had been the first one ever detonated

Oppie well knew how long it took to get from the vicinity of Eagle Hill in Berkeley to here, so, when the buzzer sounded down below, he guessed who it must be, rushing over in response to the pay-phone call he'd made. Oppie kissed Jean one last time, long and with as much pressure as he could manage, and then he made his way down the stairs.

John Strong Perry Tatlock had come at once when the stranger called exhorting him to go see his despondent daughter. He'd been expecting a call from her tonight—probably had thought it *was* her when the phone rang. But the man with the coughy, wheezy voice who'd simply identified himself as a friend said he should come at once. And so, rather than not hearing from his daughter as promised tonight, rather than receiving no answer when he came to check on her tomorrow morning and therefore deciding to break in through a window, rather than finding her dead in the bathtub, John Tatlock instead passed a wraith-like apparition wearing a greatcoat and a porkpie hat coming out of the building—from which apartment he had no way of knowing. The skeletal figure held the door for him, and Tatlock rushed past, striding up the stairs, heading on to find his Jean, their Jean, alive.

It disappointed Oppie that Professor Tatlock was a Chaucerian; he probably had little affinity for Dickens, the author Oppie had alluded to earlier that evening. But Tatlock was now at the nexus of a literal tale of two cities, *this* San Francisco, in which Jean lived, and *that* one, overwritten now and forgotten by all except one complex, tired man, in which she did not.

It was getting late, but Robert managed to hail a cab, giving the astonished driver all the money he had with him—some forty dollars in notes and change—when he dropped him off in the middle of Golden Gate Park by the Oriental Tea Garden, where one day he would walk with Stepan Zakharovich Apresyan. It was chilly and surely would grow chillier by the hour, but the numbness brought on by the temperature was almost an analgesic, and he welcomed it. Oppie found a wrought-iron park bench. A Japanese pagoda, unilluminated, a silhouette, a ghost, loomed off to one side, and words from the *Bhagavad Gita* came to him once more:

> *Vanquish enemies at arms*
> *Gain mastery of the sciences*
> *And varied arts*
> *You may do all this, but karma's force*
> *Alone prevents what is not destined*
> *And compels what is to be.*

He sat on the bench, exhausted, and tilted his head up. Before his trip he'd checked the astronomical ephemerides for tonight, so he knew exactly where to look. The moon, high in the sky, was two days past first quarter. To the east, Saturn was shining brightly in Taurus. And just about halfway between them, near the Pleiades, there it was.

An emerald in the firmament.

There could be no mistake. Oppie knew as much astrophysics as anyone: there was no such thing as a green star.

No, this was a *planet*.

A green planet.

The green planet—the green planet Mars, shining down on him from above.

Oppie lay back on the bench, pulling his greatcoat tight about him. He remembered a story by Ray Bradbury—a story the fabulist wouldn't pen for another eight years—about time travelers who'd gone all the way back to the Mesozoic to see dinosaurs. The humans were supposed to stay on their floating path, disturbing nothing, but one of them had stepped on a butterfly. When they returned to the future, everything had changed.

Would that really happen? Would such a small cause propagate out to such large effects? Johnny Von Neumann's massive I.A.S. computer, originally built to perfectly predict the weather, had failed utterly in that task. No matter how much detail Von Neumann provided to his machine, it was never enough: tiny, unaccounted-for factors really did quickly randomize atmospheric conditions. The macroscopic universe wasn't Newton's deterministic clockwork, and it wasn't the indeterminate blur that quantum theory might have suggested. Rather, reality was something else again: it was, as Teller had said of Oppie years ago, complicated and confused.

Or, in a single word, it was *chaotic*.

The Arbor Project scientists had obviously succeeded. Assuming all had gone as planned, they made—would make, had made—their first changes near the end of the Dark Ages, in the year A.D. 945—or, as Dick Feynman liked to call it, 1000 A.A., for *ante atomum*. Next year, the one that had been 1945, would now be Year One, and all subsequent years, in this new system, would be designated P.A., for *post atomum*.

But regardless of the numbering scheme used, nothing had been altered in this rewritten reality until well after the Sumerians had named the drop of blood in the night sky Nergal in honor of their god of plague and war. Mesopotamians saw a red light, too, declaring it to be the star that judged the dead. The ancient civilizations of East Asia saw "the fire star," and the Greeks and Romans, likewise detecting a sanguinary spot in the firmament, identified it with their respective gods of war, Ares and—the name that finally stuck, the one eventually used by everyone—Mars.

Progress would have been slow, and, from a distance, invisible until very late in the game. A millennium ago, in what would someday come to be known as Tunguska, Siberia, a launch facility would be built, safe in the knowledge that the explosion of an in-falling meteor in 1908 would obliterate all traces of it. From that site, Teller's super bombs would have been lobbed at the Martian polar caps, liberating the carbon dioxide there. Next, Mars would have been seeded with the cyanobacteria needed to produce oxygen. A giant magnetic parasol at the sun-Mars L1 point, designed by Hans Bethe's Patient Power group and held steady with occasional rocket bursts supplied by von Braun's team, would keep the planet safely trailing in its magnetotail, shielded from the normal solar wind that otherwise would have kept stripping off Mars's steadily thickening and increasingly more breathable atmosphere. Processes set in play a millennium ago would bear fruit—yes, God damn it, literally bear fruit!—in time for humanity to regain the garden.

In 1610, when Galileo became the first person to look at Mars through a telescope, six centuries of transformation had already occurred on that world. But the weak, imperfect lenses in his scope—not to mention the weak, imperfect ones of his own eyes—revealed nothing different than if the Martian soil and sky had remained untouched.

Time marches on, though, and eventually small changes *do* have big, lasting impacts. When Giovanni Schiaparelli initially looked at Mars through a twenty-two-centimeter telescope in A.D. 1877, Robert Oppenheimer's father Julius was already six years old, and his mother Ella—the cradle robber, as her family would later joke—had just turned eight. And when Percival Lowell published *Mars and its Canals* and *Mars as the Abode of Life*, some thirty years later, Robert Oppenheimer was a precocious toddler.

And so, yes, that the fourth planet from the sun now appeared emerald not ruby, green not red, was as yet of little consequence. Oh, it leant more credence to Lowell's observations, and to H.G. Wells's other famous novel and the radio drama Orson Welles had produced from it, but, by and large, the events of the first half of the twentieth century had unfolded in this new reality as they had in the old one it now superseded. The Wright brothers took flight in 1903. Einstein enjoyed his miracle year of physics successes in 1905. The assassination of Archduke Ferdinand in 1914 plunged Europe into war for four gory years. The rise to power of a failed painter and psychopathic madman precipitated an even longer, even larger, even more barbarous conflict two decades later. Whatever effect that pinprick of celestial light, appearing smaller than the smallest butterfly, had on human affairs, the tides of fascism and Nazism, of politics and patriotism, swelled and ebbed much the same way, and, as Wells would have it, with infinite complacency men had still gone to and fro over this globe about their little affairs, serene in their assurance of their empire over matter.

But in the middle of the twentieth century came the great disillusionment: the realization that the sun, which had shone so steadily, was bound to expel its outer surface in an incinerating sphere that would take out rocky Mercury and silver Venus and earth with its wars and so little peace and earth's craggy dead moon, but would leave intact the planet that Oppie alone remembered as having been red but now shone green.

And so: The Arbor Project.

And so: Project *Orion.*

And so: *Mariner IV,* and the first close-up photograph of the Martian surface, and the—

Oppie imagined the scene as it was now bound to unfold: the elation, the joy. The black-and-white pictures painstakingly decoded from numerical data showing—

There could be no doubt.

A river, with dark patches along both banks, its waters flowing into a circular lake, the surface of which was dappled by sunlight.

The Mars of Schiaparelli, of Lowell, of Wells and Welles. Or, at least, a close approximation of it. Waterways, to be sure, and the dimmer areas could be—should be—must be—vegetation.

It *was* there, the second home humanity needed. Yes, they could have simply (simply!) used time travel to move great batches of humans back into the past, but that would buy only a reprieve not a pardon: no matter what they did, earth would be destroyed before the middle of the twenty-first century. And, anyway, swarms of post-atomic humans in the time of Newton, or Julius Caesar, or Tutankhamen, or *Zinjanthropus* would chaotically disrupt things, making it impossible to predict how the subsequent centuries or millennia would be rewritten.

Instead, in this revised reality, thanks to Stanislaw Ulam's original idea for atomic-bomb-propelled space vessels, and Freeman Dyson's development of that notion, and Edward Teller's super technology, and the brilliant breakthrough of Richard Feynman and Kurt Gödel, and the organizational acumen of one J. Robert Oppenheimer, the key to survival would be time travel combined with—what to call it? Ah, but there already *was* a term, coined by the science-fiction writer Jack Williamson working in New Mexico some five years prior to and two hundred miles east of the Trinity blast, a bull's-eye in cosmic terms: "terraforming," engineering on a planetary scale, remaking an existing world into a form suitable for life from earth.

The Arbor Project would approach world leaders in the 1960s with word of the impending disaster and beg an exception to the test-ban treaty: there *was* a second earth waiting, as any decent observatory could now confirm, and they *did* have the means to get millions or billions of people to it. Forget von Braun's V-rockets and their paltry capacity. These arks would be *Orion* vessels, pulsing their way to the green planet, pushed along by necklaces of fusion explosions—an apt, poetic solution to the solar crisis, fighting fire with fire.

"This is my bench."

Robert Oppenheimer had fallen asleep. He woke to the words and saw the form of a man leaning over him, black against black, a void against the Milky Way like the one his calculations predicted might be formed by the death of a sufficiently massive star.

"Sorry?" said Oppie—not an apology but rather a request for a repetition.

"I said, this is my bench. I sleep here. Everyone knows that." The man's voice was rough, uncultured, but not angry.

"I'm new to the park," said Oppie. "I didn't know."

"There's another bench right there," the man said, and Oppie could dimly make out that he was pointing. "'Course, that used to be Big Jimbo's bench, but he passed away just before Christmas."

"I see," said Oppie. He struggled to sit.

"Guys like us, we pass away in the park all the time. City comes and collects the bodies."

Oppie nodded. "So I've heard."

"But you gotta have your place in the world, right? And this one is mine." He reached down to help Oppie get up. "My God, bub, you're skin and bones." The man walked him the few feet to the other bench. "Here. Just as comfy—hah!"

"Thank you," said Oppie, lying down.

"You don't look like you're long for this world."

"No, I'm not."

"That's a nice hat. Can I have it when you're gone?"

"Sure."

"Hot dog!" declared the man, and that made Robert smile. "My name's Ben. What's yours?"

Oppie thought about how to reply. The last thing he wanted was for someone to identify him to the police after he was gone—what a mess that would create! He could just say "Robert" or "Bob," and leave it at that. Or—and this tickled him—he could give his name as Arjuna, the prince from the *Bhagavad Gita* who had questioned the morality of a great war and had been persuaded by Krishna of the conflict's inevitability and his obligation to do his duty.

But, in the end, he told the truth. "My friends call me Oppie."

He heard Ben settling in on his own bench. "Unusual name—but strikes me you're an unusual fellow."

"I suppose I am."

Oh, irony, my old friend—come for one last visit, have you? He'd talked Jean out of suicide, tonight at least, but now he was about to kill himself. Yet this was different; it really was. Whereas her life had just begun, his was going to end soon anyway, and he was tired of the pain, tired of the struggle. Since there was now no way to go back to where he'd come from, tonight, with Ben for company, seemed a fine time to let go. Yes, there'd be no corpse to be cremated in 1967, but covering that up would be trivial among the clandestine tasks performed by members of the Arbor Project. And if people, bringing an end to his story, followed the instruction in his will and tossed an urn supposedly holding his remains into the sea, he hoped they would remember to weigh it down with sand.

Oppie still had the oval capsule, the size of a pea, that General Groves had given him in 1943; it had lived for years in a locked cupboard at Olden Manor, but he'd brought it along on this, his final voyage. It took most of a minute in the cold for his stick-like fingers to dig out the small hinged tin container, to remove the capsule—its rubber covering having long since cracked and fallen away—and to maneuver it with a dry tongue between his decaying teeth.

Potassium cyanide, like that which he'd painted on the apple he'd left for Patrick Blackett in 1925—long ago even when reckoning from here in 1944; even longer from 1967.

An apple. Forbidden knowledge. But there was no such thing in science. If it was knowable, it had to be known. And although the technical problems were often sweet, they were sweetest when they were solved.

Time, he knew, for his final utterance. "Good night, Ben," he said, the words slightly muffled as he continued to gently clamp his molars down on the thin-walled glass ampoule. "Let us hope for a better tomorrow—and a better world."

"Sleep well, Oppie."

J. Robert Oppenheimer, his duty done, clenched his jaw. He found the green planet once more in the sky and let it be his last sight, a beacon of hope and salvation, before he closed his eyes for good.

Bibliography

In creating this novel, I found three websites indispensable: the **Atomic Heritage Foundation** (atomicheritage.org), **Voices of the Manhattan Project** (manhattanprojectvoices.org), and Alex Wellerstein's **Restricted Data: The Nuclear Secrecy Blog** (blog.nuclearsecrecy.com).

In addition, I relied on the following books:

The Manhattan Project and the Atomic Age

Alperovitz, Gar. *The Decision to Use the Atomic Bomb and the Architecture of an American Myth.* Alfred A. Knopf, New York, 1995.

Baggott, Jim. *The First War of Physics: The Secret History of the Atom Bomb, 1939-1949.* Pegasus, New York, 2010.

Cimino, Al. *The Manhattan Project.* Arcturus, London, 2015.

Conant, Jennet. *109 East Palace: Robert Oppenheimer and the Secret City of Los Alamos.* Simon & Schuster, New York, 2005.

Coster-Mullen, John. *Atom Bombs: The Top Secret Inside Story of Little Boy and Fat Man.* Self-published, 2002.

Groves, Leslie R. *Now It Can Be Told: The Story of the Manhattan Project.* Harper & Row, New York, 1962.

Hersey, John. *Hiroshima.* Alfred A. Knopf, New York, 1946.

Jones, Vincent C. *Manhattan: The Army and the Atomic Bomb.* Center of Military History United States Army, Washington DC, 1985.

Joseloff, Michael. *Chasing Heisenberg: The Race for the Atom Bomb.* Amazon Publishing, Seattle, 2018.

Jungk, Robert. *Brighter Than a Thousand Suns: A Personal History of the Atomic Scientist.* Harcourt Brace, New York, 1958.

Kelly, Cynthia C. *A Guide to the Manhattan Project in New Mexico.* Atomic Heritage Foundation, Washington DC, 2012.

———. *The Manhattan Project: The Birth of the Atomic Bomb in the Words of its Creators, Eyewitnesses, and Historians.* Black Dog, New York, 2007.

Lawrence, William L. *Dawn Over Zero.* Knopf, New York, 1946.

Mahaffey, James. *Atomic Awakening: A New Look at the History and Future of Nuclear Power.* Pegasus, New York, 2010.

Masters, Dexter, and Katharine Way, eds. *One World or None: A Report to the Public on the Full Meaning of the Atomic Bomb.* Federation of American Scientists, Washington DC, 1946.

Nelson, Craig. *The Age of Radiance: The Epic Rise and Dramatic Fall of the Atomic Era.* Scribner, New York, 2014.

Nichols, Major General K.D., U.S.A. (Ret.). *The Road to Trinity: A Personal Account of How America's Nuclear Polices Were Made.* William Morrow, New York, 1987.

Norris, Robert S. *Racing for the Bomb: General Leslie R. Groves, the Manhattan Project's Indispensable Man.* Steerforth Press, South Royalton VT, 2002.

O'Reilly, Bill, and Martin Dugard. *Killing the Rising Sun: How America Vanquished World War II.* Henry Holt, New York, 2016.

Powers, Thomas. *Heisenberg's War: The Secret History of the German Bomb.* Penguin, London, 1994.

Reed, Bruce Cameron. *Atomic Bomb: The Story of the Manhattan Project.* Morgan & Claypool, San Rafael CA, 2015.

———. *The History and Science of the Manhattan Project.* Springer, Berlin, 2014.

———. *The Physics of the Manhattan Project, Third Edition.* Springer, Berlin, 2015.

Rhodes, Richard. *Dark Sun: The Making of the Hydrogen Bomb.* Simon & Schuster, New York, 1995.

———. *The Making of the Atomic Bomb.* Simon & Schuster, New York, 1986.

Serber, Robert. *The Los Alamos Primer: The First Lectures on How to Build an Atomic Bomb.* University of California Press, Berkeley CA, 1992.

Sullivan, Neil J. *The Prometheus Bomb: The Manhattan Project and Government in the Dark.* Potomac Books, Lincoln NE, 2016.

Teller, Edward, and Allen Brown. *The Legacy of Hiroshima.* Doubleday, New York, 1962.

Watson, Peter. *Fallout: Conspiracy, Cover-Up, and the Deceitful Case for the Atom Bomb.* Hachette, New York, 2018.

Wyden, Peter. *Day One: Before Hiroshima and After.* Simon & Schuster, New York, 1984.

J. Robert Oppenheimer

Banco, Lindsey. *The Meanings of J. Robert Oppenheimer.* University of Iowa Press, Iowa City IA, 2016.

Bernstein, Jeremy. *Oppenheimer: Portrait of an Enigma.* Ivan R. Dee, Chicago, 2004.

Bird, Kai, and Martin J. Sherwin. *American Prometheus: The Triumph and Tragedy of J. Robert Oppenheimer.* Alfred A. Knopf, New York, 2005.

Carson, Cathryn, and David A. Hollinger. *Reappraising Oppenheimer: Centennial Studies and Reflections.* University of California, Berkeley CA, 2005.

Cassidy, David. *J. Robert Oppenheimer and the American Century.* Pi Press, Indianapolis IN, 2004.

Chevalier, Haakon. *Oppenheimer: The Story of a Friendship.* George Braziller, New York, 1965.

Day, Michael A. *The Hope and Vision of J. Robert Oppenheimer.* World Scientific, Hackensack NJ, 2016.

Dyson, Freeman. *Dreams of Earth and Sky.* New York Review of Books, New York, 2015 (also contains essays about Richard Feynman and Wernher von Braun).

———. *The Scientist as Rebel.* New York Review of Books, New York, 2006.

Goodchild, Peter. *J. Robert Oppenheimer: Shatterer of Worlds.* Houghton Mifflin, Boston, 1981.

Hecht, David K. *Storytelling and Science: Rewriting Oppenheimer in the Nuclear Age.* University of Massachusetts Press, Boston, 2015.

Kelly, Cynthia C. *Oppenheimer and the Manhattan Project: Insights Into J.*

Robert Oppenheimer, "Father of the Atomic Bomb." World Scientific, Hackensack NJ, 2006.

Kunetka, James W. *The General and the Genius.* Regnery, Washington DC, 2015 [Leslie R. Groves, J. Robert Oppenheimer].

———. *Oppenheimer: The Years of Risk.* Prentice-Hall, Englewood Cliffs NJ, 1982.

Mason, Richard. *Oppenheimer's Choice: Reflections from Moral Philosophy.* State University of New York Press, Albany NY, 2006.

McMillan, Priscilla. J. *The Ruin of J. Robert Oppenheimer and the Birth of the Modern Arms Race.* Viking, New York, 2005.

Michelmore, Peter. *The Swift Years: The Robert Oppenheimer Story.* Dodd Mead, New York, 1969.

Monk, Ray. *Robert Oppenheimer: A Life Inside the Center.* Random House, New York, 2012.

Oppenheimer, J. Robert. *Atom and Void: Essays on Science and Community.* Princeton University Press, Princeton NJ, 1989.

———. *The Flying Trapeze: Three Crises for Physicists.* Harper & Row, New York, 1969.

———. *The Open Mind.* Simon & Schuster, New York, 1955.

———. *Science and the Common Understanding.* Simon & Schuster, New York, 1953.

———. *Uncommon Sense.* Birkhauser, Boston, 1984.

Ottaviani, Jim, and Janine Johnston, Steve Lieber, Vince Locke, Bernie Mireault, and Jeff Parker. *Fallout: J. Robert Oppenheimer, Leo Szilard, and the Political Science of the Atomic Bomb.* G.T. Labs, Ann Arbor MI, 2001.

Pais, Abraham, with Robert P. Crease. *J. Robert Oppenheimer: A Life.* Oxford University Press, New York, 2006.

Polenberg, Richard, ed. *In the Matter of J. Robert Oppenheimer: The Security Clearance Hearing.* Cornell University Press, Ithaca NY, 2002.

Royal, Denise. *The Story of J. Robert Oppenheimer.* St. Martin's Press, New York, 1969.

Schweber, Silvan S. *Einstein and Oppenheimer: The Meaning of Genius.* Harvard University Press, Cambridge MA, 2008.

———. *In the Shadow of the Bomb: Bethe, Oppenheimer and the Moral Responsibility of the Scientist.* Princeton University Press, Princeton NJ, 2000.

Smith, Alice Kimball, and Charles Weiner, eds. *Robert Oppenheimer: Letters and Recollections.* Stanford University Press, Stanford CA, 1980.

Stern, Philip M., with Harold P. Green. *The Oppenheimer Case: Security on Trial.* Harper & Row, New York, 1969.

Thorpe, Charles. *Oppenheimer: The Tragic Intellect.* University of Chicago Press, Chicago, 2006.

United States Atomic Energy Commission. *In the Matter of J. Robert Oppenheimer: Transcript of Hearing Before Personnel Security Board and Texts of Principal Documents and Letters.* MIT Press, Cambridge MA, 1954.

Wolverton, Mark. *A Life in Twilight: The Final Years of J. Robert Oppenheimer.* St. Martin's Press, New York, 2008.

Wernher von Braun

Biddle, Wayne. *Dark Side of the Moon: Wernher von Braun, the Third Reich, and the Space Race.* W.W. Norton, New York, 2009.

Bower, Tom. *The Paperclip Conspiracy: The Battle For the Spoils and Secrets of Nazi Germany.* Michael Joseph, London, 1987.

Goudsmit, Samuel A. *Alsos.* Henry Schuman, New York, 1947.

Huzel, Dieter K. *From Peenemünde to Canaveral.* Englewood Prentice-Hall, Englewood Cliffs NJ, 1962.

Jacobsen, Annie. *Operation Paperclip: The Secret Intelligence Program That Brought Nazi Scientists to America.* Little Brown, New York, 2014.

Longmate, Norman. *Hitler's Rockets: The Story of the V-2s.* Skyhorse, New York, 2009.

Neufeld, Michael J. *Von Braun: Dreamer of Space, Engineer of War.* Alfred A. Knopf, New York, 2007.

von Braun, Wernher. *The Mars Project.* University of Illinois Press, Urbana IL, 1991.

———. *Project Mars: A Technical Tale.* Apogee, Burlington ON, 2006 [von Braun's novel, at last seeing print in English].

Other Historical Figures

Bodanis, David. *Einstein's Greatest Mistake: A Biography.* Houghton Mifflin Harcourt, Boston, 2016.

Clark, Ronald W. *Einstein: The Life and Times.* World Publishing Company, New York, 1971.

Fermi, Laura. *Atoms in the Family.* University of Chicago Press, Chicago, 1954 [Enrico Fermi].

Feynman, Richard P. *The Pleasure of Finding Things Out: The Best Short Works of Richard P. Feynman.* Perseus Publishing, New York, 1999.

———. *"Surely You're Joking, Mr. Feynman!"* W.W. Norton, New York, 1985.

———. *What Do You Care What Other People Think?: Further Adventures of a Curious Character.* W.W. Norton, New York, 1988.

Gleick, James. *Genius: The Life and Science of Richard Feynman.* Vintage, New York, 1992.

Goodchild, Peter. *Edward Teller: The Real Dr Strangelove.* Weidenfeld & Nicolson, London, 2004.

Hargittai, Istvan. *Judging Edward Teller: A Closer Look at One of the Most Influential Scientists of the Twentieth Century.* Prometheus, New York, 2010.

———. *The Martians of Science: Five Physicists Who Changed the Twentieth Century.* Oxford University Press, London, 2006 [Leo Szilard, Edward Teller, Theodore Von Karman, John von Neumann, Eugene Wigner].

Herken, Gregg. *Brotherhood of the Bomb: The Tangled Lives and Loyalties of Robert Oppenheimer, Ernest Lawrence, and Edward Teller.* Henry Holt, New York, 2002.

Isaacson, Walter. *Einstein: His Life and Universe.* Simon & Schuster, New York, 2007.

Krauss, Lawrence M. *Quantum Man: Richard Feynman's Life in Science.* W.W. Norton, New York, 2011.

Lanouette, William, with Bela Silard. *Genius in the Shadows: A Biography of Leo Szilard, the Man Behind the Bomb.* Charles Scribner's Sons, New York, 1992.

Marton, Kati. *The Great Escape: Nine Jews Who Fled Hitler and Changed the World.* Simon & Schuster, New York, 2006 [Leo Szilard, Edward Teller, Eugene Wigner, John von Neumann].

Orear, Jay, et. al. *Enrico Fermi—The Master Scientist.* The Internet-First University Press, Ithaca NY, 2004.

Pfau, Richard. *No Sacrifice Too Great: The Life of Lewis L. Strauss.* University Press of Virginia, Charlottesville VA, 1984.

Rigden, John S. *Rabi: Scientist and Citizen.* Harvard University Press, Cambridge MA, 1987.

Rolls, Jem. *The Inventor of All Things.* One-man play about Leo Szilard performed at fringe-theater festivals worldwide since 2015.

Schwartz, David N. *The Last Man Who Knew Everything: The Life and Times of Enrico Fermi, Father of the Nuclear Age.* Basic Books, New York, 2017.

Segrè, Gino, and Bettina Hoerlin. *The Pope of Physics: Enrico Fermi and the Birth of the Atomic Age.* Henry Holt, New York, 2016.

Smith, P.D. *Doomsday Men: The Real Dr Strangelove and the Dream of the Superweapon.* Penguin, London, 2007 [Edward Teller].

Strauss, Lewis L. *Men and Decisions.* Doubleday, Garden City NY, 1962 [Strauss's autobiography].

Streshinsky, Shirley, and Patricia Klaus. *An Atomic Love Story: The Extraordinary Women in Robert Oppenheimer's Life.* Turner, Nashville TN, 2013 [Kitty Oppenheimer, Jean Tatlock].

Teller, Edward, with Judith Shoolery. *Memoirs: A Twentieth-Century Journey in Science and Politics.* Perseus Publishing, Cambridge MA, 2001.

VanDeMark, Brian. *Pandora's Keepers: Nine Men and the Atomic Bomb.* Back Bay Books, New York, 2009 [Hans Bethe, Niels Bohr, Arthur Holly Compton, Enrico Fermi, Ernest Lawrence, J. Robert Oppenheimer, I.I. Rabi, Leo Szilard, Edward Teller].

Weart, Spencer R., and Gertrud Weiss Szilard, eds. *Leo Szilard: His Version of the Facts.* MIT Press, Cambridge MA, 1978.

York, Herbert. *The Advisors: Oppenheimer, Teller, and the Superbomb.* Stanford University Press, Stanford CA, 1976.

The Institute for Advanced Study

Arntzenius, Linda G. *Institute for Advanced Study: Images of America.* Arcadia, Charleston SC, 2011.

Batterson, Steve. *Pursuit of Genius: Flexner, Einstein, and the Early Faculty at the Institute for Advanced Study.* AK Peters, Wellesley MA, 2006.

Dyson, George. *Turing's Cathedral: The Origins of the Digital Universe.* Pantheon, New York, 2012 [John von Neumann].

Feldman, Burton. *Einstein's Genius Club: The True Story of a Group of Scientists Who Changed the World.* Arcade, New York, 2011.

Flexner, Abraham, with Robbert Dijkgraaf. *The Usefulness of Useless Knowledge.* Princeton University Press, Princeton NJ, 2017.

Levy, Serge J-F. *A Community of Scholars: Impressions of the Institute for Advanced Study.* Princeton University Press, Princeton NJ, 2012.

Nasar, Sylvia. *A Beautiful Mind: The Life of Mathematical Genius and Nobel Laureate John Nash.* Simon & Schuster, New York, 1998.

Regis, Ed. *Who Got Einstein's Office? Eccentricity and Genius at the Institute for Advanced Study.* Addison-Wesley, Reading MA, 1987.

The Nature of Time and Space

Davies, Paul. *How to Build a Time Machine.* Penguin, New York, 2001.

Falk, Dan. *In Search of Time: Journeys Along a Curious Dimension.* McClelland & Stewart, Toronto, 2008.

Gleick, James. *Time Travel: A History.* Pantheon, New York, 2016.

Gott, J. Richard. *Time Travel in Einstein's Universe: The Physical Possibilities of Travel Through Time.* Houghton Mifflin, New York, 2001.

Halpern, Paul. *The Quantum Labyrinth: How Richard Feynman and John Wheeler Revolutionized Time and Reality.* Basic Books, New York, 2017.

Mallett, Ronald L., with Bruce Henderson. *Time Traveler: A Scientist's Personal Mission to Make Time Travel a Reality.* Basic Books, New York, 2007.

Muller, Richard A. *Now: The Physics of Time.* W.W. Norton, New York, 2016.

Oppenheimer, J. Robert, and Robert Serber. "On the Stability of Stellar Neutron Cores," *Physical Review,* volume 54 (1938), page 608.

Oppenheimer, J. Robert, and Hartland Snyder. "On Continued Gravitational Contraction," *Physical Review,* volume 56 (1939), page 455.

Oppenheimer, J. Robert, and George Volkoff. "On Massive Neutron Cores," *Physical Review,* volume 54 (1939), page 540.

Rovelli, Carlo. *The Order of Time.* Riverhead, New York, 2018.

Smolin, Lee, and Roberto Mangabeira Unger. *The Singular Universe and the Reality of Time: A Proposal in Natural Philosophy.* Cambridge University Press, Cambridge UK, 2015.

Thorne, Kip S. *Black Holes and Time Warps: Einstein's Outrageous Legacy.* W.W Norton, New York, 1994.

Yourgrau, Palle. *A World Without Time: The Forgotten Legacy of Gödel and Einstein.* Basic Books, Cambridge MA, 2006.

Mars and Project Orion

Brower, Kenneth. *The Starship and the Canoe.* Henry Holt, New York, 1978.

David, Leonard. *Mars: Our Future on the Red Planet.* National Geographic, Washington DC, 2016.

de Vaucouleurs, Gérard. *Physics of the Planet Mars: An Introduction to Areophysics* (translated by Patrick Moore). Faber and Faber, London, 1954.

Dyson, George. *Project Orion: The Atomic Spaceship 1957-1965.* Allen Lane, London, 2002.

Godwin, Robert, ed. *Mars: The NASA Mission Reports, Volume One.* Apogee, Burlington ON, 2000 [including Mariner IV].

Mallove, Eugene, and Gregory Matloff. *The Starflight Handbook: A Pioneer's Guide to Interstellar Travel.* John Wiley & Sons, New York, 1989.

Morton, Oliver. *Mapping Mars: Science, Imagination and the Birth of a World.* Picador, New York, 2002.

Sheehan, William. *The Planet Mars: A History of Observation and Discovery.* University of Arizona Press, Tucson, 1996.

Zubrin, Robert. *The Case for Mars: The Plan to Settle the Red Planet and Why We Must.* Simon & Schuster, New York, 1996, 2011.

About the Author

ROBERT J. SAWYER is a Member of the Order of Canada, the highest honor bestowed by the Canadian government, as well as the Order of Ontario, the highest honor given by his home province. He was also one of the initial inductees into the Canadian Science Fiction and Fantasy Hall of Fame, the first-ever recipient of a Lifetime Achievement Award from the Mississauga Arts Council, and the first-ever recipient of Humanist Canada's Humanism in the Arts Award.

Rob is one of only eight writers ever to win all three of the world's top awards for best science-fiction novel of the year: the Hugo (which he won in 2003 for *Hominids*), the Nebula (which he won in 1996 for *The Terminal Experiment*), and the John W. Campbell Memorial Award (which he won in 2006 for *Mindscan*).

He's also won the Robert A. Heinlein Award, the Edward E. Smith Memorial Award, and the Hal Clement Memorial Award; the top SF awards in China, Japan, France, and Spain; and a record-setting sixteen Canadian Science Fiction and Fantasy Awards ("Auroras"). In addition, he's received the Crime Writers of Canada's Arthur Ellis Award for Best Short Story of the Year.

Rob's novel *FlashForward* was the basis for the ABC TV series of the same name, and he was a scriptwriter for that program. He also scripted the two-part finale for the popular web series *Star Trek Continues.*

A twenty-year resident of Mississauga, Ontario, his website and blog are at **sfwriter.com**, and on Facebook, Patreon, and Twitter he's **RobertJSawyer.**

Printed in Great Britain
by Amazon

35562522R00211